DEATH ROCKS THE CRADLE

And Other Stories

The DANCING TUATARA PRESS
Books from RAMBLE HOUSE

CLASSICS OF HORROR

CLASSICS OF SCIENCE FICTION AND FANTASY

DAY KEENE IN THE DETECTIVE PULPS

DEATH ROCKS THE CRADLE

And Other Stories

The Weird Tales of
Wayne Rogers
Volume #2

Wayne Rogers

Edited and Introduced by
John Pelan

RAMBLE HOUSE

Introduction © 2011 by John Pelan
Cover Art © 2011 Gavin O'Keefe

Daughters of Pain, *Dime Mystery Magazine,* November 1934*
Killer Blood for Sale, *Dime Mystery Magazine,* November 1936
Doom Flowers, *Terror Tales,* May 1935*
Satan Stole my Face, *Horror Stories,* February/March 1936
Hell Welcomes Lonely Wives, *Terror Tales* March/April 1937
Her Lover from the Grave, *Terror Tales,* November 1935
Dead Man's Kiss, *Dime Mystery Magazine,* July 1936
Fresh Blood for Golden Cauldrons, *Dime Mystery,* September 1934**
Her Suitor from Hell, *Terror Tales,* April 1936*
Death Rocks the Cradle, *Horror Stories*, February/March 1937
Satan's Love Bazaar, *Terror Tales*, July/August 1937

*Appeared under the name "H.M. Appel"
** Appeared under the name "Conrad Kimball"

ISBN 13: 978-1-60543-707-1

Edited by Kathy Pelan and Fender Tucker

Stories from *Dime Mystery Magazine, Terror Tales, & Horror Stories*
reprinted by arrangement with Argosy Communications, Inc. Copyright
(C) 2011 Argosy Communications, Inc. All Rights Reserved.

DANCING TUATARA PRESS #22

TABLE OF CONTENTS

*Appeared under the name "H.M. Appel"

** Appeared under the name "Conrad Kimball"

THE THREE FACES OF WAYNE ROGERS

For the more prolific of the pulp authors the use of a pseudonym or two was commonplace. In some instances such as in the case of Wyatt Blassingame, the use of a secondary name was simply to accommodate having two stories in the same issue of a magazine. In what must have struck readers as an odd coincidence, "William Rainey" seemed to only appear in magazines that also featured a story by Wyatt Blassingame. The more astute readers might have noticed that there was a tremendous stylistic similarity between the two authors. By the same token, "Spencer Whitney" must have had a clause in his contract that he would only appear in issues that also featured Arthur J. Burks.

Wayne Rogers, Conrad Kimball, and H.M. Appel present a slightly different scenario, as will be seen in the contents of this second volume of Wayne Rogers' selected weird tales. All three were pseudonyms of former mainstream editor, Archibald Bittner. When Bittner made the career change from editing general fiction magazines to writing stories for the weird menace pulps and pinch-hitting on some of the more flamboyant single-character magazines such as *Operator #5* and *The Spider* he left his real name behind and assumed the identity of "Wayne Rogers".

As "Wayne Rogers" he quickly established as a dependable contributor with an appearance in the second issue of *Dime Mystery Magazine* devoted to this new genre of "weird menace". "Disappearing Death" was a solid work of novelette length and the majority of the work that was to appear under the Rogers byline would be in the 9,000 to 15,000 word range; thus insuring the author of at least being mentioned on the cover, if not having the cover art devoted to his story. While churning out a novelette or two a month may seem demanding, in the opinion of many writers (including myself) it's really the easiest length to work in for the horror story. One has adequate space to develop characters, set up a couple of red herrings and, above all, maintain a sense of dread from beginning to end.

Keeping the reader on the edge of his/her seat is always the biggest challenge in the horror genre. Doing so over 10,000 to 12,000 words is no problem, which explains why the novelette form is so popular with authors. However, Rogers was going to be given another task for Popular Publications' trio of weird menace pulps (*Dime Mystery Magazine, Terror Tales* and *Horror Stories*). While the novelette is popular with writers, the editor's and publisher's bread and butter is the short story of 5,000-6,000 words. While the longer pieces serve as the main attraction, without the short stories, one doesn't have much of a magazine. The short stories were more than just filler; in some cases, the artist didn't have time to provide a cover that represented a scene from one of the long pieces and would turn in a generic illustration suitable to the overall theme of the magazine (generally a masked fiend or lumbering brute menacing a young lady who seemingly had been surprised while undressing); in these instances the author not only had to turn work in quickly, but also had to tailor the story to fit whatever was depicted on the cover.

With the goal of satisfying editor Rogers Terrill's need for shorter pieces, "H.M. Appel" was "born" with the publication of "Baby Blood" in the February 1934 issue of *Dime Mystery*. This *nom de plume* would feature in all three publications through 1936, when the name was discarded after being used in an atypical fashion on a novelette ("We Are the Damned"), in the September 1936 issue of *Dime Mystery Magazine*. The Appel stories are quite different from the typical Rogers piece. The tales are by necessity plot-driven, usually with a trick ending and minimal characterization. As with the preceding volume (*Satan's Sin House*) we've included three examples in this book and subsequent volumes will collect the remaining Appel stories. While the Appel stories are by definition too slight to deliver the punch of Rogers' most memorable tales such as "Temple of Torment" or "Death Rocks the Cradle", I think that most readers will agree that they are clever examples of the genre and well-worth preservation in book form.

Rogers maintained a steady, high volume pace with some thirty pieces (mostly novelettes or novellas) appearing between July 1935 and October 1937. Readers may have noticed a similar authorial style in three novelettes published in 1937 under the name of "Conrad Kimball". As opposed to the very specific purpose of "H.M. Appel", "Conrad Kimball" was more in the vein of "William Rainey" or "Spencer Whitney"; a way to get two stories in the same issue of a given magazine. The "Conrad Kimball" name was debuted in 1935 in *Horror Stories* with "Hell's Actress", a story which would have been perfectly suitable under the H.M. Appel byline. Rogers didn't have occasion to use the name again until the appearance of "Fresh Blood for Golden Cauldrons", which appeared in *Horror Stories* along with "Death Rocks the Cradle". Both are among Rogers' very best work and we have included both stories in this volume.

As other assignments materialized, Rogers work for the weird menace magazines slowed a good deal, with only fifteen pieces appearing for Popular Publication from 1938-1941. However, where the quantity may have diminished, there was no compromise on quality, with some of Rogers' very best work appearing in 1940-1941. The third volume in this series will be devoted primarily to the feature-length tales from this period.

Sadly, while Rogers was still at the top of his game, many of his contemporaries had either burned out or drifted away to other genres. No one author, no matter how good, was going to be able to prop up three magazines indefinitely. Major contributors such as Arthur J. Burks seemed to have lost interest in the genre and were just going through the motions, whereas others such as Wyatt Blassingame and John H.

Knox were exploring more traditional mystery and detective tales. The dependable Henry Treat Sperry and Leon Byrne both passed away in 1939. Newer authors such as Loring Dowst and George Vandegrift weren't capable of the volume that characterized the earlier mainstays of the magazines such as Cave, Zagat, and Cummings, and the readership, jaded after nearly a decade of excess, were finding other entertainments to spend their money on. Most importantly, with the all-too-real menaces from Germany and Japan an ever-present threat, stories about cackling fiends with elaborate schemes just didn't seem to have much appeal.

One of the first on the scene, Wayne Rogers was also one of the last to leave. His pulp career had a real storybook ending as he went out with a bang. Two of his best stories ("Dracula's Bride" and "March of the Homeless Corpses") showed up in the February and March issues of *Horror Stories* and *Terror Tales*. Readers may not have realized that they were witnessing the end of an era, but by the time the two magazines hit the newsstands, Archibald Bittner was on the way to a new life in Florida operating a chain of movie theaters; when he left, Wayne Rogers, Conrad Kimball, and H.M. Appel went with him.

—John Pelan
Midnight House
Gallup, NM
All Hallows 2010

DAUGHTERS OF PAIN

BRAKES SHRIEKED as the taxi skidded to a stop, and the startled driver stared. His two passengers were flung forward in their seats.

"Look!" gasped Helen Hale, peering through the windshield into the brightly lighted thoroughfare. "That girl! She's nearly naked—"

"Not even a fan!" her companion, Bob Turcotte, agreed. "Almost ran her down." He frowned toward a crowded theater entrance on the right, where a blasé throng stood stunned to momentary silence.

"Pretty raw publicity—"

"It's Mary!" Helen's cry quavered with unreasoning dread. "Oh, I knew, something ghastly was going to happen. That's why I wired you to come? "

A bluecoat at the corner snapped out of his trance, came running toward the young woman. She was blonde and quite lovely, clad in a wisp of lingerie. Moving with halting steps over the cobblestones, slender white body pitilessly revealed in the incandescent glare, she paused directly opposite the Lyric lobby. Then, raising a red apple to her lips, she took one bite and dropped in a heap.

Turcotte leaped down, reached her side a step ahead of the policeman. A glance told the gruesome tale. The girl was dead.

"Suicide!" the officer grunted. "Now don't this beat hell, mister?"

The crowd surged forward, clamoring, peering.

"Get her into my cab." Turcotte snapped. He gathered the crumpled corpse in his arms. Helen was holding the car door ajar. The patrolman cleared a path with his club.

"Nearest hospital!" Turcotte prodded the driver, who

seemed dazed. "Stop goggling! Show us some speed."

Helen Hale pulled off her tan cloak and wrapped it around the body. Tears streaming down her cheeks, she helped Turcotte to support the limp form upon the cushion.

The policeman, perched on a jump-seat, demanded plaintively: "Ain't that a crazy way to do it? She must have got out of a parked car. Here's something that dropped when you picked her up." He proffered a length of ribbon.

Turcotte saw letters crudely printed on the strip of silk, flicked on the domelight and read:

"DAUGHTERS OF SEKHMET"

"What does that mean?" He stared at the officer.

"Search me. Suicide club, maybe. Or she might have belonged to one of those nutty nudist outfits."

Words of protest burst up in Helen Hale's throat, but Turcotte interrupted her deliberately, fearing that anything she might say would let her in for troublesome notoriety. She subsided, grieving over the girl again.

A few minutes later they swung up to the hospital receiving-platform. Following a hurried explanation, the intern shook his head. "Nothing to do. Cyanide. Anyway, it was quick and painless."

The patrolman said, apologetically: "I'll have to turn in your names. Of course it was suicide? I saw her take the dose herself? but you know how these things are."

Turcotte called another cab. While waiting, he urged Helen Hale into the deserted visitors' lounge. "Now tell me," he whispered anxiously, "who was the girl? Why did you think this was going to happen? When you met me at the station, I knew something had gone wrong."

He was a tall, good-looking, very much worried young man who had been building up an enviable record on the staff of the *Eastern* daily. His work in connection with a famous kidnapping case had won high praise.

"Oh Bob!" She controlled her voice, with difficulty.

"That's why I asked you to come sooner than we had planned? to have our wedding at once—and take me away from Chicago." She pressed a curly head against his breast, weeping.

Face puckered with trouble, he stroked her hair. "Please, don't! I can't understand. For God's sake"? his tone sharpened involuntarily—"tell me what's going on!"

"I don't know," Helen said brokenly "Mary had been acting so strangely. She was my dearest friend. After we went to have our fortunes told, she seemed terrified by evil premonitions. And now? this! Oh, why did she choose such a horrid way to die?"

Turcotte swore softly, "I'll attend to the fortune-teller. Filthy vermin, all of them. Told the poor girl something that upset her mind, no doubt. But what a pity—"

The cab arrived. "To police headquarters," he directed. "We must tell them who she was, and I'll check up with the Department. We'll have them pick up the fellow who may be responsible. Or was it a woman? Do you remember the fortune-teller's address?"

Helen's face clouded. "No, I don't. Mary received a card in the mail about a week ago. It offered a free consultation to her and to one girl friend. Just for a lark, we went. In the dark I didn't notice which streets we followed. The house was somewhere south of the Loop."

"That's bad. Was the fortune-teller a man?"

She caught her breath in an odd cry of dismay. "Bob! I can't even recall his name! He was a dark, bearded mystic dressed in white, flowing robes and a turban. It's so strange that I can't remember. I don't recall a thing he said."

Turcotte looked at her queerly. "What seemed to trouble Mary? What did she do that was peculiar?"

"The look in her eyes, Bob! As though she saw . . . Death . . . beckoning. She thought she was going to die. Some times, she would grow pale and tense; her eyes would widen and burn; twice I heard her whisper loathingly, 'Unclean! I am unclean!' Then, afterward, she wouldn't know what she had said."

Turcotte's face fell into haggard lines. His arm tightened about her waist protectively.

At Headquarters, a grizzled sergeant broke in upon their brief explanation. "Wait! Lieutenant Wayne will want to hear this." In an adjoining office, a thickset, elderly man looked up patiently. His grave eyes brightened a little at sight of Helen Hale, whose svelte slimness and soft lips drooping with grief held their own appeal.

"Yes? What is it, Moss?"

"This fellow's a reporter from New York. About that dame who done the Dutch, in front of the Lyric a while ago. ? says he knows her, that she was a nice girl? "

"All right, Moss. Let him tell it."

Turcotte recounted the known facts. Lieutenant Wayne looked at Helen. "You say you don't remember his address? Nor his name?"

She shook her head. "Only his eyes!" she burst out abruptly. "Terrible eyes that frightened me so . . ."

"Then you'd know his picture. We have a file of licensed fakers. Moss!" He turned to the sergeant. "Bring in a batch of photographs. Let her look them over."

Helen examined a great many of the prints, with no show of recognition. Then, near the bottom of the stack, she found one that made her pause. Turcotte, watching, saw her body grow rigid. The hand, which held the photograph, seemed frozen. When he caught sight of the expression upon her face, his startled exclamation cracked:

"Helen! Good God! What's the matter?"

In hushed, flat tones she murmured, "Unclean! Unclean!" With a visible effort she tried to tear her eyes away from the picture. Turcotte snatched it out of her tight-clenched fingers. A spell seemed broken. She reeled as though about to faint. He caught her in his arms.

"Bob!" She looked up at him piteously. "That's the man. Oh, I can't remember—but something horrible is yet to happen . . ." Her voice faded on a note of nameless fear.

Turcotte licked his dry lips, turning perplexed eyes toward

the officers. The sergeant's face was screwed up in a ludicrous expression of amazement. "But," he blurted, "that's Sidi Ghanna! And he's? " Noting Wayne's imperative gesture he bit off his remark.

The lieutenant said: "That girl needs a doctor. She's all upset and hysterical. Take her home. We'll do what we can."

After a moment's hesitation, Turcotte led Helen through the door. Moss followed, tapping him on the arm.

"Just a minute. She can sit out here."

Lieutenant Wayne said gruffly: "No use getting her more worked up than she is. But? tell me frankly? there's nothing funny about her, is there?"

"What the hell do you mean?"

"Don't get mad. Is she a regular customer of these yogi chaps, astrologists, and such? A little 'gone' on the subject, maybe?"

"I don't believe she ever went to one before in her life! She's the finest—"

"Sure, sure." Wayne patted his shoulder. "I just wanted to know. Because, you see—" he picked up the photograph from his desk, "this fellow, Sidi Ghanna, is *dead.*"

"Dead? Then how? " Turcotte stared at the mystic's picture. "How long has he been on record as deceased? Under what circumstances did he die?"

Sergeant Moss read from a typed slip pasted on the back of the photograph: "Sidi Ghanna. Egyptian cultist. Called himself a high priest of Sekhmet. No police record. Murdered in his study. Knife wound in back. Laid in the morgue three days, until suspect, Mulai, his assistant was picked up." Moss added extemporaneously: "I remember that yellow-faced devil. The landlady testified that two hours after Mulai left the house, she still heard Sidi Ghanna praying in his room. She gave the fellow an airtight alibi. Found the old man dead before Mulai returned."

"Well . . ." Turcotte was confused. "It must be just a striking resemblance. You might hunt for another fortune-teller who looks like him. His queer eyes give me the creeps, even if he is dead. I've got to take that poor girl home before she collapses."

In the cab, Helen Hale was shaken by spasmodic tremors. She moaned: "Don't let anything like that happen to me. Oh, Mary, Mary? what did he do to you? To die in the street, before all those staring people. Bob! I'm afraid of the eyes . . . the eyes . . ."

Perspiration beaded Turcotte's forehead as he tried to comfort the overwrought girl. She trembled in his arms, whimpering like a frightened child. It was with genuine relief that he helped her down upon reaching the North Shore cottage where she lived with her widowed mother. Mrs. Hale was quite overcome.

Turcotte 'phoned for the family doctor. The physician arrived, administered sedatives to both women. Later, when they were alone, he growled: "Damn these foreigners who unseat feminine minds with their quackery! Looks to me, Turcotte, like the result of hypnotism. Can't say how long the condition may last. You'd better stay."

The opiate had little effect upon Helen.

Throughout the long, dark hours she tossed and moaned, while Turcotte sat beside the bed, trying to quiet her. As in a nightmare she muttered broken phrases which dismayed him with their sinister portent.

"Unclean! Unclean!" There was stark terror in her pitiful cry. "Oh, the eyes! He commands! But I won't go? I won't *go . . .*"

Toward morning the girl fell into a trance-like slumber. Worn out with watching and with the nervous strain, Bob Turcotte slept in his chair until the sun was high.

Then, he carried a tray to Helen's room when she called. The girl seemed surprised.

"So early, Bob? Or did you stay last night?"

"Don't you remember?" Curiosity puckered his eyes. "I sat with you for hours, trying to chase off the bad dreams."

"Dreams?" She looked mystified. "But Bob, I didn't dream, did I? Perhaps *you* did—Her serenity, the very fact that her fears had vanished, hit him hard. What evil power had bred in her mind the hideous fright of the night before, then left it calm?

"You really don't remember? " he stammered, "about Mary?"

Helen's face whitened. Her voice fell low. "How *could* I have forgotten that?" She began to weep; not hysterically, but with the quiet grief of a girl for her chum. Mrs. Hale appeared in the doorway beckoning.

Turcotte sat in the living room and read a story in the morning *Tribune*. The traffic cop had talked. Black headlines clamored:

DAUGHTER OF SEKHMET SUICIDE

The papers denounced the authorities for permitting queer cults to flourish. A taxi-driver had supplied the only definite clue, reporting of his own accord that the girl had ridden in his cab. He had picked up two fares just outside the Loop. A man, muffled to the ears in a long cloak, and a woman, darkly clad. They had told him to park across from the theater. During the excitement, the man had disappeared. Stepping to the telephone Turcotte called Lieutenant Wayne.

"Good morning," he said. "Yes, she had a bad night . . . The gruesome business has done something to her memory. Her doctor believes both girls were hypnotized."

"That," Wayne agreed, "might account for her reaction to the picture. I suppose all hypnotists' eyes look much alike."

Turcotte said: "I believe Sidi Ghanna is still alive. Where did he live?"

"South State? No. 6517 is the address on this photograph. But don't be ridiculous! I tell you we had him in the morgue and buried him!"

Turcotte looked in an encyclopedia for the fabled Sekhmet whose high priest Sidi Ghanna claimed to be. His brow corrugated in a frown when he read that this lion-headed Egyptian goddess of destruction was sometimes known as "Devil's Daughter".

"Sounds like a hop-head's dream," he grumbled. "Ten to one headquarters will never get to the bottom of it. I'll do a little snooping of my own."

It was long past the luncheon hour when he mounted the dirty steps of a dilapidated apartment house and rang the bell. A blowsy woman opened the door a crack.

"Don't want to buy nothing today! Or? were you looking for furnished rooms?"

Turcotte pulled a dollar bill from his vest pocket and smoothed it carefully. "You might be able to tell if it is true that Sidi Ghanna is dead."

"I'll say! Dead as a smelt this year gone," she shrilled. "Didn't I find him layin' there with a long knife stuck in his back? And blood all over a nice new rug, for which I never got a nickel damages out of Mulai?"

"Ah, yes? Mulai, Does he live here now?"

"That yellow-faced imp? Do you think I'd have the likes of him around, dragging in his queer friends? I'll say not!" Her face tightened covetously. "But why are you looking for him? Maybe I can help."

Turcotte passed over the dollar bill. "Where does he live?" He tried to make his tone casual. "If I find Mulai, do you suppose he could do a bit of hypnotizing for me?"

The woman laughed raucously. "That ape? It took old Sidi to do the hypnotism stunt. He had the face for it. But Mulai—never! How could a cross-eyed man hypnotize anybody?" She started away, saying: "You wait a minute—"

Returning, she handed him a slip of paper. "Here's a bill from the transfer company. Shows where he moved all of Sidi's stuff—the old man willed everything to him—but he never paid for the hauling. They left the bill with me, and a lot of good that did them!"

Soon Turcotte found the address, in a block of vacant store buildings. He hammered at the locked door but nobody answered. There were drawn curtains in second-story windows. He circled through an alley, approached from the rear. A back door opened at his touch. The interior was dark, a musty atmosphere of disuse hanging over the place, but there was a bucket of fresh garbage at the foot of a stair.

He ascended the steps cautiously, cursing creaky boards which seemed to shout an alarm. Gun in hand, he stepped into the gloomy upper hall, began feeling his way along the wall. His groping fingers touched a doorknob. It rattled slightly. Waiting, he heard no sound. Turning the handle with care, he pushed open the portal. A blinding light flashed in his eyes. Someone swung a heavy club. He groaned and fell, pistol clattering across the floor.

It seemed but a moment later when Turcotte found himself rolling and twisting upon hard boards, but through a window high overhead he saw the pale crescent of a new moon. Hours had flown and night had fallen. There was a sweetish taste of drugs in his mouth.

Struggling to his feet he struck a match, and by its light, saw that he was confined in a narrow cubicle formed by three solid steel walls and a grating. A freight elevator. The shaft made an admirable jail. A pull at the starting lever proved the power was off. He shook the gate, looked up at the window. Leaping high, he caught a cross beam and got astride the elevator frame. The window was still far out of reach. He began climbing the cable. Fortunately, grease upon it had hardened from disuse and he managed to inch his way higher and higher until abreast the glass. Kicking out panes and sash he hooked a foot through the aperture and flung himself sidewise, catching the sill with one hand. In the dark it seemed a long way to the ground, but he risked the drop, landing upon his feet in the alley with a jolt that jarred his spine. Hurrying along the street, he passed a dingy pawn-shop, turned back. For an exorbitant price he purchased a revolver without a permit. Farther down he came to a drug store, and through the window could see public telephone booths. Going in, he dialed a number. Mrs. Hale answered. She broke into a torrent of weeping and he had to put another nickel in the slot before she quieted sufficiently to make her-self understood.

"Helen's gone!" the woman sobbed. "Something terrible has happened to her. She'll die, like Mary did—"

"Gone!" he cried hoarsely. "When? Where?"

"She seemed better—she was sitting up in bed, reading some letters the postman brought. Then I heard her shriek. I went to her room and she was cowering against the pillows, screaming, 'The eyes! The eyes!' And Bob! Someone had sent her a picture in the mail—just a pair of horrid eyes that seemed to burn right through you. I went to call Doctor Hewitt. When I returned—" Mrs. Hale's voice broke miserably again—"she was gone—*gone*, I tell you! I know she'll never come back alive."

"You called the police? No? Then 'phone Lieutenant Wayne. Tell him they've hypnotized Helen with that picture, after preparing her mind for it when she went to the fortune-teller. Tell him to throw out a dragnet for Mulai. I'm going to head her off if I can."

Turcotte ran toward the building in which he had been imprisoned. He stopped upon the corner, where he might observe people passing along two streets. Soon his vigil was rewarded. Half a block down the more dimly lighted thoroughfare a familiar form appeared, walking rapidly, looking neither to right nor left. The girl turned into the dark alley.

He ran after her, calling: "Helen! Wait—"

She was at the rear door of the storeroom when he seized her hand. She did not speak—just shouldered him aside—tugging at the latch. He caught her up in his arms and wheeled to flee. But a voice within the building snarled, "Stand still unless you want her shot." Turcotte thrust Helen behind him, reached for his gun. From a window overhead, someone dropped a heavy object. It glanced off his skull and he staggered blindly. The door burst open. Swift-moving figures bore him down.

Waves of laughter beat against Turcotte's brain . . . Malicious, hellish laughter that was, somehow, obscene. He opened his eyes, found himself sagging drunkenly against tight ropes that bound him to a chair.

Again the laughter came, a chorus of it. Shrill, demonic, threatening. He became aware of several moving forms. As his vision cleared, he saw a circle of hateful, leering faces, lighted by dark, foreign eyes in which grim fires seemed to burn.

A resonant, commanding voice silenced their raucous mirth. Turcotte's pain-dimmed eyes sought the speaker. The large chamber, which resembled the meeting place of a lodge, was shrouded in darkness save for a circle of light cast by one bare electric bulb. Striding into view came a man in vestments of white, a turban upon his head. The saffron countenance, the black crossed eyes, identified him as Mulai, once Sidi Ghanna's assistant. He paused in front of Turcotte, lips curled in an evil smile.

"You have come to a ceremony for one who is as dead. Later, you too shall pass beyond the veil."

Turcotte cursed him feebly.

Mulai stepped over to the wall and pressed a switch. Another light glowed at the farther end of the room. Turcotte uttered a cry of heart-broken grief. A black coffin loomed against a white curtain hung from the ceiling. Lying motionless within it was the body of the girl he loved. He screamed: "You've murdered her!"

He surged against the ropes which bound him. The more he twisted and squirmed, the louder Mulai's companions in crime laughed. The turbaned leader's face clouded impatiently.

"Stop it!" he grated. "All must be done with due solemnity or the effect may be spoiled." He turned, approaching the coffin, addressing Helen Hale.

"O, daughter of Sekhmet; rise and speak if you hear my command."

The girl sat up, slowly, stiffly. Her eyes opened wide. The pallid lips moved: "I hear. I obey your will."

Mulai lifted her down from the somber pier. Leading her by the hand he brought her to the center of the room. "Tonight's demonstration," he said to the half-dozen brown-faced Orientals, "shall be even more spectacular. This time I shall take steps to insure publicity. No longer shall the police suppress the truth."

He turned to Turcotte, teeth bared in a smile. "Perhaps you wonder at the nature of our plans? When one or two more girls have . . . committed suicide . . . in public places, each wearing the girdle labeled 'Daughters of Sekhmet,' I am sure that a convincing threat to the wealthy parents of other girls will produce huge cash payments to insure the safety of their children. Actual abduction will be entirely unnecessary,"

"Suicide!" Turcotte raged. "You mean *murder*! After you've hypnotized them."

Mulai smirked. "Authorities agrcc that the thing you mention is impossible. Experts will never accuse me. A person, hypnotized, will perform no revolting act that would be refused if conscious. That is why"—he frowned—"we can influence this girl to commit suicide only by making her *want to die!"*

One of the men sprang forward. Hooking his fingers in the bodice of Helen's dress he ripped the upper part away. Turcotte swore angrily, heaving and straining against his bonds. Another man tore off the girl's skirt. A third bound a ribbon round her breast, upon which was lettered:

"DAUGHTERS OF SEKHMET"

Tears of rage streamed down Turcotte's bloody face. Ropes seared his flesh. His heart pounded with superhuman efforts to break free. But the bonds held.

Mulai raised his hands and spoke to Helen again: "I bid you waken!"

Helen's taut body relaxed. She rubbed her eyes like a tired child. Then, observing her own nakedness, she gasped, whirled to flee.

Turcotte lunged and jerked with utter disregard for lacerated flesh. Helen, seeing him there, screamed:

"Bob! They'll murder us! Oh, don't let them drag me naked into the streets—"

Mulai thundered: "Is it death that you fear? Soon you will be *glad* to die!"

He jerked a cord running through staples in the ceiling.

Curtains slid back along the farther wall. At the sight disclosed beyond, Helen Hale dropped in a cringing heap. Her terrified shrieks were like dagger-thrusts in Turcotte's breast.

Within a dimly lighted booth stood a number of hideous creatures more beast than human. Their bare bodies were masses of inflamed flesh, their faces but shapeless blobs. Light glinted redly from their staring eyes. Motionless, they stood poised as though to spring.

"Lepers!" Turcotte shouted wildly. "For God's sake, run!"

Mulai's henchmen chanted: "Unclean! You shall be unclean!"

They seized the girl, dragged her toward the waiting monsters. Fear seemed to paralyze her throat muscles. Then they loosened in a wild torrent of shrieks. Supported between grinning captors, the toes of her shoes dragging on the floor, she was borne from one to another of the repulsive things in the alcove, and her flesh defiled by contact with their claws.

Frantically struggling, mouth twisted in mute agony, Helen finally collapsed. Curtains slid across the booth again.

Turcotte, blear-eyed and broken, hung in the ropes groaning wretchedly. Mulai walked to the edge of the white drape.

"Behind this screen the power of Sidi Ghanna will enter into me. Soon, in the ritual of the apple, this Daughter of Sekhmet shall find peace in the arms of Death. You know the hour—ten. The place—Drake Hotel."

A confused murmur arose among the swarthy men. Mulai commanded: "Silence! Let there be no sound after I rouse her, or the spell may be broken. Remember, I must hold her subject to my will, so that she will *want* to die. Stand motionless until she follows me."

Mulai stepped back of the curtain. It was transparent. A pale green light spread over its shimmering expanse. Seen through this chiffon veil the man seemed a nebulous figure. Soft organ music began to play. He raised his voice in a chant, making strange gestures. As Turcotte listened, he knew that Mulai was conducting a mass for the dead.

Abruptly a different, deeper voice was raised in a series of commands: "Sidi Ghanna speaks! You will sleep! You will slumber deeply. You will obey."

The figure of Mulai, behind the screen, seemed to fade. The green light changed to an aching white. In his place appeared a turbaned, bearded head of large proportions. Turcotte winced as with a terrific mental shock when he looked into the strange, hypnotic eyes of the dead Egyptian. For minutes the monotonous commands were repeated and he fought against an overpowering lassitude. Then the spell lightened noticeably when the voice changed again, to a sharper tone.

"Unclean! You are unclean! You have been defiled by a touch that is lingering death. For you, Helen Hale, in life remains but suffering and corruption. Only through the ritual of the apple may you be cleansed. I shall lead. You will follow. *You must obey!"*

Helen sat up in the coffin. Her staring eyes were fixed upon the hypnotic orbs. Her words, like an echo from the grave droned dully: "I hear. I will obey. Only, let me die . . ."

Mulai hurried out of the shadows. Taking care to not obstruct Helen's vision of Sidi Ghanna's compelling stare, he swung open a glass lid which had been dropped across the lower part of her body and lifted her out of the coffin. Draping a dark cloak around her shoulders, he turned and marched toward the stairs. Helen followed, entranced, her rapt glance riveted upon the back of his head.

A brawny forearm had locked across Turcotte's throat, choking off his outraged cry. Swift-moving hands removed ropes which bound him to the chair, lashed his ankles and wrists tightly. They carried him to the coffin, tied him there with windings of hemp across his neck so that he might not rise. Latching the glass lid over his legs they trooped out, conversing in a foreign tongue. Only the apparition of Sidi Ghanna remained.

Turcotte's brain throbbed in an aching skull. Bitterly he cursed his helplessness, writhing at thought of Helen's doom. The hypnotic tones of the Egyptian battered his senses remorselessly with monotonous commands: "You sleep. You slumber deeply. You must obey my will . . ." The fierce un-winking gaze seemed to bore into his very soul and he felt his senses swaying. Twisting his face aside, he became aware suddenly of a soft whirring sound that seemed to ema-nate from a hidden mechanism.

"Tricked!" He swore violently. "A talking picture of the dead Sidi—or movies and a phonograph!"

In blind frenzy he jerked and kicked and rolled so galvani-cally that the coffin swayed on its support, slid sidewise, crashed upon the floor. Glass in the bottom lid was shattered. His bound feet flew out. The ropes across his throat burned painfully. Squirming over upon his stomach, he groped with hands tied behind his back, seeking glass fragments stuck in the casket lid. A jagged point slashed his wrist. He sawed against it prayerfully, unmindful of the pain. The ropes parted. He squeezed out from under the cords around his neck; a moment later, he had his ankles free. Picking up a chair, he hurled it at the face upon the curtain. A smash of metal sounded. A shaft of light shot in an arc across the ceil-ing. The deep voice squawked ridiculously, then was silent.

"Phonograph, all right," he grunted, running toward the curtained booth. "Those novel-length records, made before Sidi died." The loathsome figures in the alcove proved his suspicion to be correct. Wax manikins! As he raced down the back stairs a heavy object comfortingly thumped against his thigh. They had not troubled to disarm him, accounting as one already dead. Through the alley into a deserted street he rushed. A cruising taxi hove in view. He wrenched open its door, gasping: "Drake Hotel! Police business! Stop for noth-ing—"

The driver was game. Astonished traffic cops dodged aside when the car roared past. Soon the brilliant sign of the Drake loomed ahead, but when half a block from the entranceway the driver, slapped on brakes and coasted to a stop.

"Best I can do, Captain! Traffic jam. Time for the bigwigs to be coming out from that N.R.A. meeting."

Head down, Turcotte butted through a crowd which had overflowed the street. He brought up against a roped-off space within which stood a cordon of police. A cop seized him by the arm.

Turcotte struggled and was clubbed for his pains. Dazed, he tried to explain. Suddenly a sharp cry burst from his lips: "There she is! Stop her!"

Cars arriving early had been permitted to park along the curb opposite the Drake's marquee. Silhouetted against the open door of a cab some twenty yards away, Helen Hale stood, the fatal apple in her hand.

The staring policeman's grasp loosened. Turcotte's brain functioned swiftly. No chance to reach her side in time to forestall the poisoned bite. Mulai was crouching behind the taxi, face taut with mental strain. His was the will which guided her faltering steps, that would command, "Taste the apple and die."

Turcotte's arm raised, tipped with spurting fire. Mulai pitched forward upon his face. Disregarding a policeman's hoarse warning, Turcotte burst through the cordon, dashed to Helen's side. She had dropped her cloak, just before the bullet entering Mulai's brain had snapped the hypnotic spell. Now she cringed.

Turcotte caught her up and stumbled toward a parked limousine. The door swung open and a white-haired old gentleman jumped down.

"Put her in there! Give her the robe. What ever possessed her . . .?"

Police came rushing from all directions, waving guns and clubs. Lieutenant Wayne appeared. He ordered a space cleared around the car. To Turcotte he whispered:

"Only your shot saved the girl. My men just 'phoned. They raided the place too late." Turcotte snapped: "Send them back to lie in wait. Some of the henchmen of that gang are sure to return. Now, break a way for us out of this jam."

The crowd parted before Wayne's sharp commands. The limousine crawled from its place at the curb. The chauffeur asked the white-haired old gentleman: "Where to, sir?"

"Just drive! Give them a breathing spell." He climbed in

beside the driver, cast a sympathetic glance across his shoulder. "I'd certainly like to know what happened. Whatever it was, one can plainly see that those young folks have been through hell!"

KILLER BLOOD FOR SALE

I HAD PUT IT OVER, sold a thumping big block of stock to a prospect who had eluded our best men; and my thoughts were still with the customer whose apartment I had just left, still jubilating over the substantial check that reposed in my billfold, as I walked down the hallway and pressed the button for the automatic elevator.

The car was just reaching the floor level, lighting up the diamond-shaped window in the door, and my hand reached for the knob? when a human tornado swept silently out of a side corridor and brushed me aside!

For a moment I caught a glimpse of a large-size man, of a dull expressionless face topped by a mop of blond hair, of loud, check-pattern suit? and then I was hurled to one side as the fellow flung open the elevator door and leaped inside.

Stunned by the suddenness of it, I sat there on the floor, gaping open-mouthed as a hullabaloo arose behind me and three excited men came running down the corridor. Blankly they stared at the illuminated "In Use" sign at the side of the elevator, and then at me as I climbed dazedly to my feet,

"He's gone," one of them muttered with a bitter curse. "No sense trying to catch him now. All we can do is call the police? and they'll do nothing, as usual."

From the faces of the others I imagined that they were none too sorry that their quarry, whoever he was, had escaped. They were white-lipped, wide-eyed men who had been on the verge of desperation and now breathed deeply with obvious relief. Hesitantly they turned and started back down the corridor through which they had come, and I went with them.

Went to an apartment door that stood open, and followed

them inside—and then wished to God that I had minded my own business!

The room into which I had stepped was a small one, outfitted with cheap, worn furniture; a typical furnished apartment—but now it had been lifted out of the prosaic, everyday role and had become a place of horror. Sprawled there on the floor in the center of the living room was the naked corpse of a pretty young woman—a corpse that was twisted and mangled and torn fiendishly; a corpse that must have died in screaming agony, every twinge of which was stamped indelibly on the pain-contorted face, mirrored in the horror-filled eyes!

A corpse with the throat almost torn out, the mutilated torso bathed in the flood of its own blood . . .

"This is the fourth victim," I heard a man half-whisper behind me, "and still the murdering devil is at large."

And then I knew that I had been face to face with the fiendish killer all of New York was seeking. This was his fourth victim in less than a month. All pretty young women who had seemed to come willingly to keep a fatal rendezvous with him in a cheap, furnished apartment such as this. A rendezvous that always ended in ravishment and death so horrible that the whole city was aghast.

Horrified, the gathering crowd of on-lookers stared down at the ghastly sight—but their shock was nothing to the utter terror that seized upon me and seemed to sap the strength out of my bones. To them this fearful atrocity was at least impersonal—but as I stared down at the unthinkably outraged corpse its lines seemed to blur, and in its place I could see the lovely body of Leta Barclay, my fiancée!

How Leta could be involved with anything so frightful as this, I had no idea. But as I stood there, sick and trembling, I could fairly see the shadow of the fiend who had done this thing reaching out for her, his evil tentacles coiling about her . . .

For the past month I had sensed that there was something terrifying hanging over her; something that was intangible and elusive but none the less deadly. I had seen it in her troubled, fear-haunted eyes; in the nervous tension that kept her continually on edge; in the vague and hardly discernible change that had come over her.

Ever since that night, a month before, when we had gone together to Dr. Nelson Abernathy's home to hear his brother Hubert lecture. Hubert was an explorer who had just returned from the Belgian Congo, where he claimed to have discovered the secret of the native "wireless telegraphy" by which they are able to send detailed news through impenetrable stretches of jungle with amazing speed.

"Blood is the answer," he told the two dozen guests assembled in the doctor's library; "blood answering the call of blood in the veins through which it once flowed!"

Like his brother, Hubert Abernathy was a big man with a large head, but unlike the leonine, kindly faced doctor, his flesh had been shrunken by tropical fevers until his head loomed like a thinly covered skull above his gaunt, emaciated frame. But his voice was deep and magnetic; it gripped his listeners and held them as if by a spell.

"In M'Bwami's kraal I found the answer to the riddle," he went on. "M'Bwami was the head witch-doctor in a territory many hundred miles square. More than fifty years ago he founded a brotherhood of blood by inoculating everyone in his kraal with a few drops of his own blood. As the years passed each new warrior went through the transfusion ceremony, each maiden as she reached maturity—until the vast brotherhood extended from one end of the Congo to the other.

"Through that blood brotherhood he was able to control them, to bend their wills to his—even though they were miles away from him. His people believed implicitly that M'Bwami had the power to will death—the power to impel a man, miles away, to go out and kill another man. Yes, and the power of life, as well. He had only to will it, to exert the call of his blood, and the most beautiful maidens in his domain came willingly to his hut."

I could feel a shiver pass through Leta, seated on the divan beside me; could feel her hands clutching my arm as she leaned close to me. Not only Leta felt the spell of his words. Beside her sat Marcia Poling, her best friend, and I noticed that Marcia was drinking in his every syllable avidly, while her eyes seemed riveted to his thin lips.

"M'Bwami has been dead for twenty years," he concluded, "but his people believe that he still controls them; that his blood still directs them from the grave. They claim that he appears to them, that he speaks to them—and who are we to say that they are wrong? What do we really know about the power of human blood—the psychological properties of living blood transfused from the veins of one person to another?"

In the silence that followed I could hear the soft, soughing gasp of Leta's breath, could feel her trembling as if she were chilled to the bone as her icy little hand burrowed into mine.

"He terrifies me, Chris!" she whispered. "All that talk about blood—blood *can't* do things like that to a person, can it?"

That was a month ago, but the terror that had seeped into Leta that night was even more devastating now than when it first came over her. It was changing her, making her moody and morbid—a condition that Dr. Abernathy's prescriptions seemed helpless to combat.

These ghastly murders that were shocking the city had become a positive obsession with her. With terror-filled eyes she scanned the headlines each day, and each new crime fairly prostrated her. Why? I kept asking myself that question—and the only answer that came to me was a fearful premonition that in some inexplicable way she was linked up with these appalling outrages . . .

Now, as I gazed down at that pitiful corpse, a chill coursed up and down my spine like a thin trickle of ice water—and I knew that my premonition was all too true. I knew, too, that I must get out of that apartment before the police arrived and detained us all as witnesses. Leta was in danger, and I must be free to go to her.

Unobtrusively I slipped out of that shambles and from the building without being observed. Back to the office, where my chief was waiting for me—and a short while later I was free to go to Leta.

But when I telephoned her apartment there was no answer, and tantalizing, maddening fear tightened its grip around my heart. She was supposed to be at home that night, but she wasn't there. What had happened to her? Where was she?

Those questions were hammering wildly through my brain by the time I reached my own apartment—and there was the answer, sitting waiting in the lobby for me.

"Oh, Chris," she gasped as soon as she saw me, "I had to see you; I couldn't wait. I can't keep it to myself any longer. You've got to know—"

And then she was in my arms, sobbing out a disjointed flow of terrified words.

"That terrible murderer—they've identified him. He's— he's—oh, God, Chris he's August Hinman, that nice German man Dr. Abernathy got when I needed blood—"

But already my mind was leaping ahead of her words. Hinman—he was the blood donor who had been called, six months before, when Leta lay at death's door as the result of a motor accident. It was his blood, transfused into her veins, that had brought her back to life and health.

"Jim Thompson telephoned tonight to warn me, Chris. He said he has definitely established that each of the murdered girls had received a blood transfusion from Hinman at one time or another. Oh, don't you see, Chris—don't you realize what it means? His blood flowed in their veins—that's why they went to him willingly, helplessly, when he called to them!"

Jim Thompson was a reporter whom we had met Hubert Abernathy's lecture. He was a keen newspaperman—and he had phoned to warn Leta . . .

"You remember what Hubert Abernathy said," she whispered, while stark fear leaped in her red-rimmed eyes. "M'Bwami had only to will it and the maidens came to his hut. August Hinman's blood is in my veins—more than a quart of it. He only needs to will it and—and I'll be helpless, Chris!"

Absurd! Preposterous! Vainly I rallied every conceivable argument and hurled it at her—but deep down at the pit of my stomach was an emptiness, a bottomless feeling that left me weak and shaken.

Good God—was it possible that there could be any truth to this outlandish legend? Did Leta know what she was saying? Was she doomed like those others—perhaps next on the awful death list?

Chapter Two

Throbbing Blood

"That's all rot!" I almost shouted as I clasped her hungrily in my arms—but before my eyes was the ghastly vision of that mangled corpse I had stared at only a few hours before. "You remember how the papers ridiculed Abernathy's claims. Just a native superstition. People don't believe things like that in a civilized country."

"It isn't what I believe, Chris," her voice came tonelessly. "It's what I *feel*. A terrifying change has been coming over me. At times my blood races madly—seems to be on fire. And then—then thoughts come into my mind that make me blush. It's his blood calling to me—calling to me and urging me to do things that shock me!"

Firmly I gripped her by the shoulders and held her off at arm's length while I looked deep into her frightened eyes.

"I'm not the only one," she shook her head hopelessly. "Marcia has felt it, too. She's terrified. Our reactions are the same—just as the same blood was pumped into our veins!"

The same blood—August Hinman's blood! I remembered, then. About a year ago Marcia had been suffering from anemia in such an advanced stage that blood transfusions were necessary. Dr. Abernathy had used Hinman as the blood donor.

"It's blood answering blood," Leta wailed despairingly.

"The blood in our veins answering Hinman's call. I'm afraid, Chris—terribly afraid of what he might make me do!"

This thing was impossible. It was uncanny, fantastic, to imagine that this degenerate killer should be able to influence the blood that once flowed through his veins—and yet, as I held her there in my arms, I knew that I was terrified to let her go.

The significant facts that Jim Thompson had uncovered were undeniable . . .

Jim Thompson! Again the reporter's part in this queer business leaped into my mind. It was he who had made the discoveries; it was he who had called Leta to warn her—and actually frightened her out of her wits. Perhaps these "discoveries" were trickery on his part; merely a cheap stratagem to insinuate himself into Leta's affections.

Or perhaps it was Hubert Abernathy who was at the bottom of this fiendish devilment. It was his spooky lecture that had started all this talk about blood and its power.

I hadn't liked the explorer from the beginning; hadn't liked the way his eyes traveled over Leta. There was something obscene, vulturous, about the man—just the sort who might concoct a plot as Machiavelian as this.

Gradually I managed to talk Leta out of her panic, using arguments that were for my own benefit as well as hers—arguments that I knew I could not accept even as I voiced them. Finally she consented to take a double dose of the sedative Dr. Abernathy had given her and then go to bed.

It was too late to contact Jim Thompson or Hubert Abernathy that night, but as I drove back to my apartment after seeing her home I determined to call Thompson the first thing in the morning. I wanted to know just what information he had uncovered. The first thing in the morning—

But I had hardly slipped out of my jacket and vest when the telephone rang jarringly.

"Hello, Rockwell," a man's voice came over the wire before I had an opportunity to open my mouth. "This is Thompson—Jim Thompson. I've got something here I want you to see—but you'll have to hurry. Take down this address, and then hustle over there. Make it snappy—this is just about the most important thing you ever did in your life."

Then he had hung up and I was staring frowningly at the Riverside Drive address and apartment number I had copied on my telephone memo pad. Jim Thompson—what did he want with me at that time of night?

My wonder and suspicion grew when I climbed out of a cab in front of the address he had given me. There were two police cars in front of the house, and I glimpsed uniformed men in the hallway; but Thompson was there to greet me and usher me past the police.

Without a word he led me a third floor apartment, through the short hallway and into a bedroom where several detectives were on guard, up to a bed—and then the flesh seemed to crawl on my bones while my eyes fairly popped from my head with horrified amazement!

Stretched out on that bed was the mangled body of a young man. His wrists and ankles tied spread-eagled to the bedposts so that he was helpless to move. The top of his pajamas had been torn from his body and the flesh beneath was horribly butchered. The torso was almost denuded of skin by eager, raking fingernails, and his mouth and throat were torn and savagely chewed until they were hardly recognizable!

Blood drenched the outraged corpse, stained the bed clothes and the floor. Blood everywhere—until I could feel my stomach turning over at the sight of it.

"More of Hinman's work?" I gasped as soon as I could get control of my tongue and tear it from the dry roof of my mouth.

"Maybe," Thompson admitted as he led me over to a window and pointed down into an areaway. "Maybe some of his work—but he didn't do this himself. We're going down into that court."

When we reached the paved areaway another ghastly scene awaited us. Sprawled at full length on the flagging was the crushed body of what must have been a pretty young woman.

Now her face was a mask of utter horror, her staring eyes fixed in incredible agony—as if their final vision had been a glimpse of hell itself.

Her skull was split open by the force with which she had struck, but immediately I knew that the blood which soaked her clothing and arms and made a crimson horror of her mouth was not from the broken head that had caused her death.

It wasn't her own blood—any more than the shreds of skin and grisly flesh that clotted her fingernails were her own. As I gazed down at her I had a frightful vision of what must have transpired in that upstairs bedroom before she plunged through the window to her death!

"She is Viola Mears," Thompson's business-like voice penetrated the appalling horror that had numbed my brain "I have already been able to check on her. She was one of Dr. Nelson Abernathy's patients—and she recently underwent a blood transfusion from August Hinman. That poor devil upstairs was the chap she was going to marry."

Another victim with August Hinman's blood flowing in her veins! But instead of answering his summons and going helplessly to her death she had been dispatched on an errand of barbaric murder!

My mind reeled under the undeniable evidence lying there in the courtyard before my eyes. Such things couldn't be— but they *were!* And a cold sweat broke out like a rash all over my body as I thought of Leta and what she had told me—the alien urgings in her blood—the dread that she would be called and would be helpless to do anything but obey . . .

"There's something hellishly evil on foot," Thompson was saying as he took my arm and led me back into the building, "and we've got to get to the bottom of it in a hurry or it may be too late—too late for Leta Barclay. She's your fiancée, Rockwell, but I love her, too, and I don't want to find her like that poor thing out there."

Chapter Three

Blood Lives On

There was little sleep for me that night. I tossed restlessly for hours, trying to fathom this incredible danger that threatened Leta, trying to devise some way of protecting her from it. The next morning, as early as I thought she would be awake, I drove to her apartment—but the moment I saw her I knew that Abernathy's sedative had not been very effective. Not only was she awake, but she had already secured a copy of the morning paper and read about Viola Mears' ghastly death.

There was no mention, in the article, of Jim Thompson's discovery, but Leta sensed the connection immediately.

"Viola Mears," she repeated the name several times. "I am almost certain she was one of Dr. Abernathy's patients. If she was, Chris, that means that—"

"Regardless of what it means, we're taking you to see the doctor before this things drives you into a nervous breakdown," I announced determinedly; and an hour later we were seated in Dr. Abernathy's consulting room.

Jim Thompson's discoveries and charges were foremost in my mind as I sat back and studied the elderly physician as Leta told him of her fears. Abernathy seemed worried, I noticed at once. His peaceful, benevolent looking face was not so composed as usual; it was almost haggard—and as I watched his eyes I saw that what she was telling him was not news. He knew what was coming and involuntarily flinched from it!

But when she had finished he leaned back in his swivel chair and laughed chidingly—a laugh that, to my alert ears, did not ring altogether genuine. A laugh that seemed forced, affected.

Then he was suddenly serious.

"Of course, I have read what the newspapers say about Hinman," he said soberly. "It hardly seems possible that he could commit such beastly crimes; I know him quite well, and he never impressed me as that sort of man. I have tried to get in touch with him but have not succeeded in reaching him. However, I shall not be convinced until he is apprehended and the whole truth is known. But so far as Hinman having any occult control over the blood which once flowed through his veins—that's utter nonsense.

"Perhaps Hubert may be right in his theories about the African natives—but that is Africa, where mentalities are entirely different from ours. August Hinman is an unimaginative German, interested only in the money he receives for the blood that is drained out of his veins. Once it leaves his body he never gives it another thought—you may be sure of that.

"Chris is right—your fears are entirely imaginary, Leta; even the symptoms you think you detect—just your excited imagination. We'll try you with another concoction and see if it won't give that over-worked mind of yours a bit of rest."

As he spoke he wrote out a prescription and pushed a button at the side of his desk.

Dr. Nelson Abernathy was a widower whose married life had ended in tragedy. Some ten years ago his wife had committed suicide—the climax, rumor had it, of an illicit love affair with another man. Since that time the doctor had had eyes for no other woman—except for Leta, whom he always regarded in a doting, fatherly sort of way.

Now, as I studied him covertly, I could see that he was more than uneasy. He was nervous, fidgety; and as he looked at Leta there was concern and fear in his eyes—or did I misread the telltale flicker he tried his best to conceal?

Abernathy's professional reputation was of the finest; his skill in diagnosing and treating obscure ailments was marvelous—uncanny, some of his patients claimed. He modestly attributed his success to thoroughness—and went so far in this respect that he insisted on filling all his own prescriptions rather than trusting them to an ordinary pharmacist.

In response to his ring a door at the side of the office opened and a white-coated assistant stepped in and nodded briefly to us. Dr. Arno Ecker was a large man, like his chief, but there the resemblance stopped. Unlike Abernathy, he had done nothing to take care of himself. His face, which once must have been good-looking, had become flabby and expressionless; his eyes dull; his shoulders stooped from too much bending over mixing bowls and peering through microscopes. He seemed to have no vitality, no interest in life other than puttering with his chemicals. Not a prepossessing figure. Somehow I got the impression that he had a furtive fear of the doctor—a fear that might be mixed with hatred, although why I should feel that I do not know.

Ecker took the prescription and studied it puzzledly for a moment, then backed unobtrusively out of the room.

"That prescription should fix you up all right," Abernathy turned back to Leta, "but I have another suggestion that—"

The click of the door at his back interrupted him and the doctor swung around in surprise, to confront Dr. Ecker standing uncertainly midway between the desk and the door.

"I—I am a little concerned about this prescription, doctor," the assistant mumbled doubtfully. "It is somewhat unusual, isn't it? I wondered if you realize what you prescribed— realize just what effect this compound will have?"

For a moment the color drained out of Abernathy's face; then it returned with a rush and his cheeks were suffused with an angry, glowing red, while his eyes became sharp, gleaming points of seething rage. He half rose from his chair in his sudden fury.

"I wrote that prescription in full command of my faculties," he roared. "I know exactly what it calls for, and that's what I want you to put into it. This is the third time in the past two weeks that you have taken occasion to question my judgment, Ecker, and I've had enough of it. I'll thank you to attend to your business and let me handle mine!"

With a mumbled apology Arno Ecker backed out of the room—but not before I thought I saw a gleam of malice in his eye—and Abernathy's rage subsided as quickly as it had risen. Somewhat shame-facedly he settled back in his chair and swung around to face us.

"A good man, but I have to keep him in his place. As I was

saying," he resumed, "I have another suggestion. What you need is a change, Leta. You should get out of the city for a few days so that you will have a chance to forget this thing that has been preying on your mind. And I have just the spot for you. Over the week-end I am giving a house party for my brother, Hubert, at my summer place in the Watchung Mountains, just over the river. I want you and Chris to be my guests."

The prospect of a week-end in Hubert Abernathy's company was anything but inviting for me, but before I could try to decline the invitation the doctor pressed on.

"Marcia Poling has been to see me—with a complaint very similar to yours, Leta," he said quickly. "I invited her for the same reason, and my car will pick her up this afternoon. After that we'll stop for you."

It wasn't a case of accepting or declining his invitation; the doctor accepted it for us, and before we realized it we had agreed to be ready when he came for us—but as we left his office I was almost sorry that we had come. I didn't want to week-end with Hubert Abernathy; I didn't want Leta under the spell of his dark, hypnotic eyes. But there had been no way of declining without offending the doctor.

At two-thirty Abernathy's car arrived for us and sped us across town and over the bridge into New Jersey, westward into the Watchungs. The doctor's place was a huge old wooden building set in the midst of a rambling, semi-wild estate.

"I like to preserve its natural beauty," he apologized for what seemed a lack of care.

But it wasn't the grounds so much as the building which impressed me. The old house was run down, only the shell of what it had once been. As I looked at it I could visualize it in its heyday, when the wide porches must have been thronged with laughing guests. Now all that seemed muted, gone never to return but leaving in its wake ghostly reminders of what had been.

Only then did I recall that it was in this building that Mrs.

Abernathy had ended her . . .

There were only five of us in the party: the doctor and his brother, Marcia Poling, Leta and I—and at once I knew that we were too few for a house of that size. It would have taken a party of twenty or thirty to rout the shadows from the large, high-ceilinged rooms and to dispel the loneliness that pervaded the place.

Equally soon I realized that the party was to be a failure so far as taking the girls' minds off their worries was concerned.

August Hinman was uppermost in their minds. As long as he was at large they would be in danger, no matter where they went. As long as he was free to exert the weird, incredible influence that bound them to him they believed that they would be helpless to resist.

It was night, close to bedtime, when a siren at the door brought us all to our feet, sent us flocking out onto the porch after the doctor—to stare in amazement at Jim Thompson climbing out of his coupe.

"I have news that will interest all of you," he announced. "You don't have to worry any more about August Hinman; he's dead. The police found his body in a bathtub in an empty apartment. The tub had been filled with chemicals, and the body was pretty badly eaten away—but not so far that he could not be definitely identified. So now you girls can rest in peace."

A mighty load lifted from my shoulders with that announcement. Hinman was gone—the hellish nightmare was over . . .

And then I caught Marcia's glance. She had been looking up into Hubert Abernathy's eyes, and in their depths she seemed to find the answer she sought.

"He's dead," she half whispered, "but is that the end? M'Bwami, they said, could control his blood from the grave itself—"

"What you need is another dose of medicine and a good night's sleep," Dr. Abernathy cut her short sharply. "In the morning you will be able to laugh at your fears."

His housekeeper showed Marcia to her room on the second floor, and then Leta followed. When they had gone, Thompson turned to the rest of us.

"There's more to it than that," he said crisply. "As you realize, Hinman's death wasn't suicide, doctor. He was murdered and dumped, naked, into that tub. And the murderer may very well have been the fiend who has been committing these crimes. There were no clues to the killer's identity except several flagons from which the acids had been poured— flagons from *your* laboratory, doctor. The police will probably be out here to question you about that in the morning.

"They are building up rather a bad case against you, doctor," Thompson went on. "With those flagons next to Hinman's body it become more that coincidence that all of the murdered women were your patients—patients you had treated with Hinman's blood."

"I know—I know," Abernathy gasped. "But I can't tell them anything—I don't know anything, I tell you!"

It was so late by then that Thompson accepted the doctor's invitation to stay overnight, and shortly we retired. It was quiet in Leta's room as I went to the one that had been assigned to me, but, nevertheless, I decided to stay awake that night.

Partly dressed I lay down on the bed and listened intently until the last house noise subsided. Then all was still, except the rustle of the leaves outside and the flutter of a shade in the night breeze. All quiet for what seemed hours—and then my half-dozing senses snapped alert.

That had been a noise out in the hall. I tensed and listened. There it was again—a door opening stealthily, the soft pad of feet on the hardwood floor!

Cautiously I slipped off the bed and tiptoed to my door, opened it noiselessly. In the dim illumination of the night-lighted hallway I could barely distinguish Marcia Poling's slim figure, in her nightgown, as she tiptoed from her own room to the one next door.

That was the room assigned to Jim Thompson, I remembered. Had I been spying on a prearranged rendezvous?

There would be no harm in listening a few moments at that door, I decided, and started across the hall—but before I was more than halfway to Thompson's door his terrified voice burst forth in a bloodcurdling scream.

Then I was rushing across the hall, throwing myself against that door as I shouted for help. The door was solidly built, and it was not until I had hurled myself against it half a dozen times that the lock snapped out of the wood. And then it was too late.

I knew that the moment I snapped on the light. Stretched out on the bed was Jim Thompson's mangled corpse—the top of his pajamas torn from his lacerated body, his throat a crimson horror, his eyes glazed and his face contorted in death.

And beside the bed stood Marcia Poling, blood dripping from her hands and bathing her almost from head to foot. Beside the bed she stood, staring down at it with eyes that bulged from her head as she realized what she had done.

"It was Hinman," she moaned as she wrung her gory hands. "It was Hinman. He made me do it. He came into my room and held me in his arms until I couldn't help myself. He made me do it!"

Chapter Four

Night of Horror

Behind me I heard the gasp of quickly indrawn breath, a shrill scream smothered before it was half uttered—and I swung around to find Leta standing there, her eyes round with horror, the back of her right hand crammed into her mouth to hold back the hysterical shrieks that were welling up into her throat.

"Hinman!" she choked. "Hinman! Even after he is dead the curse of his blood lives on! Even from the grave he is able to control the corpuscles that once flowed through his veins! There is no hope for us, Chris—we can't escape him!"

Before she could back away I took her in my arms and held her tight while I tried to reason with her—but the light of frantic madness gleamed in her terrified eyes. She was afraid—desperately afraid; not so much for herself as for me.

"You're going back to bed, to sleep and forget all about this," I told her grimly as I led her back to her room. "Lock the door, and I'll keep watch out here in the hall so that you will have nothing whatever to fear."

As soon as she was quiet I went back to that ghastly murder room. Dr. Abernathy and his brother had now calmed Marcia Poling somewhat and were leading her back to her bedroom. Once there they persuaded her to bathe and change her nightgown—while the doctor brought out a strait jacket he had stored in another part of the house.

Before she knew what was intended we strapped her into it and laid her out on her bed.

"It's the only thing we can do," the doctor sighed, as he locked the door of her room. "In her condition there is no telling what she may do. This way she will be safe until we can notify the police in the morning."

His hand shook as if he had the palsy, and he seemed to have aged hours in the past few minutes. I could easily understand that; my own nerves were on hair trigger edge and I wanted nothing so much as to have that night end, to see the blessed light of day once more.

Again the noises stilled, one by one, until even Marcia's wild sobbing subsided into sleep. The shadows in the dimly lighted hallway grew deeper and deeper, and Leta's doorway, as I stared at it, seemed to shrink, to grow smaller and smaller—until it winked out altogether. I caught myself that time and shrugged myself awake. And again after that, but then I must have nodded more sleepily.

Nodded until a terrified shriek knifed through me and brought me entirely awake and up on my feet in a split second. That was Leta's scream! Wildly I dashed across the hall and threw myself at her door, yelling her name, while her screams stabbed through my eardrums and tore at my heart.

Before I could batter my way inside, the door was suddenly unlocked and she sprang out into the hall, straight into my arms. She was unharmed, I saw with a gasp of enervating relief, but she was almost mad with terror. Frantically she pushed me across the hall to my own room and then dragged me inside, to slam and lock the door after us.

"Hinman—he's out there!" she gasped, between convulsive sobs. "I saw him. No, no—I wasn't mistaken, Chris—I saw him!"

She seemed wild to get away from the door, and before I realized it she had urged me over to the bed, had drawn me down onto it and was nestling close beside me. Eagerly her burning lips sought mine, clung to them—and the straps of her low-cut nightgown slipped from her shoulders, allowing the flimsy bit of lingerie to flutter down to her waist.

For a long moment I was powerless—stunned with surprise and with the wonder of her loveliness. For a long moment, while her soft, warm arms went around my neck and drew me close against her. Wild fires of desire seethed up within me at the thrilling touch of her soft flesh and my arms started to enfold her—and then I came to my senses.

This wasn't the Leta I loved. This was a strange, unaccountable person; a fearsome person who had in some way seized Leta's body and her soul. What Leta had been dreading had happened. Something—Hinman or some other fiendish power from out of the darkness—had claimed her and was bending her to its evil will.

My soul was sick within me as I struggled with her, as I gripped her and twisted her body with all my strength. Only by brute force did I manage to pin her down and hold her there until I had almost choked the life out of her. Not until she slumped back, panting and spent, did I dare to release my grip long enough to pull her nightgown back over her shoulders and to slip a pillowcase around her wrists and tie them tightly.

Completely helpless, Leta at last seemed to realize that it was useless to struggle—and with that realization the frenzy fell away from her. Tears welled up into her eyes and her body shook with sobs, but now I did not dare to untie her. Instead I tucked the covers around her, made sure that she could not get loose, and then locked the door of my room behind me as I strode out into the hall.

But the moment I swung away from my own door and started across the hall I froze in my tracks while the hair at the back of my neck rose like bristles. For a fraction of a second I was sure that I had seen another figure there in the doorway of the room that had been Leta's—sure that I had seen eyes watching me.

Then the fellow was gone, faded back into the blackness of the open doorway—and I catapulted myself across the hallway while bitter curses growled from between my clenched teeth.

Chapter Five

The Hell Above

Recklessly I flung myself into that room, groping for the wall switch and snapping on the wall lights as I plunged in. The room, I knew, was next to the one Marcia Poling occupied. Now, as I sprang through the doorway and blinked momentarily in the sudden light, I saw that a section of the paneled wall between the two rooms had slid back—and crouched there in the low, narrow aperture behind it was Hubert Abernathy!

"I know, this looks queer, finding me this way," he mumbled embarrassedly, "but don't jump to conclusions, Rockwell. Miss Barclay's screams woke me up, but by the time I got out into the hall she was going into your room with you. I couldn't help hearing what she told you about seeing Hinman, so I decided to have a look at this room and try to find out what the devil had been going on here. I found this hidden panel quite by accident as I was going over the walls, and—well, I am a lone wolf by nature and profession, so I wanted no assistance in investigating what lay behind it."

As he spoke, my eyes were prying into the opening from which he had just emerged. Now I could see that there was a compartment about two feet wide between the two rooms, and what seemed to be a stairway running upward—

At that moment the light winked out and without a sound someone landed heavily on my back. A powerful, muscular arm wrapped around my throat, drew tight beneath my chin, and a heavy fist pounded cruelly into my face. Desperately I struggled to break that grip, to slip out of it, to heave the fellow over my head, but he held on doggedly, and that sledge-hammer fist beat into my face unmercifully.

Suddenly, taking the fellow by surprise, I dropped to the floor and almost broke free. In the dim light from the window I caught a glimpse of a dull, Germanic face, of a mop of blond hair, a checked coat. With all my strength I lunged at that face, but it seemed to fade away from my flailing fist and I was borne back to the floor.

Dimly I heard Hubert Abernathy curse and then scream—a scream that ended in a groan as a heavy body thumped against the floor. Then something crashed down onto my head with stunning force and my senses swam dizzily as a sea of blackness began to overwhelm me.

Blackness and peace—until a searing agony stabbed hellishly into my chest and flickering lights danced in front of my eyes. Lights that faded, one by one, and blinked out into Stygian darkness.

When I came slowly out of that darkness I was sitting in a chair, a wood armchair, my hands lying limply on the arms. In the feeble light of an ancient lantern that hung from a gabled rafter I could distinguish piles of dusty furniture stacked around the walls, while ghostly figures hung from the rafters and dangled in thin air. An incredible place . . .

But gradually comprehension returned, and I saw that the weird place was nothing more than an attic storeroom; that the ghostly figures were only old, out-of-date suits of clothing and dresses hanging against the walls and from hooks in the beams. Only a harmless old attic—and then my heart seemed to stop beating, seemed to become a dead thing in my breast!

Those white figures standing against uprights toward the other end of the attic were no dummies, no empty suits of clothing. They were women—barefooted women clad only in their nightgowns. They were Marcia Poling—and Leta!

Marcia and Leta—tied up helplessly to those stout wooden pillars! Even as I stared, aghast, a piteous moan escaped from Leta's distended lips and her terrified eyes fastened on mine and pleaded eloquently for help.

That moan of agony wrenched at my heart and wrung an answering groan from the depths of my being. I could feel it welling up into my throat—but no sound passed my lips.

This must be some trick, I thought, leaving me sitting there facing those helpless girls. Probably the moment I tried to go to their rescue I would be pounced upon—but I had to chance that. There seemed to be nobody else in the attic, nobody watching me . . .

Wonderingly I looked down at my right hand, lying on the chair arm, and tried to lift it; but it did not move. Not a finger. Not even a muscle. It was as if the arm were a dead thing lying there.

It must be asleep, I told myself, to stem the panic that was rising in my tortured mind. It must be asleep; in just a few minutes it would be all right. But my whole body was asleep. I could not move a hand or a foot, could not turn my head, could not move a muscle!

And then I gave up trying to deceive myself and faced the ghastly truth: I was completely paralyzed! I could see, could hear, could breathe; yes, I could suffer hell's torment—but I could not move a muscle to help myself or the girl I loved more than my own life!

I writhed inwardly, struggled fearfully to recapture the use of my limbs, suffered the tortures of the damned as I strove to whip my lax muscles into obedience to my will. But it was useless—just as I knew it would be. I was utterly helpless, paralyzed. And then I remembered that stinging agony in my chest and I understood the diabolical thing that had been done to me. I had been doped, filled with a hypodermic load of some devilish concoction that chained me to that chair more helplessly and more securely than all the ropes in the world!

Chained there to sit and watch while Leta met God only knew what fiendishly conceived fate!

Perhaps if the devil who had done this thing to me waited long enough the effect of the stuff would wear off. I clutched desperately at the slightest hope—but that died still-born as my ears caught the sound of footsteps. Footsteps clumping up a flight of stairs.

The inhuman fiend was returning. Now the ghastly end would be only a matter of minutes!

In the shadows at the far end of the attic a curtain swayed. Footsteps started across the floor. A figure loomed indistinctly, came forward into the light—and my heartbeat wildly with delight!

It was Dr. Nelson Abernathy!

Frantically I tried to call out to him, but of course no sound came from my lips. But that would not matter. He could not help seeing me; I was right in the center of the attic. He was coming straight toward me . . .

Straight toward me—and past me! He passed within a foot of me but paid me no attention whatever—didn't even seem to see me!

Incredulously I stared at him while every nerve in my helpless body strove to become articulate—and then I knew the full measure of hopeless despair. I caught a glimpse of his eyes—eyes in which hell fires blazed! Eyes that were fixed in a frenzy of lust on those helpless girls!

Straight toward them he marched, while his body trembled with the wild tempest of his passion. Straight to Marcia, who was nearer to him. For a moment she did not seem to understand; thought that he came as a deliverer, but the moment his eager hands clawed at her she realized what was in store for her and her bulging eyes became wild pools of madness while she writhed helplessly in the grip of the ropes.

Avidly he clutched at her, tore the nightgown from her shoulders. Tremblingly he fumbled with the ropes, ripping them away from her ankles and then from her wrists. Before she could make a move to escape he had her in his arms, crushing his lips to hers, smothering her futile struggles as he lifted her bodily and carried her toward an ancient, dust-covered couch. Her terrified screams echoed and reechoed through the old attic.

"No, doctor—no!" she shrieked at him. But Abernathy paid not the slightest attention. A twisted smile of devilish anticipation played over his features as he dropped her on the couch, to stand for a moment gloating over her nakedness. Then he flung himself upon her, fairly enveloping her in his frenzy.

I closed my eyes at that moment, to blot out from my sight what I knew would follow—but I opened them again when the attic echoed with the creak and snapping of old wood. The ancient couch had given way beneath the burden of their combined weight, and the doctor was rolling on the floor, clutching wildly for Marcia.

Eyes blazing and mouth slavering, he climbed to his knees, started to rise—and then staggered backward as a gun roared from the shelter of the shadowy curtains through which he had come! Dazedly he raised one hand and pressed it to his side as if to try to stem the blood that was dripping out between his fingers. Groaning hollowly, he staggered to his feet, and now I saw that the light of sanity had returned to his eyes.

For just a moment he stood swaying there, while dawning comprehension and overwhelming horror mirrored themselves in his ashen face. Then he pitched forward and sprawled on the floor.

And out of the shadows, into the dim lantern light, came a stoop-shouldered, leering figure—a figure dressed in a cheap, loud patterned suit, a figure with a dull, blank face, with a shock of blond hair, with blazing, maniacal eyes. August Hinman—the man whose body the police had found almost decomposed in a bathtub full of acids!

Chapter Six

Spawn of Hate

August Hinman—now that I had an opportunity to study the man there was something vaguely familiar in the lines of that dull face, in the stoop of his shoulders. Persistently he reminded me of someone else . . .

Before I had time to rack my brain further for identification things started to happen in that attic. By superhuman effort Dr. Abernathy launched himself to his feet when he saw that evil face leering down at him. With an inarticulate cry he leaped at the fellow, his widespread fingers reaching out like claws for those triumphantly blazing eyes.

The utter desperation of his attack carried him to his mark, plummeted him full tilt into the man, his clawing nails tearing at the snarling face, raking one cheek from temple to chin. Skin and flesh tore away under those savage fingers— skin and flesh, and something else. One whole bushy blond eyebrow drew down to one side and then fell off—just as the raking nails fastened in the mop of blond hair and tugged it loose, dragged it crazily askew over one eye!

"Ecker!" Abernathy gasped in utter amazement. "Ecker— you, Ecker!" And now there was nightmare terror in his hoarse, gasping voice.

Momentarily he swayed there, seemingly held up only by the air, while Arno Ecker's hate-distorted face glared at him. Then he seemed to fold up, as if all the strength had suddenly gone out of him, and crashed to the floor, to lie still and glassy-eyed, his jaw hanging open horribly.

Arno Ecker, Abernathy's assistant! Now I realized the familiarity I had sensed in the supposed Hinman's face. The wig and eyebrows, and the complete unexpectedness of seeing Ecker there, had fooled me, blinded me to his real identity.

"Yes, Arno Ecker," the sneering devil sneered as he tossed the now useless wig aside. For a moment he glared down at the doctor, then turned to where Marcia Poling lay in a dead faint, to Leta and me, both helpless to do anything but stare at him. "Yes, Arno Ecker—you know now, but that will not matter. Just a slight change in my plans and it will be taken care of. Nobody will leave this house alive, except me. That meddlesome explorer is safely tied up downstairs—and I hardly think that you two will cause me any trouble."

Savagely he kicked the doctor's prostrate form, then glared at us with blazing eyes.

"You are probably curious as to why the good doctor suddenly became such a primitive wildman, aren't you?" he snarled. "Very simple—just an injection from a loaded hypodermic," as he drew the devilish instrument from an inside pocket and took it out of his case. "A perfect mixture of marihuana and cantharides, a mixture guaranteed to put a man into such a frenzy of lust that there is room in his mind for nothing else. The same mixture I injected into Viola Mears and into our friend Marcia so that she would dispose of that meddlesome newspaperman."

My eyes glared the rage and contempt that my inarticulate voice could not express, but Ecker basked in them; grinned fiendishly as he vented his spleen on the prostate form at his feet.

"For more than ten years I have been a slave to that devil," he gritted as he booted the doctor viciously. "For more than ten years I have had to sit by and watch him take credit for my work—watch him honored for the discoveries I made—watch him enjoy the fruits of the brilliant medical career he ruined for me. Why? Because I tried to give his poor wife the love and understanding he denied her.

"Yes, I was Mildred Abernathy's lover—the only real lover she ever had. One day the devil sneaked home unexpectedly and interrupted one of our rare trysts. The shock killed Mildred—too much for her weak heart—but the fiend held me at the point of a gun and made me fire a bullet into her body to simulate suicide. After that he held the secret of her death over my head like a sword, threatening me with exposure and the electric chair unless I obeyed his every order.

"For more than ten years I waited, but not until I heard his brother Hubert lecture did I find the perfect plan I had been seeking. Blood—the blood donor August Hinman. The thing was made to order for me. I even looked like Hinman— could easily pass for him with a bit of make-up. As Abernathy's assistant I was able to drug those of his patients I selected and then lure them to whatever rendezvous I chose.

"For more than ten years I had been denied women, while a procession of beautiful, tempting ones passed through his office. But at least I was able to enjoy my fill of them—to enjoy them doubly, knowing that the crimes would be traced back to Abernathy and end his dirty life under an avalanche of disgrace.

"Yes, I let the dirty devil attack and kill those two girls in front of you and then come in and shoot him down like the dog he was. That bullet would have brought me revenge for years of suffering, freedom from his slavery, and at the same time the fruits of his lucrative practice which will now fall into my hands. And you, my friend would have been my star witness, the one who would absolve me from all possible suspicion."

Ecker frowned and shook his head regretfully—then shrugged.

"Well it will make little difference," he concluded. "Now you will have to die also, but I won't need you. Instead of having been shot down in the midst of his orgy, Abernathy will have to appear to have committed suicide—just as his poor wife before him."

With a cunning smile he wiped the revolver clean of his own fingerprints and then placed it in the doctor's limp hand. Then he strode to Leta and tore the nightgown from her body, leering obscenely at her nakedness, while my blood boiled with impotent fury and my maddened brain threatened to burst through my skull.

Ecker saw the hell that was raging in my eyes, and he laughed callously.

"Don't worry", he assured me, "she is quite safe from me. She is to be all yours."

Again he produced that devilish hypodermic and came over to where I sat so helplessly. Now I could see that the barrel was filled with a cloudy brownish mixture—and then he had turned my left wrist and jabbed the needle point deep into my flesh.

"Half of this barrel is plenty," he mocked as he started to press down on the plunger, "but I'll give you the whole dose. I want you to enjoy yourself—and to dispose of both women for me."

Already I could feel the hellish concoction seeping through my veins; already it was crawling up into my brain and doing horrible, unclean things to me. Leta's naked body, as I gazed at it, became more desirable, more seductive, more maddeningly alluring—even while my conscious mind shuddered away from the thing that was happening to it; cowered away from the realization of what I would do to her once I was free to move.

Frantically I tried to fight down the desires that were foaming up within me, but the spell of her stark loveliness was too demoralizing.

Diabolically the fiend paused when a third of the barrel had been emptied into my system; paused and watched me maliciously to enjoy the hell of furiously contending emotions that was already visible in my eyes. From his leering face my gaze traveled back to Leta's body, drawn as if by an irresistible magnet.

Again the plunger started downward—but Leta's gasp make Ecker pause, while he turned to look at her.

"No—no," she pleaded. "Don't let him at me like that—not yet. Give me just a little longer to live—please, Arno. I'll do anything you want. See—am I not desirable? I can give you what you found in none of those other women. I can give you love—I can give you willing yielding such as you've always dreamed of. Take me first, Arno—and then you can release him, if you still want to."

Uncertainly he eyed her, and I could see the mounting desire working in him, blazing in his eyes, twitching the tense muscles of his face. Leta could see it also—and she played upon it, while every of his hellish concoction to overcome the thing within me screamed at her to stop.

Tied as she was to the upright, she swayed and writhed tantalizingly, every muscle of her gorgeous body blending in a physical poem of seductive invitation.

No man could resist that lure. Ecker's fingers trembled as he yanked the needle out of my arm; his chest was heaving and his breath panting from his half open mouth as he leaped to her side and began to yank and tear at the knots which held her helpless.

This was the bitter end, I knew, as I saw the rope fall away from her ankles. A few moments more and I would have to sit there and go through a literal hell on earth. Spasms of agony shot through me, almost blinded me with torment as they reached into every part of my body.

Every part of my body—especially my hands and feet. They were torturing me, as if a thousand needles were jabbing into them. They felt almost as if they had been asleep, as if the blood were starting to circulate again. My heart pounded wildly at that thought and I hardly dared put it to the test.

Fearfully I looked down at my right hand—and my fingers stretched apart as I lashed my muscles to obey my will! My hand moved! My leg slid forward a few inches!

Then I knew. Ecker himself had freed me; he had squirted into my blood enough of hellish concoction to overcome the effect of the drug with which he had doped me.

But he had untied Leta's wrists. He was taking her down from the upright, clutching her in his arms, starting with her toward the back of the attic!

There was no more time to wait—and I couldn't get up and struggle with him. Desperately I put every bit of strength, every bit of will power into one wild heave. It carried me to my feet, tumbled me headlong—to fall on top of Dr. Abernathy. Frantically I fumbled for the revolver Ecker had put in his hand—found it—and somehow leveled it over his dead body.

Leta saw what I was doing and understood. Suddenly she broke loose from the fiend's arms, flung herself to the floor—and my gun roared. That first shot caught Ecker in the back, but he whirled in rage—and the next four met him head on, to drop him in his tracks almost within reach of the smoking barrel.

Wonderingly I staggered to my feet. Now I could stand. I could walk. And Leta was running toward me, throwing herself into my arms.

For a moment a spasm of fear shot through me. What would I do to her now that she was so close? And then I knew—I kissed her and held her close in an embrace from which she has never since escaped!

DOOM FLOWERS

SCUDDING LIKE A wind-whipped bird before the summer squall which had dismasted her, the small sloop, *Sea Gull,* wrecked itself upon the black, snag-toothed rocks of a gloomy island shore. Thus Fred Swift and Natalie, his bride of yesterday, after heading for the Straits of Mackinac on a honeymoon cruise, came to grief eight hours out of Manistique.

Half-drowned, they gazed forlornly down, from the cliff they had climbed, to where the broken ribs of their boat were visible, caught on the foam-flecked fangs of rock. In Swift's heart the grim feeling of uneasiness grew, and his arm tightened round the waist of the tall, brown-haired girl whose soaked sailor suit clung tightly to her lissome curves. Looking back toward the grey shapes of farm buildings dimly seen in the waning light, he said:

"This is Tokeners Island. I had hoped we might miss it and strike Beaver. God knows what sort of welcome awaits us here."

Natalie's wondering glance lifted to his troubled, stern-jawed face. "What do you mean? Surely, any one will offer shelter to people just escaped from death—and as narrowly as we've escaped it!"

"We'll soon find out," was his answer. Helping her over the rubble of rock toward the smoother slope of a pasture field, he added grimly: "Don't be startled by anything that happens. There are ugly tales afloat about this lonely speck of land. It lies well off the steamer lanes. Fishermen, venturing too near, have been warned away with rifle shots. One or two men, thought to have been driven ashore here, never reappeared.

"The place was purchased a few years ago by a queer sect who settled their several families upon it and have not been seen on the mainland since. They are members of an obscure religious cult called 'Tokeners' But don't worry—" Swift managed a smile, flexed a powerful fist in mock threat. "I'll make them put us up for the night and give us a rowboat to get away in when the storm dies. See, the wind is falling now—"

Cattle were lowing dismally in the barnyard of the farm they presently approached. Raising its bleak bulk a full three stories, the unpainted house seemed vacant, its uncurtained windows staring like dead eyes. But meager crops were growing in fields stretching away toward a dark grove of pines a half-mile distant.

They passed through the barnyard gate, started across the sodden ground. Abruptly, Natalie halted.

"Look, Fred! Those cows—and horses—they have black crepe tied rounds their necks. Why, even the chickens!"

Wide-eyed, Swift regarded the animals and fowls, with their funeral marks of mourning. "Someone must have died," he said.

"Maybe they're all dead," Natalie faltered. "Oh, I'm so frightened. I have a feeling that something awful has happened—"

"Nonsense!" he affirmed stoutly. "It's just a part of their odd religion. If they were all dead, who would have hung crepe over everything? See—like over there, on the barn door and the outbuildings."

They found black crepe on the house door, too. Nor did anyone answer their repeated knocks.

Entering, they found the lower rooms deserted. Passing out to a verandah beyond, they scanned the fields and farm buildings, searching for signs of human life.

"That shed over there!" exclaimed Natalie. "The chimney is smoking. There must be someone—"

Hurrying back toward a small building near the barn they

heard a boy whistling cheerily. Through an open door then they saw him: a red-haired youngster, barefooted and clad in faded blue overalls. He was stoking a wood fire in a stove beneath a large iron kettle, and he looked up, startled, when they spoke.

"Where'd you come from? Wrecked your boat, I betcha! Now, won't there be some excitement?" his bright eyes sparkled.

"What's your name?" Swift asked. "Where is everybody?"

"I'm Peter. The folks are back in the woods at the Soul Temple, taking care of Mother Chloe. Her soul withered, so she died. They've all gone now to get ready for the planting. I'm glad I ain't got no soul yet," he chattered. "Johnnie'll get hers—then he can die at any time. I'll be the only one left that can't die without going to hell—except Warden Ludwig, of course. He'll never have a soul because he ain't got no relations to get one from."

Natalie looked at Fred, the color draining from her cheeks. "Let's go!" she whispered tensely. *"Anywhere—"*

He silenced her with a gesture, turned to the lad, who had picked up a long iron ladle and was stirring the brew from which rich, meaty odors emanated.

"Making soup?"

"Naw." The boy laughed. "Rendering tallow for the sprouting candles. Have to have them or Johnnie's soul from Mother Chloe won't grow. Then he'd die—"

As he stirred the steaming mess, examining ladlesful with boyish importance, the big perforated dipper brought to light a number of small, white bones. These he dumped into a bucket on the floor. Swift's eyes narrowed as he studied them. Suddenly Natalie uttered a quavering shriek of horror. The next dipperful had disclosed a baby's skull!

"Good God!" blurted Swift. He caught his swaying wife, who moaned, fingers pressed to her bloodless lips. "Boy! That—that thing—" he nodded toward it, mouth distorted. "Do you know what you're cooking?"

"Why, sure! It's Myra's. It died in spite of everything Father Abel could do, and it didn't have a soul yet, so it goes into the sprouting candles. That's what happens to any of us that dies without a soul. We must give our cast-off bodies to help the others grow good strong souls."

"Oh," sobbed Natalie, "take me away from this hideous place . . ."

Swift stood fascinated by the innocent demeanor of the boy at his gruesome task, wondering what madness, what horrible fanaticism, had taught him such nonchalance. The lad, sensing their revulsion, said cannily:

"Seems funny to you, I betcha. Father Abel says folks on the mainland don't understand about souls and heaven and hell. That's why he won't let none of us ever leave the island, why we don't have any boats at all. Of course, it's sorta too bad, what'll be happenin' to you—"

"What will happen?" Natalie's words rattled like shattered glass. "What will they do to us?"

"Oh, 'tain't so much what they'll do—because we all gotta die, sometime. But I reckon you're afraid of going to hell. I'm not. Warden Ludwig says it ain't such a bad place. We got it all planned to have plenty of fun if I should die before somebody leaves me a soul."

"Do you mean," Swift demanded, "that they'll try to *kill us?*"

"Oh, they'll kill you! That is—unless you're related, then only one of you'll have to die. We need fat for temple candles, to keep the souls white."

Nauseated, supporting his cringing wife on his arm, Swift cried: "You mean, they'd murder us as a part of their damnable religion?"

"Better not let father Abel hear you talk so!" The boy frowned warningly. "It's all according to the Black Book. Strangers can't live here without souls—nobody can, except the Soul Warden, old Ludwig. And we gotta have temple candles, don't we? To keep the other souls from dying. Warden Ludwig thinks that's why Mother Chloe's soul withered—because we run short of candles. We're burning only eight now—the last of them made out of two men who got washed ashore. And that ain't enough—there'd ought to be two for each soul."

"Were those men—" Natalie's question was a mere gasping whisper on her dry and trembling lips. "Were they washed ashore *alive?*"

"Oh, sure. But Father Abel fixed 'em, over there in the barn. Now you two, you're married, ain't you? You sorta act like it. Well, one of you will be all right. I heard Father Abel say that if ever two related ones came together, one could die to give the other a soul. It'll be you, I reckon—" He fixed his round, bright eyes on Swift. "Because then she could live and marry the Warden. He's been wanting a woman—"

Fred Swift felt his face bleach white with anger.

"Let any one dare touch her!" he raged. "How many people are there on this island?"

Peter closed the drafts of the stove, commenting: "I guess it's about cooked now. How many? Well, let's count 'em up. I never stopped to figure. There's Father Abel, the patriarch, and his wife, Mother Chloe—only now she's dead. Simon—he's my father and Abel is his'n—and Sarah, my ma. Johnnie is thirteen and I'm twelve, so he gets the first soul. Then there's Simon, father's cousin, and his wife, Myra. Ella belongs to them, and their last baby is in there—" He pointed to the bubbling pot. "Because it died without a soul. Like I told you. That makes ten, don't it, counting the Warden? Or is it nine? Anyway, that's all of us, till somebody comes or they have some babies that don't get sick and die."

"When," grated Swift, "will your people return?" Outside, dusk was falling, shadows thickening among the buildings. "Soon, I suppose?"

"Any minute now," the boy said cheerfully. "Then there'll be plenty of excitement. Father Abel wants to press out this tallow to make candles for tonight, when the sprouting time starts. Won't he be glad we're going to have more temple candles, too!"

"For God's sake," begged Natalie, hysterically. "let us leave before it is too late.'

"Wait." Swift held her tightly, spoke to the boy. "Doesn't a boat ever stop here? You must get supplies from some-where—the things you can't make or grow."

"Sure—the boat comes twice a year. It's due tomorrow af-ternoon. But that'll be too late to do you any good," he sym-pathized. "because Father Abel will fix one of you tonight. But then, dying ain't so bad—not that way. One crack on the head and you'll never know it was an axe that hit you.'

"Listen!" Natalie clutched her husband's arm in quivering terror. "What is it?"

Solemnly, welling out of the gathering gloom, they heard a sound of chanting. Staring through the doorway, Swift saw a procession of black-cowled figures approaching along a lane leading from the grove. Then, with a clash as of celestial cymbals, thunder clanged in the darkening sky and lighting painted the nightmarish scene with a ghastly glare. Follow-ing the wind's dying, storm clouds had piled deep above the island, and now a sudden torrent of rain obscured the maca-bre forms of the Tokeners.

Wheeling upon the boy, Swift exclaimed: "Sonny! You say I'm going to hell for want of a soul, and that maybe you'll go there, too. So let's be friends. Do me one favor—just for to-night. Don't tell them we're here! We were married only yesterday—" It seemed a queer business that he should be pleading with this serious-eyed youngster for reprieve on such grounds. "Can you understand that I want to be with her a littler longer?"

"Sure. You love her, I betcha." Blushing, the lad nodded. "I like her, too. I won't tell—but don't you snitch on me nei-ther, when they find you tomorrow. Father Abel would whip the devil out of me."

Dragging Natalie by the hand, Swift fled through the hiss-ing rain, hid behind a corner of the barn until the chanting fanatics had passed.

"Buck up!" he encouraged. "We'll be safe enough in the dark, even though the boy tells. And tomorrow we'll find a way to leave, if we have to float off on a raft."

They saw a bulky figure coming from the house, a man whose bushy beard made his head seem grotesquely huge. He entered the shed and reappeared, carrying the steaming kettle, followed by the lad. Soon a light gleamed in kitchen windows. Swift said thankfully:

"The kid didn't give us away. Now, while they're making the soul candles, is our chance to escape unseen."

Natalie pleaded: "Let's go to the farthest end of the island. We can hide among the rocks—"

"You'll suffer," he said doubtfully. "This rain is cold. If we dared risk hiding in the barn—"

"No, no!" The terrified whisper gushed out of her constricted throat. "I don't mind the wet—I don't mind anything—except those ghouls who want our bodies."

"More than that," Swift muttered beneath his breath, "I mind the one who wants a woman—"

They reached the rugged shore. Occasional lighting flashes made them crouch close to earth, lest their presence be noted by watching eyes. Circling above the line of thundering breakers, they sought a cave or overhanging ledge. But they found the going dangerous in the dark. Their hope of shelter faded.

Swift said: "Our best chance is the grove. Among the trees it will be warmer, and we'll be more secure.'

"Near the Soul temple? Oh, no—" Natalie clung to him desperately. "Anywhere but there—"

"It will be best," he insisted. "Once we get beyond the temple we'll be safe, for they've no cause to wander farther."

The rain dwindled to a drizzle and the air was still. Overhead the sky was a black, close-hung canopy which seemed to shroud the very island in crepe to match the mourners' veils. Faint flickers of lightning broke the murky shadows beneath dripping trees, and Swift stumbled forward cautiously, leading Natalie through drenched underbrush and briars. After a period of painful progress, the girl sobbed:

"Why did we come here? I'm being scratched to ribbons, and my knee hurts where I bruised it on that last log."

He caught her up in his arms. "I'll carry you."

"Put me down. You can't! You'll fall and kill us both. Fred! What—" her teeth chattered with fright—"is that light?"

An illuminated square was visible through the trees. In Swift's embrace the girl was shivering with fear and chill. A night of such exposure might well end fatally. His jaw tightened and he started toward the building.

"Sometimes audacity is the better course. If they knew we were on the island, the last place they'd search would be the soul temple. It may be the best place to hide."

A vivid, nearby lightning flash left a photographic impression of the building upon the retina of his eye: a place that was windowless, squat, with ornate cornices and a roomy cupola on top. If they could gain access to its tower—

The glazed door was closed. Swift peered through the glass. Within the low-ceilinged room, eight tall candles flared, throwing an eerie yellow light over two long tables which ranged near the side-walls. Beside each candle rose the pale green stalk of a curious flower. Some were blossoming, others not; each bloom a white or yellowish lily in the heart of which a crimson spot glowed red as blood. He saw that one plant was withered and black. Mother Chloe's?

On either side, above the tables, reared massive wooden crosses. At the farther end, upon a sable altar of rock, lay a thick black book fastened down with a silver chain. In the center of the floor, draped in somber crepe, stood a rude coffin on wooden horses. Beneath the shroud, Swift surmised, must lie the dead woman's body.

"There's a trapdoor in the ceiling," he said. "We've got to climb up there before they come. Get a grip on your nerves, dear, we'll soon be safely hidden."

Natalie swayed toward him, trembling. "You know best, but I'm afraid—"

They entered. Over the room hung a sickening odor, faintly putrid—the grisly smell of death. Swift's harassed glance searched shadowy corners for a ladder, found none. Then he saw two ends of scantling projecting from beneath the bier and knew that it had been used as a support for the coffin.

Impatiently, he swept the black shroud from the naked corpse of an elderly woman. Natalie turned her face aside, exclaiming:

"They've plugged her nose and ears and mouth with wax! You see! They haven't finished with their horrible rites—"

"The boy spoke of 'the planting'," Swift murmured. "he mentioned a 'sprouting time.' I don't quite understand—"

Hesitating, perplexed as to how he might remove the ladder without upsetting the coffin, he saw Natalie staring at the nearest table of flowers.

"A-a-h!" The cry was wrenched out of her throat. "look where they're going!" She reeled as though about to faint.

Swift steadied her, then looked. And saw that each sickly plant stood rooted in the gaping mouth of a nude form sculptured in gleaming silver. Faithfully reproduced were the bodies of men and women, along with a child or two.

A ghastly thought moved his limbs hypnotically. With outstretched finger he touched the nearest silvered cheek, jerked his hand away. No metal there! Only dry, wasted flesh drawn tight over human bones. Actual corpses had been painted. The soul flowers fed upon dead blood and tissue!

Again he examined the body upon the bier, saw that each orifice had been tightly stopped with wax. He wondered why. And, seized in the sudden grip of fear, despairing of ever reaching the cupola above, he drew Natalie toward the only exit.

Abruptly, they froze in their tracks, as a rumbling voice chanted in the night outside.

"God save us!" moaned the girl. "We waited too long—"

"No way out," blurted Swift. "Natalie . . . under the table! We must hide—"

The door swung open. Peering up carefully from their concealment, they saw a tall form enter. Gowned in black, cowled hood framing a vicious face, the man stamped across the floor carrying a bucket and brush. Candlelight gleamed on his yellow snags of teeth as he bent above the coffin.

Grinning. With swift strokes he began to silver the woman's corpse. As he painted he chanted—that he was Warden of Souls, the Companion of the Devil. Finished with his revolting task, he left off singing, began grumbling to himself.

"Time enough for a mass before they come, if I hurry. They'll be chanting—"

Snatching up a can of water, he drenched the roots of all soul flowers save one. Upon the last he looked with an expression of such utter malevolence that Natalie, watching, scarce repressed the moan of terror which rose to her distended lips.

Swiftly striding to one of the wooden crosses, the Soul Warden drew from a hidden niche behind it an oddly shaped blue bottle. Out of it he poured liquid upon the flower toward which his animosity was directed. Replacing the vial, he exerted his enormous strength to invert the cross. When he had succeeded, he prostrated himself before it, began droning the mass of Saint Secaire. Tearing part of his garments aside, making a revolting exhibition of his body, the Soul Warden went through a sensual ritual that expressed the most degraded depths of carnal lust.

His mumbled words were a meaningless gibberish until Swift realized that he was reciting backwards some hellish propitiation of the Evil One. Rising, making the sign of the cross upon the earthen floor with his left foot outthrust behind him, the Warden laughed aloud, stood the cross in its proper position, and raucously exclaimed:

"By Saint Secaire I promise soon to send plenty of souls to deepest hell! Strike the old one dead this night, Satan, and all the others shall die, too!"

With cowled head cocked to one side, as though listening to secret voices in the night, he began to shudder and groan, to clap his great hands and stamp with booted feet. Faintly, above the noise of the rain, Swift heard the Tokeners chanting eerily.

The soul Warden heard it, too. He steadied himself, visibly seeking control of the growing frenzy which possessed him. Leaping toward a table, he snuffed one of the tapers, began to crunch it hungrily between his broken teeth.

Natalie could not restrain an instinctive cry of horror.

"He's *eating* them! Eating the fat of those murdered men—"

Swift's jolting oath evidenced his utter desperation. Crawling from beneath the table he sprang erect faced the menacing shape which towered head and shoulders above him. The Soul Warden, with a howl of amazement, snatched up a length of metal pipe which had lain between the silvered corpses, whirled it about his head, aimed a killing stroke that Swift barely evaded.

"Run, Natalie! Anywhere outside—" Swift yelled to her even as he ducked.

But the girl stood paralyzed by fear. Swift leaped inside the flailing arms, drove blow after blow to the slavering mouth. The Soul Warden's huge hand clutched his throat, forced him to his knees with astonishing ease.

Natalie, roused by her husband's plight, moved galvanically. Springing upon the Warden's back she scratched at his eyes and cheeks, screaming like a Fury. The man shook himself like a great dog, flinging her aside. Then, with deliberate intent to kill, he held Swift at arm's length, raised the pipe, brought it down with smashing force.

Fred Swift moved his head instinctively. That movement saved his life. He caught a glancing blow instead of one that would have crushed his skull. Yet even that blow was enough to bring blank darkness flooding over his senses. He never heard Natalie's hopeless shriek, nor the Soul Warden's victorious laughter.

When Swift's eyes opened, the lights seemed blurred. Dim figures standing about the room resembled black, unstable shades. A deep voice was preaching sonorously. Then his vision cleared, and he strove to move.

He found himself bound to a cross upon the wall. Opposite, similarly fastened, hung Natalie's limp body, her head drooping upon her chest. He wondered if she were dead, before the anguished rise and fall of her bosom reassured him.

Standing near, regarding her with lust-reddened eyes was the gaunt figure of the Soul Warden. Kneeling in a semi-circle before the altar were two young men and their wives. Beside the dead woman's bier stood one who must, Swift knew, be Father Abel, the patriarch. With grief-stricken face upraised, grey beard floating like a cloud, his enormous hands outstretched in supplication, the man spoke on.

"You who have caused her soul to wither and die—receive her into the realms of bliss. And let Your beneficence aid the sprouting of that new soul which shall spring from her sealed lips as a token of salvation for a poor child who now lives without the promise of eternal glory."

In more normal tones, Father Abel said: "Now, children—the Ritual of the Planting."

The kneeling couples rose, gathered about the bier. From an ancient teakwood case the patriarch drew a small, dry, bulbous root. While he intoned strange prayers, one of the women filled her cupped hands with moist earth from a bucket. The other deftly removed a plug of wax from the corpse's distended jaws.

"Quickly!" urged Father Abel, "lest the life force escape!"

Black dirt dropped into the yawning cavity. He planted the bulb, tamped the mold around it. Each of the two younger men flicked water upon the bit of soil with their fingers, then all began to chant a solemn dirge.

And then Fred Swift, struggling to free his bound wrists, half-strangled by the loop of rope around his neck, cursed horribly and redoubled his efforts. Across the room, behind the backs of the intent mourners, he could see the Soul Warden—pawing the sweet curves of Natalie's body, evil hands groping over her thighs and breasts!

The sublimated terror in her brown eyes, the piteous appeal in the look she flung him, tore at his heart; bred in his mind such a depth of despair as almost dogged his senses.

Pulling upon his right arm until the flesh of his wrist was rubbed loose from the bones and his joints cracked sickeningly, Swift worked one hand from beneath the ropes. It hung at his side, a numb and bleeding thing. Wondering if the tortured fingers would find strength to deal with other knots, he moved his arm back along a limb of the cross when the chanting ceased. He feared the Tokeners might discover the progress he had made.

Father Abel, in the manner of one closing a ceremony, spoke ringingly:

"Blessings on the new soul which shall be Johnnie's! Now, light the sprouting candle."

One of the younger men stepped forward with a slim, white taper newly moulded from the kettle which Peter had tended. He thrust it into a silver holder, stood it upon the shrunken breast of the corpse. When he touched flame to the wick, the mourners wailed:

"A soul for little Johnnie! We pray that it may not wither soon."

"But all must wither in the end," the patriarch responded. "And then must the body surely die. When my soul flower faded, I shall join Mother Chloe—" He broke off, eyes bulging, stared at one of the corpse-fed plants.

"Ah, woe! Woe! It has withered even now—" Clutching at his throat beneath the billowing beard, the old man staggered in his tracks, uttered a choking cry.

Startled mourners cast quick glances toward the flower which was his life token. The plant had blackened.

Father Abel swayed and fell. His limbs jerked spasmodically, then he lay inert. One of the others bent an ear to the old man's heart, shook his head, rose up commanding:

"Soul Warden! Bring wax quickly! We must save his life force to grow a soul for Peter!"

The Warden left off his beastly stroking of Natalie's cringing limbs and hurried into the night, grumbling.

"There's no more than enough left in the hollow oak," Swift heard him mutter.

From the doorway a shrill, childish voice called: "I don't want no soul! Then I'll die, too." Three small, haunted faces peered in at the fantastic scene.

Fred Swift, brain racing with a flashing chain of ideas, regarded the withered plant through narrowed eyes. His freed hand crept behind the cross at his back, and his groping fingers found a hidden niche. From it he drew forth a squat blue bottle. Removing the rubber cork with his teeth he smelled the pungent fumes of some acid.

Replacing it, he concealed the bottle behind the cross-arm, cried:

"You, there! Which one is the son of that *murdered man? Do you want to know why the flower withered*—why your father died?"

"What do you mean? What can a soulless unbeliever know of such things?" a young man cried.

Swift faced him intently. "You are Simon? I know that your father was murdered! Believing he would die when his life token withered, he fell dead when he saw it blackened there. The one who caused it murdered him as surely as though he had used a gun."

"Who did this thing? Speak!" Simon approached the cross.

"I'll tell you—but only if you let us go free. Release my wife—unfasten these ropes on me. Then you shall know the truth."

The young man turned to the others, muttering:

"He may have proof of what I suspect. To let them go would be no sin—if they leave the island." Uncertainly, he asked: "What do you say, cousin?"

The other nodded. "We must have proof—" His voice broke queerly. "Or soon we all shall die!"

"You agree, then?" Swift exulted. "If I show you what happened, you'll let us go?"

Hard upon their assent he produced the bottle, held it toward Father Abel's son.

"Acid! Your ugly Soul Warden poured it on the roots of that flower. While we were hiding beneath the table. *I saw him do it!"*

A roar of bestial rage sounded from the doorway. The Soul Warden cried: "So you've found me out! Well, it only means sending your souls to the Devil in a quicker way!"

Simon stood the bottle of acid upon his mother's bier and looked toward his cousin meaningly. The Warden lumbered forward, snatched up the length of pipe with which he had beaten Swift.

The women screamed, darted toward the door. With savage cries he beat them into quivering insensibility. The younger men, shouting fiercely, leaped at him from two side, aiming awkward blows at his hulking body. Fred Swift, with his free hand, tore at the ropes, which bound his throat to the cross. He was desperately intent on breaking loose before the battle ended disastrously.

The Soul Warden, yelling like a maniac, brained the cousin with a single stroke. Simon proved more agile and in the whirling fight dodged round and round the coffin until, unexpectedly, Warden Ludwig gave the bier a push. It smashed against Simon's knees. As he stumbled and fell across the corpse of his mother, the metal club swung once more, caught him sickeningly against the skull, crushed it like an eggshell.

Stretching his arms aloft with a piercing cry of triumph, the Warden grinned at Fred Swift, picked up the unbroken bottle from the floor, poured acid upon the roots of every soul flower.

"I'll wither them all!" he screamed. "I'll send them all to hell!"

Striding to Swift's side, he poured the remaining liquid upon the prisoner's bare neck. Swift groaned in agony as the acid burned like fire, raised a stench of cooking flesh.

"You'll get worse that that," the Soul Warden gloated. "I'll carve your body to bits to make candles for my black masses. But you can wait till I've had some fun with *her.*" He leered at Natalie.

"Touch her, and I'll kill you!"

But even as Swift mouthed the words, he realized how futile was his threat. Twisting and squirming in his bonds, he pleaded: "Do anything you wish to me, but let her go. Haven't you done enough tonight to satisfy your master, Satan?"

"Ho!" bellowed the Soul Warden. "That one is never satisfied. Beside, I've myself to please. For a long time now I've schemed to possess this fine island, live here with my pick of their women. But that one—" Again his eyes sought the terror-stricken girl. "She's younger and prettier. So I killed the other two—"

Going over to Natalie, he ripped the clothing from her slender body, cast the shredded garments aside, pinched and squeezed her tender flesh.

"Oh, God! Let me die," she moaned. "Fred! Help me! This is worse than death—"

Swift tugged and tore at his neck rope with the might of a man gone mad. But he could not reach the knot. His bloodshot eyes turned away from the anguish of Natalie's face.

He saw a movement near the open door, glimpsed a small form crawling along the floor.

"Peter!" he gasped. "A knife—cut me loose—"

As the Soul Warden turned, the boy dodged out of sight behind the table. To allay the man's suspicion, Swift stormed: "If I had a knife, I'd cut your throat—"

"Yah! Yell your head off. I'll fix you when I get through with her."

To Natalie, as he untied one of her arms, the Warden scoffed: "You won't last long. But it'll be fun while you do. And when you're dead, I'll plant a soul flower in your mouth and burn candles made of your husband's fat, to whiten the blossom. You'd ought to like that."

Peter, reaching out from his hiding place, seized the bloody length of pipe.

"He killed all my people. I'm gonna jump up and bust him a good one," he whispered.

"No, no!" gasped Swift. "He'd not even feel it. Take one of the candles—burn the ropes from my ankles—"

The lad jerked a taper from the lips of the nearest corpse, touched flame to the hemp as directed. Swift tore at his neck rope with frenzied violence, felt the strands part where acid had bitten deep into their fibers.

The Soul Warden, his sense of smell keenly attuned to the sickly, perfumed atmosphere of the temple, must have sniffed the odor of burning. He whirled with a growl in his throat.

Peter leaped up, waving the pipe. "I'll kill you, Ludwig!" he screamed shrilly. "I'll knock your head off—"

With a grunt of contempt the Soul Warden came over and slapped the rod aside. Clamping both hands upon the slender neck, slowly and cruelly he began to throttle the child.

Natalie, still bound by an arm and both feet, shrieked a prayer for mercy. Swift, with one wrist manacled to the cross, swung his free arm outward, hooked his fingers in the Warden's collar. Snatching the man off balance, he hugged him against his chest and swung up both legs to fasten a scissors-hold around the fellow's loins.

The Soul Warden dropped Peter, gouged at Swift's eyes, lunged backward. Swift's lashed arm stretched, his shoulder cracked till he thought it was dislocated. But despite the agonizing pain, he did not release his desperate hold.

Sobbing, Peter struggled to his feet, found the iron bludgeon and swung it with all his boyish strength. It caught the Soul Warden behind the ear with sufficient force to knock him sprawling. Swift fumbled with the knot which held his aching wrist. As it loosened, the killer rose and sprang upon him with a demoniacal scream of hated.

In their rolling, threshing fight, the Soul Warden's uncanny strength told quickly. Swift lay upon his back, the other astride his middle. With one hand clamped across his face, pinning his head to the floor, the Warden bared yellow fangs and grated:

"I'll tear out your throat!"

Swift's groping fingers touched the pipe which Peter had dropped. Seizing it with both hands he thrust upward suddenly, putting all of his waning strength into the blow. A jagged end struck the Soul Warden at the juncture of neck and chin, ripped through flesh, brought red blood spurting. The man reared back with a gurgling cry, toppled, and wallowed in his own gore. Swift jumped to his feet. With merciless blows he beat at that mad fiend's body beneath him—until it was little more than a bloody, dead mess.

Young Peter crawled from his refuge under the table, spurned the dead hulk with his toe. For a second he stood staring at the naked girl.

"I'll get her some of ma's clothes," he said dismally. "Then I've got to find where Ella and Johnnie are hiding. You two can leave tomorrow, but I don't know what we kids will do—with everybody dead and us all alone."

"I know what you'll do," Fred Swift exclaimed, as he released Natalie and held her close. "We'll look after you three as if you were our very own. Without your aid, laddie . . ."

He shuddered. Then, gathering his wife in his arms, calling to the children to follow, he strode out of that hideous temple toward the bleak house, where they could find shelter until a boat came to carry them away from this island of withered souls.

SATAN STOLE MY FACE!

UP FROM THE BLEAK RIVER the icy wind swept across town, biting penetrating, cutting into exposed faces and hands, slicing through thick overcoats as if they were shoddy. It was only eleven o'clock, by the Paramount clock, but West Forty-Seventh Street was almost deserted. The few who had to be out on such a night clutched their coat collars tightly around their necks, bowed their heads to the wind, and concentrated on getting wherever they were going with all possible speed.

All except Bill Stanton. He came down the dark street, uncertainly, keeping close to the buildings that afforded him at least some measure of protection from the wind that tore right through his thin suit.

His coat collar was turned up and his shoulders were hunched to bring it up to the low-pulled brim of his soft hat, but the icy fingers of the wind reached down his neck and ran up and down his back.

His hands were thrust deep into his trouser pockets, but they were numb and blue.

Desperation gleamed in his hungry eyes. Only the desperation of exhaustion and cold could have kept him on, could have forced his reluctant feet hesitantly down the block until he stood across the way from a wide, ten-story building that stood dark and deserted. The windows were boarded up, and on the stone steps was a grimy carpet of last week's snow undisturbed by human feet.

"Olympia Hotel" read the unlighted electric sign over the entrance—and as Bill Stanton's eyes ran over the familiar letters a chill ran through him that was more penetrating, more demoralizing than the driving blasts of the near-zero gale. That pile of stone and brick was dark empty now, but as he looked at it he saw it ablaze with life—and terrifying death!

He hadn't been cold and hungry then; he had been dapper, well dressed, the popular night clerk of the Olympia, standing indolently behind the desk while he listened to a long-winded yarn from one of the guests. A big fellow with a round, florid face that was bunched up into wrinkles as he chuckled over his own yarn.

Stanton had never heard the end of that yarn. He could still see the laugh wrinkles petrify and then sag out of the fellow's face as his mouth dropped open and the color blanched out of his cheeks—as he looked with bulging eyes toward the wide staircase from which the interruption had come. *Bump—bump—bump—!*

And Stanton could still feel the prickles of horror coursing up and down his own spine as he saw what had caused that soggy, bumping noise—as he recognized the bloody, severed head that rolled and bounced down the stairs!

He gasped and muttered the name of God through chattering teeth as he stared across the street at the dark, gloomy pile that had once been home to hundreds of men and women.

That night when horror moved into the Olympia was now more than a year ago, but it and the nightmare nights which had followed were still vividly fresh in his mind—so vivid that his frost-tingling feet started subconsciously toward the corner of the block.

Since the hotel, stripped of its guests by succession of gruesome tragedies, had gone into bankruptcy, it had been closed up—with its furnishings still in place, Stanton had heard. It was that which brought him back to Forty-Seventh Street—the vague consciousness that inside those walls there was shelter and warmth. A bed—and perhaps even blankets. His shivering body cried out for those meager comforts, but the crawling horror within him held him back. There were some things far worse than weariness and cold, worse even than the death they might bring.

To go back into that empty building—to face the bobbing death's-head that had terrorized it—to grapple in the dark with the dread *thing* that had turned it into a place of ghastly horror . . .

Panic surged up in Stanton and prodded him down the street, but his suffering flesh looked back at the untenanted building longingly—and suddenly he stopped, rooted to the icy sidewalk, while he stared up unbelievingly at the boarded windows. There, on the fourth floor, he was positive he had seen a sliver of light gleaming for a fraction of a second between the close-nailed boards!

Was there someone else in the empty hotel? Perhaps someone else had broken in and taken shelter there. Then Stanton would not be alone if he went in; there would be someone there to keep him company, to help him face the *thing* if it still haunted the place. And there would be a soft bed, heavy blankets, to ease and warm his shivering body . . .

Stanton's misery could no longer be denied. It took charge of his shaking body, swept out the panic, and led his footsteps to Seventh Avenue, around to Forty-Sixth Street. There was a rooming house there with a hallway that led to a tiny back yard. He went over the wooden fence at the rear, and was in the back yard of the three-story building that stood next to the empty Olympia Hotel.

With numb fingers that glued themselves to the cold iron of the rungs he climbed up the fire escape until he reached the roof. In the darkness he groped around for what he prayed would still be there. It was—a butter-tub filled with dirt in which a sickly plant had once grown.

Stanton tore it loose from the ice that cemented it to the roof and rolled it over to the wall of the hotel. By standing on the tub he would be able to reach one of the fourth-floor windows that loomed blackly above him. These side windows had not been boarded. If he could pull himself up on that sill he could force the window, break the pane if necessary.

But that wasn't necessary. When he forced his stiff fingertips under the window it raised easily. With a sigh of thanks he pulled himself up, got a leg over the windowsill. And started to climb into the room.

Halfway in he hesitated. Strange—the place wasn't cold and dank; didn't have the smell of an empty room in a deserted building. The air inside was stale, human smelling; the room had the odor of very recent occupancy. He sniffed. Alcohol fumes were heavy in the air.

Stanton climbed in and groped in his pocket for a paper of matches, lit one and held it over his head. In its flickering light he caught a glimpse of a disordered bed, a pile of dirty clothing heaped up on a chair—*a dirty, hairy face that was leaping straight at him!*

He was bore over backward as a body catapulted into him, as clawing fingers groped for his throat, as foul smelling breath billowed into his face and a snarling voice spat vile curses at him. In the first moment of surprise Stanton could do nothing but try to defend himself blindly. Then instinct whispered that he must keep this fellow quiet; that noise would be disastrous.

By sheer desperation he rolled over and got his antagonist beneath him. Now that he no longer had the upper hand, the fellow's curses ceased.

"Help!" he croaked. Then louder, "Hel—"

Stanton's fingers closed over his mouth stifled the cry. Then he flung himself down on the fellow, his knees on the other's chest, his fists battering away at the man's head until the strangled cries ceased and the figure went limp.

Again Stanton lit a match and held it close to the face beneath him. He caught his breath with surprise and looked closer. The unconscious man was Dead-Eye Martin, a cheap crook and fake beggar who had been living at the Olympia when it closed. Stanton had no idea what the fellow was doing there now, but he was fairly certain that Dead-Eye was there for no good purpose. And he had tried to call for help—which meant that there were others of his kind in the supposedly empty building.

Quickly Stanton stepped to the bed and pulled loose a

filthy sheet. He tore it into wide strips and bound the faker's wrists and arms behind, then tied up his ankles.

Martin had his eyes open now and they gleamed with vicious hate as he snarled up at his captor. His lips parted and the whiskey-heavy breath hissed through his teeth. "You'll get yours for this, wise guy!" he snarled. "Just wait until . . . Hel—"

But Stanton was too quick for him. He slapped his palm down over the open mouth, stifled the yell, and stuffed a wad of dirty rags between the fellow's jaws. In a few minutes Dead-Eye was effectively gagged and trussed up. Stanton dumped him into the room's clothes closet and locked the door.

Then he surveyed the room by match light. Nothing there but a pile of smelly rags that served Martin as clothing. On the bureau was the stub of a candle, a pint bottle of whiskey that was nearly empty, and the black patch Dead-Eye wore over a perfectly good eye to trick the sympathetic public.

Noiselessly Stanton went to the door, turned the key in the lock, and looked out into the hall. It was pitch black and quiet as the grave—until he caught the faint echo of sounds coming up from below.

Carefully he shut the door behind him and started tiptoeing down the hall toward the stairs. A lighted match revealed that all the doors along the corridor were closed—and the familiar look of the place tugged at his memory.

He was just passing Room 410—that was directly beneath the fifth floor suite that for many years had been the home of old Hester Hallett, the eccentric recluse. Something stabbed at Stanton's heart as he thought of Miss Hallett—and of Laura Lamont, who had been the old lady's trained nurse and companion.

Laura was sweet and lovely. Her dark eyed beauty had played havoc with the blasé night clerk. It was just in front of that door—Room 510—that he had taken her into his arms and kissed her the first time, he recalled with a twinge of anguish.

Where was Laura now? He didn't even know. The night

the *thing* had attacked, the old lady had ended everything for them, just as it ended the hotel's career. The old lady never recovered from that attack; she went out of her mind and had to be confined in a private sanitarium.

Stanton could see her yet, wandering down the corridor with terror-filled eyes and talking in that frightened yet empty voice, saying over and over again:

"It came at me in the dark—just a head. No body—just a horrible shining head. It talked to me—and then it came at me—and beat me with hands it didn't have! It was just a head—but it choked me—just a head . . ."

They took her away after that, and Laura was out of a job. Bill was out of a job himself a week later, when the hotel closed. Once after that he saw Laura, but she went away on a new case, and his own luck had gone from bad to worse. No use trying to keep in touch with a girl like Laura when a fellow had nothing whatever to offer her; he'd only be a drag on her . . .

Well, he hadn't done that, anyway. He had dropped out of sight so that she could not find him even if she tried to locate him. And now God only knew where she was.

Stanton paused at the head of the stairs. The sounds from below were a little louder now, but still he could not distinguish them. Softly he picked his way down the steps to the second floor. Like the one above, it was dark and empty, but now he could see that there were dim lights glowing in the lobby below.

Crouching beside the banister he started down—and stopped short while the hair at the back of his neck seemed to stand on end. That voice—he recognized it unmistakably!

"I have never known this hotel to be so uncomfortable," it complained querulously. "My rooms are cold, and this lobby is positively frigid. I want to see Mr. Reid or—"

That was old Hester Hallett's voice, and as he crept down a few lower Stanton saw that the old lady was standing in front of the hotel desk—and Laura Lamont was there beside her.

But what brought out the goose pimples on Stanton's skin and threatened to pop the eyes out of his head was the figure standing there behind the desk. Miss Hallett was complaining to *him*—Bill Stanton—standing there in the flesh!

Chapter Two

Madness on the Stairs

Stanton doubted his own sanity as he crouched there on the stairs. That was Bill Stanton down there behind the desk. That was Bill Stanton, smiling his ingratiating smile, handing out the old blarney as he tried to josh the old lady out her grievance.

Hester Hallett recognized him and was complaining to him. Laura Lamont recognized him . . .

Stanton pinched himself until his flesh squirmed away from his punishing fingers. Was this today—or yesterday? Had something happened to him—something that had addled his mind? Perhaps hunger and privation had robbed him of his senses—driven him into delirium! Perhaps those people down there were all an hallucination—a fantastic mirage conjured up by his fevered brain.

Or was he dead? Was this the wraith of Bill Stanton crouching beside the banister and looking down on the events of his past life? Had all the last dreary year been a Purgatory—just a prelude to the hell into which he was now going to be flung?

"Mr. Reid and Mr. Wattrous aren't in just now, Miss Hallett," the startling figure behind the desk was saying suavely. "You just go back to your rooms and I'll get right after the engineer for you. We'll send up so much heat that you'll think you're on the equator!" And the voice was Bill Stanton's voice!

It was astounding—weirdly baffling, Stanton could not make head or tail of it—anymore than he had ever been able to understand the mysterious blight that had descended on the Olympia and wrecked the hotel.

When he had started to work there, several years before, the Olympia was run down, catering to the riffraff fringe of the theatrical profession and accommodating a choice collection of professional beggars and gentlemen of dubious livelihood. Hugh Wattrous, the pompous proprietor, seemed to have no scruples about the character of his guests as long as they paid their bills.

Stanton had never cared for Hugh Wattrous, never trusted him. There was something shady and devious beneath the big man's bluster, and he was slowly but surely running the hotel into the ground.

But all that had changed when Hal Reid was engaged as manager. Reid was an attractive young fellow with a host of friends and an abundance of energy. In less than a year he had raised the standard of the hotel appreciably; had succeeded in bringing in such worth while guests as Gilbert Johnson, the producer, Dr. Angelo Meltoni, the brain specialist, and Parker Seldon, the theatrical critic. The Olympia began to make money.

And then came the terror, the horrible succession of inexplicable tragedies. First the severed head rolling down the stairs! Then the fiendishly hacked corpse of a wealthy broker! The woman's body hurtling out of a tenth story window to smash to pulp on the sidewalk below!

In each case the victim had been robbed, but never was there the slightest clue to the identity of the fiendish slayer.

The attack on Hester Hallett had been the end; the Olympia closed its doors and all of Hal Reid's good work was wasted. Stanton had felt worse about that than losing his own job; he and Reid had been pals, and he knew what it meant to the manager to see the place close down.

But what lay behind those ghastly murders? Stanton had spent many an hour trying to figure that out while he walked the streets looking for a job during the past year. Hugh Wattrous? Stanton had suspected him on general principles—but what had the proprietor to gain by wrecking his own hotel? For that matter, who else would benefit by it?

Nobody, apparently. If nobody benefited—if there was no human agency behind those ghastly killings—could it be that something unknown and terrible, an evil power or a disembodied spirit such as Hester Hallett thought she had seen, had descended upon the place . . .

A gasping sob that was suddenly choked off stabbed up from below and snapped Stanton out of the daze which had come over him.

The silence that followed that muffled sob was absolute, palpable. The clerk behind the desk paused for a moment, while he eyed Hester Hallett sharply, but the suave smile on his face did not change in the slightest degree. Apparently the old lady had not heard the cry, for she continued her petulant complaint.

But Laura Lamont had heard. Stanton saw the girl stiffen, saw the color drain out of her cheeks and leave them ashen. Without a word she stared at the clerk.

Now he came out from behind the desk and took Miss Hallett's arm as he led her to the elevator.

"I'll go right down to see the engineer, Miss Hallett," he assured her, as he ushered her and Laura into the cage.

The door clicked shut—and the power droned on as the car started up the shaft. But the Olympia had been closed down for more than a year; the power had been shut off. And yet the electric bulbs in the lobby were burning, the elevator was running . . .

As soon as the elevator door closed the suave smile disappeared from the clerk's face. In its place came a gleam of eager desire, and he hurried across the lobby to the big lounge.

Stanton watched him go as if he were a thing apart, watching his own body stepping out before him. How he came to be there on duty in that deserted hotel was a problem to which Stanton thought there could be no earthly solution.

Yet he knew there was evil behind it. The chill air of the deserted lobby was pregnant with evil, the dark corners fitting hiding places for fiends. But the worst evil must be in there where that amazing duplicate of himself was heading.

Cautiously Stanton came down the stairs, crouching behind the shelter of the banister. Swiftly he dodged into a patch of shadow and made his way to the wide doorway of the lounge, slipped into the big room without being seen.

Now the restraint was thrown off in there, the cloak of quite flung aside, and a dozen coarse voices started laughing and jeering.

"Come on, beautiful; don't be bashful!" a guttural voice chuckled. "You're gonna get to like us, baby—you'll be surprised!"

"Oh—you beast!" a girl's voice gasped, and there came the unmistakable sound of a palm slapping against a cheek.

The voices rose in guffawing laughter—laughter that was pierced suddenly by a shrill scream of pain that was chopped off in the middle by the sound of another hand slapping brutally against flesh.

By now Stanton had worked his way down the side of the lounge until he stood behind a potted palm from where he could command a view of the entire room without himself being seen. And what his amazed eyes looked out on might well have been that hell to which he had feared he was headed.

The lights in the big chandelier were dark, but the place was illuminated redly by the flames of a big fire that blazed on the open hearth, a fire that was feeding on the dismembered parts of broken furniture. The flickering light played dancingly on the bestial faces of nearly a score of grinning, leering brutes who sprawled in the comfortable easy chairs they had drawn up in a two-thirds circle around the fire.

Cripples, thugs, degenerates of every sort composed that circle, and as Stanton gazed into the ugly faces he recognized many of the gentry who had once called the Olympia home. It was as vicious-looking a gathering as he had ever seen— and cowering in the cleared space in the middle of the circle was a young woman clad in a low-cut evening dress, the helpless butt of their obscene taunts!

She held her hand in front of her eyes as if to shut out the horrid sight of them, while sobs shook her trembling white shoulders. Stanton's lips pressed into a grim, hard line as he saw her terror, but there was no pity in that encircling wolf pack.

One of the thugs stole up behind her, grabbed her in his arms and forced his kisses upon her—then threw her across the circle to another lecherous devil who clutched at her gown with clawing fingers and ripped it down the front.

Frantically the terrified girl tried to keep herself covered as they tore at her and threw her helplessly from one to another, mauling her, baiting her mercilessly. A scene from hell, with men becoming monsters, and their grotesque shadows dancing weirdly on the walls behind them.

Stanton clutched the palm behind which he stood, and wondered how long he would be able to keep rein on the rage that leaped within him; how long it would be before he would fling himself into that hellish circle and tackle those degenerate fiends single-handed, suicidal as that would be.

The din rose higher. The slavering brutes were on their feet, eager hands outstretched for the dazed, half-conscious girl. Stanton clenched his fists, felt his muscles swelling— and then expelled his gathered breath softly as his eyes stared up at the balcony that served as a mezzanine on one side of the lounge.

His breath seeped out of his lungs, and the strength seemed to ooze out of his bones at what he saw there. A hideous head swam in the darkness; a head that glowed palely; a baldhead with the skin drawn tightly over the prominent face bones.

And then it spoke!

"Silence!"

The single word knifed through the din and snapped it off abruptly as the reveling thugs froze in their places and turned cowed eyes up to the balcony.

"The windows of this room have been stuffed and muffled as effectively as possible," the cold voice rasped down at them, "but they are not entirely soundproof. You fools—do you want the police in here to drag you out by the back of the neck? Don't let me have to warn you again about noise."

Absolute quiet had settled over the room, except for the

muffled sobbing of the girl who crouched on the floor.

"Another thing—this girl," the voice from that eerie head spat contemptuously. "She wasn't worth bringing in; her jewels are paste—worthless. You should have known that, Frugoni; or was it the girl you wanted? There are too many girls here already. No more—unless they have at least five thousand dollars on them. The next man who disobeys that order will regret it."

Like meek children that hard-boiled aggregation of cut-throats listened and did not dare to answer back with a single word.

"How many of you want the girl?" he voice demanded as impersonally as if it was an inanimate piece of merchandise that was being offered. "Stand up, those who want her; the rest sit down."

A dozen of the thugs remained standing and looked up at the balcony expectantly, hopefully.

"Sit down, Amberg; there is already one woman in your room," came the command. "The rest of you draw for her."

From the top of the fireplace one of the men took a pack of cards and proceeded to deal one to each of the standing men, while they crowded together and compared their draws.

"The king of spades!" came an exultant bellow. "Beat that if any of yuh kin!" And an ungainly, clubfooted giant lurched forward and grabbed the girl around the waist, clapped one hand over her mouth to stifle her screams, and calmly dragged her out of the room, toward the elevator.

The whole thing was fantastic, incredible, impossible! It couldn't happen—not there in New York, within a stone's throw of uniformed policemen, of thousands of people who would gladly tear these fiends into pieces!

But it had happened—right there before Stanton's staring eyes. Suddenly his blood was ice in his veins and a new and appalling fear gnawed at his heart. What sort of hell was this he had stumbled into? And what was Laura doing there, un-molested, among those inhuman devils? Could it be possible that she was there willingly—a part of this hellish set-up? Stanton shrank from that suggestion, tried to drive the hideous thought out of his mind, but it persisted tantalizingly. That voice which had come from the luminous head was strangely familiar, too. Somewhere he knew he had heard it before—but where?

The answer seemed almost within his grasp—yet it eluded him. And then the captive girl screamed shrilly—a frantic gasp of mortal terror—and Stanton heard the door of the elevator clang shut.

He couldn't let that misshapen monster drag her off to an unthinkable fate! There was still time to free her and get her out of that house of horror!

Ducking low, Stanton ran along the wall of the lounge and darted through the doorway into the lobby without interference. Up the stairs he dashed to the second floor. The elevator had not stopped there. Stanton rounded the turn and started up the next flight—only to crash head-on into a black figure that loomed in front of him.

For a moment he tottered while he tried to regain his balance; then he went down, and a big paw closed over his mouth while hard fingers clutched at his throat and tightened around his windpipe. Desperately he struggled to break loose, tried to pound at that dark head looming above him— but with the constricting fingers gripping his throat and the hand clamped over his mouth it was almost impossible to breathe.

His arms flailed helplessly, and they were becoming heavy, terribly heavy. Bright splinters of light danced and whirled madly before his eyes, and his pounding chest seemed to be swelling so that it must burst at any moment.

His head was lifted from the step against which it had been pressed. For a moment it seemed suspended high in the air. Then it plunged down—down into unfathomable blackness.

Chapter Three

Groping in the Dark

Stanton came back out of the veil of darkness with a start.

Blinding light poured into his eyes, and a wide-eyed, open-mouthed face swam in the radiance above him.

"Oh, it's you, is it—ye dirty masqueradin' faker!" a wrathful voice snarled. "I wisht I'd choked the life out o' ye, ye—"

Stanton batted his eyes against the flood of illumination, and gradually it resolved itself into the sputtering flame of a match held close to his face. Gradually the face above the light identified itself as that of Ben Peterson, the old fellow who for years had been porter of the Olympia.

"Ben!" Stanton gasped. "Ben—what the devil are you trying to do to me?"

The wide eyes grew rounder, the gaping mouth opened wider; and Ben Peterson's nonplussed face became a battleground for conflicting emotions. Stupefying amazement, dark suspicion and wild panic struggled visibly for the upper hand.

"Is it—is it really you, Mr. Stanton?" he whispered. "Or is it that faker that's been pretendin' to be you down at the desk that ye are? I—I wouldn't 'a' raised a hand against ye if I'd 'a' known it was you, Mr. Stanton. I thought it was one o' those dirty killers that jumped me. I'm sorry, Mr. Stanton; if I'd 'a' known I'd never have—"

The torrent of hoarse apologies flowed on, but Stanton studied the old man's face keenly. He saw, now, that Ben had pulled him up the stairs and had dragged him into a dark side corridor. What was Peterson doing there in the Olympia? Was he in league with those human jackals gathered around the fire in the lounge?

"What are you doing here, Ben?" Stanton asked quietly, and the old fellow's tirade ceased.

"There wasn't anywheres else I could go," he whined. "After the hotel closed up I couldn't find me another job—it's not easy for an old feller like me, Mr. Stanton. So I broke in through a winder here an' went back into my old room next to the boiler room. I wasn't disturbin' nobody—just sleepin' there nights, Mr. Stanton—until those dirty killers come pourin' into the place."

"How long have they been here?"

" 'Bout two weeks now—first just a couple an' then more an' more. It's awful the things they been doin' here, Mr. Stanton."

"And how long have Miss Hallett and Miss Lamont been here?" Stanton pressed anxiously.

"I dunno for sure," Ben told him. "First time I seen them was day before yesterday."

"Why didn't you notify the police when you saw what this gang were doing?" Stanton snapped suspiciously.

"I was afraid." old Ben muttered. "The cops would 'a' turned me out o' the cellar—might even've put me in jail for breakin' in here. Besides, Mr. Stanton, you know what would've happened to me if any o' that gang caught me after I turned them in. You know what they do to squealers, Mr. Stanton."

Peterson's explanation seemed sound enough, but Stanton could not quite trust him. He didn't like the old man's cringing, the darting glances of his shifty eyes; but there seemed no better course than to enlist his aid.

"Do you know what room that clubfooted fellow is in—the one who just dragged the girl into the elevator?" he asked.

"Yep," Ben nodded. "That feller's in 342—down near the end o' the hall."

"Come on." Stanton got to his feet and shook his head to clear it. "We're going down there to get her out."

Peterson started a grumbling protest but then he seemed to think better of it and followed Stanton noiselessly down the hallway. At the door of 342 they halted. Stanton tried the door, found it locked—and from behind the panel came the sound of the girl's sobbing and her captor's deep, rumbling voice.

Stanton whispered final instructions and shook the doorknob.

"Whaddaye want?" came the answering snarl, and Stanton mouthed an unintelligible reply.

The big fellow limped toward the door, grabbed the knob, snapped the key, and flung the door open. In the same instant Stanton and Peterson landed on him, grabbing him around the arms and the legs, while Stanton strove to clap a hand over his mouth.

Down they went in a clawing, pounding heap. The fight was short, but before the big fellow was pounded into unconsciousness he managed to bellow lustily—and behind them Stanton could hear doors opening along the corridor, could hear low voices calling to one another.

"Quick—grab the girl and get her down to your room!" he whispered to Peterson, as he rushed into the room, helped old Ben pick up the fainting girl, and then blew out the stub of candle that burned on the dresser.

Peterson barely made it through the doorway and out into the corridor when the clubfooted giant's neighbors closed in. One of them lit a match and held it up—to reveal half a dozen evil, snarling faces surging into the room.

Stanton hunched his shoulders and hit them low, knocking the wind out of the fellow with the match. It went out, and the darkness was filled with flying fists, swinging elbows and snarled curses. Right and left Stanton flailed as he bored his way toward the corridor, pounding his fists into faces, into bellies, kneeing and elbowing through the mob until he sprawled clear on all fours in the hallway.

Down that corridor, he knew, was a linen closet. In the dark he groped his way to it, and breathed a prayer of thanks when he found it unlocked. Stepping inside, he drew the door closed after him until it was as he had found it, open just a crack.

Through that crack he kept watch down the black hallway. Now another match was lit and the thugs were flocking into clubfoot's room. The angry mutter of their voices increased and matches were held up ineffectually in the hallway.

Then suddenly they blinked out and the thugs in the hallway quieted. And again the chill fingers ran up and down Stanton's back—although he knew that what he stared at was nothing more than human.

At the head of the dark stairway a ghostly, luminous face had appeared. Silently it came down the hallway, to the clubfoot's room, while the only noise to be heard was the scraping of the thugs' shoes on the bare floors as they backed out of the way.

The wounded man's room was empty by now, and the shining death's-head bobbed in through the doorway, while the silence of the grave dominated the place. Of course there was a human body beneath that glowing head, Stanton told himself, a human devil who held these thugs in terror of their lives—but even though he repeated that conviction to himself it could not dispel the creepy feeling that the weird performance had cast over him.

"Get the doctor from room five hundred and ten," came the cold, hollow voiced order from within the room, and Stanton shivered despite himself.

But his subconscious fear turned to something far more concrete a few minutes later when a beam of light appeared at the head of the stairway. For a moment it played on the top step of the stairs, and Stanton caught a glimpse of a woman's dress.

"Here we are, Miss Lamont," a smooth, oily voice murmured.

Laura was there, coming down the hallway!

That voice was familiar; it was an unusual voice—one that Stanton knew he should recognize.

Now they were at the door of 342, and for a moment the beam of the flashlight was reflected on the face of the man who carried it—a thin, white face with dark, piercing eyes that peered out from cavernous sockets. A face that was as unusual as the voice which issued from it—the face of Dr. Angelo Meltoni, the brain specialist who had been one of those whom Hal Reid had brought to the Olympia!

Meltoni and Laura together—answering the commands of that luminous head. Meltoni was a physician. Laura was a nurse. Could it be that the brain specialist was one of the gang, working for the fiend who hid his identity behind that floating head? Could it be that Laura, desperate for work, had surrendered and become one of them—a privileged character in this monstrous place that was worse that the grave for any others of her sex who were dragged into it?

Stanton determined grimly that he would find out the answers to those questions before Meltoni and the girl got off that floor.

"Fix him up quickly," he hear the cold voice command, "and then return upstairs."

Again the luminous head bobbed through the doorway and glided on its way to the stairway, but this time Stanton slipped out of his closet and tiptoed after it. Without interference he made his way to a side corridor that opened off the main hallway near the head of the stairs.

Patiently he crouched there until the flashlight beam again flashed down the hallway and he could hear the footsteps of Laura and Meltoni. He waited until they were directly in front of him; then he sprang, landing on Meltoni's shoulders while he shouted to Laura to wait. But the girl, if she heard, paid no attention. With a little cry of fear she ran to the stairway and raced down the steps.

"That voice!" Meltoni gasped, and he managed to twist around and swing the flashlight so that it focused on Stanton's face. "It *is* you, Stanton!" he whispered hoarsely. "Thank God for that! Thank God you're here—I have been powerless in the hands of these devils! Now at least there are two of us to fight them!"

Stanton eased his grip on the doctor's throat and drew him back into the side corridor, but he was alert for any attempt at treachery.

"What are you doing here, Meltoni?" he snapped. "Talk fast, before those cutthroats come looking for you."

"What am I doing here?" Meltoni expostulated. "Trying to escape—trying to keep my hands clean of the terrible crimes that are being committed in this place. But I am helpless, I tell you—they watch me every minute. Never have I had a chance to escape since the night they lured me into a tavern on Forty-Sixth Street. There they took me into a back room and beat me over the head. I could feel them dragging me through cellars—and then I was here, in the old Olympia."

So that was how the gang managed to get in and out of the empty hotel without being seen—through a tavern on Forty Sixth Street that undoubtedly belonged to their leader and was maintained as an innocent appearing cover for this sinister rendezvous. That explained the source of the electric power, too—a tapped wire from the tavern on the next street. A perfect set-up, Stanton admitted; once a prisoner was dragged into the Olympia all hope was gone—it was like dropping out of the world.

But Stanton was still far from satisfied with Meltoni's explanation of his part in the diabolical business.

"What do they want you here for, doctor?" he probed.

"For Miss Hallett," Meltoni answered readily. "They kidnapped the poor lady from the sanitarium where she was taken after her mind gave way. Now they have her back here in her old home. Everything they are trying to make just as it was. That is why they have that man made up to resemble you behind the desk in the lobby—so that she will feel completely at home and so that her mind will come back to her. She has information that they desire."

"And that's why Miss Lamont is here?" Stanton almost shouted his relief.

"Yes," Meltoni nodded vigorously. "They kidnapped her, too—so that everything should be just as Miss Hallett was accustomed to having it. They watch her, too—every second, poor girl."

Stanton's relief was short-lived. Meltoni's words rang ominously in his brain—like the notes of Laura's death knell!

Appalling comprehension came to him as he realized the terrible danger that hung over the girl. She was a prisoner. Once she had served the purpose for which she had been brought there she would never be allowed to escape from the hotel. She knew too much. When they were finished with her she would go the way of that other girl he and Peterson had rescued—into the middle of that ring of leering beasts, to be pawed and mauled by them and then to be dragged off screaming to one of their rooms!

"I must get back, Stanton, or they will come looking for me," Meltoni was saying. "We can't stand up and fight them—you and I. Our only hope against them must lie in surprise. I must go back to the fifth floor—to Miss Hallett's old suite. That's where they are keeping her and Miss Lamont."

For a moment he hesitated; then inspiration flashed in his eyes.

"Give me a few minutes—then come after me, Stanton," he urged. "Perhaps if we take them by surprise together we may be able to overpower the leader and force our way out of here. That is our only hope."

Chapter Four

Behind the Mask

As Meltoni's dark figure disappeared down the stairway Stanton edged his way back into the hall, tiptoed down its full length, and taking a rear stairway, hurried down to Ben Peterson's cubbyhole in the cellar beside the engine room. The door opened a crack in response to his knock and Peterson's scared face peered out, while he clutched a heavy cudgel ready to defend himself.

"She fainted on the way down here," he said, as soon as he recognized Stanton. "She's just comin' out of it now. I'm glad you're here, Mr. Stanton, 'cause I'm not much of a hand with womenfolk's."

Frightenedly the girl opened her eyes and glanced around her. One look at her surroundings and at her torn clothing, and her hysterical weeping began again, but gradually Stanton talked her out of it and made her understand that she was with friends.

"Now I'll have to leave you for a while," he concluded, "and Mr. Peterson will have to go, too. But you stay right here, no matter what happens. Don't try to escape until Mr. Peterson or I come back here for you." Then he turned to the old man. "You, Ben, slip out and get the police—and make it snappy. I'm going upstairs now to get hold of that devil with the shining head."

Armed with Peterson's heavy cudgel Stanton left the cubbyhole and started back up the stairs, lighting his way with matches to guide him through the Stygian blackness. Once or twice he thought he heard a noise behind him—something that sounded like the tap of a stealthy footstep—but when he stopped to listen there was nothing but absolute silence.

When he stepped out into the fifth floor hallway it was almost as quiet as the rest of the building—except for a low buzz of conversation that came from a room halfway down the corridor. That was Miss Hallett's suite, he saw at once, and there was light shining through the transom.

Behind that door were the old lady and Laura and Meltoni—and the fiendish devil who dominated this house of horror. Stanton clutched his cudgel with fingers that bit into the wood, and tiptoed his way to the door of 510.

That was Meltoni's voice, droning monotonously, but Stanton could not make out what he was saying. The transom, he noticed, was partly open. That gave him an idea.

Father down the hall he found a door that was unlocked. Cautiously he groped his way inside and came out with a chair, which he placed in front of Hester Hallett's door. Standing on this he could see into the room—could see the old lady sitting on a straight-backed chair and staring blankly before her; could see Meltoni crouched on another chair facing her, his eyes never leaving hers.

"Now, try to remember," Meltoni droned, "you hid some of your money in your mattress. Some of your bonds you put under the carpet. Some were in your trunks. But there were more—you remember that there were more. Where did you put the rest? Try to remember—where did you hide them so that they would not be stolen?"

The old lady's eyes were glazed and she sat as rigid and still as a statue. Her voice, when it came, seemed no conscious part of her; the words seemed to flow past her lips scarcely moving them.

"There were no others. You have them all," she said quietly.

"There was more money—much more money—and there were jewels," Meltoni's monotonous monotone droned on. "Where did you put them? Try to remember. You hid them so that they would be safe. Get up now and get them, if they are in this room—"

But Hester Hallett only repeated, "There was no more. You have it all."

And again Meltoni's voice took up his ritual. The old lady was hypnotized. Stanton could see, but even though he dominated her mind Meltoni could not draw out of it the information he sought.

After Hester Hallett went insane, Stanton recalled, her suite and her trunks had been ransacked from top to bottom. A curious collection of old currency, old bonds and valuable souvenirs of her past had come to light, but there had been rumors about a huge fortune she had once possessed and which had disappeared.

That must be what Meltoni was trying to pry from her—the whereabouts of her hidden wealth. With his hypnotism he was trying to wrest her secret from her.

Hester Hallett's face was blank and expressionless, but Meltoni's countenance was filled with cunning and evil as he leaned close to her and droned his monotonous questions. As he watched, Stanton felt all of his first suspicion of the brain specialist return with increased force.

Meltoni was in there alone with the two women—with Hester Hallett, who sat there under his influence, and with Laura, who stood by helplessly, watching the proceedings with pitying eyes. It was *he,* Meltoni, who wanted to locate the old lady's hidden wealth? It was *he* who was the fiend masquerading behind that luminous head!

And like a credulous fool Stanton had let the trickster go when he had him by the neck down there in the lower floor corridor! Stanton's eyes flashed and his jaws clamped grimly. There was still time to settle the score with Dr. Meltoni—still time to break in that door and grab the fiend by his skinny throat . . .

Meltoni's monotonous drone had stopped—and suddenly all of Stanton's rage against him evaporated.

Meltoni was *not* alone in that room with the women. He did not move from his chair, but without warning the lights snapped off—and in the air floated the livid head Stanton had seen twice before.

"Where did you hide them?" the cold, hollow voice demanded. "Where did you hide the money and the jewels?"

But again Miss Hallett's quiet voice repeated. "There is no more. You have them all."

"We're wasting time," the cold voice spat, and the lights snapped on—to reveal a weird figure standing in the open doorway of a clothes closet!

A black gown covered it from neck to feet, and on the ebony shoulders squatted a repulsive looking baldhead that was half Oriental and half negroid in its hideousness. Pasty white, it was, with mad eyes gleaming out of deep sockets.

That was the secret of the luminous head—a human devil, his head coated with luminous paint, prowling through the dark in an invisible black robe! Very human, indeed—for Stanton now saw that the fiend held an ugly-looking revolver in one black-gloved hand, and the muzzle was trained on Dr. Meltoni's stomach. From his hiding place in the closet he had had Meltoni covered all the while.

"Tie her to that bed—her hands against the head rail," the black-robed figure ordered. "Tear up the sheets."

Helpless under the muzzle of the pointing revolver, Meltoni obeyed. When Hester Hallett lay stretched out on the bed with her hands secured to the railing, the watching fiend spoke again.

"Take off her shoes and stockings. Now tie her feet to the bottom rail. Now take two of those embers from the fireplace. Jam them against the soles of her feet and hold them there until she decides to talk."

Meltoni hesitated, looked into the hideous face—and the revolver muzzle raised threateningly. With a helpless shrug he stooped over the open fireplace, picked out two blazing embers, and started toward the bed.

"No—no! You can't do that to her!" Laura screamed, but the black-robed devil knocked her out of the way and clamped his gloved hand over the old lady's mouth as Meltoni held the fire against her shrinking flesh.

That was all that Stanton could stand. Hot rage leaped within him, and he started to climb down from his chair, clutching his cudgel ready to batter that hideous head into a jelly . . .

But in that instant the chair was jerked out from under him, and he sprawled on the floor, to have two burly thugs land on him. Stanton's club was knocked out of his hand, but he needed no club in the terrific, primeval battle that followed. All that he needed were his two hard fists, to lash and pound and batter at those panting thugs as they rolled over him on the floor.

All if his pent-up rage went into that fight, and the mad joy of battle coursed through his veins like strong wine every time his fists smashed into a writhing face and drew a groan of agony. Time after time his fists smashed into a writhing face on top of him—but he hardly felt the smash of their punches. He was needed in that room; Laura, at the mercy of that black-robed fiend, needed him—and these thugs were just a nuisance in the way.

A smash to the stomach cleared one of them out of his path; a hook to the jaw sent the other reeling—and Stanton grabbed the doorknob, pushed, and the door flew open.

Inside, the old lady lay squirming and moaning, while Laura tugged at Meltoni in a desperate effort to pull the searing brands away from the suffering woman's feet. And the black-robed devil's gun was trained on Laura's breast. The black finger was tightening on the trigger!

Stanton's furious charge hurled him across the room and into that black-robed menace before the inhuman devil knew what was happening. The gun roared harmlessly in the air and then dropped to the floor, while Stanton's fists worked like trip-hammers on the hideous white face. Even in his rage his skin crawled at contact with the cold, clammy cheeks . . .

And then his feet were tangled up with the black robe. For a moment they stood there slugging each other—and the next moment they were on the floor, with Stanton on top, battering that ugly head with every bit of his strength.

Battering, battering—with such ferocity that he smashed the ugly face completely off the head!

Stanton reared back and stared, aghast, as the black-gloved hands darted up and grabbed the loosened face, to pull it back into place. Those hands were quick, but not quick enough to stop the fleeting glance Stanton caught of the face beneath what he now saw was a tight-fitting rubber mask.

It was that face that unnerved him; that left him gaping helplessly. It was the face of Hal Reid, his friend, the former manager of the Olympia!

Stunned and feeling curiously ill, Stanton got to his feet and dived for the revolver lying on the floor. With the weapon held tight against his side, he whirled on the black-robed figure who was just scrambling to his feet.

"Back up, Hal!" he commanded tensely. "Up with your hands and back up against the wall—or, so help me, I'll empty this gun into your belly!"

Slowly the black-cloaked arms started to raise and Reid began backing toward the wall. Stanton watched him like a hawk—but he forgot the two thugs in the hall. With scarcely a sound they leaped through the doorway and tackled him. Stanton went down under their combined rush, but before they could pin him he was back on his feet, the revolver moving in a threatening arc before him.

With his face contorted with savage fury, one of the thugs dodged aside and tried to dive under the gun. Stanton pulled the trigger, and the thunderous report boomed out—but the thug came on! Stanton fired again—pulled the trigger a third time in desperate panic. The fellow was almost upon him when the last shot roared from the gun muzzle—so close that the flame scorched his coat—but the bullet did not stop him!

A bulletproof vest—the answer to the thug's astounding survival flashed into Stanton's mind. But as he drove his fist into the fellow's ribs and found them unprotected he knew that that was not the solution.

There was only one other answer; the cartridges had been blanks. The gun—the gun the black-robed Reid had carried—had been loaded with blank cartridges!

That amazing fact hammered at Stanton's mind and tried to tell him something as the thugs bore him down. It still baffled him as they tied him up and flung him on his back on the bed.

But the problem was brushed from his mind when he looked up into Laura's terrified eyes and realized that now she was completely at the mercy of this wolf pack and the madman who was their leader. Her only hope was Ben Peterson and the police.

Had Ben gotten out of the hotel safety? Had he gone to the police—or had he decided that his own safety lay in flight. Torturing doubt assailed Stanton as he lay there and listened to Hester Hallett moan and toss as the blazing embers were brought back to her blistered feet.

If Ben had given the alarm the police should be there by now; they should be swarming through the dark corridors, driving these wolves before them like the inhuman beasts they were . . .

Stanton's heart leaped and pounded with wild hope as he heard the noise in the corridor. Feet—men's voices! They were coming! And then they were there at the door—half a dozen of them—cutthroats and killers!

Between them they dragged the bloody, broken body of Ben Peterson, and dumped it in a heap on the floor. Stanton didn't need Dr. Meltoni's verdict to tell him that there was no longer any life in that poor battered pulp.

Chapter Five

Brain of a Fiend

Not until Hester Hallett lost consciousness did the black-robed devil whom Stanton had once called his friend give the signal to stop the torture. To Stanton, lying there beside her, it seemed hours that she writhed and groaned, but all through that fiery ordeal the old lady had unclamped her locked jaws for only two monotonous sentences: "There is no more. You have it all."

"Well, if she can't be made to talk that way, there are other ways," came harshly from behind the hideous rubber mask that leered down at them. "Take them down to the mezzanine—Stanton, too."

The mezzanine! Dread clamped its icy fingers around Stanton's heart, for he had a sickening premonition of what that would mean—a premonition that was given fearful substance the moment he looked down into the lounge, into a ring of evil faces that flamed with lust and cruelty. They were gathered there for something special—and like the beasts they were they licked their lips in slavering anticipation!

Stanton, Laura and Hester Hallett were dragged to the edge of the balcony and tied securely to chairs, prize seats for the satanic orgy that would be staged in the shadow-painted room below them. Beside them stood Reid, his black robes almost invisible in the darkness and his luminous mask seemingly suspended eerily in the air. And in the background cowered Angelo Meltoni.

At Reid's command two of the motley gang left the lounge—to return dragging the girl whom Stanton and Ben Peterson had rescued from the clutches of the club-footed giant. Screaming and cowering in terror she was again thrown into the fire lit circle, to huddle there helplessly while that ring of degenerates baited her, tossed her from one to the other, ripped the clothing from her body and outraged her white flesh with their filthy paws.

Naked and bleeding, where their nails had ripped into her soft skin, like a cornered rabbit she looked around frantically for some avenue of escape—only to stare into evil, gloating eyes that regarded her lasciviously from every side; only to dart away as eager hands clawed out for her. Panting and sobbing, gasping for air, she tried to escape them, but they hemmed her in closer and closer—until she fell to the floor, semi-conscious, her blood staining the cold stone.

Stanton felt weak and sick at heart from that exhibition of heartless brutality—but the masked devil beside him chuckled.

"That will teach you not to try to escape when I give you to a protector," he jeered down at the helpless girl. "Fallon, maybe you can take care of her better than Olau did, but watch her—she's a flighty damsel."

While his mates laughed and guffawed, Fallon, a repulsive looking hunchback with a horribly scarred face, stalked into the circle and grabbed his victim.

"Don't worry, Chief," he boasted. "They don't none o' them get away from me! Not after I gets my hands on them—like this . . ."

And with his long fingers hooked in the girl's hair, he dragged her body across the floor to the elevator!

Before the girl's agonized screams had died away, the luminous faced mask turned to Laura, who sat trembling, her eyes fixed in terrified fascination on that row of degenerate faces that gaped up at her. Even before the words came she knew what they would be—and utter terror convulsed her features.

"It is your turn next!" Reid taunted her: "Unless, of course, you can tell me where the forgetful Miss Hallett hid the bulk of her wealth—"

"But I don't know, I tell you!" Laura screamed. "She never told me anything about it. Oh, *please,* you've *got* to believe me!"

"The only thing I will believe is where that money is hidden!" Reid snarled angrily. "I don't care who tells me where it is—but unless I have the information in the next two minutes you go down to the boys!"

Stanton pleaded with him, cursed him, reviled him, but his words made no more impression on Reid than on the rubber mask that covered his face. And Stanton's struggles made just as little impression on the ropes that bound him to the chair. One leg he had managed to kick free of the ropes, but his wrists were held tight and the ropes that were lashed across his chest held him immovable against the back of the chair.

"Time's up!" Reid announced deliberately. "Roeding! Yawitz! Come and get her!"

Eagerly two of the thugs left the pack and started up the mezzanine stairs, while Laura sobbed and quaked with fright, and while Stanton fought those devilish ropes until his boiling blood threatened to burst from his veins.

Reid saw that futile struggle and chuckled with infernal delight; came and stood in front of Stanton and laughed at him. Now the thugs, two degraded looking brutes, were on the mezzanine, shambling forward with knowing grins and spreading talons. In another few moments they would seize Laura and drag her down to the Inferno that yawned for her below . . .

Tears of helpless rage welled up into Stanton's eyes and mingled with the perspiration that ran down his cheeks. Tied up, unable to move a hand, he had to sit there and watch the girl he loved being maltreated and murdered by that rabble! Unable to move a hand . . .

Stanton tensed his cramped muscles, gripped the fingers of his bound hands—and suddenly shot out his free foot with every ounce of his strength behind it. That desperate kick caught Reid full on the knee, wrenched a yelp of pain from behind the rubber mask, and knocked him off his feet—to totter for a moment and then tumble over backward. With a dull thud his head smacked against the hard wood railing of the balcony and he fell in a heap on the floor.

The inhuman devil was down—but only for a moment. Then he was back on his feet, rubbing the back of his head and gazing around him dazedly. His thugs had started toward him, but as he got to his feet they turned to Stanton where he lay helplessly tied to the chair that had been overturned by the force of his kick.

Brutally they smashed their fists into his face as they righted the fallen chair and drew it up close to the balcony railing. Then they turned to where Laura cringed in terror, untied the ropes which bound her and, picking her up between them, carried her down from the mezzanine.

Her screams and hopeless pleas stabbed into Stanton's heart, but there was nothing he could do. During the brief melee he had managed to free his other foot, but his arms and wrists were still securely bound.

"Damn you!" he cursed Reid. "You've got the luck of the Devil himself or that crack would have split your damned skull open. But you'll pay for any harm that comes to her— you'll pay plenty!"

Trembling and sobbing Laura cowered in the middle of that hellish circle, drawing back fearfully until the heat of the blazing fire scorched her dress. And Stanton watched with aching, straining eyes, flinching as if under the lash every time the degenerates hurled an obscene remark at her or drew a fresh scream from her quivering lips.

"High card gets the lady's cute little shoe!" one burly brute proposed—and the fatal deck of cards came down from over the fireplace, to be dealt around the clamoring circle.

"Ace of spades!" howled a one-eyed beggar, before the deal was half completed—and he triumphantly tore the slipper from Laura's right foot.

Her shoes, her stockings, her dress—piece by piece their ravishing fingers stripped the clothing off her until she huddled there in the bright glare of the leaping fire in nothing but her flimsy under garments!

In the balcony above her Stanton had ceased to be a sane man; he had become a raving maniac, frothing at the mouth as he howled threats and cures at them, as he tore madly at the ropes that would not yield a fraction of an inch. If he could only get loose—could only get down there and get his hands on those cowardly fiends . . .

He was certain that he was utterly mad when he felt the rope around his chest snap and start to loosen. The rope couldn't have snapped; his strength wasn't nearly equal to that feat. But the rope *had* snapped! And now there was something cold against his wrists!

Stanton snapped his head around—and was doubly sure

that he was insane when he saw that luminous head bending over him, saw the black-robed figure crouched behind his chair.

"For God's sake, take it easy for just a moment!" Hal Reid pleaded. "Keep on yelling so that they don't look up here and see me. In just a moment I'll have you free."

Reid was cutting him loose—freeing him! The whole world was utterly mad! Stanton had no idea what it was all about, but he tensed in his chair, howled cures down into the pit, and waited, with every muscle taut, for that last rope around his wrists to snap.

It gave—and in the same moment he was pitched forward as two struggling bodies lunged into him from behind. As he scrambled to his feet he saw the black robed Reid and Dr. Meltoni locked in a furious struggle.

"You double-crossing rat!" Meltoni gritted. "Try to cross me up, will you!" And in his descending hand he clutched a wicked looking knife.

Reid managed to ward off that thirsty blade once, but Meltoni had him down and the steel flashed a deadly pattern in the reflected firelight. It would be only a question of seconds before he would drive the keen blade through the black robe and into Reid's heart.

Stanton didn't know what it was all about, but he caught a glimpse of Reid's contorted face, from which the rubber mask had fallen or been torn off—and he saw the leer of diabolical triumph that had transformed Meltoni's features into a gargoyle of unleashed hate. And he made his decision.

His upper cutting fist caught Meltoni squarely under the jaw, raised him into the air, and pitched him in an unconscious heap against the balcony railing. In a flash Stanton leaped on top of him, grabbed the knife that his fingers still clutched, and sprang to the top of the railing.

Down below there in the lounge a smirking hellion was pawing at the catch of Laura's brassiere!

Before his clumsy fingers solved the fastening his world came to a sudden end.

A hundred and seventy pounds of plummeting human flesh and bone crashed down on him, and a flashing streak of steel stabbed into his chest—to come out red and dripping!

Appalled silence blotted out the riotous tumult in that lounge, and eyes that had been glutting themselves lasciviously on Laura's nearly naked body stared in amazement at the crumpled body on the floor. Stanton made good use of their surprise. With one arm around Laura's waist, half supporting her, half dragging her with him, he made a bee-line through that circle, his red knife licking out to right and left and clearing a way for them.

Those scourings of New York's underworld had no stomach for cold steel. They shrank away from Stanton as if he were the plague, and he and Laura reached the foot of the mezzanine stairs before the boldest came to their senses and the pursuit began.

Hal Reid, stripped of his black robe and gloves, was waiting for them at the head of the stairs as they dashed up. He led the way across the balcony to a side stairs that led to the second floor. By the time they reached the landing the mob was howling behind them.

Up another flight—but by then the pounding feet behind them were much closer, and they could hear the elevator in operation. Some of the gang were using it to get above them, to cut off the possibility of escape in that direction.

"This is as far as we can get!" Reid panted. "We'll have to make a stand here."

"Up front!" Stanton snapped, and led the way on the run to the front of the building.

Frantically he groped in the darkness for a doorknob, found one, pushed, and the door swung in. Barely had they gotten into the room and closed the door behind them, turned the key in the lock, when the rabid thugs caught up with them and began pounding on the panel.

"Pile the furniture in front of the door!" Stanton shouted, as he grabbed a chair and smashed it through a front window.

Swinging it over his head like an ax he smashed it again

and again against the heavy boards that were nailed across the outside of the window. One cracked, split apart—then another. And another. Stanton grabbed the broken ends and wrenched them loose, until he could get his head and shoulders through and lean out over the street below.

Already half a dozen people on the sidewalk had stopped and were looking up curiously. Stanton forced the battered chair through the opening and dropped it, to crash to splinters on the pavement. Now other spectators came running to see what it was all about.

"Get the police!" Stanton shouted down at them frantically. "This building is full of thieves and murderers! We're trapped up here! Call the cops! Tell them to cover the tavern on Forty-Sixth Street behind this hotel—it's the way the gang will try to get out!"

Stanton shouted until he was hoarse, but several men in the gathering throng got the idea and started on the run for Seventh Avenue while others darted into nearby buildings to telephone.

Now it would be only a question of minutes . . .

Stanton turned back into the room and lit a match. Laura and Reid had piled every stick of furniture against the door and were adding their own weight to the barricade. Stanton joined them, stood shoulder to shoulder with Reid.

"I don't know what you think of me, Bill," his old friend panted. "Whatever it is, I deserve it—but I didn't do any of this willingly; you must believe that. It was all a horrible nightmare—like a drunken man who knows he is doing silly things but can't stop doing them. Only the things I was doing were hellish—and I couldn't stop myself!

"I made my first mistake when I let Meltoni hypnotize me one night in his room. He gave me dope while I was under his influence—made a hophead out of me. After that I was helpless; between the dope and his hypnotic power he led me around like a monkey. The hell of it was that I knew what he was doing but was powerless to stop him.

"He came to the Olympia in the first place because Miss

Hallett lived here and he had learned of the fortune she was supposed to have hidden away. At the same time he saw a fine opportunity to build up a gang from the yeggs and slippery characters we had around the place. He cultivated them and organized them, and then deliberately bankrupted the hotel with his deviltry so that he could use the empty building for a hangout. With the tavern he bought on the next block it was a perfect layout."

"A layout that only the brain of a fiend could devise," Stanton muttered. "And by keeping you in that masquerade outfit and pretending that he was helpless against you he had a safe alibi in case anything went wrong—an alibi that even his own thugs believed."

"It was hell—a living hell," Reid groaned. "Never for a moment was I able to get out of it until you smacked my head against that balcony railing."

The stout panels of the door were battered through and the clamoring thugs were tugging away at the furniture piled against it—but suddenly a new sound cut through the racket they were making. The wail of police sirens coming down the street, right up to the barred front door of the Olympia!

With yells of consternation the thugs stampeded down the hall.

"Then all this started over poor Miss Hallett's money?" Laura wondered aloud.

"Miss Hallett!" Stanton gasped, with a twinge of conscience. "We left her tied up down there on the balcony!"

But when the police swept through the Olympia and rounded up Meltoni's trapped thugs, the found the amazing Miss Hallett quite unharmed on the mezzanine. She had managed to free her hands and arms, and her rheumy old eyes sparkled as she pulled sheaves of paper from behind the stays of her old-fashioned corset and counted them into her lap—paper that was United States currency in thousand dollar denominations!

HELL WELCOMES LONELY WIVES

JAMES CABOT was not the only one who felt his scalp tighten as he stared down, wide-eyed and appalled, at the ghastly horror sprawled gruesomely on the pavement of the Luxonia Apartment House court. Hard-boiled reporters and headquarters men gazed at that fearful sight—and turned away with faces that were a shade whiter and jaws that were clenched grimly together.

But it wasn't the sight of the horribly broken body that sent an eerie twinge creeping through Cabot. It wasn't that he had known this woman only a few short months ago, had talked with her, watched her smile and heard her laugh at his pleasantries. It was something more—almost as if her sudden and inexplicable tearing asunder of the evil of eternity held a prophetic warning for him. His nerves quivered and tingled in rapport with something he could sense but not understand . . .

Alicia Kendall Blainey had had everything to live for. She was beautiful—even now her face, unmarred by the frightful smash that had terminated her death dive, gave witness to that. She had had social position, wealth, luxury. And romance.

Only three days ago she had returned from Reno, straight from the court where she had divorced her young husband; returned to marry Herbert Drexel, the millionaire with whom her name had been coupled for months. Only last night they had been photographed, side by side, in a gay Broadway nightclub. And now, on the eve of the wedding for which she had freed herself—she had leaped out of a twelfth story window to this ghastly death.

Why? That question hammered at Cabot's brain as he stared down at the mangled limbs that were only partly concealed by the crimsoned negligee, turned from the blood-spattered courtyard and started upstairs.

Homicide Squad men were ransacking the lavish apartment when Cabot reached it, but their search had produced few clues.

"Most promising is this crumpled envelope that was lying there on her dressing table," one of the detectives growled, "and this hunk of paper that was lying over there near the open window. Looks as if she dropped it just before she jumped out—and if we can find out who sent her that we'll probably be on the trail of a murderer."

A crumpled envelope with a Reno postmark, and a small square of photographer's paper that had been lying facedown on the floor—and the moment Cabot saw them the prickles began running down his spine! The square of paper had not been developed and was already beginning to darken, but its message was still plainly visible:

This is your last day. Tomorrow will be too late.

And beneath it the silhouetted head of an Indian chief.

Two weeks before, Jim Cabot had been in another sumptuously furnished apartment where a handsome woman lay dead on the floor, with the faint odor of almonds still clinging to her cold lips. There had been an envelope with a Reno postmark in that apartment—and a square of photographer's paper. But it had been lying face-up to the light and was browned so completely that any message it might have borne was no longer decipherable.

Julia Estabrook had been a divorcee too, fresh from Reno to contract the wealthy marriage for which she had tossed aside her first husband. She, too, had been on the eve of her wedding . . .

Cabot's blood chilled as he stared down at the death warning, and a premonition that he could not shake off pressed down upon him. Betty—his Betty—was out there in Reno. Out there to divorce him—to write *finis* to the torturing nightmare that had been the end of their romance. And in his pocket was an envelope with a Reno postmark that had seemed to become a thing alive, burning against his ribs, the moment he saw the crumpled envelope that had been lying on Alicia Blainey's vanity.

That letter was from Wendy Taylor, his sister-in-law, who was staying with Betty in the Western divorce capital. Wendy had been uneasy for several weeks. In other letters she had hinted that she was worried; had told him of queer rumors that were going the rounds in Reno—rumors about young divorcees who disappeared almost as soon as the courts awarded them their freedom.

"This town frightens me more and more," Wendy had written, "and I'll be *so* glad when we are finished and can leave it. At first I laughed at these whispered stories of missing girls. I told myself that they were the silly invention of people who had nothing else to do to occupy their time. But now the terrifying thing has struck so close to me that I can't close my eyes to it any longer.

"You remember my mentioning Dora Vaughn—the girl I met here in the hotel. She didn't have any money or family; she was just a pretty kid who wanted to go back to New York with me and try to get into a chorus. We became great friends, and I knew all her plans—but the day her decree was handed down she disappeared without a word of good-bye. I've hunted all over for her, but it's just as if the earth had opened and swallowed her up. She's gone—and I *know* she didn't go voluntarily.

"I went to the police, but they have not been able to find so much as a trace of her. Something has happened to her, Jim—I know it. Something terrible! And I have an uncanny feeling that the same thing will happen to me—to me and Betty—unless we are able to get out of here in time . . ."

Jim Cabot's brain rioted with alarm. If Wendy's ominous hunch was well founded, Betty was in fearful danger—and the thought of danger to her, especially now that he was so far away and so impotent to help her, shook and unnerved him. She was in Reno to cast him off, as these other women had rid themselves of their husbands—but no matter what a court of law might say, he knew that there was no power on earth that could destroy the bond which united them. No matter what Betty might do, he would still be hers, even though he could not keep her from this step that would take her out of his life.

Reno—in some sinister way it was connected up directly with those two women who had snatched at death when happiness was waiting for them. There was something diabolical going on out there, something that reached forth for its victims with the slimy tentacles of an octopus—and as he sat staring moodily around the little rooms that had once been Betty's, the relentless premonition became stronger and stronger . . .

And with it came galling bitterness.

Their marriage had never had a chance. It had been doomed from the start—doomed because of circumstances he could not fight. He was the descendant of an aristocratic family, the sole heir of his millionaire uncle, Finley Cabot. All through his adolescence it had been more or less taken for granted that he would marry Lenore Millard, the daughter of a family in his own circle; but Jim had fallen in love with Betty Taylor, a business girl, and married her.

And from that moment the cards had been stacked against him.

"A fortune-hunter!" his Uncle Finley had promptly branded Betty. "A nameless nobody who is after my money—but she'll find she isn't as clever as she thinks. Not a cent of mine will you get while you are married to her—do you understand that?"

Not satisfied with disinheriting him, the irate old man had had him ousted from the soft berth in the family brokerage house where he had been working, had thrown him entirely upon his own resources.

He and Betty had laughed—then.

"We don't need him and his old money, as long as we have each other," she had whispered into Jim's ear. "We'll get on better—we'll be closer to each other—without it."

Soon he had managed to land a job on a newspaper, a job with a modest salary. They had started off fine—but little by little Betty had begun to change. Hardly noticeably at first, but then more and more pronouncedly. She had become quarrelsome, irritable, flirtatious—almost brazen. Changed so completely and so bafflingly that at times he had hardly recognized her as the sweet girl he had married.

Things had come to a head one night when she came home from a dance with Keith Averill, a society playboy who had been showering her with attentions. Jim said things he did not mean in the argument that followed, and before he realized it Betty was confronting him with flushed face and dark eyes that sparkled with rage.

"I've had all I can stand of you, Jim Cabot!" she flung at him. "I've had enough of your continual bickering. I want a divorce—and I'm going to Reno to get it!"

That was two months ago. Now Betty was nearly free. She was through with him, and the rest of his life stretched ahead of him drab and uninviting without her.

His marriage had been a mess all around, he ruminated bitterly. Besides estranging his uncle, it had hurt Lenore Millard far more than Jim had thought possible; had revealed that she really was in love with him. So much so that, despite her heartache, she had remained his friend, even though her father, old Preston Millard, had forbidden her to see him. A sorry mess—but this was the end. In a week or so Betty would be back in town, and she would no longer be his . . .

That feeling of uneasiness, of impending calamity, surged through him chillingly, like a sixth sense trying to warn him. It gave him no peace, no rest. At times he could almost *feel* Betty calling to him, trying to tell him something—something that sent little chills trickling down his back and made the hair at the nape of his neck stand on end.

It was the sight of that grisly corpse spattered over the pavement that was plaguing him, he tried to tell himself—but at that moment the telephone rang startlingly, and his fingers were cold and damp as he reached for the receiver. The pit of his stomach seemed to sink through his body as he heard the operator's voice announcing a long distance call—a call from Reno, Nevada!

"Hello, Jim," came a voice, uncertain and faint with distance—and his heart leaped into his throat. "This is Betty."

For a moment her voice sounded distorted and unreal. Then he realized what was making it so quivery and uncertain Betty was crying; she was terrified!

"Oh, I had to call you, Jim!" she was sobbing into his ear. "It's about Wendy—she's gone! Disappeared just like Dora Vaughn! I haven't seen her since early this morning, haven't heard a word from her—"

"Have you notified the police?" he heard himself asking, even though he remembered how helpless they had been to find the Vaughn girl.

"No—I don't dare do that!" Betty gasped, and her voice broke hysterically. "I was so frightened—I was just going to call them—when somebody telephoned me. A man's voice—he warned me that if I went to the police I'd never see Wendy alive again. That's why she disappeared, Jim, because she went to the police with what she found out about Dora Vaughn. Dora was—"

The next word died half-uttered. Jim could hear Betty suck in her breath in a sudden gasp of horror—and then it was expelled in a piercing scream of sheer terror!

"Betty! Betty—what's the matter?" he shouted desperately—but the scream was cut short as the receiver at the other end of the line clicked down on its hook.

Chapter Two

One Who Disappeared

That wild scream knifed into Jim Cabot's brain like a white-hot dagger, rang in his tingling ears even after it was snapped off and ominous silence took its place. Vainly he shouted into the receiver and jiggled the hook. The line was dead.

At last he succeeded in signaling the operator, but it took long, interminable minutes before she was able to connect him with the Edgewater House in Reno; before the voice of the hotel clerk sounded on the wire. Additional agonizingly long minutes before he phlegmatically announced, "Mrs. Cabot's room does not answer."

"But she must answer!" Jim shouted at him. "I was just talking to her. If she doesn't answer there's something wrong. Something's happened to her. Send someone up to her room right away—"

"I'm sure you are wrong, sir," the clerk's bored voice interrupted. "Mrs. Cabot is not in her room. Her key is here at the desk."

Betty wasn't in her room. That must mean that she had called him from somewhere outside the hotel. She had been trying to evade the devils who had threatened her, but they had followed her and seized her in the midst of her terrified plea for help. She was somewhere in Reno—in the hands of Wendy's kidnapers. But where? And how could he help her?

The police? She had already vetoed that suggestion. To notify the police would mean Wendy's death—and, now, probably Betty's as well. He did not dare take that chance!

Betty was in appalling danger—a continent's width away from him; and there was nothing he could do to help her! That maddening thought pounded in his brain and threatened to drive him utterly insane. He was tied, helpless, unless he could get to her. That was it—he must go to her; must go to her at once.

But even as he grabbed for the telephone to call the air-line office, he stopped and slumped back into his chair. He was broke, down to his last couple of dollars. Every dollar that he could spare from his salary, every dollar that he had been able to borrow, he had been sending to Betty to meet her expenses.

Where could he turn for money? Not to his uncle; that would only mean a curt refusal. But where? Nowhere—the answer rose up dismayingly to taunt him as he racked his brain. His credit was exhausted . . .

And then he thought of Frank Shepard. Frank was practically the only one of his old cronies with whom he was still friendly. Frank had stuck by him when the others had drifted away. When Betty had insisted on going to Reno, it was Frank who had come to the rescue by getting her and Wendy a reduced rate at the Edgewater House, a Reno hotel operated by the syndicate of which he was the head.

Frank Shepard would advance the money without hesitation—but that burst of hope was short-lived.

"I am sorry, Mr. Cabot," the precise voice of Shepard's butler answered the 'phone, "but Mr. Shepard is spending a few weeks in Maine, at his hunting lodge. He will be away for an indeterminate period. No, I fear you cannot reach him by telegraph; his place is situated quite in the wilderness, you know."

The fear demons were holding carnival in Jim's brain as he hung up. Shepard was out—but in some way he must manage to get to Reno. Somewhere he *must* beg or borrow the price of Betty's safety; perhaps even of her life! Surely somewhere there must be another friend he could fall back on, someone he could turn to . . .

Lenore Millard! He hated the idea of asking Lenore for money, but in this emergency he would have to swallow his pride. She could help him easily, and she would not refuse. He was sure of that—but his nerves were on tenterhooks as he dialed her number, as he waited until she was called to the 'phone, and then poured out his worries.

For a moment there was silence when he had finished—and, with a flare of panic, he thought she was going to refuse. But her words quickly dispelled that fear.

"Of course, I'll help you, Jim," she was saying. "I happen to know that there is a United air-liner leaving for the coast at ten o'clock tonight. Suppose I meet you at their office in half an hour."

She was as good as her word, waiting for him at the reservation counter when he arrived—but there was a little suitcase standing on the floor beside her, and she was fingering the length of a ticket as she handed him an envelope with the money he would require.

"I've already paid for mine," she smiled as he stared questioningly. "I'm going along. Two heads may be better than one in this jam—and Betty may need me if you don't. You can tell me more about it as we drive to the airport."

Jim told her all that he knew. A dozen times he went through the recital; a hundred times he voiced the terror that was gnawing at him, that would give him no rest as the giant air-liner sped westward. Seventeen hours for the trip—but it seemed like seventeen centuries, and in everyone of them Betty might be dying; might be goaded by her devilish captors until she took the ghastly way out that had beckoned to Alicia Blainey and Julia Estabrook!

At last the flight was ended, and a taxicab was speeding Jim and Lenore to the Edgewater House, was drawing up in front of its entrance.

Jim Cabot was in no mood to be critical at that moment, but a glimpse of the hotel told him that it was a decidedly second rate establishment. He had known that Frank Shepard's hotels were not the finest in the country, but he had not supposed that they were as seedy and run-down as this . . .

But that was forgotten as he hurried across the lobby to the desk, hoping against hope that his fears were groundless; that Betty had returned to the hotel and was there now.

"Mrs. Cabot?" the sleek-haired desk clerk looked up in surprise. "Mrs. Cabot and Miss Taylor? They checked out yesterday afternoon at about four o'clock."

Checked out! At about four o'clock! Jim stared wide-eyed, as his startled brain wrested with that news. With the difference in time between Reno and New York, that was just about when he had been talking to Betty; when she screamed and the line went dead. And when they had told him she was not in her room.

There was something wrong about this. Something devilishly wrong, and Jim's temper flared as he stared into the clerk's smug face.

"You're positive about that—positive that they both checked out?" he demanded as he leaned across the desk.

"Both Mrs. Cabot and her sister?"

"That's the answer," the clerk grinned. "They're gone, bag and baggage."

"Gone where?" Jim clutched at a straw. "They must have left a forwarding address or given you some idea where they were going. It seems to me that you know a lot more about them than you're admitting."

Out from behind the door labeled "Henry Hulzman, Manager" came a tall, thin man, a man with grey hair and the severe, ascetic face of a religious zealot. For a moment he had stood listening, and now he stepped forward and took charge.

"There is nothing more that we can tell you," he said coldly. "Mrs. Cabot and her sister checked out at 4:10 yesterday afternoon. They left no forwarding address. It is not strange for a guest to check out as soon as her business in Reno is finished."

"Looks as if you're too late," the clerk added with patronizing sympathy. "I understood Mrs. Cabot secured her divorce yesterday—and now she's gone."

Gone! Again that word rang in Jim's ears with awful finality. His heart sank sickeningly as instinct whispered that there was far more to this than just checking out and leaving the hotel; something far more sinister that he could sense beneath the bland surface.

"You're sure—sure there can be no mistake?"

"There is no mistake," the manager said icily. "We are not in the habit of making mistakes on our register. Now, if there is nothing else we can do for you—"

"Yes—we'll register," Jim, decided quickly.

Somehow, as he stood there at the desk, the shabby hotel seemed to be the last tie that bound Betty to the tangible world—the last place she had been before she was "gone."

Where had she and Wendy gone? Reno is a small town, but before nightfall he and Lenore had asked that question seemingly a thousand times. And always the answer was the same—nobody knew. At the trains, the bus depots, the airport; in the hotels, the clubs, the gambling joints—nowhere was there a trace of them.

It was nearly midnight when he gave up, tired and beaten. Lenore murmured a sympathetic good night and went to her room: but even in his exhaustion he could not sleep. From the night clerk he had learned the number of the suite the girls had occupied, and now the desire to see those rooms became overpowering.

Quietly he left his room and walked up two flights of stairs. The hallway on this floor was empty, as he started down its length, checking the room numbers. 418—419— and suddenly he stood transfixed, hastily drawn back into a shadowed niche, while he stared down that row of doorways.

The door of 421 was opening—opening stealthily. For a moment it was held back on a crack; then it was pulled wide and a man stepped out and drew it shut quickly behind him. The light of a wall bracket flashed on his face as he turned— and Jim stared in amazement at the sharply chiseled profile of Keith Averill!

Keith Averill coming out of the rooms Betty had occupied, and slipping stealthily down the hall to a rear stairway!

What was Averill doing in Reno? Why was he there, prowling in the rooms that had been Betty's and her sister's? What did he know about their disappearance? Questions milled through Jim's mind as he watched the man who had precipitated his break with Betty slink out of sight. Perhaps he would find the answers behind that closed door . . .

Cautiously he let himself into 421 and switched on the light. Everything in the little three-room suite was in order. Nowhere was there a sign of Betty's occupancy—and the empty rooms in which she had lived for six weeks only added to his desolation.

What could Averill have discovered there that caused him to leave so stealthily? Averill would answer that question himself. But when Jim went down to the desk he found that the man was not registered at the Edgewater, and the night clerk knew nobody who fitted his description.

Cursing himself for a fool for letting Averill get away, Jim went back to his room, and his exhausted body lulled his frantic brain.

The sky was greying when he opened his eyes and half-propped himself up on his elbows in bed. Grey dawn was paneling the windows, but it wasn't that which had awakened him. It was something else—something startling and unnatural.

Instinctively he sensed that something was wrong. There was a strange, yet terrifyingly familiar smell in the air. And his hand—that was it; his hand was in something wet and sticky!

Slowly and deliberately he sat up—and goose pimples covered his skin as he stared down at the bed beside him. The bed sheet was stained crimson with barely coagulated blood! Blood that was spattered over the front of his pajamas—that was smeared on the palm of his hand!

Blood! Whose blood? Awful apprehension surged up horrifyingly within him, washed over him in chilling waves as he remembered Julia Estabrook's dead face, Alicia Blainey's mangled body . . .

Betty!

Tingling with horror, he sprang out of bed, and immediately discovered the trail of crimson splashes that led across the room to a closet. White-faced and trembling, he stood in front of that door, icy cold with dread of what might be behind it. Fearfully he inched it open—to stagger back aghast at the horrible sight that met his popping eyes!

In a bloody heap on the floor was the frightfully mutilated body of a young girl—a body so slashed and torn that it was little more than a gory pulp beneath a face that was a death mask of excruciating agony!

But it wasn't Betty! It was a girl he had never seen before.

Weak with relief and nauseated by that terrible sight, Jim walked dazedly to the bathroom and scoured the blood off his hand, stripped off the crimson-spattered pajamas, and got into his clothes. That ghastly corpse—how had it gotten there in his closet? How had the blood gotten on his bed, on his pajamas? Questions—questions with no sane answers.

By the time he was dressed he had gotten a grip on himself. First of all he must notify the manager. But that was no easy task. Hulzman was a man who valued his sleep, and his half-open eyes were smoldering with anger when he finally appeared—but the moment he stared into the closet and glimpsed its macabre tenant all the churlishness left him.

"My God!" he gasped in a horrified half-whisper. "That's Miss Vaughn—Dora Vaughn. She was one of our guests—but she checked out a week ago!"

Dora Vaughn! The cold, clammy tentacles of enervating terror stole through Jim Cabot and tightened around his heart. Dora Vaughn was the girl who had disappeared—before Wendy and Betty!

Chapter Three

Red Rendezvous

From the grisly corpse Hulzman's ashen face turned to Jim, and the cold grey eyes were grim with accusation. Without a word he walked to the telephone and summoned the police.

"I was suspicious of this man the moment he arrived this afternoon," he sputtered the moment the police chief and his assistant walked into the room. "He came here looking for two other girls. They were gone. They were lucky enough to escape him, but somehow he met Dora Vaughn and managed to get her up here—and you see what happened."

Vainly Jim protested, but Hulzman would listen to no explanations. His face was bleak and he pointed accusingly to the bloodstained sheet, to the crimsoned pajamas he had retrieved from the bathroom.

"I know murder when I see it," he snapped. "Chief, I demand this man's arrest before he has a chance to butcher another victim."

"Better come along to headquarters with us," the chief nodded as his fingers closed on Jim's arm—but instead of locking him up in a cell at police headquarters he led the way into his own office, motioned to a seat. "Now let's have your story," he invited.

Jim told it from the beginning, and the shrewd-eyed chief nodded his head with worried understanding.

"Hulzman was excited, or he would have realized that you couldn't have mangled a body that way without drenching the whole room with blood," he pointed out. "That body was carried to your room—was planted there."

He frowned and tapped a pencil thoughtfully on his desk.

"These aren't the first girls who have disappeared in the last few months—or the first mutilated body we've found," he admitted. "I've had other anxious relatives in this office trying to locate young women who came to Reno for a divorce—and then disappeared. And last week the Truckee River washed up a horribly mutilated corpse a few miles outside the city. There's some damned deviltry going on in this town, and I'm going to uncover it," he vowed grimly. "This is the best lead we've had."

But it was only a lead—and Betty might at that very moment be suffering the hell that Dora Vaughn must have endured before she died!

Frantic anxiety goaded Jim, now that he knew beyond doubt that Betty and Wendy were in danger even more ghastly than the suicides he had been dreading. All that day and until long after dark he and Lenore combed the town, but only maddening failure rewarded them.

Not a trace, not a clue—until they were almost back to the hotel entrance. Suddenly Jim's tired eyes narrowed, probed into the darkness. A hunched figure was darting around toward the rear of the building. With a word to Lenore, he dived after the fellow, caught a glimpse of him tugging at a rear door.

There was something familiar about that figure, something that made Jim's blood run faster. With a flying leap he lunged forward and his arms closed in a sure tackle around the fellow's middle. Together they pitched to the ground, while Jim's eager fingers clamped around his opponent's throat, forced his head back and banged it down against the flagging.

In the dim light from a nearby window he could see that upturned face—and he grunted with savage satisfaction as Keith Averill gasped and whimpered, as his eyes widened with fear and he gasped for breath as he tried desperately to say something.

"What are you doing skulking around here?" Jim demanded grimly.

"Looking for you!" Averill wheezed, the moment the pressure on his throat relaxed. "Wanted to reach you without going through the lobby—without being seen—"

"And I suppose that's why you were slinking around in 421 last night!" Jim flung at him.

"I was looking for Betty," his captive whined. "I can't understand why she disappeared. I thought there might be something in those rooms—something that would give me an idea where she went. And that's why I came here to see you. I think I have a tip, Cabot, but if I'm right it will be more than I can manage alone to reach her—"

"I'm listening," Jim gritted, as the other waited expectantly.

"I got it from a woman," Averill confessed. "She'd been drinking and became maudlin. It seems there's a place—a ranch—about twenty miles up the Truckee, where they stage some pretty raw stuff. I couldn't make it all out—and when she saw that I was trying to pump her she sobered up and became mum as a clam. But I heard enough to know that what goes on there is pretty bad. And they use young girls in their ritual—some sort of Indian ceremony—"

Jim had not believed a word Averill said—until that mention of Indians. Immediately it conjured up a picture of that Indian head silhouetted at the bottom of Alicia Blainey's death warning!

Was there a connection between that and this yarn of Averill's?

Keith Averill was a pitifully weak specimen on whom to depend. Jim didn't trust him. He might be using that tale to bait a trap—but at least there was a chance that he might lead the way to Betty . . .

"All right," Jim said, grabbing at that chance. "I'll go along with you and have a look at this place."

"And so will I," Lenore added over his shoulder—and Jim knew better than to argue with her.

Half an hour later, when they drove a hired car up to within sight of a distant group of ranch buildings, he insisted on parking the machine in a clump of live oaks and leaving her there with it. Cautiously he and Averill went forward on foot.

The big ranch house, a sprawling black blotch in the night, seemed deserted. There was a dim light in only one of the rooms, and no sign of human beings—until an amazing figure came out of a side door and started toward the river. A hideously painted Indian, naked except for breechclout and moccasins! Jim's pulses pounded, and he was close to Averill, ready for the slightest treachery, as they trailed that astonishing apparition.

Along the river a short distance, and the painted figure hailed a guard. Then he stepped forward and disappeared, swallowed up by the black bulk of the hillside. Cautiously Jim crept closer, until he could distinguish the stygian mouth of a cave, the guard sitting on a boulder beside it. As they lay close to the ground and listened, strange noises came from that black opening: a dull rumble that was punctuated by high, piercing notes—weird sounds that made Jim's scalp prickle.

"I'm going to nail that guard," he whispered to Averill.

And the next instant he leaped, bowling the sentry over by his rush and meeting him with a pile-driving smash to the jaw the moment he scrambled to his feet. Without a sound the fellow sagged to the ground.

"Quick," Jim whispered. "Take off his clothes and get into them. You can pass for him in the dark. I'm going in there."

Warily he stepped into the black orifice, edged his way slowly along a winding passageway that was dimly lit by lanterns once he was past the entrance. And as he advanced the noises became louder, rose into a bedlam of sound that reverberated through the narrow tunnel. A blast of noise that was recognizable now as the animal roar of a drunken mob; a howling din that was shot through with shrill screams of unmistakable agony!

Grim-lipped and tense, he pushed forward cautiously—and then suddenly froze where he stood as he heard a sound in the tunnel close behind him. The scuffing of a foot! There it was again. Knotted fist held ready, he crouched back as close to the wall as he could—and into the light came Lenore's anxious face!

Before he could say a word she was close beside him and her hand was on his arm, urging him forward.

"I'm going with you," she whispered firmly. "Arguing only makes our danger greater. Please don't waste any time, Jim."

Reluctantly, but hopeless to cope with her, he started forward again. Down another length of tunnel, around a turn in the passageway—and he almost stepped out into a howling inferno! Quickly he flattened himself back against the wall, drawing Lenore down close behind him so that they were not visible from the huge cavern that stretched before them.

Once that cavern evidently had been an Indian temple. The rock walls were painted with Indian symbols and hung with scalps and a variety of gruesome trophies. At one end was a throne-like dais on which a weird figure perched—a figure wearing a huge, grotesque mask and towering headdress above the ornate robes of a Navajo shaman. On each side of him squatted a barbarically painted drummer, naked to the waist, bending over the booming tom-tom that was cradled in his lap. And on the floor a score of wild dancers shuffled and contorted themselves obscenely while the rock walls resounded with their shrill screams and bestial yells.

Dancers out of hell itself those weaving demons seemed as they gyrated in the flickering light of sputtering torches. A few of them had their faces so smeared with paint that their features were unrecognizable, but the majority were almost unadorned. Wearing only the scantiest of breechclouts, they danced barefooted—women with wild-eyed faces that mirrored the depths of lust and depravity! White women with the hideous visages of infernal demons!

Round and round they danced in utter abandonment, whirling long, bloody whips over their heads—whips that dripped crimson and flecked it on their naked bodies. Whips that whistled through the air and cracked down horribly on wet, quivering flesh!

Those lashes were beating a hellish tattoo that was even more soul searing than the piercing screams of the suffering victim who was in the center of that savage circle. Each blood-spurting blow cut into Jim as if the cruel leather were butchering his own flesh. Each frightful scream stabbed into his brain—a brain that was shuddering away from the appalling possibility that that pitiful victim might be Betty . . .

For a moment the fiendish circle parted and he caught a glimpse of the stumbling, staggering figure that was the target of those hungry whips. It was Wendy Taylor—his sister-in-law!

From the ceiling of the cavern hung two stout ropes of rawhide—ropes that terminated in loops which were fastened securely through the flesh of her shoulders! Stark naked, she leaped and danced crazily under the constant goad of those merciless whips; danced until she fell backward, exhausted, to hang horribly from those taut ropes until the insufferable agony of her torn flesh brought her back onto her feet.

It was the fearful Indian sun-dance that was once used to test the endurance of newly-made braves—now converted into a ghastly ordeal for the tender body of a young girl!

Wendy's once-white flesh was scored and slashed in a hundred places, lined with ugly welts and open gashes that bathed her torso and limbs in her own blood. The cavern rang with her endless screams, with the gleeful howling of her savage tormentors. The rumble of the throbbing drums was like thunder, and blinding flashes of light continually threw a ghastly, bluish-white radiance over the shocking orgy.

Jim's blood pounded in his veins, throbbed at his temples,

and his white knuckled fists were clenched until the nails bit deep into the palms of his hands. With a muttered curse he tensed his muscles, started to lunge forward—and the cold muzzle of a gun pressed hard against the back of his neck, while a hand gripped his sleeve.

"No, you won't!" Lenore snapped into his ear. "I expected something like this—so I came prepared. Try and get away from me and I'll shoot. I'm not bluffing!"

In one of those glaring flashes of light Jim caught a glimpse of her narrowed eyes, of her tense, tight-lipped face—and he knew that she meant exactly what she said!

Chapter Four

"Light the Fires!"

Jim realized that Lenore was past the point of reasoning—and as he stared out into that cavern of horror he saw that there was nothing he could do for Wendy. Her body had already been cut to ribbons, her face hideously slashed and torn. Blood was pouring from her in streams, and it would be only a matter of a few more minutes before merciful death would release her.

Hardly believing what he saw, he stared out at that mob of prancing fiends. They were not Indians. They were whites—whites who had debauched themselves with liquor and drugs until they had sunk lower than the most primitive of the savages they aped.

The men at least hid their identity beneath disguising paint, but the women scorned disguise. They had become utter fiends, glorying in their beastly excesses, in the warm blood that dyed their hands and ran down their bare arms; naked harpies gyrating and posturing!

And with a start he recognized one of those women! And then another! Several of them were well known young society matrons—women he had seen at Newport, at Saratoga, in New York's smartest circles. Socialite women transformed into blood-lusting barbarians.

Now the bloody corpse hanging motionless from the raw-hide loops that would not let it drop to the floor, no longer held their attention. They were obeying the medicine-man's orders, arranging themselves in two facing lines about six feet apart. Two lines that led up to where a heavy post was set in the floor, with piles of wood heaped ready beside it.

The stake! And that was a hell-inspired gauntlet those eager, blood-lusting degenerates were forming!

Horrible fear tightened like a constricting band of steel around his heart and shuddering terror overwhelmed him. A new victim was about to be dragged out to face that frightful ordeal—a new victim to be thrown to those howling wolves! And that victim would be . . .

Her horrified scream shrilled through the cavern the moment she saw the grisly corpse dangling from the roof—and all the strength seemed to seep out of his leaden limbs as his ghastly fear was realized. That was Betty's scream!

Then he saw her—naked and white as she crouched in utter terror in the partial darkness at one end of that eagerly waiting double line of milling fiends. For a moment she cowered there, desperately trying to push back as they urged her forward. Then she leaped erect with a scream of agony as a whip whistled down and lashed across her back.

Again that whip cut through the air—but before it cut into her flesh she had started to run between those waiting lines, started to dodge and cringe, to stagger and grope blindly, as short, metal-tipped whips licked out at her, as spike-studded clubs slapped down on her.

Jim's eyes fairly bulged from his head, and the cords in his neck stood out like straining ropes.

"No! No! You can't!" Lenore almost screamed in his ear, and now one of her hands was twisted tightly in his coat collar while the other jammed the gun muzzle into his neck. "You *can't* go out there!"

Betty was down, rolling in agony. She was crawling to her knees, climbing unsteadily to her feet as the whips gave her no respite. Five or six steps she staggered, and then, with a despairing sob, she went down again—and in that moment

Jim hurled himself forward.

In one swift motion he upset Lenore and grabbed her gun hand, twisted the weapon out of her fingers as he threw her to the floor of the passageway and leaped out into the cavern. In that howling madhouse his rush went unnoticed until he reached the double lines of the bestial gauntlet—until his fists were smashing out right and left, knocking howling, shrieking fiends to the floor in every direction.

The unleashed fury of his charge carried him half-way down those lines, carried him to where Betty was sobbing hysterically and trying to get to her knees. In front of her he crouched, swinging his revolver in a threatening arc as he tried to hold them at bay.

But that animal pack had lost all reason, all fear. The gun did not cow them. With a savage roar they closed in on him from all sides. One futile shot he managed to fire from the weapon—and then he was overwhelmed by the screaming horde. The revolver was clubbed out of his numbed fingers and he was swept off his feet, was borne down and smothered under a sea of writhing, grappling bodies that pinned him helplessly to the floor.

"Tie her to the stake and let her watch!" he heard the medicine-man snarl savagely above the din.

Eagerly they dragged Betty to the stake and lashed her to it, heaped wood around her feet, but the medicine-man waved them aside when they tried to touch a light to the kindling.

"First she will watch," he ordered. "The fire will come later—when there is nothing more for her to enjoy! Stake him out—there in the center where she will miss nothing."

Half a dozen of the painted devils seized Jim and stripped him to the waist, then threw him down on the floor. While they held him there four spikes were driven into the hard earth and he was spread-eagled between them, his ankles and wrists tied securely with rawhide thongs. Then shavings and little pieces of wood were piled on his naked chest—and he ground his jaws together grimly.

Through narrowed eyes he watched as a match was struck and held to the brittle kindling. In a moment it ignited, the flame leaped high—and larger pieces of wood were criss-crossed and piled upon him.

Tightly he locked his jaws to fight back the scream that surged up into his throat as the flames scorched and blistered his skin; as the hot coals ate into his flesh; as the sickening odor of its burning fined his nostrils. Desperately he tried to squirm so as to dislodge that growing bonfire, but his arms and legs were stretched so tightly that he could barely move a muscle.

Around him on three sides hovered that devilish ring, leaving only one side unobstructed so that Betty could witness his ordeal. Down at his agony gloated those fiendish eyes, with the telltale pinpoint pupils of the dope addict—demon faces that leered horribly in the blinding flashes of light that were again illuminating the cave more brightly than daylight.

Sweat was beading out on his face, running down his forehead and his cheeks in rivulets. His chest had become a great, searing agony and every muscle in his body seemed to be writhing in excruciating torment.

This was the end, he knew—the beginning of an end that would drag on hellishly. There was no slightest hope now, for him or for Betty—and he groaned inwardly. He had failed dismally.

Above the howls of the frenzied women he heard her voice calling to him, pleading with him.

"I've been a fool, Jim, darling!" she sobbed. "I knew I should go back to you, but I was too stubborn to admit it—and this is what I've brought you to! I don't deserve it, Jim, but please forgive me. I love you, darling. I know that I never stopped loving you but—"

With jeers and catcalls those pitiless devils howled her down, drowned out her voice with their own gleeful cackling. Above their bedlam Jim caught snatches of her sobbing farewell—and then—suddenly the gloating fiends were thrown aside as a raging whirlwind swept through them.

For a moment his pain-filmed eyes glimpsed Lenore's

ashen-white face staring down at him as she leaped toward him. Then her foot darted out and sent the blazing brands spinning from his chest as she whirled to fight off the clutching hands that were tearing at her from every side!

Chapter Five

Hell's Bargain

Lenore was no match for that drug-maddened mob. The crazed women tore at her like wild beasts. By sheer weight they overwhelmed her, threw her to the floor and began ripping the clothes from her body. Half-naked, she fought back onto her feet and tried desperately to back away, to hold them off, but again they were bearing her down, when, abruptly, a new interruption halted them.

With a howl of terror and rage a weird-looking figure burst from the shadows at one side of the cavern. For a moment he struggled fiercely with two paint-smeared demons who tried to hold him back; then he was free and rushing into the middle of the fray. A paint-smeared masquerader like the others; but his disguise was ridiculous rather than hideous—he looked more like a clown than a savage.

Frantically he tried to fight his way to Lenore, but the women who surrounded her laughed and jeered at him.

"You can't do that to my daughter!" the absurd creature howled frenziedly, and then he whirled to where the medicine-man sat on his dais. "They can't do that to Lenore!" he screamed shrilly. "Stop them, Frank—you've got to stop them!"

Lenore—his daughter . . .

This must be delirium playing tricks with him, Jim told himself as he heard that anguished appeal. But then he caught another glimpse of the ridiculously painted figure— and beneath the clownish paint he recognized the hawkish features of old Preston Millard!

The old man was frantic, hopping around as if the floor beneath him were a red-hot griddle; but the medicine-man only shook his head.

"I've kept my end of the bargain," his voice came hollowly through the mouth of the wooden mask. "I agreed to see that Cabot's marriage was broken up; to see that his wife came out here and divorced him—and then disappeared until your daughter was able to marry him. I—"

"I don't care what you do to the other girl," old Millard raved, "but you can't harm my daughter—and you can't murder Cabot!"

"No, that will rather upset your clever plans, won't it?" the voice behind the mask chuckled evilly. "But your plans were spoiled the moment you got cold feet and came flying out here because Cabot and your daughter were in Reno. You knew that I tolerate no interference at this ranch, but you came snooping around, nosing into my business so that my men caught you. You put your neck into the noose when you did that. And now Cabot and your daughter are in it with you. Nobody comes here uninvited and goes back again."

Beneath the clownish paint Millard's face was apoplectic. He was seething with rage—and yet stricken with terror.

"You murdering double-crosser!" he snarled. "You tricked me—robbed me—and now you think you'll murder my daughter! But you won't—"

Suddenly he flung himself clear of the men who had closed in on both sides of him and catapulted himself up onto the dais. His rush carried him straight to the masked shaman who was only half out of his chair when that snarling, clawing fury hit him. Locked together, they rolled on he floor. Over and over, in a wild flurry of flailing arms and legs—until a knife flashed clear, poised for a moment, and stabbed downward.

Up it came again, red and dripping—and Millard groaned wheezingly as he relaxed his hold and slipped to the floor.

"There are knives on the cabinet," the medicine-man snarled to the blazing-eyed women as he rolled clear. "Take him!"

The shout that burst from their throats chilled Jim to the marrow. It was the exultant howl of a half-starved wolf pack closing in on the kill . . .

He looked away, looked anywhere so as not to watch that barbaric dismembering of a living man—and his eyes were caught suddenly by one of the huge masks that stood on a ledge of stone that cropped up out of the floor on one side of the cave. One of the eyes of that thing was blinking—and as it blinked a tiny flash of light was reflected from within it.

Jim concentrated every faculty on that mysterious eye, co-ordinated eye and ear—and he caught an unmistakable click; the click of a camera shutter . . .

But now the medicine-man was on his feet. One of his assistants picked up the mask that had been knocked from his head, but he waved it aside disdainfully—and Jim stared up into the snarling, rage contorted face of Frank Shepard!

Frank Shepard . . . Bit by bit Jim's stunned brain began to grasp the monstrous truth, began to piece it together. And Shepard seemed to read his mind. He strode to Jim and glared down at him.

"Yes, I'm the boss of this outfit," he snarled. "This ranch is mine—and it is a lot more profitable than my bankrupt string of third-rate hotels. I tried to keep you out of here for your own good, tried to have you jailed by that little incident in your room last night. But you couldn't be stopped. All right, now you've settled your own hash."

Bit by bit the pieces were falling into place, forming a diabolical pattern. These orgies, the inexplicable suicides of wealthy society women fresh from Reno; the flashing bluish-white lights and the camera shutter clicking in the eye of that mask; the squares of photographer's paper with the warning messages and Indian's head signature . . .

Those squares of undeveloped paper were fiendishly clever threats, devised to remind their victims all too significantly of the fearful doom that hung over them.

These women, cavorting virtually naked, with bloody hands and arms, lashing and stabbing at helpless victims—they were to be Shepard's next victims. Hidden cameras were busily making photographs of them in the midst of their fiendish excesses—photographs that would be shown to them the day the court granted them their freedom.

When they left Reno they would take with them the terrifying knowledge that a Damoclean sword hung over their heads—a sword that could be kept suspended only by paying and paying until they were bled white. Either that—or they would be exposed as human beasts when those damning photographs were shown to their prospective husbands.

Blackmail—that was the secret of this hell cavern.

"I know now just how low you are." Jim bit off the words contemptuously as he looked up at the man he had considered his friend. "But before I die I want these poor dupes of yours to know how you are going to milk them—"

Before he could get any farther two of the paint-daubed devils sprang at him. A fist smashed into his mouth and then a gag was crammed between his jaws and tied tightly around his head.

As they got back onto their feet one of the painted masqueraders brushed against a glowing ember that had been on Jim's chest and kicked it against his forearm. The red tip seared his skin and his muscles flinched away from it—until he suddenly realized the slim chance the accident might afford him.

A fraction of an inch at a time he worked the red-hot ember down his arm toward his wrist, nursing its torturing surface close to his blistering skin. If he could get it down to his wrist, down to the rawhide thong . . .

One of those howling fiends had picked up another of the burning embers and tossed it into the pile of dry wood at Betty's feet. The fagots were smoking; they burst into flame. Betty screamed wildly as the hot yellow tongues licked up toward her naked body.

"Let them roast together!" Shepard laughed, and the women began to heap fresh kindling and wood on Jim's raw and blistered chest.

But before a match could be touched to the new pyre Lenore wriggled free from the hands of the women who were holding her and ran across the cavern. Her clothing had been almost completely stripped from her, and now with a few quick motions she discarded the tattered remnants that remained and stepped out toward Shepard completely nude.

"You always wanted me, Frank," she said softly, her husky voice low and inviting. "Now is your chance to have me. Together we can make a gold-mine of this layout. With my contacts I can send you people who will make these look like small-timers. Together we can—"

She had been walking toward him, her slim arms outstretched, the supple muscles of her naked body rippling alluringly with each step, her full lips red and inviting. Shepard stared at the glory of her limbs, her full bosom, and his eyes widened.

Then she was right in front of him, her arms slipping around his neck, traveling down over his shoulders as her lips turned up to his . . .

With a strangled gasp that was a half sigh Shepard capitulated. His lips pressed down feverishly against hers while his hands clutched at her soft flesh—and the faint hope that had stirred in Jim Cabot's seared breast died stillborn.

Lenore had failed him; that left only Averill, outside at the mouth of the cave.

As if thought of the man had brought him into action, at that moment Jim caught a faint yell of surprise and pain— and he knew that Keith Averill had been surprised and overcome.

Now the ember was up against the rawhide, was burning through it as Jim curled his fingers around the bit of living coal and held it in place—but the leaping flames were up to Betty's waist. Her eyes were glaring madly and she was rolling her head from side to side as she struggled vainly to draw back from those scorching tongues.

"I can't stand it!" she shrieked. "Oh, God—just let me die!"

With the strength of desperation Jim tugged at the half-burned thong, tugged—and it snapped. His right arm was free!

But Shepard's quick eyes had seen him. He started to spring toward Jim—started, but Lenore's embracing arms held him tight. With a savage curse he tried to wriggle free, tried to tear those soft naked arms from around his neck and shoulders.

Now in a half-sitting position, Jim tugged with all his strength at the thong that held his other wrist—and the stake came flying out of the ground! With a sob of thankfulness he crouched forward and went to work on his ankles.

Lenore was watching him, clinging desperately to Shepard, her teeth sunk deep in her lip as she took the savage punishment of the cursing man's pounding fists and jabbing knees. Fearful punishment—but she hung on while her agony filled eyes begged Jim to hurry.

"Use your knives on her!" Shepard yelled to the gaping audience.

That was all they needed. In a wave they swarmed over Lenore. Glistening knives stabbed at her, were dyed red in her blood as Jim leaped to his feet.

Like searing flames those knives ate into his shoulders, his arms, but he plunged ahead. Lenore was down now, and as he saw her slump to the ground he knew that she had received her death wound—but Shepard was still safe outside the mêlée. And he was going to pay!

Jim fairly climbed over those drug-maddened fiends as he battled his way toward their master—but at last his hands clutched that Indian costume.

Fierce exultation rioted through him as his fingers tightened like steel talons around Shepard's windpipe—

But the maddened pack was on his back. They were tugging and tearing at him, seeking a fatal opening for their knives as they tried to snatch his prey away from him. It would be just a matter of seconds before one of those blades plunged into his neck or found a sheath between his ribs. Just a matter of seconds—and Jim's lips drew back over his clenched teeth as he put every ounce of strength he could muster into those viselike fingers that were squeezing—

squeezing—squeezing.

Then he was aware that there was a new note in the bedlam that roared in that cavern—a note of terror, of wild panic. The pack around him was disintegrating. Like rats they were scurrying for cover, deserting Shepard just as Jim tripped him to the floor and came down on top of him—with those relentless fingers never relinquishing their deathly grip.

Shepard had stopped fighting, stopped squirming, stopped gasping, even stopped breathing, long before Jim eased the pressure that was jamming him down against the floor. The fellow was dead, he realized at last—and that left nothing for those clutching fingers that were reluctantly loosening their grip . . .

Dazedly he looked up. The cavern was filling with policemen. They were kicking out the fire around Betty, untying her and wrapping a coat around her. And now they were at his elbow, taking his hands away from Shepard's throat and raising him from his knees.

Police . . . The chief was there—and with him was Henry Hulzman, the Edgewater House manager. The chief was coming forward.

"Fine work, Cabot!" he cried exultantly. "Fine work! But it looks as if we got here just about in time—and you can thank Mr. Hulzman for that. He's been shadowing you ever since I released you this morning. He trailed you here tonight and came hotfooting back to town to get me to catch you red-handed."

"I didn't understand," Hulzman apologized embarrassedly.

"There's a lot been going on in the Edgewater you didn't understand, Hulzman," the chief told him. "You were the front that kept the place respectable and safe. When he went off duty tonight we picked up that day clerk of yours. Bits of information I'd been gathering put him on the spot pretty bad, but he's a tight-lipped cuss. We were trying to drag the location of this place out of him when you came in and saved us the trouble. He—"

Jim left them standing there. He was far more interested in another blue-coated individual—one who flopped her far too long sleeves around his neck and sobbed happily in his arms.

"It's all been such a ghastly nightmare, Jim," she whispered. "Ever since I telephoned you. I heard a noise in the room behind me as I was talking—and when I turned around two men grabbed me. They clapped something that smelled like chloroform over my face. It made my senses swim, but I was still half-conscious when they picked me up and carried me down a back stairway to the cellar.

"They gagged me and tied me up. For hours I sat there in the dark. When they came for me it was dark outside. They carried me out through a side door that opens onto the river and dropped me into the bottom of a low flat boat that brought me to this terrible place."

"The Edgewater was nothing but a trap," Jim nodded to the chief, who was standing beside them. "Through it Shepard kept this hell cavern supplied with victims—good looking young women who had no money and weren't worth blackmailing. The wealthy ones he lured to the ranch with the promise of exciting entertainment and then drugged them until they were worse than animals, absolutely helpless in his hands."

Bitterly he looked across the cavern to where the police were cutting down the mangled corpse that had been Wendy Taylor—to where Lenore's bloodied body lay on the floor. And his eyes stared hard, unbelievingly. Lenore had moved; she was trying to lift her head!

In another moment he was kneeling at her side, lifting her head in his arms while he yelled for somebody to bring water.

"Water doesn't matter, Jim," she gasped weakly. "I am almost—finished. But before I go—I want to tell you that—I didn't know—what I was letting you and Betty in for—when I followed Dad's instructions—and began feeding Betty the drug Frank Shepard provided. Dad wanted to break up your marriage—so that you would marry me—so that your uncle would take you back. Dad wanted us to have your uncle's money—but I didn't care about that. I loved you, Jim—I wanted you for yourself . . .

"Frank said the drug would make Betty discontented—and that it would change her feeling for you and make her divorce you. When Betty went to Reno, I thought I had won—until she telephoned and you were determined to go to her. That's why I insisted on coming along: because I was afraid that if you got together—you might become reconciled.

"But I had no idea of this—of Shepard's real character—until tonight. And then it was too late. I've been a beast to both of you—but it was only—because I love you—so much—Jim."

Her eyes were closed before she finished. Her body sagged limply in his arms.

There was a hard lump in Jim's throat as he turned to Betty, and there were tears welling up into her eyes.

"She loved you, Jim," she whispered as her hand stole into his, "the way I'm going to love you—the rest of our lives together!"

HER LOVER FROM THE GRAVE

PETER REMINGTON looked down into the coffin, at the cold, dead face of his brother, and shook his head in pity. Deep in his grey eyes there was poignant regret and a vague expression of wonderment. He was no stranger to death, but now that it had struck close to him, the suddenness of it seemed to leave him baffled.

"It seems such a shame," he said softly. "He had so much to live for. He would have meant so much to the world so much to mankind. And I—I'm just a wanderer. I'd never have been missed. Yet John was the one to go . . ."

The words came from his lips subconsciously, phrasing the thoughts that had been crowding his mind ever since, two days before, John Remington had died at the height of his brilliant career. Peter had been alone as he strode into the somber parlor in which his brother's bier had been erected. Meditatively he had stood there beside the coffin, gazing down at that face so like his own.

But now there was another standing there beside him. Silently she had crossed the thick rug. A soft touch on his arm stopped his thinking aloud.

"You mustn't say such things about yourself, Peter," a low vibrant voice spoke at his side. "They aren't true."

Claire Carter's brown eyes looked up at him with gentle rebuke. They were red-rimmed, from tears, and her lovely face was pale and drawn.

Her glance shifted to the wax-like features of the man in the casket, the man who had been her fiancé; rested there a moment. Then she flashed a frightened glance around the darkened room—into the shadowy corners, at the big, shrouded family portraits that lined the walls. Even from behind their black coverings the eyes of the departed Remingtons seemed to stare austerely down at them.

The room was a cheerless, forbidding place even under normal circumstances. Now, with the death, candles lighting it eerily, it was uncanny, creepy.

Claire shivered, and her fingers clutched Peter's arm convulsively.

"I'm afraid. Peter!" Her voice was hardly more than a whisper. "Something about this room—about the whole house—seems to terrify me. It's not just that John is—gone; that he left us so suddenly. It's rather something evil— something appalling that I seem to sense in the place!"

Peter patted her hand, and was surprised at the icy coldness of her fingers.

"You're tired and shaken," he told her soothingly. "And if you're not careful you'll be hysterical. Let me take you outside for a while; the fresh air will make you see things differently."

But the outside of the big stone mansion was as cheerless as the inside. Peter had never liked the place. As boys, he and John had spent little time in it, but most of their childhood days were passed in their town home. Then, with the death of their parents, that had been given up. Peter; continually seeking out the far corners of the earth for museums and exploring expeditions, had no use for it; and John, steeped in scientific research, had moved permanently into the old Remington mansion.

On the rare occasions when Peter was at home from some distant travel, he had come out here to stay with John—and leave as soon as he decently could. It was always a relief to get away from the place, with its cheerless company.

John had been all right enough, but all his life centered on his confounded research—on the weird experiments he performed and the incredible results he achieved. He was poor company. And his assistant, Martin Lorenz, was even worse. Lorenz seemed to live only for his work. Otherwise he was as self-effacing as old Mrs. Wilmott, who kept house for them.

Claire Carter was the only cheerful soul around the place,

when she came out to visit John. They had been youngsters together—Claire and John and Peter; and when they were in their early teens Peter had imagined himself in love with the brown-haired tomboy who was destined to become one of Broadway's favorite dancers.

But he had gone traipsing off to the wilds, and John, three years his senior, had stayed at home and won the girl. That was all right, of course; John was a fine chap. But sometimes Peter had looked at the two of them together, Claire so full of life and John so wedded to this gloomy pile of masonry, and he had wondered.

But now that was all over. John was inside there, cold and still, and tomorrow, after he was placed in the big family vault, Claire would go away from this place and never come back.

Yet, still, as he looked up at the bulky brownstone structure, Peter puzzled over that indefinable question which was in his mind. Somehow he could not accustom himself to the realization that John, who had always been perfectly healthy, was now dead—gone. Pernicious anemia had culminated in a heart attack, the local physician had said. But still . . .

And there was the morose atmosphere of the place. Somehow it seemed in keeping that healthy persons should suddenly be snatched away in death in a place like this. Peter resolved that as soon as he could manage it he would get away from the property. Just leave it here for Lorenz, if he wanted it.

Then, too, it had been John's wish that, should anything ever happen to him, Lorenz be allowed to live on in Remington Hall until the work on which he was engaged was finished. Peter didn't want the place; it was not worth a great deal, anyway. All he wanted to do now was get away from it and its depressing gloom.

His decision remained unchanged that evening, after John's body had been placed in the family vault. Claire was leaving in the morning. Peter would drive her to the city— and probably stay there, he told himself.

Dinner was a cheerless meal, and after it Peter and Claire went into the library, while Lorenz, as usual, hastened downstairs to his laboratory. But the library was almost as depressing as the funeral parlor. Try as they would, neither Peter nor the girl could drive their thoughts into more cheerful channels.

"I'm going to bed," Claire announced suddenly, resignedly, as if there she hoped she might escape the depressing effect of the place.

Peter was glad, for the day had left him unnerved. Drowsiness was stealing over him—and then sleep. At least, that was the last thing he could remember, lying there on his back in the bed, slipping into little spells of semi-consciousness— little snatches of thought—little blanks of drowsiness—and then . . .

In a dream, or in a horrible nightmare, Peter Remington had once felt as he felt now; detached from himself, acting without conscious volition, going on and doing things that he could not stop no matter what he did or tried.

At first it was just blackness. Then there was a dim light, hanging from a ceiling—a stone ceiling, in what seemed to be a jagged, rocky cellar of some sort. It was a damp, musty place that was unfurnished and seemed deserted.

But, no—it wasn't deserted. There, in the center of it, was Peter, himself, walking along, peering into the darkness. And then, suddenly, there was someone else.

She screamed first; then she ran across the cellar, her frilly nightgown clinging to her figure as she raced toward him. Her eyes were large and wide with fear and her mouth was open.

"Peter! Peter!" she gasped again and again. "Oh, I knew you'd come. Oh, Peter!"

Then she was in his arms, cowering there, shaking and trembling as the tears came.

And Peter Remington viewed it all from a detachment that was absolute. Her terror struck home to him. Seeing her, there in his own arms, sent a peculiar thrill coursing through him. Yet, it was all as if he slept and, in his dream, watched himself and the feminine figure from a distance.

At last the girl stifled her sobs and pulled herself together. She backed away from the arms that had been around her, and looked up into the face that was regarding her.

Again terror leaped in her eyes—terror that was mingled with incredulous disbelief.

"Peter!" She screamed wildly. "Peter—don't look at me like that!" She was backing away from him now; fascinated horror frozen on her face. "What is it, Peter? You can't—not you, Peter! Oh God—not you!"

From his great distance Peter Remington saw himself follow her, run after her, snatch at her. His hands caught her nightdress. Snatched at the shoulder, ripped it, tore it away from her breast. His nails scratched her soft flesh, drew blood. Then he seemed to go mad . . .

His lips closed over the bloody scratches. She tried to push him away, to fight him off. But he was too strong for her. His hands pinioned her arms, held them helpless, and his lips caressed her smooth skin again and again, before he became still madder.

The cavern-like basement echoed and re-echoed with her screams. Once she pushed him away momentarily—and his teeth marks were plain on her neck. Then he was back at her, his open mouth seeking her bleeding shoulder.

All this Peter Remington saw and knew. Every twinge of terror, every shudder of horror, that passed through her reached down into his soul—yet it was as if the thing had been taken out of his control. He could do nothing about it— nothing to close that slavering mouth—to stay those tearing hands . . .

Then the blackness faded away. Peter felt ill—his head and his stomach. Light—daylight—streamed into his eyes. With a sudden start he came back to full consciousness, sat bolt upright in his bed.

That sent a throb of pain through his aching head. He lifted a hand to it, stopped the hand midway. Numbly, as if it were not part of himself, he held the hand there before his eyes and stared at it in utter horror and revulsion.

The fingernail were caked and clotted with dried blood! The dark red stains ran down his hands to his wrists! Dried blood—Claire's blood!

With limbs that felt weak and palsied he strode numbly across the room to a dresser; sick, he stood there and stared. Slowly poking his dry tongue out of his mouth, he edged it along his red-stained lips. A bit of that hellish crimson stain cracked off. It dissolved in his mouth, and he tasted the salty tang of human blood. Claire's blood!

Peter Remington stood there a long while, studying himself, trying to read behind the horror that looked out at him from his own eyes. This was he, Peter Remington. He was right there in his bedroom, as he had been the night before. He had been asleep. Now it was daylight. Birds were chirping outside in the trees. The world was real. But this was no nightmare. There were dried blood on his hands and on his lips.

Dazedly Peter washed—scrubbed that awful stain out from beneath his nails. Then he dressed. He was not thinking; the ability to think rationally seemed to have left him. He dressed automatically, and like an automaton he left his room and went downstairs.

There were things he had to do, of course. He had to drive Claire to the city. Still more, he had to leave this place— forever; get as far away from it as possible, so far that he would no longer even be able to remember it.

His footsteps sounded hollowly on the uncarpeted stairs. Deathly silence lay over the place. At the foot of the balustrade Peter turned to the right and opened the parlor door. The room was as the undertaker had left it, the gloomy portraits on the wall hardly less melancholy than when they had been hidden by black shrouds.

Peter closed the door softly. Then he crossed the hallway and stepped into the library. It, too, was empty. He sat down in a chair near the fireplace. He must think. That was the only thing to do, he kept reminding himself; he must think.

But thoughts would not come. His mind spun dizzily and

he kept repeating to himself an absurd rhyme from Mark Twain: "Punch, brothers, punch with care, punch in the presence . . ." Over and over and over it went crazily through his head—until a sharp sound broke the heavy stillness.

A board squeaked on the stairway. Peter sat up more rigidly. Another squeak. Footsteps on the stairs. Someone was coming down. He stood up.

It was Claire, wearing her hat and coat, and with a little bag in her hand. But when Peter started toward her, she froze there on the stairs, backed up against the wall, her hands raised as if to hold him off. Her eyes were wide, her mouth was open and she seemed to be trying to speak.

Then the words came, stumblingly.

"No—no—go away. Don't come—near me. You . . . You . . . No—no!" her words were coming faster; her voice was rising. "How could you? Peter—you—oh, how could you? Don't touch me! Don't—!"

Her voice cracked on a high note, ended in a scream. Peter was quite close to her now. Even in the dim light he could see her quite clearly—*and he could see teeth marks on her neck!*

"You're upset, Claire," he told her. "You've had too much of this. I must get you out of here right away."

With wide, burning eyes she watched him, as if she could not believe the words she was hearing. And her lips kept moving, repeating, "No—no—no," endlessly.

"I'll get the car and start you home immediately," he told her, as he started toward the door.

"No—no," she insisted. "Please—" she said the name as if it were some curious foreign phrase that suddenly had cropped up unaccountably in her mouth—"don't do anything more to me. Let me go. Martin will drive me down. I can't— can't be near you!"

Again her voice rose hysterically, and now there was another noise on the upper landing. A door had opened and footsteps came to the top of the stairs. Martin Lorenz stood there.

For a moment he looked down at them questioningly. Peter

stared up . . . Lorenz wasn't much to look at; he was ordinary, the sort of man one forgets ten minutes after having met him—colorless. Peter had never liked him—hadn't disliked him, either, for that matter. Just regarded him as a nonentity, a fixture of John's laboratory.

Now Lorenz started down the stairs and Claire rushed up to meet him, as if he were a God-sent haven of refuge.

"Drive me to town, Martin!" she begged. "Now—right away . . . I don't want to stay here another moment!"

"But I understood that Peter was to drive you—" Lorenz began, but she choked him off excitedly.

"Please, Martin, I want you to drive me—not Peter. Please, Martin, for my sake!"

Peter tried to interrupt, to explain; but Lorenz seemed to grasp the situation. He nodded reassuringly to the girl and, over her head, made a gesture of understanding to Peter.

"She's near the breaking point," he said matter-of-factly. "It will be better if I drive her. I'll get the car immediately."

Claire followed him out to the garage, and in a few minutes Peter heard the sound of a motor. Then it passed the door, went down the driveway and faded away in the distance.

Peter was alone, and now that the excitement was past, drowsiness was creeping over him again. Mrs. Wilmott was not up yet, so he made some coffee and fried a pair of eggs for breakfast. That helped some, even though the drowsiness persisted somewhat.

But now he could think clearly. That horror last night, he realized, was no nightmare. The blood under his nails and on his hands, the teeth marks on Claire's neck—they told their own ghastly story. Beyond that the whole occurrence was a bewildering blank.

He had gone to bed. He had waked up in bed. During the night he had been somewhere—in some ghoulish chamber where he had lost his senses. That chamber, he decided, must be somewhere in this castle of gloom.

Peter decided to investigate. He knew the upper floors of the building fairly well, but he had never paid much attention to the basement since John had taken it over and converted it into a laboratory.

From the living room he went down the stairs to the laboratory, and switched on the light. The place was a maze of scientific apparatus, the walls lined with cabinets of chemicals. Leading from the main room were several smaller ones, anterooms, storerooms and one where animals were kept to await their turn in the experiment room.

But nowhere could Peter find any place that resembled the cellar-like cavern in which he had been last night.

Again his eyes felt heavy and drowsiness threatened to close them. Peter shook his head angrily. There must be something in all these cabinets, he told himself, that he could take to keep himself awake. One by one he searched them, until he came to a bottle half-filled with white powder and labeled caffeine. That would do the trick.

He measured out three grams, mixed the powder with water, and then gulped it. Putting the bottle back in the cabinet, he resumed his search. Somewhere down here, he told himself, there must be a cellar-like place with a stone ceiling.

In the animals' room he made a discovery. In one wall, almost blending with the concrete, was a door which he had not noticed the first time he had glanced in. Now he approached it curiously. There was no knob—just a keyhole. In order to open it one had to have the key.

He got down on his knees and tried to get a purchase with his fingers along the edge or at the bottom. There didn't seem to be any—

Grating upon its hinges, the door behind him, the one leading to the laboratory, closed! A key turned in the lock with a quick metallic click as Peter got to his feet and sprang across the little room. He threw his weight against the door, but it held solidly. Twice more he tried to force it and then a strange giddiness came over him so that he could not make another attempt.

The air was becoming heavy—and sweetish. The electric light bulb was becoming smaller and smaller. It was fading, fading.

Peter groped out blindly. Then the light blinked out altogether, and he floated off in the all-pervading blackness.

That's where he found the jagged, rock-hewn cavern—in
the blackness. Gradually the blackness gave way and Peter
saw a dim light hanging from the ceiling. The place was evidently a sub-basement beneath the cellar, its rough supporting pillars carved out by hand!

He got a better look at the place, now. The walls seemed to
be off somewhere in the blackness, but the light revealed the
heavy pillars clearly enough. One of them was lighter than
the others—almost white.

Gradually his eyes focused on it, and again numb horror
clutched at his heart. There was a body tied to that pillar—a
white, rigid figure from which came low, intermittent moans.
Then he could see the face, now staring around the cellar in
wild terror. Claire Carter's face!

Her outer clothing had been removed and she stood against
the pillar wearing only her shoes and stockings and her
silken underthings. Ropes bound her ankles and were looped
over her breast.

Again Peter Remington stared as if out of a nightmare, and
again no muscle or nerve of his body would respond to the
wild rioting of his heart. To his amazement, he saw himself
rising up as if out of the floor.

Now he saw that the middle of the cavern which, the night
before, had seemed to be solid stone or concrete, had become
a great, gaping hole. Out of that blackness climbed a figure
that Peter Remington recognized as himself. It stepped out
onto the solid floor, and pulled out a ladder after it. For a few
moments *this* Peter was gone while he carried the ladder off
into a far corner of the cellar. Then he was back, standing
there before Claire.

Again her wide eyes stared at him. Again her lips were
moving—and Peter Remington gradually made out what was
saying.

"Peter! Peter!" her voice was dazed, hurt, stricken. "Why
are you doing this to me, Peter? Surely, I never harmed
you—never hurt you, Peter. I—I loved you."

Something wild and joyous leaped in Peter Remington's heart. She loved him! Memories of those days when he had considered her his sweetheart came rushing back to him. Then Claire had not forgotten all about them!

"You loved me," he heard himself saying, as his figure stood there facing the tied girl. "You loved me—and yet you were going to marry John."

"I couldn't help that," she gasped. "You did not seem to care—and John wanted me."

"So you were going to marry John, although you didn't love him. You were going to give him the husks of the affection you held for me—going to let him marry a woman who loved another man."

Peter Remington felt as if he must burst out of his body. In some way, he must break from this nightmare—spring forth and stop himself from saying these things. He could feel the blood pounding in his veins, could feel his heart beating cruelly against the walls of his chest.

Then, just for a moment, he could feel the perspiration pouring down his face—and a numb ache in his wrists.

"Please, Peter," the girl's voice came to him again. "Untie me and let me of this terrible place. Please—oh, please, Peter!" Her voice rose to hysteria. "You killed Martin! Don't kill me, too!"

"You were going to make a fool of John," Peter heard himself saying again. "Once you loved him; but you found out that his money was nearly gone. And then you fell in love with Peter and Peter's money. You were going to betray my brother for me."

"No—no!" Claire screamed. "I didn't know about John's money . . . I didn't care about it . . . I wasn't going to—!"

Again Peter Remington felt suddenly cold as her voice broke off in a choking sob. He could feel the perspiration rolling off him—feel the ropes around his wrists and his ankles. And he could think naturally once more!

With a sudden wild burst of relief he knew that the Peter out there on the floor of the cellar was not the real Peter Remington. That Peter was a fake—a masquerader. But who could he be?

As he listened, the man's voice went on and on, accusing the girl of infidelity, accusing her of ulterior motives, accusing, accusing. Jealous accusations poured from his lips . . .

Jealous—that was it! The Peter out there, that masquerading Peter, was jealous. But who would be jealous of Claire? Who would utter such accusations?

Peter Remington felt very sick and weak as the answer to that question came to him. Only John Remington, who lay dead in his grave, would be jealous because his fiancée loved his brother. Only John would know of his own financial condition, which was news even to Peter.

But John was dead and in his grave . . .

Then came another rush of staggering thoughts. Peter remembered John's experiments: how his brother had brought back to life animals that had been definitely dead. He remembered John's peculiar malady—how, in the prime of life, he had been stricken and died. John had been striving to find the secret of bringing back to life humans who had passed through the veil of death.

He had found it! That was John out there on the cellar floor—John disguised as Peter!

Peter realized sickeningly that he and John looked a great deal alike. It would not be difficult for John to disguise himself so that, in that dimly lit cellar, he would pass for Peter— even fool Peter himself!

A cold terror that was far worse than his former horror seized Peter. It had been maddening to see himself out there torturing Claire—to think that he could be doing such things. But it was far more dismaying to realize that the fiend was his own brother—probably driven insane by jealousy.

John, a madman! Claire in his hideous power!

Peter could not move a muscle to help her. Every atom of brain energy and will power he martialed in a desperate determination to drive his muscles to answer the dictates of his will—but not a nerve quivered. Instead, he slipped back into a drowsy fog.

When he came back to reality, the pseudo Peter was still there before Claire, jeering at her.

"Well," he was saying, "I don't want a second-hand love. You belong to John, and I'm going to send you back to him. But before you go, I want you to dance for me. I have been away so much that I've had little opportunity to see you dance. Now you'll have a chance to dance for me alone."

Claire had ceased arguing. She no longer tried to plead. Her eyes seemed riveted on the face of her tormentor, as if they must break through his cruel determination and force him to be merciful. But he paid no attention.

"Such a dance none of your Broadway audiences ever saw," he chuckled. Now, with fresh horror, Peter recognized even John's voice. The drug which held him powerless was wearing off, he told himself; his senses were becoming more keen and he could see through the masquerade which at first had deceived him. That voice was not his own—he should have recognized that sooner. It was John attempting to disguise his own voice.

"There is your stage!" the voice went on, and the imposter pressed a button in the pillar close beside Claire's head.

The dim light that had lit the cellar was drowned out in the white glare of a powerful bulb and reflector that hung directly above the dark pit. Immediately the blackness vanished, and Peter saw that the pit was in reality a circular tank, evidently made of steel. It was at least a dozen feet in diameter, and the top was flush with the level of the cellar floor. How deep it was, Peter could not tell, from where he was.

Where *that* was, puzzled Peter, also. So far as he could make out he was sitting down—it seemed—with his outer clothing gone. Evidently he was somewhat behind a partition of some sort, for, while he could see what was going on in the cellar, Claire had not seen him when her anxious eyes were scanning every corner of the cellar.

"You will not need these, for your dance," Claire's tormentor said, as he kneeled beside her and took off her shoes, then slipped off her stockings. "Instead, I have a little ointment that will facilitate your steps."

From a dark portion of the cellar he brought a jar. Diving his hand into it, he brought out some sort of salve or liquid, which he rubbed over the girl's legs and feet. Then he untied the ropes, which bound her and started pushing her toward the edge of the tank.

Peter mentally lashed his will power until he felt that the blood vessels and veins in his head must burst—but no muscle responded. Desperately he struggled to cry out, but his lips would not move to shape a single syllable.

"No—no!" Claire was screaming again. "Peter! Please, Peter—not in there. Oh, God—Peter! There's a skeleton in there!"

"Only a dog—a large dog," the masquerader chuckled. "He could not dance well enough—so he died. But, of course, you will do much better."

Then she was at the edge of the tank. For a moment she struggled there, with the strength of desperation. Then one bare foot slipped off the rim and kicked out into space. Then the other. For a moment the man held her dropped her there; then he dropped her and she disappeared into the tank.

Her terrified scream came to Peter's ears. Then only her low, tortured moaning sounded . . .

Now the man who pretended to be Peter Remington disappeared again in the darkness of the cellar. In a few minutes he returned, wheeling what looked to be a large bottle such as is used to supply spring water. Again he disappeared, to reappear with another bottle. Four in all, he brought.

Then he stood on the edge of the tank and looked down. With a fiendish grin on his face, he rolled one of the bottles to the edge, and sent it plunging down to the metal floor of the tank. Peter heard the smash, as the bottle crashed into pieces, and the girl's wild scream.

"Your assistants," the man on the rim of the tank, jeered. "You don't know them, so perhaps I had better introduce you. These little fellows are *dinoponera grandis*—or 'great, terrible ants', as the Brazilians call them. I'm afraid they're hungry—and they're very partial to that sweet mixture you have on your legs. When they reach you, you had better begin your dance."

Dinoponera grandis—the dread *tucanderos* of the Brazilian jungles! Peter Remington knew what that meant. Never would he be able to erase from his mind the memory of that tragic expedition he had led up the Amazon—the picture of one of his bearers, spread-eagled on the ground, daubed with a honeyed concoction, and then swarmed over by a horde of savage ants.

The ground had been black with them. In waves they had swept over him, their terrible mandibles sinking into his flesh and tearing remorselessly. Peter often heard that dying man's scream in his sleep. By the time the rescuing Brazilian troopers had arrived the poor devil was nothing but a heap of stripped bones.

This devil on the edge of the tank was dropping thousands of *tucanderos* down into that pit to swarm over Claire's nearly naked body!

Peter's whole figure seemed to vibrate, to palpitate, with the tensity of his struggle. Yet no muscle moved. Flashes of fire danced before his eyes like a Fourth of July celebration; the taste of blood was in his mouth, the smell of it in his nostrils.

Then again the cellar whirled giddily, waves of darkness swept before his eyes. He seemed to be falling into that pit, but when he hit bottom and again opened his eyes, the lids moved!

Another bottle crashed to the bottom of the tank—and the fiend had a third at the rim.

Peter moved a finger, a toe. He squirmed around, and ascertained that he was bound to a chair. But a moment's investigation told him that the ropes were not very secure. The devil who had tied them had depended upon whatever drug he had used on Peter to keep him helpless.

The tang of caffeine mingled with the blood taste in Peter's mouth, and he thanked his lucky stars for the inspiration which had prompted that dose, which was beginning to counteract the drug John had given him at some time or other. Now he set to work in earnest on the ropes—tugging, tearing, straining. They were giving—but it seemed to take an eternity to get them loose enough to slip off. He had only minutes—seconds! For he knew full well how quickly the dread *tucanderos* did their work.

There was agony, now, in Claire's screams. The voracious insects were attacking her!

"Dance!" the devilish masquerader cheered. "Dance for your life. Don't let those fellows start on you—they've been especially trained to eat human blood. Once they start your blood flowing, Claire Carter's last dance will be over very soon."

The fourth bottle crashed to the bottom of the tank—and Peter Remington tore his bleeding wrists free from the ropes. In an instant he was bent over, tugging away at the ropes around his ankles. Then they, too, were free.

He could see now that the chair to which he had been tied was placed behind a partition about four feet high. His captor had figured it cunningly so that only the top of his head would show above the partition, thus concealing him while giving him a full view of all the hellishness going on before him.

Peter's vocal muscles responded as quickly as the others.

"John!" he screamed, the moment he was free from the chair. Then he leaped over the partition and was racing for the tank. He had to get Claire out of that hell first of all.

But that yell had warned the tormentor. Instead of running, he turned and faced the charging Peter. Amazement showed first in his face; then fiendish hatred. It flashed from his eyes and his lips curled up in a bestial snarl.

He met Peter, head on, but out of a sheathe at his waist he drew a wicked looking knife. Peter caught the wrist of his knife-hand as their bodies thudded together. His own fingers were weak and still partly numb from the drug and the ropes which had bound him. But he clung relentlessly and put every bit of his strength into the pressure on that wrist. At last he heard the knife clatter to the hard floor. Then he saw it—and kicked it away into the darkness. He did not want that knife himself; even though John had become a mad fiend, Peter could not have plunged the blade into his own brother.

Now that the knife was gone, his opponent seemed to gather new strength. They rolled and fought on the floor. John seemed the stronger, and Peter was fighting desperately to save himself from a knockout as he was pinned to the floor under his opponent.

"John!" he panted again and again, but the mad-eyed devil only grinned and fought more ferociously.

Peter put all his strength into an upward heave; almost got free. But again his opponent was on top. They had rolled to the edge of the tank. Claire's pleas came like stabbing knives to Peter. He squirmed, thrashed, heaved—and they plunged over the edge together!

With a thud they landed on the bottom of the tank, and this time Peter was on top. Desperately he hammered away at his opponent, and out of the corner of his eye he saw Claire— and almost lost the grim battle then and there!

She was running about wildly, threshing her arms round, rubbing her hands frantically up and down her legs—and with every sweep she brushed away hundreds of big black ants, each over an inch in length. They were swarming over her legs—fairly coating her body to her waist—and the light of tortured insanity blazed in her eyes: the madness of sheer, stark, uprooting terror.

Her movements were becoming slower. She was panting for breath. In a few minutes more—

The black insects were already swarming all over Peter, stinging him; but he hardly felt their bites. With new and merciless determination he turned back to his opponent. Brother or not, this man had to die so that Claire might have a chance for life.

But when he looked down at the man he was battering, Peter could hardly see John for the ants that were swarming over him. They had fairly inundated him—tearing away at his bleeding face, at his gasping mouth, at his throat. Then Peter saw the blood that was flowing out from under his brother's back. The tormentor had fallen on one of the bottle fragments and blood was spurting from a wound—hastening the doom that already swarmed over him.

When Peter tore loose from the grasping fingers which clutched him, the masquerader had not sufficient strength to get back on his feet.

In a bound Peter was across the tank, had grasped Claire, swept hundreds of the torturing insects off of her, and hoisted her against the side of the tank.

"Grab the top and pull!" he shouted.

Then she was up, with a final boost that got her over the top. Peter turned back to confront his opponent, but now there was only a heap of swarming ants on the bottom of the tank—thousands of hungry, voracious killers!

"Give me your hand! I can pull you up!" Claire called, as she leaned over the edge.

Peter reached up and took her hand, braced his foot against the side, and jumped. He caught the top—and then was over, to sit on the floor while he spat ants that clung, biting, to his lips, swept them off his body by the hundreds, and ground them beneath him as he rolled.

Claire helped him to the best of her ability, then clothed herself as best she could in the torn dress, which John had ripped from her and thrown on the floor near the pillar.

"Come on," he panted to Claire, as he held out a supporting arm. "In the laboratory I'll find something to ease those bites for you."

Near the laboratory door Peter found his suit where it had been flung into a corner of the hallway. Evidently John had taken some of his clothes off so that the ants could do their savage work more easily. John had meant to throw his own brother into the pit—after he had watched Claire die from the vicious attacks of those rending little inch-long killers.

As Peter, rubbed soothing oil on her legs, Claire told him of her flight from Remington Hall, how Lorenz had gotten out of the car to open the estate gate, how he had been dragged back into the trees, how he had screamed, how she -

had started to run back to the hall, and how the man she had thought to be Peter had pursued her and caught her when she stumbled and fell.

"It doesn't seem possible he could have been John!" she gasped, when Peter had told his story. "But," she admitted, "if he was jealous, he chose a fiendish way to torture me—making me think that you were doing it, Peter."

Even that admission was not sufficient to dispel Peter's agony of spirit. Heavyhearted, he led the way from Remington Hall. How had John applied to himself the method by which he had restored animals to life—*after he had died?*

Peter told Martin later of the hideous things which had happened and questioned him particularly about the power his brother had discovered by which life could be restored. The man told him that he himself had applied the electrical invention to John's body, but that it had failed to work. Peter was puzzled. Then, slowly, it came to him; and he believed he understood.

That was why John had taken such pains to make sure he would not be embalmed when he died! Wealth and a family vault had made it possible not to comply with the state law requiring the embalmer's fluid. His brother had given Martin orders to apply the electrical invention, but it had not worked until *after* his body had been placed in the vault—and its door was not locked because, since childhood, John had always had an overpowering fear of being buried alive. The electrical invention had worked late, as its inventor had planned. John had come to life in his burial shelf—escaped from the family vault to attempt his crazed, jealous vengeance.

Peter Remington shuddered, and Claire slipped an arm lovingly around his waist. An overpowering feeling of deep despondency swept over him. His own brother! Then at the pressure of Claire's arm, he looked into her face; saw her sweet, sympathetic smile. He felt better. Perhaps in the bliss he would have with the girl he loved—had always loved—he might with time find a happiness that would gradually erase from his mind the fearful, tragic memory of his brother John.

DEAD MAN'S KISS

TEN FORTY-FIVE—fifteen minutes more of life! Alice Mason shuddered and glanced around the big living room, now so funereally quiet, its distant corners black wells of brooding silence. Restlessly she paced to a window, to stare out into the thick, fog-laden darkness. In fifteen minutes they would unlock his cell door and lead her brother, Arthur, on that last short journey to the little green door and the ghastly room that lay beyond it. Often she had seen gruesome pictures of the death chamber in the newspapers, and had pitied the poor wretches who were dragged into it. And now it was Arthur, the brother she had known all her life but never quite understood, who was waiting there for the summons to be plunged into eternity!

Fifteen minutes more . . .

Outside, the night was stygian, its blackness unbroken by a single light, the thick darkness heavy with moisture that was dropping and splashing suddenly from the trees. Each plopping drop seemed to tick off those last few minutes.

Inside, the stillness was broken only by Shirley's sobbing and the endless pacing of Alice's feet. They were alone in the big house, those two; alone to sit through the nerve-wracking death watch together. Their friends and neighbors had stayed away, ostensibly so as not to intrude on their privacy—but actually, Alice knew, because the threat that hung over that house filled them all with a nameless terror.

She had been hoping and praying that Myron Taylor would be there to lend her strength, to share that last frightful hour with them—but Myron was Arthur's attorney. He was carrying on the useless fight to the bitter end, hopeful to the last that the governor might intervene and commute the death sentence.

But now even that last faint hope was gone. The governor would have acted before this—and Myron had promised to 'phone them the moment he had good news. It was too late; the grim machinery of the law was grinding on relentlessly.

"It was all my fault!" Shirley sobbed for the thousandth time. "I shouldn't have encouraged Phil. If I hadn't done that he wouldn't have come here, and Arthur wouldn't have— killed him!"

"Please, dear," Alice tried to soothe the younger girl, "it's nobody's fault. We've been over that so many times. There's no answer to it—the whole thing is a horrible, ghastly nightmare! If we could only close our eyes and wake up to find that it was all past!"

"Wake up!" Shirley chattered hysterically. "I'll never sleep again! Whenever I close my eyes I'll see Arthur's face the way he glared at me when I left the witness stand. I'll never get the sound of his voice out of my ears. I killed him, Alice—my words damned him!"

Ten Fifty . . .

Alice closed her eyes as if to shut out sight of her sister's agony—and in place if it she faced the stabbing memory of that unforgettable day in the courtroom. All during the trial Arthur, who was more than ten years her senior, had been his usual composed, tight-lipped self. But that day, as Shirley had finished her unwilling testimony, his iron control had slipped. For a moment he had broken loose from his attorneys and sprung to his feet.

She could see him now as he stood there, shaking his fist at them and roaring, "You've signed my death warrant, you two, and I'll not forget it. They may kill me—but they can't keep me away from you!"

Horrified silence for a long moment—then a babble of noise: the judge's pounding gavel, the prosecutor's outraged protests, his own counsel's warnings and attempts to quiet him. And then Arthur sank back in his chair, once more his cold, taciturn self.

They had been doing the best they could for him, she and

Shirley, but in the hands of the prosecutor they were help-less. He had wrung from their unwilling lips the few simple facts the state needed to build up its case of premeditated murder.

Over and over again Alice had reviewed those facts. They were so few, but so damning. Shirley had been going out with Phil Stewart, and Arthur had objected. He had ordered Phil from the house, had threatened to kill him if he ever came back. Then that terrible night of the tragedy—Arthur was standing in his study over Phil's body when she and Shirley ran downstairs, the bloody poker with which Phil's head had been bashed still in his hand.

Arthur claimed that Phil had broken into the house, was burglarizing it, and that he fought when Arthur discovered him. But old John Stewart, Phil's bitter, vindictive father, had produced a note in Arthur's handwriting asking Phil to come to the mason house that night.

"Premeditated murder!" roared the state, and the prosecu-tor insinuated that there was something abnormal about Ar-thur; that his guardianship over his sisters was not natural or moral. "Fired by this incestuous jealousy, he invited young Stewart to the house that night and deliberately murdered him," he charged. "This wasn't the first time he interfered with the girls' male friendships. Only two months before the murder he quarreled with Henry Lang, his partner in the jew-elry commission business, and terminated the partnership because of Lang's interest in the young ladies."

Under his searching cross-examination Alice had had to admit that she knew of no other reason why the partnership had been dissolved; and Shirley had to testify to the quarrel she had overheard between her brother and young Stewart—had to admit the threat of death Arthur had shouted at Phil Stewart.

The details were so meager and so damning, and Arthur's defense had been so weak, so futile. There was only one ver-dict possible. Arthur had signed his own death warrant, but he did not seem to realize that.

After the trial—after he was removed to the death house—

he had steadfastly refused to see either of his sisters; had returned their letters unopened. His hostility had remained unshaken, and his enraged threat hung over their heads to make the ordeal of those last heart-breaking weeks even more terrifying.

Ten fifty-five . . .

Shirley was watching the dock with wide, distended eyes; watching it as if it were clicking off the few remaining moments of her own life. The girl was very close to an hysterical breakdown, Alice knew, but there was nothing she could do. It was all she could do to hang onto her own fast-slipping control.

The house seemed so huge, so empty—and yet populated with so many terrifying shadows and resounding with so many eerie sounds. For weeks after tragedy the place had been thronged with policemen and detectives, besieged by curious sightseers, but gradually they had stopped coming. Alter the death sentence had been imposed there was only Alice and Shirley and old Barbara, their cook and housekeeper. Barbara had stayed for a while growing more uneasy each day, but finally she had broken down and given up.

"I can't stand it any more, Miss Alice," she had sobbed. "Mr. Arthur seems to be all over the house. I hear his voice whispering and I hear him walking. And last night I saw his face looking at me from my window. It's just as if he was dead already and come back to haunt us!"

After that Alice and Shirley were alone—alone with the swiftly passing hours and their own terrified thoughts.

Arthur had never been very close to them. He was naturally aloof and reserved, not given to sentimental demonstration. But, of course, they loved him—now, when he was irrevocably lost to them, they realized how much.

But he had always been somewhat strange and mysterious. Alice had never been able to understand him—and that added to the horror of this eternal Gethsemane she was enduring. If she only *knew,* it would be easier—but she didn't. The reasons behind that ghastly night of tragedy were shrouded in the mystery of Arthur's close-lipped personality.

Had it been murder? Had Arthur deliberately lured Phil Stewart to the house and killed him to stop his attentions to Shirley? And was there actually something to the prosecutor's insinuations that Arthur was not a normal man . . .?

Alice shuddered and glanced at the clock.

Ten fifty-nine . . .

"One minute more," Shirley moaned. "They are coming for him now, Alice! I can see them!"

Alice slipped her arms around the girl's quivering shoulders. Somewhere in the old building a floorboard creaked loudly, as if someone were walking on it. And outside the wet splashing of drops of condensed fog. Only seconds left now . . .

Eleven! The hour of death! Now there was no hope, or Myron would have 'phoned. Now the keepers were at Arthur's cell door, leading him down that last length of corridor, through the little green door, seating him in that barbarous chair! Alice could visualize every horrible detail—could see the executioner reaching out his hand for the lethal switch . . .

Suddenly every light in the room dimmed and seemed to sputter.

"Oh, God!" Shirley moaned. "They're killing him! That's the way the prison lights dim when—when they pull the death switch!"

Cold horror closed its fingers around Alice's heart and petrified her as she stared at one of those dimmed, flickering bulbs. The death chair was taxing the prison power—but the prison was nearly a hundred miles away! It was impossible that the chair should affect their lights; incredible that the power of half the state should be impaired to speed Arthur Mason's soul to eternity!

And then the lights blinked out entirely.

Blackness that was almost palpable flooded them after the light. Alice groped her way through it toward a desk drawer where there was a flashlight, while Shirley's chattering burbled into a moan of terror. A moan that was shot with the shrill notes of madness.

Blackness and stillness broken only by Shirley's blood-curdling hysteria. Alice fumbled in the drawer and found the torch, snapped it on, and an arc of light shot across the room illuminating it unnaturally.

"The current must have gone off," she said, more to hear her voice uttering a sane commonplace than anything else.

But the moment she lifted the telephone instrument to her ear the "hello" died on her lips. The line was dead, muted with that complete quiet which meant that there was no current. The lights and now the telephone . . . If there had been an electrical storm she could have understood it, but surely this fog had not been able to interfere . . .

Shirley had followed her into the hallway, tugging at her sleeve and whimpering frightenedly.

"Don't leave me along, Alice! I'm afraid—I'm terrified! Let me stay with you—close to you!"

And then her voice stopped, a word chopped off in the middle as if the motivating force behind it had suddenly been extinguished; and her fingers dug into Alice's arm like talons.

"There's somebody else here—" Her voice was barely a whisper; more a gasp of expiring breath.

But Alice had already sensed that other presence, although she heard no sound. Cold perspiration oozed out on her forehead, on the backs of her hands. Her flashlight turned tremblingly, wavered its beam down the hall toward the door—and then she could no longer feel it in her nerveless hand.

There, inside the doorway, was Arthur, coming toward them!

The beam of light shone full on his haggard, contorted face, now thin and drawn after his months in the death house, and lined with veins that stood out like livid bluish welts, as if the fearful current were still coursing through them. The light shone on his prison clothes; on the slit trouser leg with the horribly blackened limb showing through it. Shone on his hands, now gnarled and clenched, as if they still gripped the arms of that fearful chair.

Beads of perspiration stood out on his glistening face, on the taut, straining muscles of his throat—and his dark eyes blazed at them with deathless animosity. For a moment his head bent forward—and there was the white patch where his head had been shaved to receive the death-dealing electrode.

He had made no sound as he came through the outer and inner doors, and now he was coming toward them noise-lessly!

Alice gasped, and her heart seemed to stand still within her panting breast. The long moments seemed to become an eternity—an eternity that was terminated by the shrill peal of doom that was Shirley's wild scream.

"God in heaven!" she shrilled. "He's come for us!"

Abruptly the clutching fingers loosened their bloodstained grip on Alice's arm. The scream wheezed into a sigh, and Shirley's body thumped to the floor.

Alice tried to bend over her, tried to interpose her own body between her unconscious sister and that silent, ghastly thing that was advancing on them. But her muscles would not obey her will. Her knees were weak and trembling. All strength seemed to have gone out of them—but they were propelling her backward. She was backing down the hall-way, backing toward the stairs that led to the upper floor.

She couldn't leave Shirley there at the mercy of that in-credible thing that, only a few minutes before, had been their brother. She couldn't—but there was no way in which she could stop herself. The inhuman looking caricature of her brother was coming forward faster now, his slippered feet making no sound on the carpeted floor; and as he came, his clothing seemed to billow in the slight breeze of his passing as if it were made of nebulous, gossamer stuff.

Alice was backing, backing—frantically now, while shud-dering horror coursed through every part of her. She was al-most running backward toward the stairs. And then the crea-ture lunged for her!

Something bumped into her foot, slammed against the back

of her knee. She was losing her balance—falling. The light waved wildly in her upthrust hand—and lighted only the grotesque, agony twisted face that loomed above her!

That was all that Alice saw—just the twisted, sweat-glistening features, the corded neck, the mad eyes—and something crashed against the back of her head and the darkness that was all around her swept over her and pushed her down, down into a pit of bottomless night.

She was lying on something soft when she opened her eyes, something soft that seemed to be suspended in utter blackness. In blackness that must have drowned all sounds by its intensity. Unearthly quiet and stygian darkness—this must be the tomb, panic whispered to her terrified brain. This was the grave and she had been buried alive—that was Arthur's revenge for the wrong he thought she had done him!

But one isn't fastened in a grave with one's arms stretched above one's head and one's feet held taut. There was something queer about that. She tugged at her arms, and something cut cruelly into her wrists. They were tied, lashed to something that held them securely; and her feet were fastened to something at the other end of whatever held her.

And then she caught the sound that must have hammered at her fogged mind and brought her back to consciousness—a lock snapping back, a door squeaking open. Someone—or something—was coming into the place where she was, was coming toward her!

A match burst into flame, touched the stub of a candle—and in the weak, flickering light she saw that she was in her own room, stretched out helplessly on her own bed. And over her leaned the horrible twisted-featured thing that had been her brother!

His eyes were looking down at her, blazing at her with a savage glare that was a mixture of hatred—and something else that chilled her blood even more than the appalling reality of his impossible presence there in her room. His eyes, evil pools in the candlelight, gleamed with stark, unfettered lust!

Frantically Alice tried to shrink away from him, tried to twist her body to the far side of the bed—but he leered down at her derisively, and his body shook with silent laughter. One gnarled, twisted hand stretched forth and gripped the neck of her dress—and the touch of the still clenched knuckles was clammy and cold. So cold that even after they had passed, her skin prickled and radiated an icy glow where they had been.

He was ripping her dress down its full length, tearing the cloth away from her body. The cold fingers were tugging at her under-garments, sending the penetrating chill of death through her blood. She tried to scream, but her tongue was a dead thing in a dry, parched cavern. Only her eyes seemed to be functioning, and they were fixed and staring with overwhelming horror.

He was stripping her—and in that moment the prosecutor's insinuations came back to her! He had been right. Arthur, this brother she had never really known, was a horrible, unthinkable degenerate—and now death had swept away the last barriers, unleashed the full force of his ungodly passions! Now he had come back from the grave itself to have his way with her!

Somehow her frantic brain must have gotten command of her throat muscles for now she heard her own voice in her ears.

"Arthur," it begged, "you can't do this to me—you mustn't!"

For the first time he spoke—if that seared, toneless whisper could be called speaking. All the vitality seemed to have burned out of his voice, leaving it only the hollow, lifeless shell of what it had been.

"I told you they could not keep me from you!"

Her eyes, round with speechless horror, stared up at him—and saw that the light of the candle shone through his clothing! But not through his body; that was still opaque against the light. And then she noticed something more—a curious, detached discovery in that moment of sickening horror. There on her dressing table beside the sputtering candle lay a leather case in which Arthur used to keep precious stones that had to remain in the house overnight.

She had seen the case a day or two before Phil Stewart's death, but not since then. And now Arthur had come back for it—come back from the grave to take his wealth with him!

But he couldn't do that. There was no wealth beyond the grave. There was an end of things mundane here on earth. Arthur couldn't . . .

The evil eyes were glaring down exultantly at her nakedness. The cold, clammy hands were roaming over her body, leaving a chill trail on her shrinking flesh—and new terror surged through her. Wildly she threw herself sideways on the bed, tearing and tugging at her lacerated wrists until one of them, bathed in blood, slipped out of the rope that held it.

This horrible creature—this inhuman thing—couldn't be Arthur. It was a creature of this world, a human fiend come to loot and rob . . .

Her freed hand lashed out and grabbed at his shoulder—but the cloth of the prison clothes seemed to melt away under her fingers. It fell away like down and left her clutching at emptiness. Again her frantic fingers groped for him—touched his twisted face—and the dead flesh gave way beneath her touch, oozed out between her fingers!

And then the wild screams, pent up far too long, burst from her lips and pealed through the room in her abandonment of soul-shaking horror.

His harsh, whispering voice was drooling obscenities into her ears, cursing vilely and muttering an exultant paean of evil satisfaction and triumph. But she hardly heard him as the reverberations of her own screams filled her ears. Wild, abandoned, half-insane screams that seemed to well up of their own volition out of the innermost recesses of her squirming, writhing body!

Oddly, she though she heard those screams echoed from somewhere downstairs in the silent house—and then she knew that they were, when his slimy, cold hand closed over her lips and gagged her horridly. They *were* being echoed downstairs—by pounding on the door, by the crash of glass, by running footsteps. They were coming up the stairs, pounding down the hall toward her room.

That hell-spawned creature heard them, too, and his eyes blazed with new rage as he sprang to the door and turned the key in the lock. But now her released lips were again giving full vent to her terror.

"Alice!" That was Myron's voice shouting in the hall. "For God's sake, Alice, what's the matter?"

She tried to tell him, tried to control those awful screams that were welling up from her throat and mold them into intelligible words, but again that obscene hand clasped down over her lips—and the candle was snuffed out, plunging the room into pitch blackness.

Myron was throwing his weight against the door now, beating upon it with a chair. The panels were splintering, giving way. The door was coming down—and the foul creature that held her half smothered tensed, ready to spring the moment Myron came plunging into the room.

He would be overcome before he had a chance—if he *had* any chance against this fearful thing of the dark half-world! He would be pounced upon and throttled before he could recover his balance, unless . . .

Alice's every instinct recoiled with revulsion and nausea surged up in her, but she twisted her mouth open—and closed her sharp teeth in the palm of that loathsome hand! Closed her teeth and clenched her jaws with every ounce of strength there was in her body.

And now the creature became articulate. No longer was his voice a hushed, lifeless whisper. His lusty howl was pain-filled, and his curses were snarling and savage as he smashed his fist into her face and forced her to unclench her teeth.

"Look out!" she screamed the moment he was free. "It's Arthur—he's come back for us, Myron. Look out—"

The rending of timber and the snapping of hinges told her that the door had given way, that Myron was hurling into the room. Then there was a rush of bodies, panting, cursing, the thud of vicious blows, the gasp of constricted breath. They were rolling on the floor, tumbling and crashing around the room—Myron and that incredible thing that had been her brother. But what possible chance had Myron against a creature such as that?

Frantically she tugged at the wrist that was still imprisoned—and then it was free. She could sit up in bed and tug at the ropes that were lashed around her ankles. They were loose, untied, and she staggered from the bed and groped over the top of her dressing table. There was the candle stub—and a paper of matches.

Trembling fingers fumbled in their eagerness, and then the candle caught the match's flare—and she drew back from where two bodies threshed and struggled at her feet. But the furious battle was almost over. Myron was squatting on top of his nearly naked adversary and was choking him relentlessly while he banged the creature's head in a tattoo against the floor.

Solid, substantial blows that shook the floor as they thudded against it, Alice noticed as she stared down at the waning struggle. There was nothing ghostly or ethereal about that head—and then she saw that Myron was tearing the very scalp off it; tearing off a scalp that seemed to be on top of another scalp! A wig, of course! And there was no shaved spot in the thick head of hair that lay beneath it.

With a choking gurgle the creature stiffened and went limp; and now she saw that his ghastly, agony-twisted face had become an unrecognizable, formless pulp. Myron was scraping at it, scooping off hands full of the battered flesh!

But it wasn't battered flesh. It was clay or putty—make-up material of some sort—and out from beneath it came the thin, aristocratic features of Henry Lang, Arthur Mason's former partner.

"Don't wonder that you're surprised!" Myron panted. "I'd be, too, except that I had a pretty good hunch that I'd find this fellow somewhere around the premises. If Arthur wasn't such a close-mouthed, stubborn ass Lang never would have gotten this opportunity. Only this afternoon, with the death chair waiting for him, he told me about this packet of jewels; told me where I could find them so that I could divide them between you and Shirley."

"Then he forgave us—before he died!" Alice gasped.

But Myron was grinning up at her.

"Right and wrong," he chuckled. "He forgave you—but he's not dead. When I heard about this packet of jewels I began to see the light. That was what Phil Stewart came here for—to steal those jewels. The only one besides Arthur who knew he had them was Lang, so I put two and two together and figured that Lang had hired Stewart to burglarize the house, probably even hired him to pay attention to Shirley as that he could have an opportunity to look over the place. On the strength of that theory I persuaded the Governor to grant a stay of execution. Tried to telephone you, but the line was dead."

He had gotten up from the almost naked body that sprawled on the floor, and Alice bent over, curiously, to lift a tattered piece of the clothing that littered the floor. It was soft and light, almost downy in its texture. Now she recognized what it was—cleansing tissue!

"Specially made for this masquerade," Myron nodded. "Lang had been trying to get in here to search the house for those jewels ever since Phil Stewart's attempt failed, but there were always people around. Then he hit upon taking advantage of Arthur's foolish threat. First he got rid of old Barbara by scaring her out of the house. Then he prepared to give you and Shirley a dose of the same medicine the moment Arthur should have been dead. A wig, ghost clothing, a built up face, and plenty of some sort of grease with a menthol base to give his hands a cold, clammy feeling—that fiendish getup was enough to terrify anyone. Shirley's still lying in a faint downstairs.

"Arthur broke up with him because he discovered that Lang was crooked—so Lang planned to avenge himself by stealing these gems and at the same time taking something else that he'd been coveting for a long time."

Myron's voice stopped. He looked at Alice as though he

had just now realized the full terror of the thing she had gone through. "Darling!" he murmured, and his arms closed around her waist and drew her trembling body close against him. "He'd have succeeded if I'd been a few minutes later," he said huskily. "The Governor granted us a reprieve in the nick of time!"

FRESH BLOOD FOR GOLDEN CAULDRONS

THE DESOLATE HOWLING of the December wind—that was what filled the old house with eerie noises. The wind rattling the windowpanes, whining mournfully through cracks and down the chimney, scurrying dry leaves across the porch floor like the rustle of stiff old dresses. Nothing but the wind—but it wasn't the wind that caused that unmistakably stealthy creaking!

Lucille Jordan shivered and glanced covertly across the open fireplace to where Ellen Craig cowered in the depths of a big armchair. The mounting terror that was turning her own heart into a thing of ice was mirrored, stark and staring, in her friend's wide eyes.

"That—that was a door opening!" Ellen whispered, her frightened voice so low that it could hardly be heard above the moan of the wind.

"Silly!" Lucille tried hard to make her brittle laugh sound natural; tried to conceal the fact that her own heart was in her mouth, that she was straining her ears fearfully, dreading a recurrence of that terrifying sound. "It's just the wind . . . you ought to be used to it by now—"

"I'd never get used to this spooky old place!" Ellen shuddered. "I don't see how you can stay in such a house. The first two days I was here weren't so bad—but now it's getting under my skin. There's something wrong with this place, Lu. Perhaps it *is* haunted, the way that old woman I met in town this afternoon told me. Haunted by lost souls, she said—and tonight I can fairly feel them gathering around me, hemming me in!"

Haunted by lost souls . . . The chills ran down Lucille's spine as she remembered the first time she had heard the old woman croak those words, remembered the knowing shake of her grey head and the sly wink of her rheumy old eye. But Lucille laughed; she *had* to laugh—Ellen was dangerously close to hysteria.

"That was old Mournful Mary," she scoffed. "She's only a crack-brained gossip that nobody pays any attention to. Just an old woman with a penchant for mouthing ominous-sounding nonsense."

But even as she pretended to scoff, she was recalling the first morning Mournful Mary came to clean the house—the day after she and Keith had arrived in Arondale. Keith had already gone down the hill to the town, to begin his duties in the laboratory of the Beauchamp Glass Works, and Lucille was launched upon the task of making a home of this house that was really too large for them, but was the only thing available on the residential hill.

"You needn't bother tryin' to tell me anything about this place," said old Mary as she took charge of things. "I've set it to rights so many times for new tenants that it's gettin' to be a sort o' ritual with me. I know every nook an' corner of it."

And then as she rested after scrubbing the kitchen floor:

"Your husband's gone to work in the glass works, eh? In old Paul Beauchamp's lab'ratory, I suppose? Generally it's lab'ratory people that take this house—an' start off so bright an hopeful, just the way you're doin' now. But they all end up the same. Where are they now? Lots o' folks in town've been wonderin' about that.

"Brilliant men, they've been—I've read their diplomas an' things from all sorts o' colleges an' universities; not only in this country, but them foreign places, Paris an' Germany an' such like. But none o' them could suit old Paul. One after the other, they left—disappeared only the good Lord knows where. An' then another came to fill the place, just like you're doin' . . ."

By the time the house was cleaned Lucille was on the verge of hysteria. The position that had seemed such a wonderful opportunity for Keith had taken on the grim aspects of a snare.

But when Keith came home that night he scoffed at the old

woman's croaking and made Lucille promise not to employ her again.

"Perhaps Mr. Beauchamp is hard to please," he argued. "Most of the others didn't make the grade—but I can't see that working in the laboratory did anything to harm John Havelock. This is just the opportunity I've been hoping to find, and I'm certainly not going to let any old crackpot scare me out of it. Not only do I get an excellent salary, but I have the use of a splendidly equipped laboratory for my own work after hours. With the facilities I have here my invention should be perfected in a short time—and when I put that across I'll be even more successful than John Havelock!"

That was six months ago—and since that time Lucille had had many an opportunity to ponder the old cleaning woman's words . . .

Again the wind howled dismally—and Lucille's blood chilled in her veins as her straining ear seemed to stand off her head to catch every faint surreptitious sound. What was that? The stealthy tread of footsteps on the porch?

Her body seemed to be a stiff, ice-sheathed automaton, an automaton with curiously quaking knees, as she got up from her chair and walked to the door to the hallway. Fearfully her trembling hand reached out into the darkness and switched on the hall light. Reassured by the light, she drove herself down the hallway to the big front door, stared out through the panel window at its side.

The porch was empty, of course. No sound but the wind flapping a loose radio wire against the side of the building. Nothing but the wind—yet Ellen was shuddering in terror when she came back to the living room.

"I can't stand any more of this, Lu," she gasped through chattering teeth. "I'm going home tomorrow—as early as I can get away!"

Ellen was going home—and then would be alone again, so terribly alone! Lucille's heart sank and she caught her under-lip between her teeth to hold back the tears that threatened to brim into her eyes.

Perhaps the glass works did nothing to physical bodies of its employees, but did take something away from them. Their personalities? Their souls? Lucille didn't know—but she did know that she had lost Keith during the six months they had been in Arondale.

Something had come over him, had changed him completely. He was no longer the thoughtful, considerate man she had married less than a year ago. Now he had no time for her, hardly seemed to know that she existed. He appeared to have lost all interest in her. Everything was his work.

"In just a little while." he dismissed her protests again and again "my invention will be completed. Then I'll turn everything into gold for you!"

But Lucille didn't want everything turned into gold. She didn't want to sit, lonesome and terrified, in that big house night after night while he strangled everything that had made their life together so lovely before they came to Arondale.

It wasn't only that he was away from her; there was something more than that—something unwholesome and evil that she could sense but could not identify. She could read it smoldering in Keith's eyes. He was afraid, too—and she trembled for him, even though he would not confide in her and she did not know what it was she feared.

Cooped up there in that big house on the hillside, overlooking the works and the town that housed the laborers and their families, yet so remote from them, she had been miserably— lonesome had had too much time to think and brood. That was why she had invited Ellen, her best friend, to spend a few weeks in Arondale.

But Ellen had been quick to react to the unbearable loneliness, to sense the lowering threat that seemed to hang over the place like a black cloud. Her imagination had peopled the darkness with figures she was sure she saw lurking around the house, darting in and out between the trees and clumps of evergreen shrubbery.

To quiet her, Lucille had drawn all the blinds in the living room—but a sudden gust of wind whistled through one of the window ventilators and the shade blew high in the air, slipped its roller and rushed toward the ceiling with a thunderous bang. Ellen's shrill scream echoed the report of the blind, and Lucille whirled toward the window just in time to glimpse a face peering in from the darkness!

For a split second the light outlined it indistinctly, and then it was gone—but in that fraction of time she was almost certain that she had recognized the avid eyed face of Albert Engel.

Engel was a co-worker of Keith's, another of the experimental laboratory assistants. From the moment he had met Lucille his hungry eyes had betrayed his interest in her, and since then he had made little attempt to conceal his liking or his resentment against Keith for the way he had been neglecting his wife.

There was something about his dark, penetrating eyes that frightened Lucille; something about the intensity, the barely repressed emotion, of the man that made her shy away from him, made her go out of her way to avoid him. And now he was out there in the darkness, prowling around the house, spying on her . . .

But before she had time to consider that, another blast of wind slammed the back door—and brought out the gooseflesh all over her petrified body. She had locked that door securely less than an hour ago!

Someone had unlocked it! Someone was back there in the kitchen! Shaking with terror, she darted to the Governor Winthrop desk, yanked opened the top drawer and grabbed the little revolver she kept hidden there.

Now the noise on the porch was plainer. It was unmistakably the clump and shuffle of feet! There was someone at the front door! A key was turning stealthily in the lock—the door was creaking open on protesting hinges!

Somehow Lucille's trembling limbs carried her to the living room doorway, out into the hallway, to fumble for the light button—but before she could switch it on again she heard the muffled sound of feet rushing toward her. In the black darkness she could sense someone or something almost upon her.

Without conscious effort she pulled the trigger, and the revolver barked—once, twice—and then something flung itself upon her.

She could feel bare arms slithering around her, foul breath panting in her face, long, talon-like fingers groping for the gun. Frantically she kept it in front of her and pulled the trigger—again and again. The reports were muffled, almost drowned, by the body that pressed close against the muzzle. There was the stench of burned flesh, and then the arms relaxed their grip around her. With a moan of agony something backed off down the hallway, and then fell to the floor with a crash—just as Ellen shrieked wildly in the living room.

Lucille was on the verge of swooning when that horrified scream shrilled out and steadied her. With the revolver still clutched in her ice-hard hand, she staggered back into the room she had just left. Now it was empty.

"Ellen! Ellen!" she called frantically, but now utter silence had closed in on the house; even the wind seemed hushed and watching.

Through room after room she ran, flashing on the lights to reveal no sign of the girl who had been there only a few moments before. All of the downstairs rooms back to the kitchen. Like the others, it was empty—and now the kitchen door was securely locked—from the outside!

Cold tentacles of terror gripped her clammily, threatened to sap the last bit of wavering strength from her quaking body as she staggered back into the living room, out into that ghastly hallway. Now her fumbling fingers found the electric button, switched on the light—and she stood transfixed, staring down at the horrible creature that lay sprawled in its own blood on the floor.

The thing was a man—or what had once been a man. Almost naked, his emaciated body was little more than skeleton, an incredibly filthy sack of bones. His matted grey hair was straggly and unkempt; his nails long, dirt-encrusted talons; his boney face whiskery and grimy.

But what struck eerie terror into her soul was a certain

something in that dead face that told her this was no ancient derelict. The wide forehead, the well-molded nose, the sensitive lines that could still be detected around the thin mouth—beneath the grime and neglect were evidence aplenty that this repulsive looking creature was really a young man. A young man prematurely and horribly aged. A young man who had once been cultured and brilliant . . .

Who was he? How had he been reduced to that shocking condition?

As she stared down at the dead face, the chill fingers of apprehension stole around her heart and seemed to slow its beat. Suddenly Mournful Mary's croaking voice rang in her terrified brain:

"Brilliant men they were—but where are they now? One by one they disappeared only the good Lord knows where!"

Chapter Two

Dying Warning

Almost inarticulate with terror, Lucille managed to reach the telephone, managed to make the operator understand that she wanted to talk with the glass works. Interminably she sat with the receiver glued to her ear, while every shadowy corner of the room seemed to spawn ghastly creatures like that one lying out in the hallway.

She could hear the operator ringing, could hear the buzz of the glass works phone—but there was no answer. Keith must be there, at work in the laboratory, but she could not reach him, could not call him to her aid. She was altogether alone . . .

Instinctively her mind flashed to John Havelock, and she asked the operator to call his number.

Havelock was the outstanding alumnus of the Beauchamp laboratory, a brilliant young inventor who had outgrown the glass works and Arondale. His inventions had made him a fortune and he now had an elaborate laboratory of his own in New York, but sentiment still held him to the town in which he had made his success. He still kept his old house on the hill and occasionally spent a few days in it.

Those days had come to mean more to Lucille than she was willing to admit. Left alone so continually by Keith, she had found sympathy and understanding in Havelock. Wrapped up as he was in his work, the inventor still knew how to interest a woman, how to take her mind off her troubles, how to be tender—With a little shiver of trepidation Lucille had asked herself just how much John Havelock meant to her; whether she had made a tragic mistake in marrying Keith and if this was the inevitable awakening . . .

Her heart leaped with relief when his questioning voice came over the wire, when it lifted with pleasure as he discovered who was calling him—and then filled with quick concern when he heard her gasp out an incoherent account of what had happened.

"Stay where you are," he clipped firmly. "I'll be right over."

But once she had put the receiver back on the hook the wind howled dismally and a thousand eyes seemed to be peering in at her from the black rectangle of the shadeless window. As she stared around the terror-haunted room she knew that she could not stay there alone in the house with that horrible corpse! Anything was better than to sit there helplessly while the unknown thing that had carried off Ellen came back and seized her also.

She *couldn't* do that! She would get out, run to meet Havelock. Fearfully she picked her way past the gruesome thing in the hall, and then flung out through the front door, to go racing down the street as if all the fiends of hell were pursuing her.

She was more than halfway to Havelock's house before he met her and gathered her under the protection of his overcoat, to hold her trembling and sobbing in his arms.

"You'll catch your death of cold!" he scolded as he led her back to the house. "Running around on a night like this without a hat or a coat—and then you'll wonder why you come down with pneumonia—"

Lucille hardly felt the cold. It meant nothing to her, nothing compared to that grisly thing she had left lying in the hall. Her skin seemed to crawl as Havelock led the way over the threshold, into the hallway—and then her staring eyes threatened to pop out of her head!

It was gone! The hall was empty! There was no sign of the corpse! No sign of the revolver she remembered having dropped beside the telephone!

Room after room they searched the house, but the corpse had vanished as completely as if it had never been there. Even the bloodstains appeared to be gone from the dark brown hall carpet. It was as if she had imagined the whole thing—and as he looked up into Havelock's eyes she read doubt and concern in them. He thought that she was hysterical—thought that her mind was slipping!

"He was lying right there on the floor, halfway to the door," she repeated as if to convince herself as well as Havelock. "I saw him, John. I knelt right down beside him. He was dead—he couldn't have moved—and he's gone. Oh, I *did* see him, John—you must believe me!" She insisted as Havelock gently patted her shoulder. "I'm not—not crazy. He *was* there—and Ellen is gone. How do you account for that?"

"Probably went out to hunt for you," Havelock shrugged, "if you're sure she didn't go for a walk and leave you alone in the house? You've been alone entirely too much the last few months, that's the trouble; your nerves are mighty close to the snapping point. Before I do another thing, I'm going to take you over to Dr. Eldon."

"I don't need a doctor," Lucille begged. "We can't take time for that while Ellen may be—may be dying!"

"You're trembling like a leaf, and if you don't look out you'll be the one who is dying," Havelock overruled, and five minutes later he had her in Dr. Eldon's office.

"Nerves more than anything else," the physician pronounced after he had taken her pulse and examined her. "I'll give you a sedative—something to quiet your nerves and bring your pulse down to normal."

"But, doctor, it isn't my nerves," she protested. Then she was telling him everything, from the first eerie noise to the discovery of that incredibly empty hallway where a ghastly corpse should have been lying.

Keenly his wise old eyes probe hers as she babbled on. Understandingly he nodded his head.

"This isn't the first time I've heard a tale like that," he admitted. "Paul Beauchamp ought to be ashamed of the way he works those young fellows of his and keeps them away from their wives. Some day one of them will go out of her mind, and then Beauchamp will wake up."

But it wasn't Beauchamp, Lucille knew. Keith's hours were not too long; all this overtime work was for himself—devoted to this invention which he would not discuss other than to assure her that it would prove to be the wand that would turn everything into gold for them.

"Next we'll hunt up that husband of yours," Havelock decided as they left the doctor's office and started for the glass works.

The long, low buildings that housed the Beauchamp plant were dark and silent when Havelock routed out a watchman and got him to admit them. The great, shed-like shops through which they passed were only dimly lighted overhead and reflected the dull glow of the banked furnaces. Through the empty shops to the laboratory at the rear of the first floor; but it, like the rest of the plant, was dark and deserted. Keith was not there.

"Probably he started for home while we were at the doctor's," Havelock hazarded as they turned from the empty rooms—but Lucille was puzzled and uneasy, and her alarm was tinged with vague, hardly definable suspicion.

It was still too early for Keith to be quitting work; he never came home until much later than this. And there was the telephone call she had tried to get through to him. If Keith had been there he should have gotten it, for after regular hours the wire was connected directly with the laboratory . . .

When they got back to the house it was as she expected:

Keith was not there. There was no answer to her ring and she opened the front door with her key, while her pulses started to pound and she steeled herself for another glimpse of that terrifying hallway.

"I don't like the idea of leaving you here alone, Lucille," Havelock hesitated on the porch. "Perhaps I'd better go in with you and wait until Keith comes home. Maybe—"

Suddenly he stopped short—and in the silence that followed the night seemed to be filled with stealthy sounds. Dimly in the darkness Lucille saw low-crouched figures scurrying across the porch, saw one of them leaping at Havelock. Frantically she screamed a warning, but before he could whirl around to defend himself it had fastened itself on his back; long skinny arms were wrapping around his neck, choking him.

In the same instant clutching hands grabbed at her, sharp talons dug cruelly into her flesh. About her she could hear the slither of bare skin, could smell the stench of unclean bodies. The creature she had killed in the hall must have come back and brought with him his fellows from the pit of hell!

Lucille's frightened scream rose to a shrill crescendo of blind terror.

As if that mad scream had conjured him up out of nowhere, the blood-smeared face of Albert Engel suddenly loomed in front of her, came lurching toward her surrounded by those grotesque demons. In hysterical panic she threw herself back, back, as far away from it as possible.

Now the porch had become a wild stampede, a fantastic thing out of a nightmare. The night echoed to the slap and pound of fists, the scrape and scuffle of shoes and bare feet, the panting of labored breath. Bodies were lunging and pitching all around her, hands snatching at her, grabbing her arms—and in the midst of the pandemonium she went down, slipped to the floor in a half faint.

Feet kicked and thudded around her, trampled on her; bodies fell on her, heaved upright again to rejoin the fray—and then she was dimly aware that the struggle had ceased. The noise had quieted down to a low gasping that seemed to be right beside her.

Slowly her eyes opened and became accustomed to the darkness. The porch now seemed to be deserted and quiet except for that gasping noise close to her. Gingerly she extended a hand, and her fingers touched something warm and sticky, felt farther and identified the body of a man stretched out on the floor at her side.

Shakily she got to her feet and opened the front door, to reach inside and switch on the porch light. On the floor at her feet lay the battered, broken body of Albert Engel. His breath was coming in a gasping wheeze and death was already beginning to film his eyes, but he was trying to talk, striving desperately to tell her something. Lucille knelt down beside him, raised his head so that she could put her ear close to his bloody lips.

"Be careful—of Keith," he gasped. "There is . . . something unbelievably devilish . . . going on at the works. Beauchamp—he's gotten Keith into it. For months Keith's been working . . . to lower the melting point of glass. He's brought it down—from seven hundred degrees—to less than three hundred. That must be for diabolical purposes I can only guess at—"

Blood gurgled up in his throat, began to choke him, but he fought it down. Wildly his eyes sought hers, pleaded with her to understand—and again barely it intelligible words came through the bloody foam that fringed his lips.

"A secret passage . . . door behind the big supply cabinet . . . the rear of the laboratory . . . Push it aside—"

Horribly the death rattle sounded his choked throat. Albert Engel gasped convulsively. The figure in her arms was a corpse . . .

Chapter Three

Gold Agony

Gently Lucille lowered the bloody head to the porch floor and got to her feet. Blindly she ran through the hallway and to the telephone in the living room, gasped Havelock's number into the transmitter. Eons of breathless waiting—but there was no answer, just as she had expected. Havelock had not run out and deserted her. God only knew what those weird devils had done to him!

There was nobody else to whom she could turn for help. The other residents on the hill were comparative strangers to her—and, besides, instinctively she knew that this was not a situation in which she could call upon outside help. Keith had become involved in some unthinkable wickedness, and if he was to be saved from it she must save him herself. To bring in others might only be to betray him.

She was alone—altogether alone and on her own in that demon-haunted house. Again panic began to surge up within her, began to turn her blood to water, began to fill the shadowy room with lurking menace. Then Engel's dying words flashed back into her mind.

The secret passage he had mentioned was her opportunity, her only opportunity. It might lead her to Keith—perhaps in time to save him from the consequences of what he was doing.

Resolutely but with trembling limbs and darting eyes that peered fearfully at every patch of Stygian darkness, she ran most of the way back to the glass works, slipped past the sleepy watchman, and darted through the empty shops to the laboratory. A dim light burning above the doorway barely illuminated the room, but sufficiently to outline the big supply cabinet at its rear.

Lucille's heart sank as she saw the size and weight of that cabinet; it would take a squad of men with ropes and crowbars to budge it. As she expected, it did not even shake when she threw her weight against it. But Engel had told her to push it aside . . .

Systematically she pressed and pushed against it from every angle, went over every inch of one side without success. Then the other side, from top to bottom—and suddenly, as she pressed against a low section near the wall, it bellied in slightly and the big cabinet slid away easily and quietly before her. Behind where it had stood was a door in the white wall so snugly fitted that it was almost imperceptible. Like the cabinet, it opened noiselessly when she pressed against it—opened onto a flight of stairs that led downward into blackness.

What sort of evil den was at the foot of those steps? She didn't know—was afraid even to conjecture; but she knew that she had no choice. Perhaps Ellen was down there, help-less. Perhaps Keith was there. She must go down!

Her leg tingled as she lowered one foot to the first step. The tingle rose like cold water creeping up her body as she went down, down into the blackness. Steps that ended in a short, low passageway. Lucille groped her way along it until it ter-minated at a door.

Cautiously her icy hand found a handle, gripped it and be-gan to draw the door inward, a fraction of an inch at a time, while her wide staring eyes peered through the opened crack—and then seemed to petrify in her head, to stare with amazement and horror at the weird scene before her!

The place into which she peered was an underground crypt, a combination chapel and scientific workroom—and ghastly torture chamber! At one side was a black-draped altar with a huge skull in the center, fitfully illuminated by wavering blue flames that licked out of the open top of two smaller skulls set on each side of it. The skulls of children—of babies, those must be—she realized with a shudder that ran chillingly through her whole body.

Behind the altar, leaning negligently upon an inverted cross, was a life-size image of Satan with grinning face and shining, almost human eyes.

Satan's evil gaze was fixed on the center of the room where a weird, demoniacal looking figure, clothed from head to foot in a black robe and cowl, was busily at work over a small melting furnace that roared with intense flame. Above the furnace was a cauldron-like metal pot in which something was bubbling and stewing heavily.

But those peculiar appurtenances sank into obscurity as the crack in the doorway grew wider and Lucille stared with horrified eyes at the rest of the room's contents. Elevated above the furnace at an angle of forty-five degrees was a bed-like arrangement that she recognized as a rack—a fiendish rack on which the naked body of a young girl was stretched! Moans of awful agony came from her writhing lips and streams of blood were dripping from her body, and carried down to the cauldron.

The girl's agonized moan was echoed by a groan of utter anguish that came from the other side of the room—and now Lucille could see what appeared to be three glass cases standing in a line on the opposite side from the altar. Each was about three feet square and five feet high; in each stood a man, with only his head projecting above the top. The victims were imbedded in solid blocks of glass!

Incredulously her gaze turned back to the Machiavellian master of this infernal chamber. From beneath the black hood she caught a glimpse of an unrecognizable chalk-white face, as if the creature were a shade from beyond the grave. Intently he occupied himself with the horrid contents of his hellish crucible, utterly deaf to the moans and prayers of his victims.

And at the head of the rack was another black-robed devil!

Lucille had not noticed him before, but now she saw that he was bending over a wheel that controlled the diabolical mechanism of the contraption—that set in motion the spike-studded surfaces that were tearing the girl's back to shreds!

A gasp of horror sprang to her lips, was beaten back into her throat by her clenched fist, as the full significance of that frightful set-up burst upon her brain. Those inhuman devils were Beauchamp—and Keith! That was Keith, her husband, operating that ghastly wheel with such appalling skill!

"I know nothing about gold—nothing, I tell you!" the tortured grey-head moaned, as that hellish barbarity went on.

The rack wheel creaked, and the girl's scream cut him short—an ululating cry of excruciating agony that knifed into Lucille as if the infernal machine were tearing at her own body.

"Please!" the old man begged. "Please don't hurt her any

more. She is all that I have—and she can't stand any more
pain. She's done nothing to you—and you will gain nothing
by killing her. I tell you—"

Stony silence greeted his heart-rendering plea, but the terrible wheel stopped turning, the corners of the machine moved,
slowly inward and the girl's taut body relaxed. The black-
robed devils went to work at her ankles and wrists loosened
the cruel iron grips that had sunk deep into her flesh. Together they lifted her from the torture bed—and then turned
her over, to refasten her, *face down on the bloody spikes!*

When Lucille stared at the girl's fiendishly butchered back
a wave of nausea swept over her, threatened to overcome her.
From neck to heels it was a raw, bleeding mass of torn, lacerated flesh—a crimson horror into which the sharp spikes had
dug savagely.

And now they were biting deep into her breasts, into the
soft flesh of her unprotected stomach. Her screams pealed
from her lips in a steady stream—a shrill cacophony of pain
unendurable.

"I know what you want to know!" the frantic grey-head
screamed as the perspiration ran down his face in rivulets. "I
know what you want! I'll tell you—I'll tell you anything, tell
you everything—if only you will stop torturing her. I'll
talk—I'll talk . . ."

Without a word the black-robed monster behind the rack
left his post and stepped across the room. When he returned
he was carrying a telephone-like apparatus that he adjusted
over the old man's mouth and strapped firmly around his
head.

"Then talk!" he grated harshly, and a cold shiver ran
through Lucille and seemed to sap the strength from her
limbs, for the voice was Keith's as she had heard him once
when he was beside himself with rage!

The apparatus, she quickly saw, was the transmitter end of
a Dictaphone, connected by a wire to a cabinet at the side of
the room. Frantically the old man babbled into it. She could
barely hear the low hum of his muted voice, but from his

sweating, anxiety-twisted face, she knew that he was omitting nothing that might win mercy for his daughter.

While he talked the hellish torture stopped, but the moment his voice quieted the rack wheel began to turn afresh and the girl's screams keened out deafeningly. And that indescribably bestial torture went on uninterrupted, until her body was a ghastly thing of mangled flesh from which the last spasm of agony had been drained, the last flicker of life sapped.

The moment she died the inhuman monster who presided over the cauldron became tremendously excited. Like a mother watching her infant, he hovered over it, grasped it carefully with metal hooks that gripped its edge and, with the help of his assistant, lifted it from over the furnace and placed it in a cooling tank. Beside himself with impatience, he paced up and down continually until the cauldron was sufficiently cool to handle; until it could be upended to spill out onto the stone-topped table a hemisphere of metal about ten inches in diameter.

Eagerly he pounced upon the half ball, scrutinized it closely—and all the enthusiasm ebbed out of him.

"Lead—only lead!" he mumbled in bitter disappointment. Lucille recognized beyond a doubt the high, cracking voice of Paul Beauchamp.

But suddenly he tensed—and then fairly leaped into thin air. Frantically he ran to a nearby cabinet and grabbed up bottles of acid, scurried back to the table and began to apply their contents to the metal with trembling fingers. And then his cackling voice whooped out in a wild shout of exultant delight!

"Gold! Gold! I've made it!" he shrilled triumphantly. "See—the bottom of this precipitate is solid gold!"

Fondly his fingers parted and caressed the metal while he chortled with childish satisfaction. Proudly he held it up so that the dull eyes of his glass-imprisoned captives could gaze at it.

"My ancestor, the Compte Francois de Beauchamps, was the greatest alchemist of his time, the greatest of all history—but I have out-done him!" he crowed. "When he came back from leading Joan d' Arc's armies he set himself to discover the secret of transmutation, of turning base metals into gold. More than eight hundred people were put to death in his castle before the stupid authorities arrested and executed him. But, near as he came to the secret, he never actually achieved a perfect transmutation—although they claimed that drops of pure gold were found in the ashes of the pyre on which he was burned.

"I have followed in his footsteps. I have carried on where he left off—and now I have succeeded! I have made gold! Compte Francois pointed the way correctly—through agony . . . through ecstatic suffering the miracle is wrought. I am on the right track. A partial transmutation now means that soon I shall succeed completely. Soon anything that I drop into my crucible will be turned to gold—I will be a second Midas with a wand of gold!"

Lucille listened to his mad harangue with utter horror. The wand that would turn everything into gold—those were Keith's very words!

Chapter Four

Hell's Altar

Beauchamp's enthusiasm had risen with his gloating recital. Complete success, he was sure, was within his grasp, and he was wildly impatient to seize it. From his helpless auditors he whirled toward a door at one end of the underground chamber.

"Bring in the new one!" he shouted loudly. "We'll strike while the iron is hot—and this time our success will be one hundred percent!"

From the side room two degenerate wrecks of men, even more repulsive looking than the one Lucille had killed in the hall of her home, came in response to that command. After them they dragged a rolling platform on which Ellen Craig crouched in a position of utter fear and horror!

Lucille stared—and her sharply indrawn breath soughed

through her tightly clenched teeth. Ellen was naked—naked and helpless! For, as the low platform was pulled into the center of the room, Lucille saw that she was covered with glass—imprisoned in a thick shell of glass.

"Oh, God! What are you going to do to me now?" she wailed, as she stared terror-stricken, around the strange room. "Please let me go! Oh, please listen to me! Please . . . Please . . ."

Her voice was rising, breaking hysterically as she must have gained some inkling of what was in store for her.

Beauchamp rubbed his hands together, and the chalk-white mouth, half revealed by the partially pushed-back cowl, was twisted in a grimace of satisfaction, twitching in eager impatience.

"Quick! Take her out of that and strap her in place!" he snapped at his groveling servants. "There is no time to lose."

While Beauchamp knelt before the black-swathed altar and indulged in hellish rites of devil-worship, the misshapen creatures beat against the glass shell with hammers. Instantly cracks spider-webbed through it, and then it fell away from Ellen's body in a thousand pieces—but before she could spring clear those dirty, talon-like hands darted out and grabbed her, lifted her bodily and carried her to the waiting rack that was still wet and warm from the body of its last victim.

"No—no! Not this! Oh, God—no!" her shrieks rang through the room as her body was stretched out on the spiked bed and fastened securely. "Oh, God Almighty—save me!" she prayed to her deity—and as a hellish obligato for her screams, came the rumble of Beauchamp's voice mouthing the unholy names of the Prince of Evil. Eagerly he took the short, thick leaden ingots which his assistant handed him and placed them in the crucible, set it back in position over the furnace and turned on the hissing, roaring flame.

From a drawer of the Pandora's box that served him as a cabinet he lifted a hypodermic syringe, filled it from one of the bottles the closet contained, and walked over to where Ellen lay sobbing and pleading. Quickly he jabbed the needle

into her taut arm, emptied the loaded barrel into her veins—
and instantly the girl became a writhing, squirming mad
woman.

"I'm burning!" she screamed as she threshed on the sharp
spikes and drove them, unheeded, into her flesh. "Oh, God—
my whole body is on fire!"

The muscles of her splendid body stood out like bands of
steel as she strained in her agony. And then the devilish
wheel at the side of the rack began to turn, set in motion the
half dozen spike bristling rollers that ate into her back as they
revolved—with Beauchamp's assistant operating it skillfully
so as to inflict the utmost pain.

Incredulous with the sheer horror of what she saw, Lucille
watched the monster she knew was her own husband. What
had Beauchamp done to him? By what ungodly machinations
had he succeeded in transforming what had once been a lov-
able, considerate man into a callous murdering fiend?

Something snapped in her reeling brain as she heard Ellen's
tortured screams and saw the blood spurt from her wounds
and start down the drains to the waiting crucible. Unmindful
of her own peril, she flung herself through the doorway and
into that underground inferno.

"Keith! Keith!" she heard her own voice screaming wildly
as she sped toward the rack. "Stop it, Keith—*stop it!*"

Startled, the hooded figures whirled, chalk-white faces that
were a pallid blur beneath the cowls glared at her; but instantly wily old Paul Beauchamp grasped the situation—and
met it.

"Stop her!" he spat an order to those shriveled wrecks of
men. "Grab her and tie her up!"

Midway to the rack they intercepted her; their bony arms
wrapped around her like grisly spider legs and smothered her
frantic struggles. Heedless of her pleas, they dragged her to a
stout chair, threw her into it and lashed her securely to its
legs and back.

To make certain that she was securely tied, the black-robed
assistant left his post at the torture wheel and came to her

side, tested the knots and nodded with satisfaction.

"Keith!" she panted as he bent over her. "Listen to me, Keith! Look at me—*please,* darling!"

But he ignored her pleas. Only his hands strayed over her body—and their touch was sensuously caressing. As they followed the ropes across her breasts she caught a glimpse of the square-set ruby ring she had given him for a birthday present—and again she burst into sobbing pleas.

A hellish chuckle, deep in his throat, was his only answer—and he turned back to grasp the wheel and start turning it slowly, slowly downward. Hours and hours that frightful ordeal seemed to take—hours and hours of screams and groans, of tearing flesh and running blood. Once the ghastly room blurred before her eyes and she knew that she was fainting—but when she came back to her senses the horribly mutilated thing that had been Ellen Craig was still twisting and squirming on the blood dripping spikes. Hours and hours before merciful death was able to put an end to her agony.

Again Beauchamp was hovering over his cauldron, waiting until the last breath had gasped from his victim's lips before he lifted the crucible from the furnace and set it to cool. Again he was feverishly testing the half-ball of metal that clumped out onto the tabletop.

"Gold!" he breathed softly. "Better than last time! Nearly half of it is pure gold!" Then his voice rose, shrill and wildly excited, as he shouted to his assistant, "We're going on with the work!" To the cringing animated skeletons, "Clear the rack! Put this new one in place! Hurry—there's no time to lose!"

Lucille had been tugging away constantly at the ropes that bound her, had succeeded in partially freeing her hands, but she needed much more time to liberate herself. And now the hooded assistant was at her side, was beginning to tear at her clothing as the slave creatures lifted her from the chair and held her before him.

Hopelessly her glance darted around that fearful place, even though she knew that there was no faintest hope of aid or mercy from its denizens.

Quick, panting breath came from beneath the cowl that was right in front of her, as Keith's hands ripped open the neck of her dress and his fingers came in contact with her naked flesh. They caressed it lingeringly, sensuously—and then froze where they were while he turned to peer behind him.

Behind the altar, behind the life-size image of Satan, a commotion had started. The snapping of wood, the scrape of feet—and Lucille suddenly realized that the staring eyes were blank; were empty holes in the diabolical face! For a moment the image swayed, tottered, and then tumbled headlong as the bound, gagged figure of Keith Jordan pitched after it and rolled helplessly on the floor!

That barbarous monster in the black gown wasn't Keith! Her husband had been tied hand and foot and imprisoned behind that image, forced to stare out through its eyes and watch the hell that was going on there—the hell that his own wife was blaming on him!

A tremendous weight seemed to lift from Lucille's shoulders as the full significance of what had happened dawned upon her. In that crazily ecstatic moment she wanted to laugh. But her humble, apologetic eyes sought Keith's.

"I'm sorry, darling!" she half-whispered; and in the depths of his dark eyes she read the message he was unable to speak—he understood.

Savagely Beauchamp's bestial assistant pounced on him and dragged him to his feet.

"All right! If you won't stay put we'll fix you so that you'll have no choice!" he snarled thickly.

Back into the chair the slaves dropped Lucille while they went to the black-robed devil's assistance. Mute with horror, she watched as Keith's clothing was stripped from him, as he was pinioned to the floor and his body was anointed with a thick, salve-like oil.

Then, while the slaves held him upright and cowered as far as possible from him, Beauchamp's assistant came forward gripping the nozzle of a metal hose that was attached to what seemed to be a pressure tank. Deliberately he twisted the nozzle, and a fine spray sizzled from it and began to coat Keith's body glisteningly from throat to feet.

That was molten glass they were spraying on him! Lucille watched with staring eyes that would no longer close as the coating of glass thickened until the slaves released him and he stood imprisoned helplessly in a casing of glass.

Only his head was free, and now the gag was ripped from between his jaws—to release a flood of pent-up curses and maledictions the moment he recovered the use of his mouth.

"Engel, you dirty skunk!" he shouted at the black-robed assistant. "You needn't hide behind that hood—I know who you are! I've been wise to your slimy game for some time! I've been watching, waiting to trap you red-handed, but you were too devilishly cunning for me. You want my wife, I know that—and now you've got us both—"

Engel! Lucille was sure that she had seen Albert Engel's dead body lying on the floor of the hallway. But it had disappeared—vanished unaccountably. Perhaps, after all, she had been tricked . . . Engel, she knew, was fond of her. Often she had surprised him eyeing her hungrily.

That was why those fingers had run over her naked flesh so lasciviously a few moments ago . . .

Purposefully she twisted and squirmed, wriggled her body beneath the ropes until she managed to drop the torn dress down from her left shoulder so that it fell nearly to her waist, completely revealing the rounded contour of one naked breast. Deliberately she ripped a bit of the cloth—and the black hood turned full face toward her.

Beneath its shadowing brim she caught a glimpse of a chalk-white mask of a face, of burning eyes that were fixed on her bosom, but now Paul Beauchamp reached the end of his patience.

"Enough of this!" he cried irritably. "We've wasted time enough! Put her on the rack and let us get to work. I am ready!"

With a rush the scurrying slaves were at her side, were pulling her up from the chair—and Lucille saw the gates of ghastly death opening wide to receive her!

Chapter Five

Desperation Stake

"I don't know what you want, Beauchamp," Keith turned to the robed figure at the furnace, "but I'll do anything you say. I'll slave here for you the rest of my life—without pay, without anything—if only you will let her go! I can't tell you anything about this hellish alchemy you're practicing; I don't know anything about it. If you think I do you've been misinformed—tricked by Engel, there, who is using you so that he can have my wife."

But his pleas lost their earnestness, lost their conviction, as he realized that they were hopeless; realized that nothing he could do or say would have any effect on those inhuman fiends.

And then her view was cut off as the cowled assistant loomed in front of her, as his hands reached down and seized her dress, tore it in tattered rags from her body. Again she could sense the passion that pounded in his veins; could detect the sharp intake of his breath, the surreptitious caress of his clamp fingers as he stripped the undergarments from her limbs while the slaves finished untying the ropes that held her ankles and wrists.

He was her one slim chance—the last feeble ray of near-hope for herself and for Keith . . .

Deliberately she pressed her warm body against his hands tantalizingly, while she smiled invitingly at the white mask of which she could see only part under the folds of the cowl. Wantonly she contorted and exposed herself in a way that no man could resist—and then, suddenly, she had slipped free of the clutching talons that gripped her and was in his arms.

"Stop, Lucille, stop! You can't do that!" Keith's protests rang in her ears as he divined her purpose. "You can't give yourself to that filthy beast—not even for our lives!"

Lucille steeled herself to the horror in his voice and pretended not to hear. The lips beneath the cowl were close to hers; the eager hands were moving caressingly over her slim figure. If she could only reach the beast in this man—could capture and hold it for a few minutes . . .

But Paul Beauchamp would stand no more delay. With a snarl of impatient anger he ran across the room and grabbed her arm, yanked at her brutally and started to tug her toward the waiting rack.

Frantically she clung to the man in her arms, glued her lips to his in a kiss of utter abandon—and the arms around her stiffened, held her back as Beauchamp tried to tear her away!

With a scream of rage the glass works owner threw himself at his assistant. The hood flew back from his bald head and his round, pudgy face, daubed from ear to ear with chalky white paint, was twisted into a grotesque mask—like a circus clown pretending emotion. But there was no pretense about the eyes that flared out from between the white lids. They were the eyes of a madman.

Like the darting paw of a cat his arm snaked out, clawing fingers reaching for the face of the man who had dared to resist him. Triumphantly they ripped the edge of the cowl to bare the whitened features not of Albert Engel, but of John Havelock!

Havelock's eyes were grim—hard, murderous eyes that seemed to blaze with devilish fire as they glared out of his set, white face. Without a sound his fist swept up from his side and crashed with savage force into Beauchamp's face— to send him staggering back against the wall before he collapsed in a still heap.

Lucille's desperate gamble had succeeded, but now fresh fear gnawed at her pounding heart. Had she gone too far— overplayed her hand? Havelock's arms were around her; his hands were pawing her boldly; his lips were ravishing hers bestially. In vain she tried to hold him off, to evade his hot mouth. Helplessly she was lifted in his strong arms. He was going to carry her off—where?

That question was answered all too quickly, when Havelock set her down on the rack! Firmly he held her there while the slaves obeyed a nod of his head and rushed forward to secure her hands and feet!

Keith was shouting amazed recognition. Beauchamp was moaning as he groveled on the floor. Vaguely Lucille heard them—but it was John Havelock who held her attention, held her fascinated.

The John Havelock whose company she had enjoyed, whose sympathy she had welcomed. Now all the warmth had gone out of his kind, understanding eyes. They had become hard and coldly calculating, narrowed slits of icy slate grey.

"Havelock," Keith was repeating the name wonderingly. "Then it isn't the secret of gold transmutation that you're after. Such folly wouldn't interest you—"

"No" the inventor laughed contemptuously. "I am interested in something far more practical and valuable than that. Beauchamp, the poor, doddering old fool, thinks he's been making gold because he melted down the bars I carefully prepared for him—bars of lead with cores of gold. He's been having a great time torturing and murdering people; helping me to extort their secrets from men he thought were would be alchemists like himself. Actually, I have been very carefully picking his victims—his assistants in the laboratory upstairs—picking promising inventors who had something worth divulging—"

"And you've been taking advantage of his crazy obsession to rob innocent men of their secrets and their formulas— stealing their life's work from them in their agony!" Keith flung at him, as he began to understand the full extent of the man's fiendish depravity. "You've been giving them to the world as your own—making a fortune and an international reputation on the inventions you looted from the suffering brains of their creators!"

"Quite correct;" Havelock agreed complacently. "Then I make docile morons of them—like the ones I sent to kidnap Lucile and Ellen tonight. She shot one of them before I changed my tactics." He grinned boastfully. "But unfortunately the game is about over. Too many men of science have been disappearing with their wives or daughters. So tonight will be the wind-up. But before I close up shop I intend to have the formula for pliant glass which I happen to know you have perfected.

"Many of the men who died in this room took days to accomplish it, Jordan—days of watching their loved ones dying by inches while they stood there helpless in their glass prisons. But there isn't time for that now. So you're going to talk in a hurry—or you will stand there and watch your wife in my arms before I torture her to death on that rack! Make up your mind in a hurry."

As he spoke he took hold of the wheel at the side of the rack, twisted it—and the corner sections of the apparatus slid out until Lucille was spread eagled so cruelly that her bones seemed ready to snap out of their sockets. Another turn—and the bed of the hellish contraption sank until the blood-clotted rollers beneath it were against her skin; until the sharp spikes were eating into her soft flesh!

The agony of those sharp points was almost unendurable. Her senses swam under it in a red haze. Through it she could see Havelock, now without his cowl and robe, coming toward her; could see him climbing up onto the apparatus beside her.

Lust and evil desire gleamed hotly in his eyes, as he stared down at her nakedness—and then he was taking her in his arms. She could feel his weight upon her, driving those hellish spikes deeper and deeper into her bleeding body.

Then her mouth was open—open until her wide-stretched lips threatened to split: and out of her straining throat came a shriek that seemed to go on and on and on. Deafening it rang in her ears—seemed to blend with the red haze that enveloped her. Endlessly, until another noise broke through it, roared above it. That was Keith's voice; she recognized dully, Keith's voice . . .

"You win, Havelock!" he was shouting frantically. "I'll talk! I'll tell you anything you want to know!"

Keith's voice . . . She heard it rambling on, carefully dictating the technical details of a scientific formula. Now the agony had lessened. Havelock's body was no longer pressing her down onto the spikes. He was standing in front of Keith, carefully taking down every word in a memo-book.

At last he was finished. With a nod of satisfaction he slipped the book into his pocket and came back to the rack, back to that awful wheel; but this time when he turned it the spikes receded and the corners moved inward. Gradually they released her agonized limbs.

"I really didn't intend to go through with it and kill you," he grinned down at her. "I was quite confident that my bluff would work—and one of the sweetest rewards I have been promising myself is that lovely body of yours—but under more comfortable circumstances than this. This underground room is all wired, ready to be blown up so that what went on down here will never be discovered. The explosion will be attributed to an accident, and that will be the end of it. But you won't be here when that happens. I'm taking you to my own house. For the past few months I've seen that you no longer love your husband, Lucille. You will soon forget him—after the explosion—and as my wife you will have all the luxury and entertainment you' desire."

Lucille tried to struggle, tried to break away from him, but she was helpless in his arms when he lifted her off the rack and started with her toward the floor above. With brimming eyes she looked back at Keith—and utter despair over whelmed her as she realized that this was the last time she would ever see him.

The last flicker of hope died within her as they reached the door and Havelock stooped to slide a tiny switch that was concealed in the wall paneling. The mechanism that would wipe out that hell hole was in motion! Once through that portal there would be nothing that anyone could do for Keith— but just as Havelock's hand gripped the door handle old Paul Beauchamp summoned the desperate strength to leap to his feet.

"Lies! All lies!" he shouted madly. "I heard your lies—but I know better! I, Paul Beauchamp, have discovered the secret of transmutation that men have sought all through the ages— and now you are trying to rob me of it! But you shan't—you shan't—"

In a frenzy he flung himself upon Havelock, and his old

limbs seemed suddenly endowed with superhuman strength a he rained blows on the man he was sure intended to defraud him. Havelock had to give ground under that berserk assault, had to release Lucille so as to defend himself.

At last she was free—but what could she do? Helplessly she watched as Havelock sparred for an opening and then dived in to secure a deadly grip on the old man's throat, a grip that tightened relentlessly. Frantically she tried to free Keith, but her hands were useless beating against the thick glass shell, and there was nothing that she could find to use as a hammer.

"Run!" Keith pleaded again and again. "You can still get away, darling—and there's nothing you can do for me. Please—"

Paul Beauchamp's limp body dropped to the floor—and Havelock turned, started back to recapture her . . .

He was only a few yards away when Lucille put all of her strength into a running charge that hit Keith at the waistline and toppled him over onto the floor. The crash and tingle of breaking glass was sweet music in her ears as she leaped over his prostrate form and threw herself at Havelock. Tightly she wrapped a her arms around him, to cling to him desperately until he brutally tore them loose and knocked her aside.

But that was all the time Keith needed. Like a leaping hound he came up from the floor, and his right fist, still encased in its glove of glass, pounded into Havelock's face. Blood spurted from the mangled features and Havelock staggered back, but he was not finished. With a bull-like bellow he catapulted himself at Keith, took another punishing smash to the face but got his clutching arms around his enemy and pitched with him to the floor.

Now Keith's glass-swatched fists were a handicap rather than a help. Havelock hunched his head down between his shoulders and avoided them while his fingers sought constantly for Keith's throat. Over and over they rolled—and in the rolling the glass gloves were cracked and battered, transformed into jagged knives that ripped the fiend's face to a bloody pulp; that slammed him back, squealing for mercy, onto the wicked shards of glass that littered the floor where Keith had fallen.

In a hundred places the razor edges cut into his body before a jagged spear point sliced into his jugular and sent his life-blood gushing and spurting over the sizzling cauldron that had been fed by so many of his victims.

Dazedly Keith staggered to his feet when Lucille tugged at his arm and shouted into his ear. Frantically she urged him through the doorway and up the stairs into the laboratory, out into the empty shop before the whole rear of the glass works rose from its foundation and then crashed to the earth in a terrific detonation.

Thrown flat on the floor by the force of that blast, Keith got to his knees and crawled to where Lucille lay. Anxiously he cradled her in his arms until her eyes fluttered open—and then his lips were crushed to hers. In the fervor of that embrace they both knew that they had refound something they had lost—something that was infinitely precious and worth all they had endured to reclaim it!

HER SUITOR FROM HELL

SOMETIMES AT NIGHT, when a high moon glints on the surface of that dark pool where first I encountered the shrinking death, doubt and terror cleave my brain with their dagger-strokes, and I despair of ever regaining my normal physique and health. Sometimes in my sleep I seem to feel again the hideous torpidity of mind, the loathsome human fluidity of bone and muscle, that rendered me an inert jellyfish shrunken to the a proportions of a child. But science yet may save me . . .

We were celebrating my thirtieth birthday, here at the old Louisiana plantation where our family, the Paynes, have lived for a century past. On every hand the grounds are guarded by a barrier of forbidding swamps through which a hard road leads to various plots of high land now cultivated by white tenants, once tilled by my grandfather's black slaves. During the year since Grace and I were married the old manor house had been modernized in various ways, and foremost among improvements was a gleaming, white-tiled outdoor swimming pool designed to take the curse off torrid summer days.

When the scorching sun had dropped behind a surrounding wall of moss-draped cypress trees, Grace proposed a cooling dip. Although our guest. Doctor Hemerich Koop, made some small objection, soon we coaxed him into a bathing suit and led him to the brink of the inviting basin. Grace ran to the end of the springboard, her delicately molded form poised as lightly as a mocking bird's upon a swaying bough. Arcing through the air in a clean dive that sent drops sparkling upward, she rose to the surface laughing and called:

"Come in! It's delightful!"

Then, her face sobered as she floated there regarding the

two of us with thoughtful eyes.

I sensed the comparison she was making and knew the reason. Doctor Koop, whom I had employed, ostensibly to manage a small private hospital upon the plantation for the benefit of tenant families, but actually to safeguard the health of my bride, was one of her school day lovers whose doglike devotion had endured through adolescent years. As one of an adoring dozen she had given his aspirations no serious thought until, with college behind him and a profitable profession ahead, he proposed marriage and she told him it could not be.

With disarming candor she had confessed that she wanted a husband whose physique would match her own bodily health and strength; because she desired numerous children and there must be no heredity taints that might prevent the growth of tall sons and lovely daughters.

Koop's years numbered the same as mine, but I stood six feet two in my stockings and tipped the scales at two hundred weight. He was a scrawny man of five feet four and a childhood injury had left his back slightly hunched. Beneath his bulging brow dwelt a brain whose keenness mine probably never would attain, although I did well enough at managing the estate.

Hemerich Koop also guessed the tenor of her thoughts. Smiling, he said heartily:

"What a gorgeous pair of animals you are! In with you, Ralph, and have your fun. I'll sit and watch."

With the sense of something akin to pity I plunged, sympathizing with the hopelessness of his plight, yet selfishly glad in the knowledge that his fondness for Grace would result in especially watchful care. That meant a great deal to a young couple expecting to raise a family in the depths of a swamp forty miles from the nearest city.

It meant more than that to me, five minutes later, when a monstrous face was thrust out of a clump of shrubbery a few yards away and the idiot, Pedro, began snarling obscene Spanish oaths which frightened Grace into a fit of trembling hysteria.

Following a final gust of vile curses Pedro hurled some curiously shaped object which splashed into the pool near where Grace clung to me. Then he scuttled into the swamp before I could call a servant to catch him.

I held my wife in my arms, sitting upon a bench beneath the pergola, while Koop ran to the house for his small black bag. Returning, he gave her a sedative. Between us we strove to calm her fears, insisting that the half-wit's outburst was meaningless, but still terrified she cried:

"He has grown more bold! It has a dreadful meaning! That old crone, Zell Mendez, is slowly goading him to the point of murder. They mean to *kill you,* Ralph, because of the accident that crippled him."

I laughed the idea aside, but even Hemerich Koop's dark-browed face betrayed deep concern. Uneasily, he said:

"All the tenants talk of the threats Zell Mendez makes against you. They fear her curses. Superstitiously, they believe that she is in league with the devil. Sometimes, I wonder. Sorcerers have performed strange deeds which science cannot fathom."

"For God's sake, Koop!" I exclaimed. "You don't mean that you believe in such twaddle?"

He smiled, grimly. "Not as witchcraft, if that's what you're thinking. But we live in a swamp, Ralph, and I must con fess that some of the secrets of swamp herbs and poisons handed down from one generation of voodoo practitioners to another have not yet been solved by the medical profession. Did you read, last spring, of the man in Bay St. Louis whose stature is slowly shrinking? Who has been dwarfed to the size of a child from a height of six feet? Not only is he said to be suffering from a curse, but similar cases have been recorded in Barbados and in Porto Rico. It *makes* one wonder—"

Angrily, I seized the bottle of brandy he had brought from the house and gulped a steadying drink. Grace said, tearfully:

"Why should she blame you, that old, old witch, for an accident that was unavoidable? Three people swore that Pedro Mendez darted out of the brush, squarely in front of your car—"

"Forget it, dear," I said, inwardly shuddering at the recollection of a stunning impact, the sickening crunch of flesh under heavy wheels, the screams of the stricken idiot when my speeding roadster felled him. "Doctor Koop did everything possible for the poor fellow. And neither Pedro's curses, nor his mother's, will mend his crooked legs nor harm us."

Hemerich Koop was looking toward the glassy surface of the pool.

"What did he throw at you when he was swearing there? I saw something queer splash—"

"I'll see." Standing on the brink I scrutinized the white bottom, saw a small blue bottle lying in the deep end exuding an inky cloud. "There it is. I'll fetch it up."

I dived. The immersion cooled my excited blood instantly. But, even as I enjoyed the pleasant sensation, blighting fear struck home. *Cooled me?* I felt chilled to the bone! My limbs seemed frozen. Neither arms nor legs function. In a state of complete paralysis I glided to the bottom. The air in my lungs slowly raised me to the top but I hung face downward, helpless. By no force of will could I command the movement of a single muscle.

When my tortured lungs rebelled and I could no longer forestall the gasp which filled them with water in a drowning flood, I heard Grace's shrill cry of alarm echo as from a great distance. Then a black coma enfolded me.

The time which followed was marked by vague periods of light and darkness. Occasionally, I realized that I lay in a hospital bed, that a doctor and a nurse came and went, that I had not drowned but was alive.

Days and nights passed like a blur of delirium, studded with moments of excruciating agony, broken by terrifying dreams in which the idiot's face appeared to leer at me as I suffered there, while he gibbered of escape from pain through use of some exotic drug contained in a small bottle of hellish midnight blue. At last, after an eternity of nameless terror, there came a phase of clear consciousness, yet so weak had my strange illness left me that I could not raise my heavy eyelids and, perforce, without a sign of life lay listening to the voices of Doctor Koop and Grace.

"He is wasting away to death!" My wife's anguished tone was sharp with grief. "It is Zell Mendez's curse! Ralph is doomed. You cannot save him."

"Now, now, my dear," the doctor chided. "Don't give up hope so easily. He lives! And while there's life there's hope aplenty. If only I could tell—" His voice thinned on a troubled note. "Whether this queer shrinkage is the result of a drug—or something worse—"

"You've said that before!" There was near frenzy in Grace's cry. "You, too, believe it is a curse! That old Zell Mendez has bewitched him—"

"Nonsense!" Koop snapped sharply. "Of course it must be the work of a drug. But, unfortunately, the small blue bottle which Pedro threw into the swimming pool had quite emptied itself before I went back to recover it. Analysis of water from the tank produced no satisfactory results because of great dilution. We have not yet discovered the nature of the poison."

"If Zell Mendez could be forced to tell!" Despair edged my wife's sweet voice. "I've pleaded with her, but she only laughs, showing her yellow hag's teeth in a gloating snarl, calling down still more terrible curses upon poor Ralph's head. Oh, will he ever be conscious again? Or will he die?"

Try as I might I could not open my eyes nor give any sign that life was burning more brightly within me, that all was not lost. Grace came to the bedside. I felt the warm touch of her fingers upon my cold and flaccid hand. In her stifled sob there was a note of sheer horror, the reason for which I did not then comprehend.

"Somehow you must stop this horrible thing, Hemerich!" she exclaimed. "At any cost. Call in specialists to aid you, use every resource that money can buy, before it is too late."

"My dear Grace," Hemerich Koop said, "money won't help, nor can any specialist. I am doing my best to influence the outcome of this peculiar seizure and no one could do more."

His words cheered me as I lay there a motionless, helpless hulk, for I knew the keenness of his brain, his thoroughness in seeking the solution of difficulties. If only he could contrive to ease the worries with which Grace was besieged.

They left the room together. I heard the door open and close. Then, for hours it seemed, I was plagued by visions of vicious faces leering. The unwholesome countenance of old Zell Mendez loomed above the foot of my bed, snaggle-toothed, wild-eyed, stringy grey hair straggling across her leather cheeks. I thought the broken lips mouthed venomous curses over and over, and never in life or death would she forgive the accident that had crippled her son.

Pedro's malignant visage tormented me after his mother's dimmed and faded. A moron at best, he was pop-eyed and pimply. His forehead sloped straight away in line with a long, pointed nose, and his chin receded obliquely to form a snouted face like a hog's. After my car had smashed his legs and left them but flopping clubs upon which he stumped about with the aid of two canes, Pedro's appearance was enough to frighten women and children. His witless tongue forever drolled profane obscenity.

Lying there in my torpid state, seeming to hear the foul threats he voiced, suddenly I was obsessed with fear for Grace. What if the idiot sought to vent his spleen upon her? Alone in our big house, save for black servants, she would prove easy prey for him. The thought shocked me into wakefulness. My eyes snapped open, they widened with consternation, and my jaw hung loose at sight of the ugly face peering through an open window near my bed.

"Pedro!" I gasped. "Is it you? Did I hear you talking?"

"I meant every word of it," he whispered, shrilly. "And why not? Now, you're no better than me.

"Filthy beast!" I rasped, weakly. "If I hear that you've so much as looked at Grace I'll horsewhip you. And should you attempt to molest her I'll break your back with my two hands."

"Y-a-ah! Your hands! Look at 'em and tell me how much breakin' they can ever do. You'll never get off that bed alive. Don't you know that your finish is all planned?"

Pedro loosened the screen and swung it aside. I thought he intended to clamber in and murder me but a streak of stubbornness kept me from calling aloud for help. With all the force of my will I strove to lift the hands he mentioned so contemptuously, but could not. Powerless as a babe, I demanded hoarsely:

"What do you want? What do you mean to do?"

Pedro grinned, his eyes shining redly like two mirrors of hate. His subdued laughter jangled.

"I'll do everything I said—after you're dead. She won't listen till you're gone. But now that you look worse than me, your pretty wife'll let me love her once you're out of the way."

A red haze of hate suffused my brain and for a space I could not see clearly. Then the spasm passed and I found him leaning through the aperture, balancing a tiny blue bottle upon his palm.

"Take it!" Pedro invited. "Quick death, easy death, without any pain. Ma wanted me to slip it into your grub, to make sure you die. But 'tain't worth the risk. You're dyin' now. Take it, yourself, so your wife'll quit cryin' about you and listen to me."

"Get out!" I raged. "Go away from that window before I yell for help. I'll have you shot—"

Pedro drew back hurriedly.

"That ain't no way to act," he complained, "after I came to do you a favor. Here! I'll leave the bottle in this corner. Nobody'll see it and you'll want it soon." He refastened the screen.

After a long, gloating look at me Pedro disappeared. A low-flung shaft of light from the setting sun glinted upon the blue bottle and I stared, fascinated, wondering if in truth I might soon want the poison.

Why had the idiot: "Now that you look worse than

me . . .?" I remembered Doctor Koop's comment concerning a strange "shrinkage" that puzzled him. Did he mean my skin, the wasting of my flesh? I shuddered at thought of freakish human skeletons I had seen, struggled in a blinding effort to gain control of my limbs, almost succeeded.

After I had fallen back, gasping, upon the pillow a harrowing fear possessed me. Something was horribly wrong! I must get up and away! To Grace . . .

What the ensuing effort to rise cost me in mental strain and mortal agony only God can realize. If there be such a thing as actual power of mind over matter, then it was that which, in the end, gave me command of my muscles again. Striving to the point of deadly nausea, beset in every joint by dreadful pains which nearly drove me mad, at last I forced myself to a sitting position, swung my legs down from the bed. Clinging to the white iron framework I made an effort to stand, although at first my knees buckled miserably.

Dimly, I perceived the door of a closet across the room. On hands and knees I crawled to it, seeking a robe or other covering for my nakedness. I reached for the knob three times and failed, before I could draw myself erect. Swaying there, I found inside a suit of my clothes which Grace must have brought as a childish means of bolstering hope that one day I would wear them home. Dragging garments from the hooks I crawled back to the bed again. After a grueling ordeal of rising and seating myself, I drew on the dark grey trousers and managed to stand. Dazedly I stared down at their absurd length, noting that the legs were *at least a foot too long!* Fumbling in the pockets I found a familiar purse. Yes, indubitably they were mine. Turning a little, then, I caught a glimpse of my reflection in the glass of a window that was closed. A cry of horror burst across my lips at sight of the revolting figure there darkly revealed.

A dwarfed and hairless monstrosity! My bald skull bulked far too large for the scrawny neck and stunted frame which supported it. Deepset eyes were gloomy caverns beneath my brow. My nearly fleshless jaws were those of a Death's head. Lips paper thin and tightly drawn.

My broad shoulders had narrowed and were hunched like those of a deformed child. My long and powerful legs were shrunken to spindling, bony shanks from which the last vestige of strength was swiftly ebbing.

Staring at the odious reflected shape I felt my reason sway. Loosing a rendering scream I toppled upon the floor and sank into a bottomless abyss of blackness in which my sufferings were extinguished with the appalling slowness of creeping death.

But I lived. When next I knew that death's groping clutch had missed me, it was to find myself again reposing in the hospital bed. The voices I heard, and the spoken words, dispelled an awful lethargy which gripped my brain but did not break the chains of weakness that shackled my leaden limbs.

"Ah, God! I can't bear to look at him." It was my wife's despairing cry. "No curse has done this! It is the poison." I listened to her muffled sobs of horror.

Doctor Hemerich Koop was speaking but I could not distinguish the things he said. When my eyes flicked open I saw that he held Grace in his arms and was whispering with lips pressed close against her golden hair. She broke away and whirled to face him, her cheeks flushed with anger and dismay.

"You dare say such things to me! While Ralph lies dying—"

"As well say 'dead' my dear, for soon he shall be. And even though I were to keep him alive, would you not choose me small and ugly though I am, in preference to the jellylike thing which was once a man? Ah! He is watching us! See him quivering there like a viscous blob upon the sheet."

"You demon!" Grace screamed in chattering frenzy. "Not Zell Mendez—but you! *You* did this—"

"And why not? He stole your love from me."

"As though I ever could have loved a hunched and evil creature!"

"I am a man!" Koop thumped his narrow chest proudly. "I am active and strong. My brain is fine. Look, now, at the one who thought himself superior. Is not Ralph Payne a disgusting sight? He little resembles that 'father of tall sons and lovely daughters' of whom you boasted."

Grace approached on laggard feet and stood beside my bed. Tears streaming, she touched my torpid arm, my bony face, crying bitterly:

"I love him! His soul lives despite the ruin you've made of his magnificent body. Oh, what have you done to him? What blight have you wrought?"

Doctor Koop came near and hatred glowed in his eyes as he grinned down at me.

"It was a master stroke," he bragged. "The strategy of using Zell Mendez and her half-wit spawn as pawns in my little game. For days on end she voiced her threats to all she met, after the accident. There are fifty witnesses to swear that she contemplated the murder of Ralph Payne and made Pedro help her plan it. Now, both are jailed, accused of poisoning your husband by contaminating the swimming pool, and no one ever shall hear of the clever operation that I performed upon his throat."

Grace stared, and so did I, my powers of speech paralyzed as yet although my tongue curled and twisted in an effort to talk.

"You operated on Ralph? Why?" My wife's eyes were round with terror. "Oh, tell me what you've done to him. Is there no cure?"

"I could cure him—but at a price you may not wish to pay. Another might, if he were skilled in the science of the glands and knew what I have done. Prevailing upon Pedro Mendez to hide nearby and toss a bottle of common poison into the pool after frightening you, I let Ralph drink of drugged liquor from a bottle I brought, knowing that we'd have to rescue him from his dive. The numbing effect of the drug I used is instantaneous. That gave me an excuse to bring him here to the hospital. With only a simple-minded Cajun girl to help I planted a globule of metallic compound at the base of the parathyroid gland where it would immediately create sufficient pressure to halt the gland's functioning. The result, as you see, was swift decalcification of his bones, a shrinking of stature, a wasting of flesh. He is like a thing of rubber and jelly, now, as death approaches."

"But he could be cured?" Grace pleaded. "Oh, say that he can be saved!"

"Of course. By removal of the pressure, and with proper treatment, in a matter of months he might regain his normal size and health. But who shall grant him that boon, my dear?"

"You shall! Hemerich! You say you love me. You must be kind. Restore him. We'll forgive and forget. Stop this madness and use your skill to make him a man again."

"You heard my terms. I mentioned a price—" Koop's smile was lecherous. He seized Grace in his arms and sought her lips. "The price is yourself—mine for always. And you must answer now!"

Never shall I forget the play of torturing emotions that swept over my dear wife's face as she fought to submerge her revulsion, to find the courage to endure an odious ordeal. She gasped:

"What do you mean—for always? Not after he is well?"

"If I grant him life," Koop said, harshly. "it must be without you, and he shall never know. At best, his mind might not be restored completely. It will do no harm to make certain of that."

Comprehending his horrible intention to render me a witless hulk endowed with life, Grace threw herself upon her knees and pleaded piteously. Roughly, Koop thrust her suppliant hands aside.

"If I only wanted you now, I'd take you. It must be of your own free will and for always."

Again, weakening, he put his skinny arms about her and pressed his repulsive lips to hers. Grace tore herself free; she struck him with her open palm, and dropped in a sobbing heap upon the bed beside me.

"Let me die with Ralph!" she moaned. "Don't touch me. Only let me die—"

Hemerich Koop's swarthy face paled greyly. I knew, then,

that he had expected victory. Failure seemed to drive him mad.

"Die? Never, you fool! I'll keep the pair of you alive so long as the spark can be held within your rotting bodies! You shall endure the same operation, Grace and in turn shall become as he is. Bones of rubber and flesh of jelly, while your brain melts in harrowing helplessness. If you love him so, you shall lie beside him and dream of the ecstasies that you will know no more."

Springing upon Grace, Koop bound her hands with a towel, likewise her ankles. Dashing out of the room he returned with a hypodermic syringe and plunged the needle into her arm. Soon my wife's frenzied struggles ceased. Removing her bonds Koop leaned across her motionless body and peered into my starting eyes.

"You know! I can read the suffering there! Both must live to suffer endlessly. While I watch over you day by day and laugh at two strong lovers who coveted 'tall sons and lovely daughters'!"

His harsh mirth echoed in the room. He opened the door and called.

"Addie! Come here!"

A dull-eyes Cajun girl appeared, fear written large upon her stupid features Koop exclaimed:

"The lady is sick. You must help me operate!"

He carried Grace out. The girl cast a frightened look at me. I thought her lips moved in soundless pity, that she felt an urge to render aid, but stark terror held her captive and she followed Koop obediently.

Once more I set my mind to the task of making the flesh obey. If only I could move, roll off the bed, crawl to the room where Grace lay helpless beneath his hellish hands. This time I could not. My greatest effort served only to elevate my head a trifling way. But in that brief instant a downward glance encompassed my shrunken legs and I groaned in trembling horror. The two limbs lay coiled awry upon the sheet like rubber tubes in which no semblance of bone remained. Koop had spoken truly. I was but a jelly like blob of slowly liquefying matter that was scarcely flesh. The shock seemed to disintegrate my brain and consciousness faded.

Grace was lying upon a bed which had been moved into the room before I awakened. Someone had turned me upon my side so that I might see her there when the torpor lifted. A white bandage encircled her throat and her eyes were wide and staring. Both wrists and ankles were caught close to the iron framework by broad straps to hold her prisoner. Her quivering lips formed a whispered query:

"Ralph! Can you hear me? Can you speak?"

For long moments I fought the rigidity of throat muscles, then croaking words grated across my dry teeth.

"Yes, I hear. Oh, God! I see—"

"He operated on me! Soon I shall be *as you are!*" The dread sentence of doom gushed out of her very soul, a gulp of anguish.

"How long?" I gasped.

"A week, he said, before the gland is seriously affected. Oh, there is no hope—"

Koop's voice sounded at the doorway. His hateful visage was framed there, grinning.

"Oh, yes there is, my dear. I might yet reconsider—if, within the week, you decide that life with me is preferable to living putrescence."

I found the strength to curse him, to utter threatening prophecies of retribution. Doctor Koop only smiled.

"You have revived considerably, as a result of treatment last night while you were unconscious. I want you stronger—that you may suffer more! While you lie there, waiting, watching."

He stepped away to Grace's bed, threw back the coverlid, tore her gown away. Lust gleamed in his hot eyes but hunger for vengeance and the will to torture prevailed. He turned aside, muttering:

"Watching! Seeing her lovely form shrivel and shrink. There'll be wrinkles and bony angles where you knew curves

and tender maiden's flesh. Love will be smothered in revulsion as you watch each other disintegrate and become two dwarfed, disgusting things with only brain cells living."

Koop went out, saying as he departed: "Soon the treatment will make you ravenously hungry, Payne. In an hour or so I'll bring you food and feed you with my own hands. For you must live! To see and suffer . . ." His brittle laughter echoed from a distance.

Grace was weeping. I could think of no cheering thing to say. Stupefied, I lay resigned to the inevitable. But soon I experienced a faint sensation of life, of circulation, in the arm which lay crushed beneath my body. Koop's remark flashed across my mind. "You will be stronger. The treatment last night—" Hope flared faintly. Strong enough to move, to crawl, to exhaust the last faint spark of life force seeking aid for Grace?

I thought of our isolated position in the swamp, then remembered the telephone. But the instrument in the outer office might as well have been miles away. Feverishly, my frantic brain struggled with the problem of what might be done if I found some vestige of strength restored. My wandering gaze paused at the nearest window. An idea sprang into being.

"Grace!" I exclaimed. "There may be a fighting chance. If you could free an arm or leg. Try it!"

Pitifully, she looked at me and shook her head, but I urged frantically:

"Try! Twist and try!"

Grace began to writhe, to tug and struggle. Faint moans of pain escaped her tight-drawn lips as the straps cut skin and flesh. At last, she said:

"I've one foot loose. But, Ralph, I can't do any more."

"Plant your heel against the wall," I cried. "Push Hard! Force your bed against mine, and shove me nearer to the window. It's only a matter of inches—"

Grace succeeded in doing what I asked. Our beds collided and the impulse of her thrust skidded my cot against the windowsill, rolling me upon my back as I made a desperate effort in that direction. Lying there, then, I tried to move my hands, found new life in the fingertips but none in my arms. Slowly, gropingly, nails scratching at the bed linen and mind savagely intent upon accomplishment, I dragged one hand in fractional jerks across the sheet onto the window ledge, and seized the tiny bottle that Pedro Mendez had hidden there.

The trivial muscular feat that followed exhausted me more than I can express. With the prize precariously clutched between thumb and forefinger I worked my hand back by the power of fingertips alone until it reached my body. Three attempts I made to raise that left arm and failed. Then, like a crawling worm, I made it creep across my chest until it met the other. In a little while, when the cold sweat of weakness beaded my brow and nearly all my strength was spent, with my right hand I laid the vial in Grace's palm. Her fingers closed upon it.

"What—"

"It means escape," I exclaimed. "Hide it!"

"I don't understand."

Her eyes sought mine. I rolled my head and whispered:

"It is *poison.*"

Doctor Hemerich Koop came later, bearing a well laden tray. His forecast was correct. I knew the pangs of hunger but the viands he carried interested me less than the bottle of wine. Placing the food upon a table, he turned to smile at Grace and said:

"You've hurt yourself struggling. One strap was poorly fastened. Why not agree to my proposals and have them all off?"

My wife looked up at him long and moodily. One could scarcely recognize her voice when, chokingly, she said:

"I can't bear it! *To be like him!* Oh, God! I can't—"

"You mean—" Doctor Koop leaned above her, eagerly. "That you have counted the cost of hopeless love for the thing that he has become?"

"My love is dead!" she stormed, hysterically. "I was faithful, I was true. But Ralph Payne is gone! There remains only

. . . that!" She swung her eyes toward me and quickly looked away.

Koop exclaimed: "Then you'll come to me? Oh, this glorious."

Awkwardly, in his haste, he fumbled at the straps which bound her. Casting them aside he caught Grace in his arms and helped her to arise.

"My dear one. My lovely one," he gloated. "Always I've watched you, wanted you. And now you are mine!"

With a shuddering sigh Grace pushed his pawing hands aside, forced a shrill laugh, crying:

"Yours I shall be, but don't ever call it love. It's the price I must pay>"

"Have it your own way," he snapped. "So long as you do pay."

"Don't be angry," Grace pleaded. "I am upset and unnerved. Perhaps a little of that wine—"

He snatched up the bottle, smiling again.

"Of course. It's just the thing!"

Pouring two glasses he raised one and turned to me in mock salute.

"Now, Ralph Payne, you'll have something more to watch. Here's to greater suffering."

Grace lowered the glass from her lips, face white as death, exclaiming:

"Drink your toast to me! Have I not deserved it?"

Koop's countenance split in an evil grin.

"You're improving, my dear! We'll get along famously."

Grace took his glass, half emptied, and gave him hers.

"The better to seal our bargain, Hemerich!" she cried, and a laugh like an echo from hell rattled upon her bloodless lips.

Koop tossed off the drink at a gulp. He started violently. A terrible tremor shook his scrawny frame from head to foot. Collapsing. He screamed:

"Poison!"

The man expired before he struck the floor. Grace crashed her glass against the wall and swayed as though she might faint.

The door opened. Addie, the Cajun girl, stood gaping there.

"I watched through the keyhole," she whispered. "Is he . . . dead?"

"Dead!" I shouted, relief strengthening the voice in my throat. "Executed just as we planned it."

"He was a devil. He put a curse on you," she mumbled stupidly.

"The telephone," I gasped, as vague fears for the future flooded into my brain. "Help my wife to it, Addie. Quickly! We must lose no time."

Grace steadied herself. Hope flamed in her eyes.

"I'll call Doctor Carondelet at New Orleans. He'll operate on us. We'll both be saved."

~ ~ ~

Perhaps we shall be. I am not yet well. But, sleeping or waking, my beloved is always near. The soft caress of her hand, the sight of her loveliness unimpaired, give me hope and courage. When gaily she measures the inches added to my stature during the month, and playfully runs slender fingers through my newly sprouted hair, I feel sure that ere the year ends I will dare appear again in the haunts of men, as tall and muscular and proudly fit as before I was stricken by the shrinking death.

DEATH ROCKS THE CRADLE

THE CHILD'S SOBBING grew fainter, lapsed into a drowsy murmur, and then was lost entirely beneath the soft crooning of a lullaby as little Abbie's blue eyes closed at last in sleep. Standing unobserved in the doorway of the nursery, Jerry Caldwell smiled indulgently as he watched the lovely picture his sister Katherine made as she bent over the cradle of her three-year-old daughter, every line of her face and posture eloquent of adoring mother love.

And then the spreading smile on his lips froze—slowly receded as his eyes clouded and a vague uneasiness stirred within him and settled chillingly around his heart.

There was something more than admiration in the avid look with which Katherine regarded the sleeping child, in the protecting way she hovered over the cradle. Instinctively Jerry sensed more than material devotion in her white, strained face. Unaccountably he saw stark terror there— haunting dread. For a moment it was as if a veil had been drawn back and he had glimpsed a soul in torment!

"Such utter devotion is not good for a woman," a thick voice whispered at his ear. "If anything should happen to that child it would mean the end of everything for Katherine."

Noiselessly Jerry backed away from the doorway and turned to face Lothar Zimmerlie, his father's associate. He had never liked Zimmerlie, and now the man's words rang ominously in his ears and at the same time stirred his resentment—just as he resented Zimmerlie's place in this household, resented the man's constant attentions to his widowed sister. Zimmerlie was almost twice Katherine's age and Jerry distrusted his motives for wanting to marry her.

"But I thought that Abbie was getting along nicely since Katherine brought her here and put her under father's care?" Jerry questioned as they walked quietly down the carpeted hallway. "What danger is there—"

"True," Zimmerlie's guttural voice cut him short. "It isn't illness. That is nothing. No, it isn't *that* we have to fear." He seemed to be talking to himself, thinking aloud. "The illness is the least of the dangers that hang over her. *That* we understand and can fight . . ."

His voice had sunk almost to a whisper, and now it trailed off into nothingness, leaving his half-uttered thoughts suspended enigmatically, tantalizingly hinting at incredible possibilities.

Again Jerry was gripped by the vague sense of uneasiness, the indefinable feeling of lurking evil, of impending calamity, that had been bothering him ever since he had arrived at the house early in the afternoon. Again he heartily regretted that he and Leta Sawyer, his fiancée, had stopped off for this over-night visit on their way to a vacation in Canada.

It was only because Dr. Eustace Caldwell, his father, had announced his intention of disposing of the family estate in order to secure more money to devote to his medical research that they had interrupted their vacation plans. This would probably be Jerry's last opportunity to visit the Adirondack Mountain home in which he had been raised—but had he suspected how greatly the atmosphere of the place had changed he never would have stopped.

It was no longer the home he had once known. Everything was subtly, indefinably changed. Not only the Caldwell estate, but the entire countryside, the whole village of Henleyville. Changed as if a cloud of blanketing horror hung over it and obstructed the sun; made men look at each other from the corners of narrowed eyes, darkly, suspiciously, hatefully.

On their way through the village that afternoon he and Leta had come face to face with that horror—and drawn back aghast. Coming out of a store with an armful of purchases Leta had suddenly stopped in midstride and caught her breath with a gasp of pity.

"Oh, the poor little thing!" had burst from her lips before she could check the words and prevent her voice from reaching the ears of the mother of the vacant-eyed little cripple who had caught her attention.

Jerry saw the woman's malignant glare turn on them, but he hardly noticed it as he stared, fascinated, at the pitiful little travesty of a child. Blank eyes gazed out of a loose, expressionless face; the mouth hung open, with drooling lips and half-protruding tongue; the head lolled from side to side as if it were too heavy to remain upright. Shamblingly, the twisted, wasted little body dragged itself along the street. What should have been a healthy three or four year old boy had become a pathetic, human scarecrow—a flower blighted just as it emerged from the bud.

Listlessly the youngster struggled along, until his dull eyes spied a Negro coming down the street. A split-second of horrified, stony staring—and then he was transformed into a shrieking, clawing obscenity, clutching frantically at his mother as if he would seek refuge in her very body!

"The black man!" he wailed almost inarticulately. "He's come to get me again—the black man! Don't let him hurt me again—oh-a-a-h—he's comin'—he's comin'!"

The panic of utter terror threw the child into a convulsion, dropped him writhing and moaning to the sidewalk. At the youngster's first screams a crowd had begun to gather, and when Jerry tried to push back, to bar the sight of the suffering child from Leta, he found that they were ringed in. Drawn, bitter faces stared down at the wriggling form.

"It's little Willis Armlin," he heard a man growl to someone behind him. Then he realized the full significance of that twisted little body.

The Armlin child had been kidnapped about six months ago and had later reappeared wandering aimlessly around the village one night in his present brainless, half-paralyzed condition. There had been four such unexplained disappearances in Henleyville during the past six months, and three crippled wrecks of children had come back out of nowhere, worse alive than if they were dead.

Jerry had read brief accounts of these strange disappearances in the New York newspapers, but their horrible sig-

nificance had not actually come home to him until he stood
there looking down at the pitiful spectacle on the sidewalk—
until he saw the bitterness and bleak despair in the eyes of
those around him.

Those eyes became hard and baleful when they turned on
him as he started to lead Leta back to the car. For a moment
he thought the crowd did not intend to let him pass; that they
would block his way and hold him there. Then, sullenly, they
gave way, and he was through.

"One o' the Caldwell's," he heard a gruff voice mutter as
he passed—and the string of blistering oaths that followed
mention of his name brought out prickles of gooseflesh on
his suddenly taut skin.

Why, he did not know. These people has been his friends
and neighbor all during his childhood, yet now he sensed that
their attitude toward him had changed. Their was no mistaking the vindictiveness of those curses, no mistaking the hostility in those bleak eyes and grim faces. For no reason that
he could imagine their liking had turned to hatred . . .

All afternoon his mind had been going back to that scene
in the village, trying without success to fathom the undercurrent of antagonism that had flared openly for a few moments.
Even though he could not understand it, he knew that it was
real—and fraught with danger. And then, as he stood watching his sister standing over the cradle of her daughter, the
thing had reached out for him again and clutched him chillingly.

Was this the fear, the dread, the indefinable emanation of
evil he had sensed almost from the moment he stepped into
his father's house? Had the horror that dominated the village
penetrated his old home and laid its paralyzing hand on
Katherine and the others?

Jerry didn't know, but as he thought of it, the blood in his
veins seemed to chill and become sluggish. His sixth sense
scented danger and warned him to get away—to take Leta
away—before it was too late. Early the next morning they
would leave, he resolved, and meanwhile they would spend
the evening at the movies. That would at least get her away

from the depressing atmosphere of the house.

With a curious feeling of relief he drove into town and parked his coupe behind the theater, but if he hoped that the screen drama would take his mind off the worry that was plaguing him he soon realized his mistake. With unseeing eyes he watched the screen while his brain sought persistently to fathom what it was that was disturbing him, what it was that his sixth sense was trying to warn him against.

Jerry's home had never been a very cheerful place, he reflected. His mother had died when he was still a young boy, and shortly after that his Aunt Margaret had moved in to keep house for her brother-in-law and take care of Jerry and Katherine.

Margaret was the wife of Dr. Caldwell's ne'er-do-well younger brother, Rolfe. They had had one child, Sanford, who was left a hopeless cripple by an attack of infantile paralysis that had necessitated amputating his legs above the knees—and then was further deformed when he was horrible scarred in a fire. Shortly before this second tragedy Rolfe had disappeared, taking with him part of the local bank's cash.

Beside these blood relations, the household had consisted of Lothar Zimmerlie and Morris, a huge Negro whose life Dr. Caldwell had saved by an operation in New Orleans and who had become the surgeon's abject slave.

Jerry had gone off to college and then had entered business in New York. Katherine had grown up and married, had borne a child and been widowed; and now she was back in her father's home so that he could treat a malady that threatened to cripple little Abbie.

Dr. Caldwell was a taciturn individual who lived only for his work. He had dedicated his life to a search for the cure for infantile paralysis and was completely immersed in his research and experiments; so much so that his children hardly felt that they knew him. Margaret Caldwell, likewise, was not a cheerful soul; her own experiences had soured her and left her cold and impersonal.

Not a very cheerful household, but, even so, the Caldwell home had never been so gloomy, so impregnated with an almost palpable air of tragedy, as it was now . . .

Jerry was still wrestling with his problem as he and Leta came out of the theater and started back to the parking space where they had left the car. There were others bound in the same direction, but that would not account for the large, excited crowd that was milling around in the parking space.

Something was the matter, he knew at once—and again the premonition of danger tingled through him. There were several hundred people in that crowd, but the angry rumble of their voices quitted as he and Leta appeared—gave way to a hush of expectancy.

All too readily the crowd made way for them, and then he saw that it was his own car that was the center of the excitement. Saw, too, that it was not where he had parked it. Instead, it now stood in front of two other cars so that they could not get out until his was moved.

So that was the trouble—a couple of irate car owners waiting for him to get his coupe out of their way . . . Strange that a little parking tangle should cause such excitement . . .

The owner of one of the boxed-in cars had evidently opened the door of the coupe to release the emergency brake, and it was through the open door that the milling crowd was gaping. Something in their attitude, in the awe and horror that stamped the faces of those nearest to the car, warned Jerry. Cold prickles snaked their way down his spine as he stepped forward. Then his eyes threatened to bulge out of his head and his body was bathed in clammy perspiration!

In the bottom of the coupe, partly jammed up behind the emergency and the controls, was something white that was half covered with a piece of oilcloth. Something ghastly white!

Through the other door of the car a flashlight lanced and centered its beam accusingly on that white shape—and a wave of sickening horror swept over Jerry as he saw that his first shocked glance had not been mistaken. That ghastly white thing was the naked, twisted body of a child!

Chapter Two

"Lynch Them!"

"The dirty murderer! He had it hidden up there under the cowl! You saw it fall down when I released the brake, Jim! The dirty baby-killers—they come here an' sit through a movie with this pore thing out here in the car! Waitin' till we went home so that they could dump it out in the street an' leave it there!"

A dozen voices were shouting and screaming at once, but Jerry heard them only dimly, only subconsciously, as he stared down at that twisted, broken little body—in *his* car!

"It's little Junior Frieling," he heard someone explain to newcomers. "He's dead—in Caldwell's car."

Junior Frieling—the last of the four kidnap victims. Junior had been missing for more than two months, and not the slightest trace of him had been found although the posses from town had searched every square foot for miles in all directions. Not the slightest trace until tonight—and now he was lying there, dead, in Jerry's car . . .

Rough hands grabbed at Jerry, seized his arms and pinned them behind him. Heavy fists lashed out at him, thudded into his face, pummeled his body before cooler heads in the crowd intervened and gave him some protection. Leta had been dragged away from his side, and now she was frantically trying to protect herself from a screaming mob of women that hemmed her in on every side.

"I don't know anything about this!" he shouted, desperately trying to make himself heard above the clamor. "If I had killed that child I wouldn't bring the body here and leave it in my own car, would I? If I did, I wouldn't leave my car parked this way so that someone would be sure to open the door and find it! Give me a chance to investigate—"

But they would not listen to him. His voice was drowned out by yells of rage as the mob worked itself up to fever heat. His words were smashed back into his mouth as horny hands slapped across his lips.

"Lynch them!" someone howled. "Get a rope an' string them up!"

"Tar and feathers first!" came another savagely yelled suggestion. "Tear the clothes off them!"

"No! No! You can't do that! Leta screamed; and Jerry caught a glimpse of her as the frenzied women grabbed at her dress and began to tear it in ribbons from her body.

The sight of her terrified face gave him the will to do what he had not been able to do for himself. With all his strength he suddenly whipped his arms across his chest and tore loose from the hands that were gripping him. Head down, like an enraged bull he charged straight into the thick of the mob, his pistoning fists battering a way toward Leta.

The members of that mob were eager to kill him, to tear him limb from limb, when he was helpless—but none of them was over-anxious to step in the way of that berserk charge and risk a battered face. They fell away before him— and then a shout went up behind him; a shout and the crash of breaking glass, the scream of rending metal.

By the time he reached Leta's side she was almost free, her tormentors of a moment before now eagerly swarming to the rapidly demolishing coupe. The windows were smashed out, the tires cut to ribbons, the doors and hood torn off, he saw as he glanced back into the howling vortex of the mob. And now a torch was being applied to the wreck.

They were taking such delight in this opportunity to vent their rage that Jerry was able to fight his way past the few who still stood in his way and to drag Leta with him, out of the parking lot and onto the street. It was almost deserted, except for a few cars in front of a nearby restaurant. Jerry led the way toward them on the run, while Leta tried to cover herself as well as she could with the tattered remnants of her dress.

A lout of a fellow standing beside one of the cars leered at her bared shoulders, then glanced down approvingly at the silken clad legs exposed by her up-held dress.

"Looks like you need a taxi, Jerry." He grinned as he held

open the door. Jerry recognized Claude Barnes, a fellow he had known when they were kids. "Hopin an' I'll run you out to your place."

Any car was a God-send at that moment. Gratefully Jerry climbed into the rickety runabout and helped Leta in beside him. Before the mob realized that they had gotten away and came swarming out on the sidewalk after them, Barnes had crossed the main square and was heading out the farther end of town.

"Looks like you run into a bit o' trouble," he chuckled as if the thing were a huge joke.

"Plenty," Jerry panted. "And without the slightest idea of what it's all about. This whole town seems to have gone crazy."

"Well, now, you gotta admit they've been given cause," Barnes argued as he took advantage of a passing road-light to cast a probing glance at where Leta huddled as close to Jerry as she could. "Maybe you'd be a bit crazy yerself if you had a kid that was swiped and brung back the way these kids've been. Of course, I don't take it that it's any o' *your* fault—but you can't blame them for holdin' it against your old man—"

"Against my father?" The exclamation burst from Jerry's astounded lips. "What has he got to do with it?"

"Well, of course, I don't rightly know," the driver began with obvious relish. "Maybe they've got it all wrong, but folks around here think that he's the one who's responsible for these kidnappin's. We know all about this infantile paralysis experimentin' he's doin'—that was all writ up in a city paper a while back. Of course, the paper said he only uses animals an' such like, but folks around here are wonderin' about that. These youngsters that come back have been experimented on—they've got cuts an' scars on them an' parts o' them are missin'. Who else would wanta do anything like that to them? Nobody but your old man—if he's usin' the kids for his experiments."

Jerry listened with amazement that held him mute, but at

last he recovered his voice.

"That's ridiculous!" he snorted. "No medical man would do anything like that to human beings—to helpless children. He would have to be an inhuman fiend—a madman."

"I ain't sayin' it is or it ain't," Barnes shrugged. "I'm only tellin' you what folks are sayin'. One o' them youngsters, you know, was found wanderin' around the road near your place—an' now they found this one in your car—"

He left the rest to inference, and as Jerry pondered what he had just heard his amazement was streaked with doubt, with fear that welled up within him no matter how he tried to fight it down. He could not believe that his father would have a part in such hellish business. But he realized that he actually knew very little about the doctor, except that he was bound up entirely in his work, that it occupied him to the exclusion of everything else and that he was ready to sacrifice anything for it.

Anything? Just how far *would* Dr. Caldwell go if he felt that success was within his grasp, that he was on the verge of a discovery that would be a boon to all mankind? Jerry asked himself that question, and a chill coursed through him as he realized that he could not answer it—that he was afraid to answer it!

Dr. Caldwell's laboratory had always been a forbidden place, open only to himself and Lothar Zimmerlie. Jerry had seen it only when there was no work in progress. But often, as a child, he had wondered about it, had speculated on what went on within it—and now that speculation had taken on new and dreadful significance.

Was it possible that beyond those closed doors the kidnapped Henleyville children were being used as human guinea pigs?

That thought was shocking, staggering—but even as Jerry recoiled from it he remembered that newspaper article Barnes had mentioned; remembered how furious his father had been when it was published. The unwelcome publicity had made him incoherent with rage.

Why? Because he was afraid to let the world know what

was going on behind his laboratory doors? Because he was afraid of interference—of investigation?

Barnes had swung in through the arched gateway to the Caldwell estate. His headlights were tunneling through the blackness of the tree and shrub bordered road, just beginning to pick out the white porch columns in the distance, when his foot lifted from the throttle and the car coasted along in comparative silence while he leaned forward and strained to listen.

Plainly through the night came the sound Jerry also had heard—the wail of an infant! Then suddenly it was cut off, muffled as if a hand had been clapped over its mouth or a blanket thrown over its head—but the eerie sound still echoed in Jerry's ears and seemed to chill him to the tips of his toes.

A child's cry in the woods at that hour of the night—it was weird and unnatural. Almost as if they had heard the ghostly wail of that little corpse that had sent the townspeople into a frenzy!

Barnes jammed his foot down on the brake, and Jerry saw that his face was ashen, his teeth chattering. Wild-eyed, he stared out into that tunnel of light—and for a fraction of a second the headlights played full upon the figure of a woman running across the road. Then she was gone, swallowed up by the thick shrubbery. But not before they had all recognized Jerry's sister, Katherine. Katherine, with a small, blond-haired child clasped in her arms.

That child was Abbie, Jerry told himself with desperate insistency. But what was Katherine doing out at that time of night? Where had she been with the baby, alone and on foot?

There was an explanation, a simple and rational explanation, which he would hear as soon as he got into the house, he assured himself doggedly as he strove to deny the nameless terror that was gnawing away at the pit of his stomach. It would all be clear as soon as he got inside the house and talked to Katherine . . .

"Don't bother to take us any farther," he told Barnes as he

shoved a folded bill into the fellow's hand and opened the door to help Leta out. "It's just a few steps more, and you can swing around here for the road back to town."

"Just as you say," the driver mumbled, but now his movements were slow and awkward, and he swung the car widely so that its lights centered for a long moment on the spot where Katherine had disappeared.

Almost reluctantly he stepped on the gas and rattled off down the road, while Jerry heaved a sigh of relief.

With one arm around Leta he led the way across the moonlight spotted grounds to the house, climbed the steps to the porch—and then stopped dead still, certain that they were not alone in the night. There in the bushes at the side of the house he was sure he had heard someone or something move.

Again that telltale half-sound—and he was off the porch in a leap, racing toward a clump of shrubbery he had seen move ever so slightly. At the same moment there was a wild scramble of feet, a dark form sprang from cover, and in a bright splash of moonlight he was almost certain that he caught a glimpse of the heavy-featured face of Lothar Zimmerlie!

Then it was gone. Again the quiet of the night was broken only by the hum and chirp of insects.

Puzzled, and angry with himself for not having been quicker, Jerry went back to the porch and into the house with Leta. He'd have a question or two to ask Zimmerlie about that performance. But when they got inside, the lower floor was dark except for a night-light in the hallway.

After he had kissed Leta good night at the door of her room, he tiptoed across the hall to his sister's room. Not a sound came from beyond the closed door and there was no response when he tapped gently upon it. Could it be that she was still out there somewhere in the night with able? Could that be why Zimmerlie was skulking in the bushes?

Jerry's puzzlement turned to anxiety. Softly he turned the knob and opened the door, peered inside. And in the re-flected moonlight he saw that Katherine was asleep in her bed, the sheet crumpled low under one nightgown-clad shoulder.

Quietly he tiptoed his way across the room to the door of the nursery. There in her cradle lay Abbie, fast asleep, her curly blond head burrowed into her pillow, one little arm around the plush rabbit that was her inseparable sleeping companion.

Thoroughly mystified, Jerry tiptoed his way back into the hall and to his own room—almost convinced that the woman he had seen in the moonlight had not been his sister.

Chapter Three

Demon of the Night

Little Willis Armlin screaming and squirming on the sidewalk; Lothar Zimmerlie leaping up from behind a patch of shrubbery; the body of Junior Frieling wedged under the cowl of his car: Katherine running through the night with a child in her arms; the mob howling and tearing at Leta . . . Those horrible pictures were all tumbling through Jerry's mind in a wild, kaleidoscopic maze as he dozed off to sleep—but it seemed that his eyes had hardly closed when they blinked open again and he propped himself up on his elbows in bed.

That queer thumping and creaking he had heard was not a part of his wild imaginings. He had actually heard it, out there in the hallway. There it was again—a muffled thudding, a dull clanking. Noises that he could not identify but that made the hair at the nape of his neck stand on end!

Noiselessly he let himself out of bed and catfooted to the door, opened it softly and peered out into the hallway—and for the second time that night his body was bathed from head to foot in sudden perspiration. Coming out of Katherine's room was a huge black creature, almost a formless mass of shadow in the darkness of the hallway. And it held a child's limp body dangling under one arm!

Mechanically it stalked down the hall with that unearthly

clank and thud.

For long moments Jerry crouched there in the doorway, spellbound, gazing at that incredible creature that *must* be another figment of his overworked imagination—but it wasn't. Fascinated, he watched it reach his doorway and go, clumping steadily toward the other end of the hall. Into his mind flashed a picture of the Armlin child in convulsions on the sidewalk, of the Frieling child's twisted corpse . . .

If that creature, whatever unholy spawn of hell it might be, made off with Abbie they would not see the child again until she was like one of those poor, tortured victims!

That dread thought catapulted Jerry out of his doorway as if his legs were made of Indian rubber. Right at the creature he flung himself, his arms spread wide for a tackle that would bring the thing to the floor. Straight to the mark his flying leap carried him—but when his arms closed around the creature's knees it was as if he had flung himself against two steel pillars.

Half-stunned by the impact and numb with the pain that tore through his bruised shoulder, he reeled back and landed in a heap against a hall table that went over with a crash. Now the creature had dropped the little one and wheeled clumsily on his attacker. Inexorably he bore down on Jerry until he towered above him. Then huge black hands reached down and fastened like steel claws in his shoulders.

Not until then did Jerry find his voice—and then it was too late. The moment he started to yell one of those powerful fists closed around his throat and half-throttled him.

Desperately he struggled, but even as he flailed away at the monster he knew that it was useless, knew that he was helpless against this creature. His feet kicked harmlessly against those iron hard legs; his fists thudded with as little effect on the almost equally hard arms and torso—and the strength was fairly running out of him.

His senses were beginning to swim, his breath barely sufficient to keep his tortured lungs from collapsing—when he saw the door of Zimmerlie's room open a trifle. That would mean help! But the door opened only a crack and no wider, and no help came from behind it.

Helplessly Jerry bent over backward as the merciless hands at his throat tightened their pressure and forced him down. Then another door opened just across the hall, and Leta stepped out to see what was causing the noise. The light in her room was turned on, and as she stood there in the doorway her slim figure was silhouetted perfectly through the sheer nightgown she was wearing.

One shoulder strap slipped down over her arm as she shrank back with a gasp of terror, and the light modeled half of her bosom alluringly.

Jerry heard the creature catch its breath; saw the blazing eyes in the black face turn to the girl and fasten their gaze greedily on the rounded white flesh before she could pull the nightgown back into place. The vise-like fingers at his throat had stopped their constricting, had loosened as the monster stared with avid, hungry eyes.

That was more of a break than Jerry had expected. Summoning every last ounce of his waning strength, he threw himself backward while he smashed at the black head above him. One of the creature's hands was torn loose. The other began to lose its grip. Jerry was almost free when the monster's head pivoted back, a snarl of rage rumbling from its throat. One of those huge fists raised, and came down with the force of a sledgehammer. And then the blackness rushed in over him; blackness that was shot through with horrid streaks of nausea.

Vaguely he heard that curious clanking and thudding, heard it grow dimmer until it seemed to fade entirely. Quiet after that. Unnatural quiet that was appalling after the fury of that ghastly struggle.

He should not be lying there on the floor doing nothing. Jerry knew that. He should be up on his feet after the monster—should be up looking after Leta . . .

Determinedly he fought his way up out of the blackness, shook the dizziness out of his head and groped his way up to his knees. The hallway was empty and quiet. No sign of the black creature or of the child it had been carrying. But there

was a heap of white over there in front of that doorway—
Leta!

While his heart pounded so that it fairly shook his body
and his quaking knees threatened to give beneath him, he
crawled over to that still white heap, bent while terror
clutched at his throat with a grip more torturing than the
black creature's vise-like fingers.

The nightgown had been ripped down the front and pulled
to both sides so that her naked body was almost completely
revealed. It was so white and still. In the dim light from the
doorway it did not seem that her bosom was moving. That
meant she was *dead!*

Frantically he flung himself over her, pressed his ear
against chest. Her heart *was* beating—faintly, but *beating!*
And then a breath of air soughed through her lips. She had
only fainted; she was alive!

"Thank God! Thank God!" The two word prayer of
thanksgiving gasped from him a dozen times as he chafed
her hands and worked over her until she revived and could
be helped back to her bed.

During all that struggle there had been no sign of Katherine. Surely she must have heard—unless the monster had
left her lying dead in her bed . . .

Fearful of what he would find, Jerry crossed the hall and
stepped through the open doorway of his sister's room. She
was lying there just as she had been earlier in the night,
sleeping peacefully—sleeping while her child was dragged
off to an unthinkable fate!

Feeling as if he were walking into a death chamber, he
stepped into the nursery—and the world seemed to rock and
sway crazily around him. Abbie wasn't gone—she was there,
just as she had been before, fast asleep with her bunny
clutched to her side!

Was this all a hideous nightmare, or was he having hallucinations? Was he mad—roaming through a weird inferno of
his own conjuring? That must be it . . . How else could he
have seen Abbie out there in the black creature's arms when
she was peacefully sleeping here in her cradle?

That terrifying thought was given added substance when Katherine's voice spoke to him from the doorway.

"What—what are you doing in here at this time of night, Jerry?" she asked in a voice that was uncertain with amazement. "I heard a noise and thought it was Abbie—"

"Is that the only noise you heard?" Jerry whispered, while the tide of fear rose up within him. "Didn't you hear someone else in here—someone taking Abbie out of her cradle and through your room? Didn't you hear any noise in the hallway?"

Katherine's eyes were round and a look of fright—fright for him—came into her face.

"Why, Abbie is there, asleep in her cradle, just as she has been all night," she answered him in tones that were meant to be coaxing, humoring. "There could not have been anyone here or I would have heard; you know how lightly I sleep—"

It was incredible—terrifying if what she said was true . . .

But it *wasn't* true! For a split second Katherine was off guard, and Jerry caught a glimpse of the utter terror that was lurking in the depths of her eyes. In that moment he knew that she was lying, lying desperately!

But why?

Had she willingly let that black monster take Abbie out of her cradle? And who was the creature? Could it have been the doctor's big Negro servant, Morris?

Jerry hurried back to his own room and got into his clothes. Then he went to Morris' room and tried the door. It was unlocked, and the Negro was in his bed, snoring so thunderously that the windows fairly rattled. Morris wasn't sufficiently adept as an actor to pretend that noisy sleeping.

Methodically Jerry searched the other rooms one after the other. His father's bed had not been slept in, but that was not surprising because it was Dr. Caldwell's custom to work in his laboratory far into the night. Lothar Zimmerlie was not in his room either, although his bed had been disturbed as if he had been lying down on top of the sheets in his clothes. That left only Sanford, the cripple . . .

His bedroom and his mother's were in a separate wing of the house. His door was closed when Jerry reached it, and no sound came from the room—but the moment Jerry's fingers touched the doorknob a veritable fury flung across the little hallway and launched into him, swept him savagely back from the door.

"What are you doing here?" his Aunt Margaret demanded as her thin fingers fastened like talons in his shirt and pushed him back. "What are you doing at that door? Tell me why you're snooping around here in the middle of the night!"

"What's Sanford been up to?" Jerry snapped. "Why are you afraid to let me open his door?"

"He hasn't done a thing! Nothing—nothing at all, I tell you!" she chattered. "He's been in there all night. He's asleep—I won't let you disturb him!"

Her eyes blazed with fury and she was trembling with rage—or was it fear? Jerry hadn't time to determine that then. With one arm wrapped tight around her shoulders holding her helpless, he turned the knob and gently opened Sanford's door.

In the moonlight that streamed in through the windows the room looked like a fantastic junkshop, cluttered up with odds and ends of electrical equipment and mechanical gadgets with which the cripple amused himself. Near the center stood his empty wheelchair, and at farther side Sanford lay in his bed, his closed, his chest rising and falling gently with the peaceful breathing of undisturbed sleep.

Softly Jerry drew the door shut—but before the latch clicked back into place his hand froze on the knob, his ears straining to catch the muffled sound of a struggle, of a scream and a moan of agony, from somewhere on the lower floor of the house!

Like a sprinter at the bark of the starter's gun he raced to the stairs, took steps three and four at a time, but when he reached the ground floor all was quiet. The hallway seemed empty and disturbed, until he reached the rear of building, a few feet from the back door, and almost stumbled over a body that was sprawled on the floor.

It was Lothar Zimmerlie, his face twisted in agony, the fingers of one hand tightly clenched on a tattered fragment a child's night dress. His throat had been ripped out horribly and his neck was broken, twisted back over his shoulder by terribly powerful hands!

Blood from his severed artery had spurted over the floor, and leading away from it Jerry found the bloody print of an incredible foot or hoof. A thing nearly twelve inches in diameter, composed of numerous camel-like pads . . .

Two prints of that amazing foot—and then the track was lost at the back door.

Chapter Four

Crimson Dawn

Unquestionably Lothar Zimmerlie had died in the cruel hands of that black creature. But why? Trying to rescue the child? But *what* child? Abbie was sleeping soundly upstairs in her cradle . . .

Jerry was completely nonplussed as he knelt over the scientist's broken body. But the answer to these mystifying questions, the answer to all this hellishness, he was convinced, was right there in that house. And it must be in the only part he had not searched—the wing that housed his father's laboratory.

Grimly he started for it, resolved that he would search those rooms no matter how much his father might object. Some ghastly devilment was being perpetrated in that house, and he intended to put a stop to it before it brought them all to their doom.

His blood chilled as he remembered that howling mob in the parking space—how nearly they had wreaked mad vengeance on Leta. Her innocence was no protection against them. Once they got altogether out of hand they would murder her horribly, strip her and tear her limb from limb. With that mob in the village and this fearsome creature roaming the house the girl was in deadly peril!

But just as he reached the short hallway that terminated at the heavy door which closed off the wing of the house devoted to Dr. Caldwell's laboratory and its auxiliary rooms, his father was locking the door for the night.

"Just a moment, Dad," Jerry called determinedly. "Before you lock that door I'd like to take a look around your laboratory."

Dr. Caldwell turned his bushy grey brows raised in surprise.

"You know I do not permit that, Jerry," he said quietly. "For your own good, I cannot allow you past this door. The experiments I am conducting are too dangerous—the malady with which we are dealing is too contagious—to allow intrusion."

With an air of finality he turned the key in the lock and then thrust it into his pocket as he started down the passageway.

Jerry studied him intently—analyzed the cold grey eyes, the sharp-featured, Vandycked face—and realized with a sinking heart that he hardly knew this cold, unemotional man of science who was his father. What were those experiments that were too dangerous to be seen? What was going on behind that locked door? He would have given a lot to know, but he realized that only by physical force could he hope to enter the forbidden laboratory.

"Perhaps what you say is so," he admitted resignedly, "but you may have to open that door to a number of people before very long. You know about the kidnappings that have been going on around here lately, and about the condition in which the children have been returned. But do you realize that the people in town are blaming you for that? They say you are using the children in your experiments. Tonight somebody put the Frieling child's body in my car, and we were nearly lynched. They wrecked the car and burned it."

Again the bushy grey brows lifted.

"That was an unfortunate experience," Dr. Caldwell conceded, "but you will be able to collect insurance on your car. These sorts of things happen in the life of a scientist; we have to expect them." He shrugged contemptuously. "That is always the reaction of the ignorant, layman when something happens which he cannot understand—blame it on the black magic of the man of science. There is nothing to fear in such mob hysteria."

He was utterly calm, entirely unruffled by what he had heard. So much so that complacence riled Jerry.

"All right," he snapped, "but come along with me and I'll show you something you can't dismiss so easily."

With a feeling almost of satisfaction he led the way to the rear of the building and switched on the hall light, to reveal Lothar Zimmerlie's mutilated corpse sprawled on the floor.

"There's some sort of beast loose in this house—and here is some of his handiwork," he announced grimly, as Dr. Caldwell stared down at the corpse of the man who had been his associate for more than twenty years. "I've searched every part of the house for it—except your laboratory."

A shadow of regret passed over Caldwell's face and he shook his head—more with annoyance than sadness.

"Too bad," he murmured dispassionately. "Lothar was a valuable assistant. It will be difficult to find his equal. But you may rest assured that there is no wild creature in my laboratory—if that is what you expected me to admit to you."

Cold and unemotional as a cake of ice.

Zimmerlie's death had failed to shake or horrify him—and again Jerry wondered fearfully what sort of man Dr. Eustace Caldwell really was!

"Lothar?" Katherine's anxious voice cut in on Jerry's troubled thoughts. "Has anything happened to him?"

She was coming down the hallway, a negligee hastily thrown over her nightgown. Too late Jerry tried to step in front of the gruesome spectacle on the floor. She had already seen it—and in the next moment she had brushed him aside and dropped to her knees beside the corpse, to give way to a wild paroxysm of weeping.

"He did his best," she sobbed, her words hardly intelligible between hysterical outbursts. "He tried to protect me—that's why he is lying here! He gave his life for me—for me and Abbie—to save us! Oh, Lothar! I told you we couldn't fight it . . ."

Her frenzied raving was almost incoherent, but when Jerry tried to question her she suddenly became mute. Her eyes filled with shuddering terror, as if she had just realized what she had been saying, and he noticed that her cowering glance darted fearfully to her father, as if it was his presence that had silenced her.

The cold, unmoved man of science; the terrified, nearly prostrate girl; the mutilated corpse on the floor—in some inexplicable way they all tied in with this damning thing Jerry had sensed hanging over the house, but as he glanced from one to the other he could not find the key to this ghastly mystery.

That night of horror was nearly over. Dawn was beginning to lighten the eastern sky. With daylight Jerry resolved that he would have a look into that locked laboratory . . .

"No matter what else you may be willing to do, we've got to notify the sheriff about this," he reminded his father. "I'm going to telephone him now."

But when he tried to call the operator there was no response. The line was out of commission. That was some more devilment; undoubtedly the line had been cut so as to isolate the house. Grimly he stalked out the front door, to trace the line and try to discover what had been done to it— but before he was down the porch steps Leta's terrified scream knifed through him and brought his heart up into his throat!

He had forgotten all about her in the excitement of the past hour, had forgotten that she was alone and at the mercy of that inhuman black monster!

Grisly fear spurred him in a mad race back into the house, up the stairs to the second floor. But when he gained the top of the stairs he knew that he was too late. The door of her room was standing open. Before he ran to it he knew what he would find—the room was empty. Leta was gone!

Something seemed to die within him as he stood there in the doorway, staring into that terribly empty room. She was - gone—dragged off—and only God Almighty knew where the monster had taken her! As if to mock him, from the distance he could barely catch the sound of muffled clanking, could barely distinguish the whine of pulleys.

And then silence.

That whine—it was made by the cables in the little, hand-operated elevator that had been built at one end of the hall-way so that Sanford Caldwell could wheel his chair into it and hoist himself from one floor to the other. The black creature had made a get-away by means of the cripple's elevator.

Dimly in the nap of the hall carpet outside Leta's room Jerry could see the print of those huge, many-padded feet. Then he was up on his feet, racing for the lower floor, only to pause at the foot of the stairs and listen while new terror coursed chillingly through him.

That howling and yelling outside was the mob from the vil-lage. Like a ravening pack of wolves they were encircling the house, were tramping on the porch, ringing the bell, pounding on the windows. Shouts and curses—loud, profane demands that the door be open—and the first rock hurtled through a pane of glass.

As if the tinkling glass was a signal, the mob charged the door, hurled themselves against it bodily, and sent it crashing in under the sheer weight of their furious assault!

Chapter Five

Hell's Procuress

Through the breached doorway the mob swarmed into the hallway, armed with clubs and stakes, with horsewhips and pitchforks. At their head was a bearded giant with blazing eyes and craggy features that worked continuously under the stress of his unrepressed emotion.

"Where is he?" he yelled as he strode forward with gnarled fists clenching and unclenching at his sides. "Where's the murdering baby-killer that stole my Beth?"

The howl of the pack at his back fairly shook the house—but above it a cold, calm voice rang out authoritatively as Dr. Caldwell stepped forward to confront them, unafraid.

"What is the idea of this intrusion, John Gowan?" he demanded of the bearded giant who glared at him. "Why have you broken into my house with this crowd of loafers?"

For a moment the sheer effrontery of it cowed them, kept them quiet. Even John Gowan lost his bluster—and in its place came an abject breakdown that was pathetic.

"I want my young 'un," he babbled, while tears blurred his eyes. "Give her back to me, Doc, an' I'll get these fellers out o' your house. You *gotta* give her back to me, Doc—you can't do to her like you done to the others. You can't do that, Doc—not to my young 'un—"

"I haven't any idea what you're talking about, Gowan," the doctors voice cut him short. "I haven't seen your child or any of the others. Now get this mob out of here before you all land in jail."

But now the others had found their voices, and again the building rang with their enraged yells. Gowan was pushed aside and heavy hands grabbed hold of the doctor and pinioned his arms behind him. Out of the crowd stepped Claude Barnes, delighting in his sudden importance.

"Beth Gowan was kidnapped last night," he snarled at Caldwell. "Snatched right out o' her crib, she was—an' I know who snatched her. Your daughter there!" He pointed an accusing finger at Katherine, who stood, ashen-pale and cowering, at Jerry's side. "I saw her sneaking back here to the house with the youngster in her arms. So did your son—if he's man enough to admit it. We saw her plain in the light o' my headlights!"

"That's enough talk!" a loud voice bawled from the doorway. "The kid's here in the house—let's find her!"

And like an avalanche they surged forward, sweeping Jerry and his father and sister with them. In vain Dr. Caldwell tried to keep them out of his laboratory, but they scoffed at his threats and warnings. Without waiting to find the key they went at the door with axes and clubs, splintered it and tore it from its hinges.

Over it they swept into the laboratory, to mill around uncertainly until someone found the electric button and switched on the light—to reveal a ghastly scene that held them tongue-tied and gaping-mouthed!

Katherine's horrified scream broke that tense silence as she tried to fling herself forward, but Jerry's arm lashed out and clutched her, held her back. Aghast, he stood staring into that white-walled room that had become an antechamber of hell itself.

The walls of that room were lined with cages in which Dr. Caldwell kept the animals he used for his experiments—but there were no animals being used in the ghastly business that occupied the center of the place.

Side by side on twin white operating tables lay the naked bodies of Beth Gowan and little Abbie! Their curly blond heads were almost alike—but there the similarity ended. The Gowan child's body had been drained of blood until it was ashen white and shrunken so that the little bones stood out— a skeleton barely covered over with skin. Abbie's body was pink and healthy.

Rubber tubes strapped to their arms and attached to a softly chugging machine told the grisly story. Beth's lifeblood had been pumped out of her body and into Abbie's!

Jerry tried to close his eyes to that macabre scene; tried to close his mind to a realization of what had occurred—to the diabolical thing his father had done. So this was the reason that locked laboratory door could not be open . . .

A plethora of horror overwhelmed him, nauseated him, as he stared at that pitiful, shrunken body—and at that instant Katherine broke away from him and raced across the laboratory.

With wide, horror-brimmed eyes she stared down at her baby's closed eyes, at her still face. Like a woman in a trance she bent over the little body and pressed her ear to Abbie's breast—and the poignant moan that sobbed from her blanched lips was the epitome of all agony, the hopeless cry of a soul that has plumbed the uttermost depths of despair!

Like a madwoman she whirled on her father, her wild eyes blazing insanely in her grey-white face.

"You did it, you murdering monster! You killed her!" she screamed. "I brought you the others whenever you wanted them! I sold my soul to the devil to satisfy you—and now you've taken my baby!"

Dazed with horror, Jerry listened as those ghastly, damning accusations poured from her lips; as she shrieked bitter, hysterical curses at her father. His sated, numbed brain could hardly understand the words she was saying, could hardly grasp the enormity of the frightful thing that had been done there in the house that had once been his home . . .

And then Katherine's shrill voice was drowned in the awful roar of the mob—a mob whose blood lust was worked up to the killing point!

"That's where our children all went!" Gus Frieling shouted to his neighbors.

"That she-devil snatched them and brought them here so that her butcher of a father could rob them of their blood and brains to give them to her own brat! Baby-killers!"

"Baby-killers!" Fifty hate-maddened voices took up the shout as the mob, completely out of hand, rushed at the Caldwells.

Jerry tried to argue, to plead with them as he fought desperately to defend himself nobody heard him. The laboratory had become a frenzied maelstrom of flying fists and threshing bodies, a bedlam of screaming women and howling, cursing men. In waves they swarmed over him and bore him down, but time and again he struggled back to his feet and tried to fight his way to where Katherine was being horribly manhandled.

For a brief moment Dr. Caldwell's bloody head reared above the mob as he climbed onto a low platform and tried to beat them off with his ineffectual fists. Then he went down, just as Morris, the huge negro, came charging through the press, his only thought to fight his way to the doctor's side.

"There's the nigger that helped her!" someone howled above the din, and in the next moment a dozen of them were at him, climbing on his back, hanging from his arms, pounding away at his face.

Jerry saw him submerged, dragged down like a gallant old buck surrounded by a pack of wolves—and then he had all he could do to keep his own feet. From every side they lashed out at him. Fists smashed into his face, thudded against his chest, pounded into his back, caromed off his shoulders. For every one that he managed to parry he took half a dozen jarring, strength-sapping blows.

His arms ached and had become as heavy as lead; his whole body screamed with pain—and his reeling brain kept reminding him that it was hopeless; that all the rest were gone and that it would be only seconds now before he would join them in oblivion. Only seconds . . .

In front of him he saw a heavy club raised—poised for the blow that would brain him. He knew that he could not duck that blow, knew that he could not ward it off, but instinctively his left arm raised up to protect his head. With a vicious sweep the bludgeon descended and battered down his defending arm as if it were a thing of straw.

Frightful agony shot through the bruised limb—and then something exploded in his brain; something that filled the whole world with glaring light that faded and faded even as he was slipping down, down into endless blackness.

For a long while Jerry lay there in a coma. For an eternity, it seemed, as he struggled sickeningly through recurrent waves of nausea; as he fought his way back almost to consciousness only to lapse back into the darkness. In one of those brief intervals of near-consciousness he was sure that he heard the mechanical clank and thud of the black creature—that he saw the monster looming in the laboratory doorway, only to be blotted out by the enveloping darkness.

But when he finally opened his eyes and dragged himself up onto one elbow, there was no sign of the creature in the wrecked laboratory. All around were overturned table, broken cases, trampled equipment. Blood-spattered wreckage on every side.

With an agony effort he got to his feet, staggered across the room to drop down beside the blood-covered, horribly battered body of his sister. What those vengeful devils had done to her was appalling. Jerry did not see how the breath of life still remained in that broken body, but her eyes were open and she was moving her battered lips, trying to tell him something.

Through a bloody froth her words finally came as he propped her up in his arms and bent his ear close to her mouth.

"It was true—what I told them," she gasped. "I did it—I took those poor babies from their cribs, but I couldn't help it, Jerry. God knows I couldn't help it! For months it's all been . . . such a horrible nightmare. Ever since that night about six months ago when I woke up and saw father standing in the nursery, in front of Abbie's cradle. He was dressed in his operating uniform—even his cap and mask. I could only see his eyes . . . and they were blazing wildly. They fascinated me. At first they terrified me, and then I didn't seem to mind.

"He was waking Abbie—going to take her to be used in one of his experiments—for the benefit of mankind, he said. At first I thought he was mad, but I could see that he meant to do it. Then I was terrified. I begged him to spare her. I promised to do anything—if only he would let her live. He looked at me with those burning eyes . . . and he said, 'Yes, you will do anything. You will do as I tell you. You will go to Orrin Armlin's house tonight and bring me the child. Do you understand? You will bring me the child—and you will never say a word about it to anyone, not even to me. Never a word. Do you understand?'

"I promised to obey him. I stole the youngster. I know now that he hypnotized me, Jerry. He held my mind powerless, so that I could not do a thing. The next day I wanted to talk to him—wanted to tell him that he must give the child back to its parents. But I couldn't say a word. I wanted to—and something within me would not let me even mention it. Oh,

God, it was horrible!"

"But why didn't you just take Abbie and get out of here?" Jerry interrupted. "Why didn't you come to me?"

"I couldn't," Katherine's voice was weaker, barely audible. "Abbie was so sick then. Father had told me that I brought her to him—just in time. He was giving her treatments, and without them she would have died. I couldn't take her away—and I couldn't go to you, because of the strange, controlling power he exerted over me. Not even to Lothar—but I think he suspected. He kept watching me, kept trying to help.

"But nobody could help me—just had to do as I was told. Five times he came to me like that—at night—and told me to bring him a child. Five poor, innocent victims. I was so horrified at what I was doing . . . it was driving me mad. I think I might even have given up . . . let him take Abbie but by that time I had no more will of my own . . . I just did as he ordered. And always I had that ghastly secret locked up inside of me . . . and I could not tell anyone—could not even denounce father . . . tell him . . . what a beast he was . . ."

Merciful death put an end to that ghastly confession, and Jerry lowered the outraged body gently to the floor. She had paid terribly for what she had done—paid in blood and suffering for the diabolical scheming of an inhuman fiend. And that fiend was her own father—was *his* father!

Painfully Jerry staggered back to his feet and surveyed the wreckage about him. Now he noticed that the air was peculiarly thick, acrid. It was tinged with smoke! Now he was sure of it—a thicker gust had just come down the hallway. The building was on fire!

Dazedly he groped his way across the room, almost stepped on little Abbie's body. As she rolled away from his foot, he noticed that one arm seemed to move toward her face—and then a half-whimper escaped from her lips! Quickly he scooped her up and held his head against her chest. Her heart was still beating and her chest was moving. She was alive! Alive and left there to be burned to death . . .

Perhaps there were others still alive in the building. Perhaps Leta was in one of those rooms, tied up and helpless, waiting fearfully for the flames to reach her!

With the baby in his arms he made his way to the door, across the dead body of black Morris, and out into the passageway. Once he got out into the main hallway he saw that the building was on fire on all sides. Smoke was gushing up from a dozen different points, and the crackle of flames was all around him.

It took only a few minutes investigation to tell him that the fire was incendiary. The enraged mob had closed all the shutters and bolted them from the outside, barred and nailed the doors, then set fire to the house. The place was an infernal fire-trap for whoever might still be alive within it—a funeral pyre to destroy the evidence of the murdered corpses on its floors.

Leaving the unconscious baby at the foot of the stairs, Jerry raced up the steps and ran from room to room, searching frantically for Leta, frantically calling her name, to be sure that she had not been left there to be cremated alive.

The flames were spreading with alarming speed. By the time he reached Sanford's quarters that section of the building was all ablaze. Through the flame-ringed doorway of the cripple's room he could make out his Aunt Margaret's body crumpled up on the floor—could see Sanford slumped forward in his blazing wheelchair!

There was not a chance in a thousand that either of them could still be alive in that cracking furnace—but even if they had, Jerry could not possibly have reached them.

The blazing ceiling of the upper hallway was beginning to tumble in as he sprang clear and bolted for the stairs. Leta was not on the upper floor, and he could find no trace of her in the roaring lower rooms. Finally the heat drove him back, forced him to pick up his unconscious charge and stumble down the stairs to the cellar.

Even down there the smoke was thick, but Jerry groped his way purposefully toward the rear. In his childhood there had been a doorway in the rear wall that opened onto a tunnel which terminated in a natural cave. It would be a way of escape, unless the tunnel had fallen in or been filled up.

Readily his fingers located the familiar door, slid down the rusted metal surface and grasped the heavy latch. It lifted easily and the door swung open on well oiled hinges. Puzzled as well as pleased, Jerry lit a match and held it up in the dark tunnel. Then he bent down and held it close to the dirt floor.

There, in the thick dust, were many impressions of the black creature's curious footprints! This tunnel evidently led straight to its lair!

For a moment Jerry hesitated—but the roaring crash behind him told him that he had no alternative. The blazing house was collapsing, cutting him off from the cellar.

Grimly he started through the tunnel.

Chapter Six

Spawn of Hate

Jerry Caldwell was frantic with worry about Leta as he made his way along that underground passageway. It was as if he were deserting her, leaving her to a horrible fate back there in that roaring conflagration. Hopelessly he plodded along through the darkness—and then suddenly his pulses leaped with excitement.

Faintly he had caught the sound of voices at the other end of the tunnel—Leta's voice, pleading with someone!

That spurred him on at a cautious half-trot. And soon a dim light appeared ahead of him. As he came nearer he saw that a door had been fitted into the cave end of the tunnel. It was partly ajar and he could see into the rock-walled grotto.

The place was much as it had been in his childhood, but now it was lighted by dim, lantern-shrouded electric bulbs and was filled out with furnishings; a white table and many-drawered cabinets, several curious chairs, a couch.

On that couch, at the far side of the cave, lay Leta! She was lying on her back, bound hand and foot—and beside her sat Jerry's father!

That *couldn't* be Dr. Caldwell—but it was! Even from the

rear Jerry could recognize him, could glimpse the familiar Vandyck, the curly grey hair. He was bending over the girl, fondling her—and Jerry could just catch his low-spoken words.

"Aren't you being stubborn? Isn't it foolish to suffer like this—and the way you will very shortly?" he was arguing coaxingly. "I can take care of you and get you out of here safely—if you will be nice to me. It wouldn't be so hard . . ."

Unctuous, wheedling words that were filled with foul suggestion! Jerry's blood ran cold as he listened to them—as he watched his father's hand straying over Leta's body, watched him unfastening her clothing as he pretending to be untying the ropes that held her fast. Helplessly she submitted to his caresses, to the indignities of his exploring fingers.

"Hurry!" she panted as her terrified eyes darted to a doorway at one side of the cave. "Oh, please hurry—before that horrible creature comes back. You *can't* leave me here for him!"

"Don't worry, I'm hurrying," the old man chuckled. Now Jerry noted that his voice was different than usual; it was convulsed with passion that made it deeper, harsher than he had ever heard it.

And when Jerry momentarily caught a full view of his face there was something different about that, too. Perhaps it was the dim light of the cave, but his features seemed to have become demoniac; more hard and cruel than Jerry had even seen them.

The man he was looking at had the build and features of his father—but suddenly Jerry knew that he was not Dr. Caldwell! He was an impostor, a devilish masquerader . . .

At that moment the clanking, thudding noise began again, grew louder, and from the side door of the cave the black monster stalked mechanically into the main grotto. Now Jerry could see that the creature was a little over six feet tall, dressed entirely in unrelieved black. The flat features and curly mopped head were those of a Negro—until the black hands reached up and removed the face and hair entirely!

The whole thing was a cleverly devised mask that fitted

over his head—and beneath it was the horribly scarred and distorted face of Sanford Caldwell, the legless cripple!

That hideous gargoyle of a face twisted into a leer as Sanford looked down at the girl, and then he saw what the old man had been doing. Immediately the scarred features convulsed with rage and the fires of hell kindled in his murky eyes. Pivoting clumsily, he stalked toward the couch—and Jerry saw that the whole lower half of his body, beneath the loose black trousers, was a piece of machinery; a machine that he operated by means of a lever at his left side. The feet were huge, wide-spreading, mushroom-like clusters of pads that enabled him to keep his balance as he operated his artificial walking apparatus.

"It was a mistake to bring this girl here," the old man started to scold. "You should have let her burn with the rest of the tribe. Dead she was safe, but here she'll be a constant source of danger. And you shouldn't be fooling around here now. There's no time for that. You've got to get back to the building in your wheelchair so that you can be discovered by the fire-fighters. They must be there by now—and unless they find you near the blaze there will be difficult explanations to make. Come on—I'll help you to get back."

But Sanford's eyes were blazing with fanatical rage and he paid no attention to the other's ranting. Instead, he gave a short, low whistle, and out of the side room scuttled a misshapen, nearly naked creature that had once been a man—a horribly crippled, gaunt and emaciated creature that scurried along on all fours and seemed more animal than human.

"Take him, Dan!" Sanford snapped, and the monstrosity leaped into the air and threw himself upon the old man's back; skinny arms wrapping around him, clawing hands holding him helpless until Sanford stood in front of him.

Sanford's huge, black-gloved hands shot out and fastened like vises in his shoulders. As easily as if the old man were a doll, he lifted him and carried him to one of those curious chairs; sat him in it and pressed a button near its base.

Immediately two stout metal rods rose up from the heavy

arms of the chair; rods that passed just inside the old man's elbows—and then his whole body became convulsed, taut and straining, as a torturing current of electricity shot through it and threw him forward against the rods.

"Now, my dear father, I'll take care of the rest of the party—especially of the young lady who seems to interest you so much," Sanford sneered. In a flash Jerry understood the resemblance the old man bore to Dr. Caldwell, and the difference.

This was Rolfe Caldwell, his uncle!

On the wall of the cave hung a surgeon's uniform and mask. Now Jerry understood how his uncle had been able to impersonate the doctor so successfully. In that all-covering costume it was no wonder that poor Katherine had taken him for her father, and once she had yielded her will and obeyed his devilish commands her doom had been sealed.

Now I'll show you how a young lady should be handled," Sanford chuckled, and his mechanical steps started in Leta's direction.

Shuddering terror and revulsion were mirrored in her face as she struggled with the ropes, trying desperately to squirm out of his reach. It was useless, and her pitiful moan of despair was the surrendering of all hope.

Jerry had been crouching there in the partly open doorway waiting for an opportunity that would be certain. If he could leap out and pounce on Sanford's back, throttle him before his scuttling slave came to the rescue . . .

But now there was no more time to wait. Putting the unconscious baby down at one side of the tunnel, he pushed open the door—and immediately a bell began to ring clamorously!

With a snarl of rage Sanford whirled on him, and in the same instant the crippled monstrosity leaped. Before Jerry could fight clear, those gaunt, spidery arms were twining around his legs, fastening their grip at his knees so that he could not move. Then Sanford was gripping him with his incredibly strong hands, dragging him to another chair beside Rolfe Caldwell.

Again a button was pressed and two metal rods shot up out of the chair arms. Jerry struggled desperately to break loose, but Sanford's grip was like iron—and the moment h released it the prisoner was held by a force even more irresistible. Livid fire tore through him, tingling every cell in his body, drawing his limbs up so that it seemed the bones must snap. Helpless to move a finger, he strained forward, held mercilessly in place by those diabolical rods that stopped his tortured body from catapulting across the cave.

By now Rolfe Caldwell had been reduced to a blubbering, whining wretch. Tears flowed from his eyes and mingled with the streams of perspiration that ran down from his forehead.

"You can't do this to me, Sanford," he pleaded. "I'm your father."

"I'm remembering that," the black clad cripple answered, and there was unholy satisfaction in his voice.

"I gave you the apparatus that lets you walk," the old man babbled on frantically. "If it wasn't for me you wouldn't be able to get out of your chair. Remember, Sanford, it was my idea to inflame the mob against Eustace so that they would wipe out the whole family and the estate would go to you. It was my idea to set fire to the house so that the mob would be blamed for the killings. I've done all the planning, Sanford— I provided the dummies of yourself to leave in your room when you were out—I took care of the children and planted them where they would do the most harm—I arranged everything. You need me, Sanford; you can't handle things without me!"

But Sanford only laughed in his face, a hard cruel, exultant laugh that sent chills down Jerry's back. Once he had heard a madman laugh like that as he was being laced into a straightjacket . . .

"Not anymore, I don't need you," Sanford chuckled. "You've served your purpose fully, my dear father. Yes, you brought me these mechanical legs—but let me remind you that it is your fault that I lost my real ones. If you had given me proper care they never would have had to be amputated.

And let me remind you that it is you to whom I am indebted for this scarred face. If you had not run off and deserted me I never would have been caught in the blaze that left me the way I am today.

"Someday, I knew, you would come back. Someday I would have a chance to pay you back for what you did to me. Someday . . . You can't imagine how I planned for that day. And then, when you came and made yourself known to me, I knew that my time was at hand. All that I had to do was obey you like a poor, half-witted fool. Nothing to do but let you arrange everything for me and set the stage so that I could take command—and turn *you* into the same horrible sort of freak you made out of me!"

As he spoke he had stalked to one of, of the cabinets, and when he came back he carried a blow-torch. With maddening deliberation he lit it, turned up the flames so that it changed from yellow to a hissing, sparking blue. Slowly he moved it toward Rolfe's face, held it just out of reach—and then shoved it forward so that the flame lapped up the goatee, swept around the screaming victim's skull and denuded it of hair.

The old man howled and screamed in utter agony, but that terrible flame never turned away from him. Over his mouth, his nose, his ears, it played. Down his chest, his arms, his legs, so that his clothing caught fire and fell away in charred bits. And still that relentless flame hosed over him.

His screams echoed and reechoed through the low cavern. The stench of his burning flesh filled the place. Leta moaned and turned her face away. Jerry shouted at the grinning fiend behind the torch, pleaded with him—but Sanford only contorted his hideous face into a horrible caricature of a smile.

'Don't be impatient, my dear cousin," he mocked. "Your turn is coming very soon. As soon as I am finished here. All my life I've hated you for your handsome face—for the way you have with women. They flocked around you—and shuddered away from me. But now I'm going to change that. When I am through with you they will run screaming at sight of you. They'll think I'm a beauty by comparison!"

His bestial chuckles mingled with his father's screams as the biting flame of the blow-torch ate into the old man's flesh, right through it to the bone, and hissed away there until the very marrow was scalded out of it. Half-cooked alive, Rolfe Caldwell still clung to consciousness while his body was maimed and broken.

"You need not worry about the young lady being a source of danger to me," the fiend assured his writhing, screaming victim. "She will never leave this cave. So long as she is able to interest me she will remain as she is—but once she fails to satisfy me I'll make of her a thing that nobody on God's earth will ever recognize! But I hardly think that will be necessary. She will stay here as my mistress; and you and Jerry will stay here as my abject, broken slaves—just like Dan, here. You wouldn't think that Dan was once one of the best electricians in New York, would you? He came here to install this electrical apparatus for me, and then he stayed to—er—test it out.

"You will be like him, both of you—crippled, shambling wrecks; brainless and docile, ready to obey me in whatever I order . . ."

He was fairly slavering as he reveled in his hellish triumph, but his words had lost their power to terrify Jerry. Already he could feel that terrible flame eating into his flesh, roasting him alive, turning him into a broken thing for whom death would be a blessed deliverance.

In a few minutes now the warped-brained fiend would be finished with his father and would turn his wrath on Jerry . . .

And after that it would be Leta's turn to endure a hell even more ghastly and unendurable!

Jerry's sweating face turned compassionately toward the girl—and saw that she was partly free! While Sanford was engrossed with his Satanic pastime she had been struggling with the ropes that bound her wrists, completing the work that Rolfe had started!

Her arms were free. Now she was working at her ankles, frantically untying the knots, kicking the ropes loose. They fell away—but instead of springing to her feet and running she still lay there, tugging at her clothing, rolling and twisting . . .

With a little moan she slid off the edge of the couch and rolled to the floor—and as she scrambled to her feet her clothes fell away and she was almost naked!

With a angry snarl Sanford whirled on her—but the snarl faded from his lips and his eyes fairly goggled out of his head as she tugged at the last intimate bits of feminine attire and let them fall at her feet, to stand there completely nude—nude and subtly inviting!

The blow-torch was forgotten in his hand as he stood staring at that lovely body—as she walked toward him with a smile on her lips and her white arms outstretched. It fell to the floor, unheeded, before she reached him; before.

Desperately, frenziedly, Jerry tried to regain the slightest control of his taut muscles, but they were rigid, like bands of steel. Fiercely he tried to turn his eyes away so that he would not have to watch what was going on there right in front of him—would not have to endure the additional agony of seeing Leta giving herself unreservedly to this monster!

Her arms were encircling him, pressing him close to her naked body. Her lips were glued tight to his misshapen mouth—but she was pushing him backward, backward farther and farther . . .

Streams of perspiration trickled down Jerry's crimson face as he fought his knotted muscles, as he strained against those diabolical metal bars that held him back. If only he could reach forward a few inches more—even an inch . . .

Sanford must have realized at the last moment what was about to happen. Suddenly he braced himself and tried to push Leta away—but at that instant Jerry's superhuman efforts bore fruit. His knees inched forward that last little distance—and touched the fiend's metallic legs!

Instantly there was a flash, the dry smell of an electrical discharge, and the power went off as the fuse blew out under the additional strain of electrifying Sanford and the girl in his arms.

For seconds that seemed eternities Jerry sat there while his body recovered from the effects of the current that had his hungry arms encircled her and his eager hands, quickly stripped of the black gloves, pawed over her alluring curves, held it rigid. Then he was free, flinging himself at the snarling fiend.

"Get him, Dan!" Sanford howled in terror, but Jerry's fist met the brainless cripple's rush—smashed him down.

Dan toppled out of the way, and then Jerry reached his objective. His fist pounded into Sanford's face just as the inhuman devil's arms closed around him.

Once those steely fingers closed around his windpipe Jerry knew that he would be finished. His throat would be torn right out of his body, just as this monster had done with Lothar Zimmerlie. But he was almost helpless in Sanford's grip. Those vise-like fingers were paralyzing him, threatening to snap his bones. One hand was stealing steadily across his chest, getting nearer to his throat . . .

Bracing his toes against the floor Jerry put everything he had in a sudden heave. For a long moment the fiend swayed, fought desperately to retain his balance, but the artificial feet were not quite up to that test. Then he toppled over, still clutching Jerry in his punishing grip.

But the moment they crashed to the floor, Sanford let out a howl of agony—a howl that was echoed by frantic yells and screams. Into Jerry's nostrils floated the odor of freshly burned flesh, of singeing hair and burning cloth.

There on the floor beneath Sanford, was his own blowtorch, the roaring flame eating into his skull!

Frantically he tried to wriggle away from it, but his own shoulders held it in place, and now Jerry was deaf to his screams, to his pleas ands promises. Not until the last breath had gasped out of his body and his twisted soul had joined his father in death did Jerry relax his hold and stagger to his feet—to the soft haven of Leta's open arms.

~ ~ ~

With Abbie in his arms and Leta at his side, Jerry led the way out of the cave and into the woods at the rear of the Caldwell estate. Ahead of them they could hear the roaring shouts of the volunteer fire-fighters—but they were altogether unprepared for the dejected, grey-haired figure they found watching the ineffectual attempts to save his home and workshop.

'Thank God you're safe!" Dr. Caldwell gasped when he saw them, and for once there were tears in his cold, unemotional eyes. "I? Well, the mob from town thought they were going to hang me, but the sheriff and some of his deputies put a stop to that. He's going to give me a chance to prove that I had nothing to do with these kidnappings—"

"That'll be a cinch when we take him back to the place we just left!" Jerry laughed happily—but it is doubtful whether his father even heard him.

Again Dr. Caldwell was all physician as he knelt beside little Abbie and examined her critically, as he felt her pulse and tested her heart. The grey head nodded with satisfaction as he looked up into their anxious faces.

"She's perfectly okay," he announced in his usual stiff, professional manner. "Drugged, is all. In an hour or two she will be as well as ever."

Which, Jerry and Leta felt, was all that anyone could ask.

SATAN'S LOVE BAZAAR

Chapter One

The Devil Makes a Pledge

MURDER IS NOTHING NEW or particularly startling in the life of a district attorney, and we had had plenty of homicides in Jordan City: drunken killings, gang slayings, insurance murders, crimes of passion—the usual run that any city D.A.'s office handles year in and year out. My two terms had hardened me, and I thought I could take things of that sort in my stride. That was before Sheriff Jackson brought in Lute Brunner from hills. That was before . . .

Six hours after the dull-witted farmer clumped into my office the whole city was recoiling in horror from the details of his ghastly crime. The office itself still seemed to reek with the fetid odor he had brought into it; a nauseous, acrid odor that had impregnated his ragged clothing and stamped him as the foulest monster I had ever encountered.

A "hex murder," the newspapers called it, but the deeper I delved into the maze of ignorance and superstition that was its background the more I wondered how any human being— any creature molded in God's image, could descend to such a level. To kill in the heat of passion is one thing; even to murder cold-bloodedly, to remove someone who stands in the killer's way, is understandable—but the thing that Lute Brunner did . . .

Stolid-faced, dull-eyed, hardly appearing to be interested in what I was saying, he sat across the courtroom and stared at me as I gave the state's case to the jury.

"Gentlemen," I said, "I want you to visualize in your own

minds, if you can, that scene in the woods on the side of Shiloh Mountain. Dusk is deepening into night as this man, Lute Brunner, creeps through the brush until he is within a few feet of old Hetty Mears' lonely cabin. For days he has been planning this deed, timing it carefully, picking just the right spot so that she will not see him when she steps out of her door.

"Crouching there in the brush he waits until this half-crippled, sixty-five year old woman hobbles out to draw water for her evening meal. Silently he leaps upon her and clubs her over the head. Then he ties up her unconscious body, lashes her wrists and ankles securely with baling wire he has brought with him.

"Callously he drags her to her own outdoor fireplace and slips ropes through her bound wrists and ankles, fastens the ropes to two trees and draws them tight until she is suspended helplessly above the dead coals of her noon fire. Deliberately he piles up fresh fuel beneath her and sets a match to it.

"Like a fiend out of hell he stands there as the flames catch her clothing and burn them from her writhing body. Like an inhuman devil he stands gloating there while her screams ring in his ears, while her flesh sears and blisters—while she roasts alive! Right in the smoke of her disintegrating body he stands, glorying in her agony, until the stench of her cremation has saturated his clothing as thoroughly as this monstrous deed has stained his soul!

"A crime so foul it is incredible that a human being could have conceived and executed it! And what excuse does he offer for this barbaric outrage? Why did he put this helpless old woman to death in the most horrible way known to man? Why—"

Lute Brunner answered for himself. Before I could give the answers to my rhetorical questions—before I could tell them that Hetty Mears had died because the butter in his churn would not set, because one of his cows went dry out of season—he was on his feet, interrupting me.

"She was a witch," he repeated. It was the only defense he

had made. "She put the sign on me. Fire is the only thing that kills a witch, so I burned her—burned her till there was nothing left to come back and do me more harm. You don't understand, Mr. Taylor, but maybe some day when the sign is on you—"

Frank Dixon, his attorney, was on his feet, vainly trying to quiet him, to drag him back to his place at the counsel table. The judge's gavel was pounding, bailiffs were starting toward him. Brunner gave up. With a shrug he sank back into his chair, into the semi-coma that had characterized him all through the trial.

No, I didn't understand how any human being no matter how uneducated or how superstitious, could be driven to commit such an unforgivable atrocity; and before I finished my summation I knew that the jury agreed with me. Lute Brunner's conviction was a foregone conclusion—but as my eyes traveled over the spectators they came to rest on a stalwart, leonine-headed individual sitting over among the hill people, and the edge was taken off my satisfaction.

Abel Fleming was a power in the hills; was the power in that wild, thinly populated territory that stretched beyond the state road. Like a feudal lord he ruled the ignorant inhabitants who cowered in fear of his supposed supernatural powers.

Weird tales drifted down from the scattered shanties of his domain; whispered tales of the influence of his evil eye, of the dread hex by which he kept his followers in subjection—tales of men who disappeared, men who mysteriously withered and died when they had aroused his displeasure. But always there was nothing but whispers; never actual testimony from the frightened hill-folk, never direct evidence that could be used to pin anything criminal on the reputed hex-doctor.

Calmly, his big, strong-featured face revealing neither satisfaction nor disapproval, Abel Fleming listened, and when I sat down I felt his eyes upon me. They were dark eyes that studied me without betraying the slightest hint of what was going on in the unfathomable mind behind them.

Unquestionably Lute Brunner was guilty of the murder of Hetty Mears, but every hour that I had spent preparing the case against him I had become more and more convinced that it was Abel Fleming who should have gone to the chair for the crime. Nowhere was there the slightest lead to impli-cate him, no¬ where anything direct that I could lay my fin-ger on—yet I could fairly see his dominating figure looming in the background, pulling the strings that operated his pup-pets for undisclosed motives of his own.

There was something uncanny about that situation—and now, as my eyes encountered Fleming's basilisk stare, I had the weird feeling that he knew exactly what was going on in my mind; that he was chuckling inwardly, secure in the knowledge that any attempt to involve him in the crime would be futile . . .

The jurymen filed out of the courtroom—and were back again in record time. There had been no worth-while de-fense, but the speed with which they reached their verdict of guilty, was something of a blow to Frank Dixon, the attorney the court had appointed for Brunner's defense. Dixon had worked hard on a hopeless case, trying vainly to forestall a decision that was a foregone conclusion, and my sympathy went out to him.

That was the story with most of Dixon's cases—hopeless from the start; yet he was ambitious and worked with a zeal that was worthy of better reward. The court knew that he was always available for appointment as counsel and that he would give every case the best possible handling, and as a result he had been defending a raft of cheap crook cases which netted him very little and were not much help in fur-thering his ambition—which, I believed, was to succeed me in the district attorney's office.

If that was Dixon's ambition, but I knew that it was doomed to failure. With the fall reopening of court I was to resign my office to accept an appointment to the district court bench, a reward for the drastic anti-vice campaign I had conducted until Jordan City was purged of most of its undesirables. But it had already been decided in the county committee of the dominant party that my friend and assistant, Neil Blanchard, was to succeed me—unless Cliff Mason, a formidable opponent, was able to defeat him in the primaries.

That didn't leave much hope for Dixon, but, nevertheless, as his client was led off to his cell I could not help feeling sorry for him and admiring the hopeless fight he had waged against a case that would have taken the heart out of most attorneys.

The picture of Brunner's ghastly crime, of the helpless old woman roasting to death like a chicken spitted over a fire, had spread a miasma of horror over the whole courtroom. I detected it in the eyes of the jurors, in the white face of the judge, in the low murmurs of the spectators as they shuffled out. It would be a long time before any of us would forget that grisly picture.

All during the afternoon it haunted me, despite my efforts to shake it off, and it still weighed on me as I left my office for the day and set out for the Charity Bazaar being held by the Jordan City Civic Club, of which I was one of the directors. Each June we staged this bazaar in the city's largest auditorium and devoted a week to raising money to finance our charity program for the year. All the best people in town took part, and the event had come to be quite a social function.

This was the opening day, the first glimpse I had had of this year's layout, but almost as soon as I walked into the comfortably filled auditorium I was surprised and not very agreeably impressed. Pretty young Flora Campbell, who stepped up to sell me a program, was dressed in a costume that would have attracted plenty of attention on any beach. Her bare legs and stomach and her almost equally revealed breasts were startling there in that brightly lighted room.

But that, I soon discovered, was the keynote of the affair. Instead of the pleasant, easy formality to which we were accustomed, this year's edition of the bazaar had been "livened up" to the point of being decidedly risqué—the work of a

Broadway director who had been imported to stage it for us.

As I wandered from booth to booth, from attraction to attraction, I became more and more disappointed—and vaguely apprehensive. But it was not until I reached Evelyn Owen's booth that my disapproval became personal. Evelyn was my fiancée, was to become Mrs. Garry Taylor in the fall when I became a judge, but she had been very secretive about her stunt in the bazaar.

When I reached her booth I saw the reason why. She was selling kisses at five dollars apiece!

"Don't be a jealous silly!" she laughed at me when I protested. "You're frowning like an old bear—and everyone's looking at you. For five dollars you may kiss me—and from present indications I'll need a bit of kissing before the day is over; there don't seem to be many men who think my kisses are worth that much."

"But any Tom, Dick or Harry—" I started to object.

"Any Tom, Dick or Harry," she mimicked. "You know right well, Garry Taylor, this bazaar is patronized almost exclusively by members of our own circle—so what difference will a few kisses make?"

She was right in that; our bazaar seldom attracted any but the society element of the city—men who might have lightly kissed her at any time without paying five dollars to help provide milk for hungry youngsters. Perhaps I was unduly jealous. I tried to tell myself that—but, somehow, I didn't like it, and my curious uneasiness increased.

Not until some time afterward did that half-sensed apprehension take more definite form. I was at the ticket window, and suddenly found myself staring into the dark, compelling eyes of Abel Fleming as he handed over a dollar bill for his admission. The hill people had never come to the bazaar in previous years, and Fleming's presence sounded a tocsin of alarm in my brain. Vividly his presence recalled to my mind the courtroom scene—recalled the ghastly picture of that helpless old woman burning to a crisp over a roaring fire . . .

The knowledge that he was there at the bazaar, that he was

inside mingling with my friends, with Evelyn, would give me no peace. Shortly I found someone to relieve me and went back into the auditorium—and immediately I knew that a sixth sense had been warning me, had been urging me back inside!

Shocked and outraged, I started across the hall to where Abel Fleming stood at Evelyn's booth. He had stepped up onto the raised platform and was taking her in his arms—but instead of the jocular peck which most men took for their five dollars he was crushing her to him passionately! One arm was around her, bending her head back into the crook of his elbow while his lips enveloped hers lingeringly; and the other hand was stealing up under her breast, cupping its rounded fullness in his fingers!

For a moment Evelyn struggled with him, tried to push him away, but then her efforts ceased and she seemed to relax in his arm as his fingers bored into hers. The next moment I was across the hall and my fingers fastened in his collar. In my rage I yanked him back so furiously that he toppled off the low platform and fell to the floor—to be met with a fist to the jaw the moment he was back on his feet. That blow floored him again, and I stood waiting for him to get up, waiting to unleash the fury that was raging like hot fire in my swollen veins. I hoped he would come back.

Half a dozen of my friends intervened before the fight could go any farther and started rushing Fleming to the door. But before he was past me he set his feet solidly and flung their hands off his arms. Blood was trickling from the corner of his mouth and his dark eyes were like coals of fire in his white, set face as he stood there, glaring his savage hate.

"I'll go—you don't have to throw me out," he grated. "You can put my body out—but I'll still be here with you every moment. You'll know that I'm here—and before you close this bazaar you'll come up into the hills and beg me to come back and have free run of it!"

Even after he had gone we stood staring at each other, white-faced and shaken; wordless until a low, gasping moan snapped us out of our semi-trace. That moan came from

Mary Corbin, standing right beside me. Her face was ashen under the rouge of her Oriental dancer make-up, and her eyes were widened to great pools of terror.

She began to sway backward just as my hand slipped around her waist—and then she was trembling and sobbing hysterically in my arms.

Chapter Two

The Unseen Director

Each year it was the custom of the Ladies Auxiliary of the Civic Club to serve supper between the afternoon and evening sessions of the bazaar for those participating in it. Usually those meals were jolly gatherings, but tonight the festivity was subdued; hushed, as if a pall of tragedy hung over us all.

As I sat beside Evelyn I noticed that the business of eating was receiving concentrated attention all around me. Whether we would admit it or not, uneasy superstition had already clamped its cold grip on us. Abel Fleming's reputation was a potent thing, even in the city—and the picture of malignant picture he had made as he hurled his curious threat was still vivid in every mind.

As soon as we were finished I went back to my place at the door, and it was several hours before I had an opportunity to go inside again to see how the bazaar was progressing. It was Neil Blanchard who came out to get me.

"Better come inside and have a look around, Garry,' he said uneasily. "I don't like it worth a damn."

The moment we got back onto the floor of the auditorium I knew what was bothering him. The whole atmosphere of the place had changed; just how I could not be sure, but I sensed it in the faster tempo, in the undercurrent of hysteria. The laughter was louder and more boisterous; the dancing was wilder and more spectacular; the expression on the faces of the performers was more excited, more feverish.

"You get it, don't you?" Blanchard turned to me as we

passed booth after booth. "The whole thing is degenerating into a honkytonk performance. It's getting altogether out of hand, and the first thing you know we're going to have trouble. You can thank Berleigh Parker, our expert director, for that. He laid this thing out so that the emphasis is on sex wherever you turn—and now the party's running away with him."

Business was flourishing wherever we looked. Lines stood waiting at the central dance floor where the "dime-a-dance" hostesses were charging half a dollar for their services. Crowds were flocking in to see the Oriental dancers and the peepshows. Evelyn and her co-workers were having all too much patronage to suit me at their kiss-selling booth. Even the fortune-tellers had customers waiting in line for their services—which were more than satisfactory, judging by the grinning faces of those who came out of the curtained booths.

Rushing business everywhere—but in every case the activity had become feverish, and the women were almost beyond themselves with excitement. I agreed with Blanchard; there was trouble in the air—and instinctively my eyes again strayed anxiously to where Evelyn was offering her lips to any man who had five dollars. She was laughing provokingly as another customer stepped up on her platform; was holding up her lips invitingly as he took her in his arms—and the chill of apprehension that trickled down my spine clashed with the hot anger that reddened my face!

The stage end of the auditorium had been partitioned off into a small tableau theater. Blanchard drew me into line with the jostling crowd of ticket-purchasers, and we got inside just as the curtain went up to reveal a very effective living reproduction of a famous painting of an artist and his model.

Betty Blanchard, Neil's wife, was the model, standing on the dais. Her arms and shoulders and feet were bare and she was holding a loose white robe around her body so that the rounded tops of her breasts were just visible above it. The artist, brush poised in hand before his canvas, was looking at her before putting in the next stroke.

A ripple of applause ran through the audience, but it was the scattered applause of the uninitiated. The others were waiting, expectant—and then they were rewarded. Betty's robe seemed to slip from her fingers and almost dropped to the floor. Just in time she caught it—but for a long moment she stood there before them stark naked!

Neil gasped as the crowd whooped with delight. I could see the hot blood running up into his cheeks, but as I watched him out of the corner of my eye I was sure that he had not seen what was plain to me. That slip was not accidental; it was carefully planned—cleverly performed so that the seeming accident had a much more arousing effect on her audience than if Betty had stood there in the nude when the curtain rose.

The excited gleam I caught in her eyes betrayed her, and I knew that the thing was intentional—just as I could see that she fairly reveled in the wanton display of her charms.

But even as I understood what she had done I sought vainly for what had prompted it. For some time I had been aware that Betty was having a flirtation with Harry Graber, the man who posed as the artist, but even that would not account for her making such a public exhibition of herself . . .

As the curtain came down Neil Blanchard came to life and started grimly for the stage door, on the outside of the little theater. I was right at his heels as he stormed in behind the scenery and confronted Betty and Graber.

"How did that happen?" he demanded furiously; and before either of them could answer, "why haven't you anything on under that sheet?"

Betty stammered something about getting into the spirit of the pose, but Blanchard had already whirled on Graber.

"It strikes me as very odd that just you and Betty, out of all the others, should have been cast together for that scene," he said significantly. And I knew then that he had not been altogether blind to what was going on for the past few months. "And it strikes me as even more odd that Betty gets into the spirit of her work so completely that she strolls around here behind the scenes practically naked with you—"

Rage was blazing in his eyes and his lips were drained of color, but Graber backed away, frightened and shaken.

"I don't know anything about this, Neil," he protested. "I had nothing to do with what she wore. What happened was as much a surprise to me as to you. But Betty isn't the only one—the girls all seem to have lost their heads. I never saw them like this before; they're throwing themselves into these poses so completely that we don't know what to expect next."

"That's Parker's work," Blanchard swore bitterly. "He has the women so worked up with his damn sexy ideas that they don't know what they're going."

"I thought of that," Graber nodded agreement, "but I have a hunch that the responsibility goes farther back than Parker. He's only doing what he was hired to do, but you remember it was Cliff Mason who proposed an outside director in the first place. He's the one who engaged Parker and brought him here."

Cliff Mason . . .

I hadn't much use for the man. Aside from political differences, I felt that he wasn't trustworthy; and I blamed him for preventing me from scoring a complete victory in my vice crusade. Mason was attorney for Joe Steckel, owner of a notorious night-club and the man we believed to be the head of Jordan City's vice ring. Our campaign succeeded in convicting most of his lieutenants, and we managed to clean up the Golden Horseshoe, his night-club, and put it on a respectable basis, but we weren't able to nail Steckel himself—thanks of Cliff Mason's questionable tactics.

But even though I disliked the man personally, I could see no reason why he should want to debauch the charity bazaar . . .

A wild disturbance outside in the auditorium suddenly swept all thought of Cliff Mason out of my mind and keyed up my every nerve. Waves of applause, loud cheers and raucous shouts of encouragement rose in a riotous din. That demonstration sounded more like the drunken ovation a stag performer might receive than anything to be expected at the bazaar.

Grim-lipped I hurried to the stage door and stepped out into the hall, to find a boisterous crowd gathered around the barker's platform outside the Oriental dancers' booth. Mary Corbin was in the center of that platform—and as I looked at her I felt the hot blood rushing up into my cheeks and my hands balling into fists at my sides.

Mary was a very sweet girl—and at one time I had been close to marrying her. That was before Evelyn Owen came to Jordan City; but even though Mary was no longer my sweetheart I still held a very genuine affection for her—and the thing she was doing shocked me almost as much as if it were Evelyn up there on the platform.

With utter abandon she was throwing herself into one of the most sensual dances I had ever seen. One by one she had discarded her garments as her gyrations became wilder and wilder, until she wore nothing but a few veils—and even those dropped to the platform before I could make my way through the tight-packed crowd. Stark naked she postured before her audience, turning slowly so that every line, every intimate curve of her body was revealed to their feasting eyes!

Slowly and deliberately she turned at first, then faster and faster until she was pirouetting like a top, whirling with dizzying speed, a flesh-white column that went round and round—until it crumpled and sank to the floor in a sprawled heap!

"She's fainted!" the scared barker shouted as he bent over her. "Get a doctor, somebody—quick!"

We carried her into the booth and stood aside while Dr. Wilkins worked over her. Strange, half-intelligible words were coming from her hardly moving lips. He bent close and tried to catch what she was saying, but in a few minutes he gave it up and shook his head puzzledly.

"'Able' is about the only word I can distinguish," he said

doubtfully. "Evidently something she doesn't think she is able to do—"

But cold terror was stealing into my breast and clutching at my heart until it seemed that its beating must stop. Able— she wasn't saying "able!" In her half-conscious delirium she was muttering "Abel"—was talking to Abel Fleming, who had promised that he would be there with us every minute that the bazaar was open!

There seems to be no indication that she was drugged," the doctor frowned, "yet there is no doubt that she is in some sort of trance, under some sort of spell. About the only thing I can do is administer a sedative."

From his bag he took a hypodermic needle and filled it, but just as he was about to press the point into Mary's side the seizure left her. For a moment she sat up and her frightened eyes turned from one to the other of us while she covered her breasts with the shawl that had been thrown over her. Then she burst into hysterical tears and sagged forward, limp and close to collapse.

She had been under some sort of spell, the doctor had said—and she was calling Abel Fleming by name . . .

As I stared down at her, sobbing brokenly in the arms of one of her friends, I remembered Fleming's malevolent face—remembered the startling effect his glaring eyes had had upon her. Perhaps Mary was more psychic, more sensitive, than the rest of us. Perhaps she had known then what his threat would mean—had known what we all faced . . .

In that moment the vague, indefinable apprehension that had been growing within me began to crystalize; became transformed into an eerie fear of something that my mind would not admit was possible—but that my intuition shuddered away from in terror!

Chapter Three

Death Steps In

That night it seemed the bazaar never would close, but

when the auditorium finally was darkened and I started home with Evelyn the fear that was riding me found plenty more on which to feed. She was there beside me in the car physically, but that was all. Mentally she was so far away that she was hardly aware of my presence.

So far away—where? Cold perspiration seeped out on the back of my hands as I asked myself that question—and shied away from the answer that thrust itself into my mind. Was she, like Mary Corbin, already hearing Abel Fleming's call? Was that why she was so distracted, so absorbed with her own thoughts? Because his devilish power was beginning to exert itself over her?

Surreptitiously I watched her, and saw that when she did look at me it was with a peculiar, calculating expression such as I had never seen in her eyes. It was as if she was studying me, weighing me, speculating on what I might do . . .

Her unusual behavior baffled me, and added fuel to my growing terror. Whatever it was that was coming over her, it had its source back there in the bazaar, I knew; and the surest way to combat it was to keep her out of that place. But how?

"I don't like the way the bazaar is being run this year," I plunged into the thing desperately, "and I don't like that job of yours a little bit. It's cheapening, Evelyn. That's what's the matter with the whole bazaar—it's cheap and bawdy. Do something for me, darling; stay away from it tomorrow. Give it up; there will be plenty of others to take your place, and I'd feel a lot happier knowing that you are not taking part in it."

But even before I finished talking, I knew my cause was lost. Her eyes were becoming cold and hostile, and her little jaw was hardening into lines of determination that I could not mistake.

"I've promised, and I'm going through with it," she said doggedly. "You're simply being very silly, Garry, and I won't listen to you. If you insist, we're going to quarrel, and I'll go ahead with it anyway. Nothing you can say will stop me."

Her voice was rising excitedly, and as I looked deep into

her eyes I knew it was no use. She was anxious to go back there tomorrow, was looking forward to it eagerly, and she resented my interference as if I intended to deprive her of something on which she had set her heart.

There was nothing I could do but shrug and let the matter drop, but all the next day my thoughts kept reverting to the bazaar, dreading the afternoon hour at which I knew it would open. That was a hard day for me, aside from the worry that gnawed at me unceasingly. I was tied up all afternoon and booked for a dinner engagement that kept me until nearly nine o'clock.

By the time I reached the bazaar the evening session was going in full blast—and it took only one look to tell me that last night's session had been tame compared to this one. The moment I stepped into the auditorium I was shocked by the spirit of wild abandon that ruled the place.

And tonight, I saw with added misgivings, it was not only our usual people who were in attendance. Word of what had gone on the night before must have been passed around the town, and as a result most of the worst elements of the city had flocked to the bazaar. They were crowding the aisles, leering at the women, snickering and making vulgar comments as they cheered them on to further excesses.

"Look at this place," I tried frantically to make Evelyn see what was going on around her. "It's a bedlam. We've got the scum of the town in here—and you women are encouraging them and leading them on. I don't know what's come over you—"

But she laughed at me.

"That's all in your imagination, Garry," she chided. "None of the other men seem to mind. Why should you? I can't understand why you've become such a Puritan all of a sudden. There seems to be something on your mind that's making you suspicious and disagreeable—and I don't like it."

She was right about the other men of our circle, I had to admit that. They seemed to have entered into the spirit of the wild revelry as completely as the women. Was the fault mine? Was I worrying too much? I tried to answer those questions honestly, but I didn't know. I realized that during the day my thoughts had been with Abel Fleming far more than they should have been—seeing him hold Evelyn in his arms and kissing her, seeing him glaring his hate and hearing him rasping his threat. Perhaps that was it; perhaps I was stupidly playing the fellow's game by letting his ominous-sounding words harass me . . .

I tried to forget my suspicions, but the fear that was gnawing at my heart was not a thing with which I could argue. If only I could get Evelyn out of there and keep her out . . .

I was passing one of the fortune-tellers' booths at that moment, and Connie Haemer slipped up to my side and linked her arm through mine.

"I haven't had a chance to read your palm yet, Garry," she coaxed as she smiled up at me. "You'd better come in now. My last customer was so well satisfied he said he would bring back an army."

Connie was Evelyn's best friend. If anyone could influence her, Connie would be the one. Perhaps I could convince her of the danger I feared; perhaps I could persuade her to get out of the bazaar and take Evelyn with her. Anyway, it was worth a try.

With that intention I went into the dimly lighted booth with her, and the curtained doorway closed behind us. The booth was just a little cubbyhole with a small table in the center and a padded bench running around three sides of it. A draped overhead lamp and a number of cushions completed the furnishings.

Connie seated me opposite her across the tiny table and took my right hand in hers. Before I could say anything she began her palaver, so I grinned and thought I'd let her go through with it. But in a few moments I noticed that this fortune-telling was taking a peculiar turn. Connie was rubbing my hand, caressing it with warm fingers that made little excursions past my wrist and up my sleeve. She was not looking at my palm at all. Instead her eyes were fixed raptly on my face—eyes that sparkled with excitement; that were warm with desire and invitation.

Now she was leaning over the table toward me, and I noticed that the folds of her loose gypsy blouse had divided and fallen apart so that her unconfined breasts were almost fully exposed. They were rising and falling rapidly with the quickening breath that was panting out through her eager, parted lips. I tried to rise, but for a split second that brought my face closer to hers across the table—and her arms slid around my neck as her lips captured mine and held them in a kiss so intense that I could taste warm blood in my mouth!

Connie, too, was in the clutches of this thing that had settled over the bazaar! Forcibly I tore her arms from around my neck and plumped her back onto her bench while I dived through the curtained doorway. Now I knew that I was right; that bazaar was going stark mad—and some-where in the background a fiendish devil was chuckling as he watched it degenerate into a Bacchanalian rout!

As I shot out of that booth I almost ran headlong into Neil Blanchard. He looked at me curiously and then nodded his head.

"You've had a taste of it, too, eh?" he grunted. "I've heard what's going on in those booths. It's almost as bad out here, for that matter. The whole bazaar's gone cuckoo, if you ask me—and that's just what Burleigh Parker wants."

Bitterly he surveyed the frenzied activity on all sides, and then turned back to me.

"You know that this place is full of reporters and newspaper photographers, don't you? From the New York papers, every one of them. How'd they get here? Parker sent for them, of course. He's deliberately staging an orgy here so that he'll get his name and pictures in the papers and re-establish himself on Broadway. He's been slipping out of the lime-light lately and needs something like this to put him back in the headlines."

As he spoke I saw the flare of the cameramen's flashlight bulbs as they snapped pictures of the frenzied dancing going on in the center of the hall—dancing that would have been more in place in a voodoo debauch . . . I went looking for Mr. Burleigh Parker.

In one of the wings behind the stage I located him, and cornered him before he had a chance to evade me. His eyes were frightened and he was trembling as I grabbed him and pinned him back against the wall. Perspiration beaded out on his forehead as I demanded to know what in hell he thought he was doing with our bazaar, but then he found his voice.

"I don't know what's happening here, Mr. Taylor," he protested. "I've directed other bazaars like this one—but never one that got out of hand like this. It's becoming a madhouse out there. I can't control it. And frankly I don't like it. I'll do anything I can—anything you say—to stop it; but the women won't listen to me. They pay absolutely no attention to my orders."

"How about those newspaper men? Why did you send for them?" I flung at him.

"That's another thing I don't understand," he shook his head helplessly. "I didn't send for them—but somebody must have. They were tipped off to be on hand tonight for something big, and that has me worried. The way things are going out there, God knows what will happen . . .

I think I can generally tell when a man is lying, and Parker impressed me as telling the truth. He seemed to be a very much worried young man; a director whose show had been taken out of his hands and was running away with him. I told him I'd see what could be done and would call him as soon as I could use him—and then something happened that drove Burleigh Parker from my thoughts entirely.

As I was retracing my steps down the dressing-room lined corridor toward the stage door a white figure darted from the stage and slipped into the narrow passageway. Instinctively I flattened myself into one of the doorways, just in time to catch a glimpse of Betty Blanchard poised alertly in front of one of the cubicles two doors farther down the corridor.

She was naked, except for stockings, slippers and what appeared to be an open negligée; and the furtive way she glanced up and down the dimly-lit passageway, before she opened the door and darted into the dressing room, told me that there was more trouble afoot. Whatever it was, I decided

Neil Blanchard ought to know about it—in a hurry.

I hurried down the corridor to try to locate him, when suddenly the stage door flew open and a raging fury burst into the narrow passageway. Eyes wild and glaring, lips drawn back over clenched teeth, his face contorted into a mask of ferocity, Neil Blanchard leaped straight at me, swept me out of his way and dashed past—to fling himself into the dressing room where Betty had just disappeared.

I heard the key click in the lock before I could recover my balance. Vainly I raced back up the corridor and hammered on the closed door. Frantically I called to him and demanded that he let me in.

There was no answer but Betty's terrified screams.

Desperately I threw my weight against the door and tried to batter it in, but there wasn't sufficient room in that narrow corridor to let me get a running start. Behind the stage, I remembered, there was an axe posted for fire protection; but it took minutes—hundreds of precious seconds—to run down there and get it. More long minutes wasted while I battered a hole through the door so that I could squeeze my way inside.

And then it was too late.

Harry Graber lay dead on the floor. His throat was literally torn out, the cords and spouting arteries severed as if a raging beast had been clawing at them. The moment he saw me Blanchard leaped up from his mangled victim and threw himself at his wife, cowering naked in a corner. His blood-dripping fingers fastened in her throat and closed like terrible vises, while streams of thick saliva drooled from his clenched jaws. The man had become a veritable fiend, a creature gone utterly mad with rage and avid blood-lust!

Betty's eyes were bulging out of her head and her face was turning purple as I fought with him, but still I could not break that terrible death-grip—until three other men came to my rescue. Not until a club crashed down on Blanchard's head and knocked him senseless did those bloody fingers loosen. Not till then did the mad light fade out of his eyes.

We had saved Betty's life—but not before Neil Blanchard had stained his hands with murder . . .

"I'll be here with you every moment!" Abel Fleming's bitter voice rang in my ears. "You'll know that I'm here—and before you close this bazaar you'll come up into the hills and beg me to come back and have free run of it!"

I could almost hear him mocking me now—could almost see him shaking his huge head with satisfaction. Two women driven to the verge of insanity, one man dead and another stamped with the brand of Cain—and the bazaar was only two days old!

"What will happen next?" I asked myself, while in the back of my tortured brain terror spawned the glimmering of a mad idea that took root in desperation.

Chapter Four

Call to Hell

The crowd outside in the auditorium was unaware of the ghastly tragedy backstage, and the club directors, hastily summoned, were afraid that panic might result if it were announced. It would be better, they decided, to let the bazaar run and close it as early as possible that night.

Personally, I was in favor of closing it for all time, but I was overruled. I noticed the others looking at me as if they thought I was out of my head. But they were older men—and they didn't have a lovely fiancée out there selling the intimacy of her lips to any degenerate who had five dollars to offer . . .

Anxious and on the point of rebellion, I went out through the stage door and from its slight elevation scanned the milling crowd in the hall. Apprehensively my eyes sought out Evelyn's booth, some thirty or forty feet from where I stood. What I saw made the icy grip on my heart tighten. The kiss-selling booth was doing a capacity business—and as I watched I saw that the caresses Evelyn was giving were no mere formalities. Her lips were clinging to those of the men who took her in their arms, and each left her more spent and panting than his predecessor!

At least I would put a stop to that!

Determinedly I started toward the booth, but before I was down from the short flight of steps leading to the stage door Cliff Mason pushed his way through the throng and grabbed my arm excitedly. His eyes were troubled and his handsome face was furrowed with lines of worry.

"I can't find my wife, Garry!" he hung onto me as I tried to get past him. "Gwen's disappeared. She left the dance floor, where she was hostessing, half an hour ago. Nobody has seen her since. The last I saw of her she was dancing with Joe Steckel—?"

"Steckel!" I had no idea that the nightclub proprietor was at the bazaar, and his name exploded from my lips. "You mean to say that fellow had the damned gall to show his face here among decent—"

The indignant exclamation wilted on my tongue and my eyes almost popped out of my head as I saw Steckel himself. He was at Evelyn's booth—had her in his arms and was covering her lips with a lingering, wet kiss! She clung to him weakly as he relinquished her, and I saw him bend down and whisper something in her ear—something that brought an obscene grin to his fat face!

"Four or five of the women seem to have disappeared," Mason was saying. "Somehow they must have left the hall without being seen . . ."

But I hardly heard him. A red haze had risen before my eyes and the roaring in my ears drowned out the sound of his voice. If I could have gotten my hands on Joe Steckel at that moment I would have torn the life out of him just as Blanchard had murdered Harry Graber. But by the time I reached Evelyn's booth the racketeer had disappeared in the dense crowd.

"You're getting out of here, Evelyn," I ordered firmly. "Tell the other girls to quit, too. This bazaar is closing—now."

For a moment she stared at me rebelliously, and then her expression changed. Perhaps it was the livid rage in my eyes, perhaps it was my strained face—but rather than fear I thought I detected a hint of cunning, of satisfaction, in her eyes . . .

It took us more than half an hour to close the booths and get that hilarious, catcalling crowd out into the street. When I climbed into my car beside Evelyn I was exhausted, physically and mentally. Again I sensed almost immediately that there was something strange about her. But it was different from last night when she hardly seemed to know that I existed. Tonight she clung to my arm and snuggled warmly against me. When I glanced down at her face as we stopped for a traffic light she was smiling up at me, and her eyes were aglow with something that puzzled me and at the same time sounded a note of alarm in my brain.

There was something expectant about that half-hidden gleam, something secretive; as if she was looking forward with delightful anticipation to something which I knew nothing about. Strangely, the touch of her hand on my arm brought out the goose-pimples on my skin, and I had all I could do to keep from shying away from her. Yet, as I gripped the wheel and kept my eyes resolutely on the road ahead of me I knew that I was afraid of her for reasons which I could not possibly have put into words.

"You're coming in, aren't you, Garry?" she invited when we reached her apartment and I stood in the doorway.

"There was nothing unusual about that. I had often gone in with her to have a cup of tea before going home and thought nothing of it—but tonight the idea frightened me—and suddenly I knew why. It was the insinuating, wheedling tone of her voice; it was the arch, inviting look in her eyes, the way her hands caressed me and tried to draw me inside. She was trying to lure me into her rooms like a prostitute working on a reluctant customer!

When I demurred and tried to back away she slipped into my arms and her lips were pressed hotly to mine. Soft, coaxing sounds came from the depths of her throat and her hands slid inside my coat, went around me and caressed my body as she tried to draw me into the foyer. Right out into the corridor she pursued me with her eager lips and her soft, sensuous invitations—until I grasped her hands and forced them away from me, forced her back into the apartment and slammed the door on her.

My knees were weak and shaking when I got downstairs and stepped into the street, but as I was about to get into the car a sixth sense sounded a warning in my brain; it seemed to be dragging me back, holding me there. On a sudden hunch I drove the car to the other side of the street and a little farther down the block, and then came back to a point from which I could watch her doorway.

In less than twenty minutes she came through the lobby and I could hardly believe my eyes as I stared at her! Her face was brazenly daubed with paint. Her mouth was a scarlet gash, and she was wearing an extremely low-cut gown that clung to her figure and accentuated its every line. Sinuously she glided through the doorway, proceeded down the street, with a provoking hip-swinging gate!

My heart was in my throat as I cautiously followed her on the opposite side—and then I fairly dropped in my tracks as she sidled up to a husky passer-by, a total stranger. She smirked at him invitingly in the manner that has but one meaning the world over!

Horrified amazement seemed to glue my feet to the sidewalk for an eternity—and then I was free, racing across the street, grasping her by the arm and pushing her away as I thrust myself between them. Evelyn's heavily mascaraed eyes flashed with rage, and the fellow's hand clamped down on my shoulder and whirled me around.

"What's it your business, buddy?" he demanded nastily as he shoved his ugly face close to mine.

It was some minutes before I could identify myself and straighten things out with him, and by that time Evelyn had run off and hailed a taxicab. Fortunately I just caught the address of the Golden Horseshoe, Joe Steckel's place, as she gave it to the driver.

Quickly I ran back to my car and followed her—but as the machine sped along I literally sweat blood. What in God's name had happened to Evelyn? Two days ago she was a sweet, normal girl. In less than forty-eight hours she had been transformed into a sex-crazed wanton! Before my very eyes I had seen her changing, had seen everything that was fine and sweet and clean about her crumbling and going to pieces—until she had actually become a street-walker—and not for the money!

All in the short space of time since Abel Fleming's lips had been crushed against hers . . .

Abel Fleming! He had made good his fiendish boast; his damning specter had hovered over the bazaar every moment from the time he stepped foot into it. In some unholy way he had bewitched it, had turned its earnest workers into sex-mad animals—and now he had cast his hellish spell over Evelyn. That was the only way account for her behavior.

But, I vowed grimly, I would not go begging him to come back to the bazaar that had ejected him. No—I would not go back to him for that. But if any harm befell Evelyn I would hunt out that black-dealing monster and settle the account with him, without help of the law but my two hands!

A block before I reached the Golden Horseshoe I drew up to the curb and parked the car, for I had no intention of parading in the front door of Steckel's gilded sin spot.

During the vice investigation I had proved that, while the upstairs rooms of the club were kept fairly respectable, it was downstairs that the deviltry was staged. If Evelyn was in that place, it would be downstairs that I would find her.

Carefully I made my way through a nearby building and over fences until I was in Steckel's back yard. From a yard two doors away I had salvaged a broken automobile spring that might be useful to pry open a window if I could gain admittance in no other way—but when I reached the basement door of the Golden Horseshoe I found it unlocked.

Noiselessly I let myself into the dark hallway and flattened against the wall, listening to the boisterous gayety of a drunken party. The uproar was coming from farther down the corridor. Cautiously I inched my way along until I stood in the heavily draped doorway of a large basement room where a score of people were dancing to the sensuous music of an Oriental orchestra. Utterly crazed, they seemed, completely under the spell of that weird threnody—especially the women, who wore so little clothing that complete nudity would have been less licentious. Bitterly, I thought of the strange happenings at the bazaar.

Half a dozen of the Civic Club women I recognized in that cavorting throng. Gwen Mason was among them, and the others were the wives of our most influential citizens; the wives of men who had backed me to the limit in my vice crusade. Eminently respectable women gone mad with lust!

But Evelyn was not among them. Anxiously I strained my eyes to peer into every shadowy corner of that tremendous place—and then suddenly the hair at the nape of my neck seemed to stand on end.

That was the sound of a creaking board! There was someone in the hall behind me! More than one person—many feet seemed to come running from all directions as hands grabbed for me and yanked me out into the corridor. From every side Steckel's roughnecks closed in on me and, too late, I realized that the whole set-up was a trap, the inviting basement door purposely left unlocked so that I would walk into it.

Desperately I threw myself to the floor and scrambled a few yards on all fours. Now the darkness was in my favor, and before they could switch on a light I was back on my feet, blessing the inspiration that had made me pick up that broken spring and take it with me. Like a flail I swung it around my head, and in a moment the hall was filled with howls of agony as the heavy bludgeon smashed into snarling faces and caromed off broken heads.

At one side of that corridor I knew there was a stairway that led up to Steckel's office on the floor above. In the darkness I tried to grope my way toward it—and when the light snapped on it was only a few yards ahead of me. Savagely I smashed the blood-reddened spring down on two more heads and then darted up the steps, just as a revolver thundered and a bullet whistled by my ear.

Steckel was in his office, frantically diving for a desk drawer as I burst in on him, but the spring caught him on the side of the head and knocked him spinning across the room before he could grasp the weapon he kept cached there. In an instant I was after him, the murderous spring raised over his head to bash out his brains.

"Where is she? What have you done with Evelyn Owen?" I snarled at him, while my arm fairly itched with the urge to bring that spring down across his terror⌐ distorted face.

"She's gone!" he whined. "She ain't here any more, I tell you, Taylor. She's gone—up in the hills with Abel Fleming!"

Something snapped inside of me as the meaning of his babbled words penetrated the fog of rage that clouded my brain. Something snapped—and I became another person. Garry Taylor, the district attorney, ceased to be at that moment. In his place, in his body was a madman—a madman with a hellish idea that had been festering in his brain suddenly bursting forth in full virulence and blotting everything else from his consciousness!

Chapter Five

Hex Doom

With one hand firmly gripping Joe Steckel's collar, forcing him ahead of me as a shield, and the other wrapped around the blood-spattered spring, I battled my way out of that sordid joint. Not until I was out on the sidewalk did I fling the slobbering night-club man away from me and run for my car.

I did not know whether or not to believe Steckel—but now that seemed immaterial. There was only one thought in my mind: I wanted to get my hands on Abel Fleming. The hex-man had become an obsession with me. I could see nothing but his hateful face in front of me; could hear nothing but his voice in my ears.

Fleming was behind all this weird deviltry. It was his hell-spawned spell that had transformed Evelyn, and the only way to free her from its demoralizing clutch was to kill him. Again and again I went over that liturgy, until the blood was pounding in my veins and my brain was on fire as I jammed the throttle down to the floor-boards.

A quarter mile below Fleming's cabin I stopped the car and leaped out onto the rutted road. Cautiously I picked my way up through patches of brush and trees until I was at the edge of his clearing. A light blinked feebly through the grimy window of his one-story cabin—and I felt as if I must howl with exultation!

Stealthily I crept up to his door, until I could peer through the window beside it and see him sitting at a table, counting bills by the light of a lantern—entirely oblivious of the retribution that hovered over him. Now he was mine!

That door had no lock. Noiselessly I grasped the latch and pressed it down—and then I catapulted into the cabin, smashed my fist into his jaw as he turned in his chair. Before he could get to his feet I knocked him reeling across the room. Then I was after him, smashing away at him with both fists. All ideas of fair play were thrown to the winds as I tore into him. This devil fought helpless women with the unholy powers of darkness; to overcome him I would use any weapon—like the chair I swung over my head and brought crashing down on his skull . . .

Abel Fleming tottered for a moment as blood gushed from his torn scalp; then he wilted and thudded to the floor. My whole being tingled with mad delight as I looked down at him. It was as if Lute Brunner stood there in the cabin beside me. I could hear his voice plainly in my ears:

"Fire is the only thing that kills a witch, so I burned her—burned her until there was nothing left to come back and do me more harm. You don't understand, Mr. Taylor, but maybe some day when the sign is on you—"

Yes—I did understand! Vaguely I had sensed this ever since I staggered away from the sight of Neil Blanchard's hands stained crimson with Harry Graber's blood. Vaguely I had sensed what I must do—now I knew! I must kill this devil creature—must burn him to a crisp so that Evelyn would be freed forever from his damning spells!

Fleming was a heavy man, but I seized him by the collar and dragged him out of the cabin. By the light of his lantern I found two trees with strong crotches, growing not more than ten feet apart. They would do splendidly! With the hexman's axe I cut down another and trimmed its trunk until I had a stout pole sufficiently strong to sustain his weight.

With ropes from the cabin I lashed his wrists together, around the pole so that he would hang vertically and burn slowly, from the feet up! God forgive me! . . . It took all of my strength to upend the pole and place one end in the crotch of one of the trees, then I hoisted the other up into place with the aid of a heavy forked stick.

With eager haste I piled leaves and brush on the ground beneath him, covered them with fresh-cut sapling and what died wood I could find around the place. A noble pyre that would wrap him in flames as soon as I put a match to it!

Fleming opened his eyes just as I took a paper of matches from my pocket and struck one. He was trying to say something, mumbling incoherent words—but I laughed at him and held the match in front of his eyes. Deliberately I thrust it into the leaves and kindling—and a fierce satisfaction welled up within me as a column of smoke curled upward and was then shot through with flame!

In the course of two short days I had slipped back hundreds of years. The district attorney who could not comprehend how a human being could stoop to do the thing that Lute Brunner had done was doing it himself! I realized that and I laughed—laughed wildly as the smoke puffed my way and wreathed around my face! All reason had left me; in its place was only a frenzied determination to exterminate this creature so that Evelyn would be free from the ungodly spell he had cast over her.

The flames were creeping up through the brush, licking up at Fleming. His trousers were beginning to scorch, to smoke from the heat—and if I had had a bellows I would have knelt and spurred the blaze on!

But suddenly I tensed, while surges of rage mounted within

me. Someone was coming—someone who would try to interfere; would try to stop my grisly work! My fists clenched
and I eyed the dark path grimly. A girl who came running
through the bushes. A girl I knew—Mary Corbin!

"I can't let you do this, Garry!" she panted as she flung
herself at me and grasped both of my arms with her hands. "I
hate you—or I thought that I hated you—for tossing me
aside for Evelyn Owen. But I can't go through with it! I can't
let you make a murderer of yourself! I knew what you would
do—that's why I followed you here to stop you. Please,
Garry, put out that fire before it gets any bigger—there's still
time to save yourself! . . . Oh, you won't listen to me!"

When she saw that I made no move to do as she begged,
she tried to do it herself. Frantically she kicked away some
of the burning branches and reached down to drag others off
the pile, but her flimsy evening dress must have caught on an
outstretched twig. I heard it rip—and when she backed away
from the flames the whole front of it was torn so that her
lovely voluptuous breasts were naked.

"Oh, I can't do it alone, Garry—please help me!" she
pleaded, and then she had her arms around me and was kissing me feverishly.

It had all happened so quickly that I was half-dazed, but as
she clung to me something was trying to penetrate my stu-
por—a familiar odor that tugged at my memory . . .

Mary Corbin's face was right in front of me as she
clutched me; her naked breasts were pressed against my
chest—and that familiar odor was very close to them. I
glanced down at their creamy whiteness—and the odor was
stronger. In the top of her dress I located it; a handkerchief
tucked into the top of her sleeve—a handkerchief with the
perfume that Evelyn always used!

Before she saw what I intended I plucked it out and held it
up to the light. Yes. It was one of Evelyn's expensive lace
handkerchiefs! That meant that Mary Corbin knew where
Evelyn was—that she had been with her—had taken that
handkerchief from her!

She read the dawning understanding in my eyes and tried

to dart out of reach, but I grabbed her and hauled her back, held her firmly in front of me while I looked straight into her eyes.

"You know where she is," I said grimly. "Tell me."

Her lips were tightly sealed and her eyes were inscrutable.

"All right," I clipped, as I started to drag her toward the path that led to the car, "then I'll take you back to town and you'll show me where—or you'll wish you had!"

With the heels of her shoes digging into the soft loam she braced herself and tried to hold back, fought furiously to stop me—so frantically that her torn dress ripped to shreds and hung in tatters below her waist. Down over one white hip it slipped—and then she wriggled her body and it fell from her altogether. Naked except for her stockings she stood there in the firelight and held her arms wide so that her every charm was revealed to me.

"Let's not fight any more, Garry," she pleaded softly, while the flickering flames painted thrilling highlights and intriguing shadows on her undulating figure. "Look at me, dear. Take me! I can give you more that she ever could. Garry . . ."

But again my grim eyes betrayed me and told her that her efforts were useless. Suddenly her fists clenched and raised above her head and her pretty face was convulsed with ugly rage.

"Have it then—you asked for it!" she screamed at me. "Your lovely Evelyn is one of Steckel's women now. You'll find her in one of his rooms—if she isn't too busy to see you! If you still want her you can have her—after Steckel's gang gets finished with her!"

Gradually, as I stood watching her ranting and raving like a madwoman, I sensed that she was trying to keep me there; that she was deliberately striving to detain me. But why? Quickly I looked around me on all sides. Through an opening in the brush I was sure that I was a flash of white—sure that I heard the snapping of a twig! Instantly I started toward the sound, just as a ragged old crone darted from the path and scurried into the brush!

More by sound than by sight in the almost pitch-black night I flung into the bushes after that old hag, followed the sound of her flight until the undergrowth thinned and I found myself in another clearing. It was a clearing that ran up the side of the hill to where a denser patch of blackness loomed ahead of me. Daring an instant's flash of a match, I saw that the stygian patch was the mouth of a tunnel; a tunnel that wound as I groped my way along it and abruptly debouched into a lantern-lit cavern.

Suddenly framed in the cavern mouth, I stared across the rock-walled chamber in shocked amazement—stared at the low, blanket-spread couch where Evelyn lay moaning, her ankles and wrists securely lashed to it. Only a few tattered shreds of clothing still clung to her nearly naked body, and her tear-stained face was a picture of hopeless despair—but the moment she saw me her eyes filled with wild concern!

Instinctively I ducked to one side as I caught her warning—just in time to avoid a fist that swung savagely at my jaw. The vicious blow smashed into my shoulder and almost knocked me down. It was the old crone. Then she was leaping in at me, pounding my head with a barrage of blows. She had amazing strength, and it was all that I could do to cover myself and back away from her onslaught.

Evelyn's moans and the sight of her wide eyes, fearfully watching the struggle that would decide her fate, stabbed at my heart and filled me with desperation—but as I sparred and backed around the cave I began to feel the terrifying conviction that I was no match for this old woman. It must be something more than human strength that was driving me back, that was dazing me, sapping the strength from my arms. Something unnatural, demoniacal, that brought the hag charging in relentlessly at me . . .

Witches and hex-men, I had heard, were able to change their form at will—were able to assume the guise of beasts or other humans. That must be it—this creature must be Abel Fleming! This cave was where he had imprisoned Evelyn— was where he had lured me deliberately so that he could batter me into submission and murder me before her eyes!

I was reeling groggily, so battered that any good punch might have dropped me in a senseless heap, but that appalling thought sent me charging forward with berserk fury. One wildly swung fist missed, but the other caught the hag on the jaw and knocked her across the cave—thudded her back against the farther wall.

The roof, at that point, was quite high. The rock wall ran up to a height of about nine feet and then gave way to several feet of yawning blackness that separated it from the stalactite-hung ceiling. Out of that black pocket rumbled a shower of pebbles and stones, loosened by the jar—to be followed by a slide of huge boulders.

All except one crashed down onto the cave floor—but that one struck the venomous old harridan squarely on the top of the head! I heard the sickening sound of splintering bone as the skull beneath her cowl-like shawl was battered in, and then she lay like a heap of dirty rags on the floor!

I thought I knew what to expect when I knelt beside the body and drew back the bloodied shawl. I steeled myself for the gruesome sight—but I was flung back on my heels with astonishment when I stared down into the dead face of Frank Dixon! Hardly believing the evidence of my eyes, I lifted the grey wig from the crushed skull and wiped the make-up from the dead face. But there was no mistake. The masquerader was none other than the attorney!

I tried to conceal the grisly sight from Evelyn as I sprang up and ran to the couch where she was tied, but she had already seen.

"He must have been crazy," she half-sobbed as I worked over the tightly knotted ropes that held her. "He told me that he loved me—that he wanted to marry me. He promised me all the money and all the luxuries I wanted. He boasted how rich and powerful he was. You've been wrong about Joe Steckel, Garry. He was just one of Frank Dixon's men, taking orders from him. It was Dixon who owned the Golden Horseshoe and controlled the terrible vice ring you broke up.

"He was so sure of himself—and so sure that I was helpless to do anything but obey him—that he told me how he was going to have the whole city in the palm of his hand. He started all that trouble at the bazaar to get rid of you and Neil Blanchard. Neil will go to prison if he escapes the electric chair—and Dixon told me that you were dead already—"

"That's what he thought," I commented grimly, as I realized that Dixon and Steckel had purposely lured me to the Golden Horseshoe to meet my death. "But even with Neil and me out of the picture, I don't see why he was so sure he'd have such clear sailing. With us out of the way, Cliff Mason would have been a safe bet for district attorney this fall—"

"That was just what Dixon planned," Evelyn nodded. "He told me that he could handle Mason; that after tonight Mason and the rest of the big-shots in Jordan City would be very quiet and obedient."

In a flash of understanding I grasped the fiendish thoroughness of Frank Dixon's careful scheming. Gwen Mason and those other women in that orgiastic revel in the basement of the Golden Horseshoe . . . They had been carefully selected and lured there so that they and their husbands would be completely in the power of Dixon and his gang. Doped with cantharides and other aphrodisiac drugs at the bazaar suppers, the women had been led into a sensuous debauch— and photographed—which would be held over the heads of their husbands as a club to keep them from any attempt to make trouble.

"And all the while I have been blaming Abel Fleming," I thought aloud as I freed Evelyn from the couch and helped her into my coat.

"Fleming was just a helpless tool," she volunteered as soon as I mentioned the hex-man's name. "Dixon laughed at the way he used him to fool you. While he was working on Lute Brunner's defense he found that Abel Fleming had really engineered Hetty Mears' murder—and he uncovered evidence that would have proved it. Dixon threatened to expose him unless he did as he was told, and forced him to come to the bazaar and pick a fight by kissing me so that you couldn't help seeing it. Fleming's rage and the threat he made were just staged to frighten us . . ."

Before she was finished I had grabbed the lantern from the wall of the cave and was leading the way out through the entrance tunnel on the run. Suddenly I had remembered that I had left Abel Fleming tied up helplessly over a blazing fire! Perhaps by now he was roasting to a crisp! My hands were stained with his blood . . ."

But as soon as we reached the clearing I saw that the hex-man had not died in the flames. He was no longer suspended over what was left of the scattered fire. A few feet from it the charred remains of his woolen trousers still smoldered on the ground, but he was nowhere to be seen. Quickly I ran to his cabin and yanked open the door—but the inside was as deserted as the clearing.

Abel Fleming was gone.

Curiously I stepped through the doorway and looked around the room. There was something different about the place, something that was not as it had been when I was there half an hour earlier. Then I saw what it was, and my brows knit in puzzlement. The door of a closet stood open. Painted on the inside of it was an unmistakable full-length, life-size picture of Frank Dixon.

That was an odd place for a painting—but odder still was the way the top of the door had been hacked to pieces . . .

Evidently it had been opened and then the top had been curiously chopped in with an axe that lay on the floor beside it. The savage blows had cut the wood to splinters—had ripped down into Dixon's head and battered the whole top of it!

An icy stream trickled down my spine as I stared at that mutilated effigy—and remembered how Frank Dixon had died a few minutes before with a rock shattering the top of his skull . . .

Suddenly the empty, shadow-haunted room seemed fairly alive with lurking evil; with uncanny, unearthly evil that chilled my blood. I wanted to get out of there—out into the clean, fresh night air. My arm went around Evelyn's waist, and as I helped her along the straggling path to where the car waited I wondered—had Frank Dixon, with all his fiendish craftiness, finally meddled with something that was too powerful, or too unthinkably evil, even for him to handle?

RAMBLE HOUSE's

HARRY STEPHEN KEELER WEBWORK MYSTERIES

(RH) indicates the title is available ONLY in the RAMBLE HOUSE edition

The Ace of Spades Murder
The Affair of the Bottled Deuce (RH)
The Amazing Web
The Barking Clock
Behind That Mask
The Book with the Orange Leaves
The Bottle with the Green Wax Seal
The Box from Japan
The Case of the Canny Killer
The Case of the Crazy Corpse (RH)
The Case of the Flying Hands (RH)
The Case of the Ivory Arrow
The Case of the Jeweled Ragpicker
The Case of the Lavender Gripsack
The Case of the Mysterious Moll
The Case of the 16 Beans
The Case of the Transparent Nude (RH)
The Case of the Transposed Legs
The Case of the Two-Headed Idiot (RH)
The Case of the Two Strange Ladies
The Circus Stealers (RH)
Cleopatra's Tears
A Copy of Beowulf (RH)
The Crimson Cube (RH)
The Face of the Man From Saturn
Find the Clock
The Five Silver Buddhas
The 4th King
The Gallows Waits, My Lord! (RH)
The Green Jade Hand
Finger! Finger!
Hangman's Nights (RH)
I, Chameleon (RH)
I Killed Lincoln at 10:13! (RH)
The Iron Ring
The Man Who Changed His Skin (RH)
The Man with the Crimson Box
The Man with the Magic Eardrums
The Man with the Wooden Spectacles
The Marceau Case
The Matilda Hunter Murder
The Monocled Monster
The Murder of London Lew
The Murdered Mathematician
The Mysterious Card (RH)
The Mysterious Ivory Ball of Wong Shing Li (RH)
The Mystery of the Fiddling Cracksman
The Peacock Fan
The Photo of Lady X (RH)
The Portrait of Jirjohn Cobb
Report on Vanessa Hewstone (RH)
Riddle of the Travelling Skull
Riddle of the Wooden Parrakeet (RH)
The Scarlet Mummy (RH)
The Search for X-Y-Z
The Sharkskin Book
Sing Sing Nights

The Six From Nowhere (RH)
The Skull of the Waltzing Clown
The Spectacles of Mr. Cagliostro
Stand By—London Calling!
The Steeltown Strangler
The Stolen Gravestone (RH)
Strange Journey (RH)
The Strange Will
The Straw Hat Murders (RH)
The Street of 1000 Eyes (RH)
Thieves' Nights
Three Novellos (RH)
The Tiger Snake
The Trap (RH)
Vagabond Nights (Defrauded Yeggman)
Vagabond Nights 2 (10 Hours)
The Vanishing Gold Truck
The Voice of the Seven Sparrows
The Washington Square Enigma
When Thief Meets Thief
The White Circle (RH)
The Wonderful Scheme of Mr. Christopher Thorne
X. Jones—of Scotland Yard
Y. Cheung, Business Detective

Keeler Related Works

A To Izzard: A Harry Stephen Keeler Companion by Fender Tucker — Articles and stories about Harry, by Harry, and in his style. Included is a compleat bibliography.

Wild About Harry: Reviews of Keeler Novels — Edited by Richard Polt & Fender Tucker — 22 reviews of works by Harry Stephen Keeler from *Keeler News.* A perfect introduction to the author.

The Keeler Keyhole Collection: Annotated newsletter rants from Harry Stephen Keeler, edited by Francis M. Nevins. Over 400 pages of incredibly personal Keeleriana.

Fakealoo — Pastiches of the style of Harry Stephen Keeler by selected demented members of the HSK Society. Updated every year with the new winner.

Strands of the Web: Short Stories of Harry Stephen Keeler — 29 stories, just about all that Keeler wrote, are edited and introduced by Fred Cleaver.

RAMBLE HOUSE's LOON SANCTUARY

A Clear Path to Cross — Sharon Knowles short mystery stories by Ed Lynskey.

A Corpse Walks in Brooklyn and Other Stories — Volume 5 in the Day Keene in the Detective Pulps series.

A Jimmy Starr Omnibus — Three 40s novels by Jimmy Starr.

A Niche in Time and Other Stories — Classic SF by William F. Temple

A Roland Daniel Double: The Signal and The Return of Wu Fang — Classic thrillers from the 30s.

A Shot Rang Out — Three decades of reviews and articles by today's Anthony Boucher, Jon Breen. An essential book for any mystery lover's library.

A Smell of Smoke — A 1951 English countryside thriller by Miles Burton.

A Snark Selection — Lewis Carroll's *The Hunting of the Snark* with two Snarkian chapters by Harry Stephen Keeler — Illustrated by Gavin L. O'Keefe.

A Young Man's Heart — A forgotten early classic by Cornell Woolrich.

Alexander Laing Novels — *The Motives of Nicholas Holtz* and *Dr. Scarlett*, stories of medical mayhem and intrigue from the 30s.

An Angel in the Street — Modern hardboiled noir by Peter Genovese.

Automaton — Brilliant treatise on robotics: 1928-style! By H. Stafford Hatfield.

Away From the Here and Now — Clare Winger Harris stories, collected by Richard A. Lupoff

Beast or Man? — A 1930 novel of racism and horror by Sean M'Guire. Introduced by John Pelan.

Black Beadle — A 1939 thriller by E.C.R. Lorac.

Black Hogan Strikes Again — Australia's Peter Renwick pens a tale of the 30s outback.

Black River Falls — Suspense from the master, Ed Gorman.

Blondy's Boy Friend — A snappy 1930 story by Philip Wylie, writing as Leatrice Homesley.

Blood in a Snap — The *Finnegan's Wake* of the 21st century, by Jim Weiler.

Blood Moon — The first of the Robert Payne series by Ed Gorman.

Bogart '48 — Hollywood action with Bogie by John Stanley and Kenn Davis

Calling Lou Largo! — Two Lou Largo novels by William Ard.

Cornucopia of Crime — Francis M. Nevins assembled this huge collection of his writings about crime literature and the people who write it. Essential for any serious mystery library.

Corpse Without Flesh — Strange novel of forensics by George Bruce

Crimson Clown Novels — By Johnston McCulley, author of the Zorro novels, *The Crimson Clown* and *The Crimson Clown Again.*

Dago Red — 22 tales of dark suspense by Bill Pronzini.

Dark Sanctuary — Weird Menace story by H. B. Gregory

David Hume Novels — *Corpses Never Argue, Cemetery First Stop, Make Way for the Mourners, Eternity Here I Come.* 1930s British hardboiled fiction with an attitude.

Dead Man Talks Too Much — Hollywood boozer by Weed Dickenson.

Death Leaves No Card — One of the most unusual murdered-in-the-tub mysteries you'll ever read. By Miles Burton.

Death March of the Dancing Dolls and Other Stories — Volume Three in the Day Keene in the Detective Pulps series. Introduced by Bill Crider.

Deep Space and other Stories — A collection of SF gems by Richard A. Lupoff.

Detective Duff Unravels It — Episodic mysteries by Harvey O'Higgins.

Diabolic Candelabra — Classic 30s mystery by E.R. Punshon

Dictator's Way — Another D.S. Bobby Owen mystery from E.R. Punshon

Dime Novels: Ramble House's 10-Cent Books — *Knife in the Dark* by Robert Leslie Bellem, *Hot Lead* and *Song of Death* by Ed Earl Repp, *A Hashish House in New York* by H.H. Kane, and five more.

Doctor Arnoldi — Tiffany Thayer's story of the death of death.

Don Diablo: Book of a Lost Film — Two-volume treatment of a western by Paul Landres, with diagrams. Intro by Francis M. Nevins.

Dope and Swastikas — Two strange novels from 1922 by Edmund Snell

Dope Tales #1 — Two dope-riddled classics; *Dope Runners* by Gerald Grantham and *Death Takes the Joystick* by Phillip Condé.

Dope Tales #2 — Two more narco-classics; *The Invisible Hand* by Rex Dark and *The Smokers of Hashish* by Norman Berrow.

Dope Tales #3 — Two enchanting novels of opium by the master, Sax Rohmer. *Dope* and *The Yellow Claw.*

Double Hot — Two 60s softcore sex novels by Morris Hershman.

Double Sex — Yet two more panting thrillers by Morris Hershman.

Dr. Odin — Douglas Newton's 1933 racial potboiler comes back to life.

Evangelical Cockroach — Jack Woodford writes about writing.

Evidence in Blue — 1938 mystery by E. Charles Vivian.

Fatal Accident — Murder by automobile, a 1936 mystery by Cecil M. Wills.

Fighting Mad — Todd Robbins' 1922 novel about boxing and life

Finger-prints Never Lie — A 1939 classic detective novel by John G. Brandon.

Freaks and Fantasies — Eerie tales by Tod Robbins, collaborator of Tod Browning on the film FREAKS.

Gadsby — A lipogram (a novel without the letter E). Ernest Vincent Wright's last work, published in 1939 right before his death.

Gelett Burgess Novels — *The Master of Mysteries, The White Cat, Two O'Clock Courage, Ladies in Boxes, Find the Woman, The Heart Line, The Picaroons* and *Lady Mechante.* Recently added is A Gelett Burgess Sampler, edited by Alfred Jan. All are introduced by Richard A. Lupoff.

Geronimo — S. M. Barrett's 1905 autobiography of a noble American.

Hake Talbot Novels — *Rim of the Pit, The Hangman's Handyman*. Classic locked room mysteries, with mapback covers by Gavin O'Keefe.

Hands Out of Hell and Other Stories — John H. Knox's eerie hallucinations

Hell is a City — William Ard's masterpiece.

Hollywood Dreams — A novel of Tinsel Town and the Depression by Richard O'Brien.

Hostesses in Hell and Other Stories — Russell Gray's most graphic stories

House of the Restless Dead — Strange and ominous tales by Hugh B. Cave

I Stole $16,000,000 — A true story by cracksman Herbert E. Wilson.

Inclination to Murder — 1966 thriller by New Zealand's Harriet Hunter.

Invaders from the Dark — Classic werewolf tale from Greye La Spina.

J. Poindexter, Colored — Classic satirical black novel by Irvin S. Cobb.

Jack Mann Novels — Strange murder in the English countryside. *Gees' First Case, Nightmare Farm, Grey Shapes, The Ninth Life, The Glass Too Many, Her Ways Are Death, The Kleinert Case* and *Maker of Shadows.*

Jake Hardy — A lusty western tale from Wesley Tallant.

Jim Harmon Double Novels — *Vixen Hollow/Celluloid Scandal, The Man Who Made Maniacs/Silent Siren, Ape Rape/Wanton Witch, Sex Burns Like Fire/Twist Session, Sudden Lust/Passion Strip, Sin Unlimited/Harlot Master, Twilight Girls/Sex Institution*. Written in the early 60s and never reprinted until now.

Joel Townsley Rogers Novels and Short Stories — By the author of *The Red Right Hand: Once In a Red Moon, Lady With the Dice, The Stopped Clock, Never Leave My Bed*. Also two short story collections: *Night of Horror* and *Killing Time.*

John Carstairs, Space Detective — Arboreal Sci-fi by Frank Belknap Long

Joseph Shallit Novels — *The Case of the Billion Dollar Body, Lady Don't Die on My Doorstep, Kiss the Killer, Yell Bloody Murder, Take Your Last Look.* One of America's best 50's authors and a favorite of author Bill Pronzini.

Keller Memento — 45 short stories of the amazing and weird by Dr. David Keller.

Killer's Caress — Cary Moran's 1936 hardboiled thriller.

Lady of the Yellow Death and Other Stories — More stories by Wyatt Blassingame.

League of the Grateful Dead and Other Stories — Volume One in the Day Keene in the Detective Pulps series.

Library of Death — Ghastly tale by Ronald S. L. Harding, introduced by John Pelan

Malcolm Jameson Novels and Short Stories — *Astonishing! Astounding!, Tarnished Bomb, The Alien Envoy and Other Stories* and *The Chariots of San Fernando and Other Stories.* All introduced and edited by John Pelan or Richard A. Lupoff.

Man Out of Hell and Other Stories — Volume II of the John H. Knox weird pulps collection.

Marblehead: A Novel of H.P. Lovecraft — A long-lost masterpiece from Richard A. Lupoff. This is the "director's cut", the long version that has never been published before.

Mark of the Laughing Death and Other Stories — Shockers from the pulps by Francis James, introduced by John Pelan.

Master of Souls — Mark Hansom's 1937 shocker is introduced by weirdologist John Pelan.

Max Afford Novels — *Owl of Darkness, Death's Mannikins, Blood on His Hands, The Dead Are Blind, The Sheep and the Wolves, Sinners in Paradise* and *Two Locked Room Mysteries and a Ripping Yarn* by one of Australia's finest mystery novelists.

Money Brawl — Two books about the writing business by Jack Woodford and H. Bedford-Jones. Introduced by Richard A. Lupoff.

More Secret Adventures of Sherlock Holmes — Gary Lovisi's second collection of tales about the unknown sides of the great detective.

Muddled Mind: Complete Works of Ed Wood, Jr. — David Hayes and Hayden Davis deconstruct the life and works of the mad, but canny, genius.

Murder among the Nudists — A mystery from 1934 by Peter Hunt, featuring a naked Detective-Inspector going undercover in a nudist colony.

Murder in Black and White — 1931 classic tennis whodunit by Evelyn Elder.

Murder in Shawnee — Two novels of the Alleghenies by John Douglas: *Shawnee Alley Fire* and *Haunts.*

Murder in Silk — A 1937 Yellow Peril novel of the silk trade by Ralph Trevor.

My Deadly Angel — 1955 Cold War drama by John Chelton.

My First Time: The One Experience You Never Forget — Michael Birchwood — 64 true first-person narratives of how they lost it.

Mysterious Martin, the Master of Murder — Two versions of a strange 1912 novel by Tod Robbins about a man who writes books that can kill.

Norman Berrow Novels — *The Bishop's Sword, Ghost House, Don't Go Out After Dark, Claws of the Cougar, The Smokers of Hashish, The Secret Dancer, Don't Jump Mr. Boland!, The Footprints of Satan, Fingers for Ransom, The Three Tiers of Fantasy, The Spaniard's Thumb, The Eleventh Plague, Words Have Wings, One Thrilling Night, The Lady's in Danger, It Howls at Night, The Terror in the Fog, Oil Under the Window, Murder in the Melody, The Singing Room.* This is the complete Norman Berrow library of locked-room mysteries, several of which are masterpieces.

Old Faithful and Other Stories — SF classic tales by Raymond Z. Gallun

Old Times' Sake — Short stories by James Reasoner from Mike Shayne Magazine.

One Dreadful Night — A classic mystery by Ronald S. L. Harding

Pair O' Jacks — A mystery novel and a diatribe about publishing by Jack Woodford

Perfect .38 — Two early Timothy Dane novels by William Ard. More to come.

Prince Pax — Devilish intrigue by George Sylvester Viereck and Philip Eldridge

Prose Bowl — Futuristic satire of a world where hack writing has replaced football as our national obsession, by Bill Pronzini and Barry N. Malzberg.

Red Light — The history of legal prostitution in Shreveport Louisiana by Eric Brock. Includes wonderful photos of the houses and the ladies.

Researching American-Made Toy Soldiers — A 276-page collection of a lifetime of articles by toy soldier expert Richard O'Brien.

Reunion in Hell — Volume One of the John H. Knox series of weird stories from the pulps. Introduced by horror expert John Pelan.

Ripped from the Headlines! — The Jack the Ripper story as told in the newspaper articles in the *New York* and *London Times*.

Rough Cut & New, Improved Murder — Ed Gorman's first two novels.

R.R. Ryan Novels — Freak Museum and The Subjugated Beast, two horror classics.

Ruby of a Thousand Dreams — The villain Wu Fang returns in this Roland Daniel novel.

Ruled By Radio — 1925 futuristic novel by Robert L. Hadfield & Frank E. Farncombe.

Rupert Penny Novels — *Policeman's Holiday, Policeman's Evidence, Lucky Policeman, Policeman in Armour, Sealed Room Murder, Sweet Poison, The Talkative Policeman, She had to Have Gas* and *Cut and Run* (by Martin Tanner.) Rupert Penny is the pseudonym of Australian Charles Thornett, a master of the locked room, impossible crime plot.

Sacred Locomotive Flies — Richard A. Lupoff's psychedelic SF story.

Sam — Early gay novel by Lonnie Coleman.

Sand's Game — Spectacular hard-boiled noir from Ennis Willie, edited by Lynn Myers and Stephen Mertz, with contributions from Max Allan Collins, Bill Crider, Wayne Dundee, Bill Pronzini, Gary Lovisi and James Reasoner.

Sand's War — More violent fiction from the typewriter of Ennis Willie

Satan's Den Exposed — True crime in Truth or Consequences New Mexico — Award-winning journalism by the *Desert Journal*.

Satans of Saturn — Novellas from the pulps by Otis Adelbert Kline and E. H. Price

Satan's Sin House and Other Stories — Horrific gore by Wayne Rogers

Secrets of a Teenage Superhero — Graphic lit by Jonathan Sweet

Sex Slave — Potboiler of lust in the days of Cleopatra by Dion Leclerq, 1966.

Sideslip — 1968 SF masterpiece by Ted White and Dave Van Arnam.

Slammer Days — Two full-length prison memoirs: *Men into Beasts* (1952) by George Sylvester Viereck and *Home Away From Home* (1962) by Jack Woodford.

Slippery Staircase — 1930s whodunit from E.C.R. Lorac

Sorcerer's Chessmen — John Pelan introduces this 1939 classic by Mark Hansom.

Star Griffin — Michael Kurland's 1987 masterpiece of SF drollery is back.

Stakeout on Millennium Drive — Award-winning Indianapolis Noir by Ian Woollen.

Strands of the Web: Short Stories of Harry Stephen Keeler — Edited and Introduced by Fred Cleaver.

Summer Camp for Corpses and Other Stories — Weird Menace tales from Arthur Leo Zagat; introduced by John Pelan.

Suzy — A collection of comic strips by Richard O'Brien and Bob Vojtko from 1970.

The Great Orme Terror — Horror stories by Garnett Radcliffe from the pulps

The Hairbreadth Escapes of Major Mendax — Francis Blake Crofton's 1889 boys' book.

The House That Time Forgot and Other Stories — Insane pulpitude by Robert F. Young

The House of the Vampire — 1907 poetic thriller by George S. Viereck.

The Illustrious Corpse — Murder hijinx from Tiffany Thayer

The Incredible Adventures of Rowland Hern — Intriguing 1928 impossible crimes by Nicholas Olde.

The Julius Caesar Murder Case — A classic 1935 re-telling of the assassination by Wallace Irwin that's much more fun than the Shakespeare version.

The Koky Comics — A collection of all of the 1978-1981 Sunday and daily comic strips by Richard O'Brien and Mort Gerberg, in two volumes.

The Lady of the Terraces — 1925 missing race adventure by E. Charles Vivian.

The Lord of Terror — 1925 mystery with master-criminal, Fantômas.

The Melamare Mystery — A classic 1929 Arsene Lupin mystery by Maurice Leblanc

The Man Who Was Secrett — Epic SF stories from John Brunner

The Man Without a Planet — Science fiction tales by Richard Wilson

The N. R. De Mexico Novels — Robert Bragg, the real N.R. de Mexico, presents *Marijuana Girl, Madman on a Drum, Private Chauffeur* in one volume.

The Night Remembers — A 1991 Jack Walsh mystery from Ed Gorman.

The One After Snelling — Kickass modern noir from Richard O'Brien.

The Organ Reader — A huge compilation of just about everything published in the 1971-1972 radical bay-area newspaper, *THE ORGAN*. A coffee table book that points out the shallowness of the coffee table mindset.

The Poker Club — Three in one! Ed Gorman's ground-breaking novel, the short story it was based upon, and the screenplay of the film made from it.

The Private Journal & Diary of John H. Surratt — The memoirs of the man who conspired to assassinate President Lincoln.

The Ramble House Mapbacks — Recently revised book by Gavin L. O'Keefe with color pictures of all the Ramble House books with mapbacks.

The Secret Adventures of Sherlock Holmes — Three Sherlockian pastiches by the Brooklyn author/publisher, Gary Lovisi.

The Shadow on the House — Mark Hansom's 1934 masterpiece of horror is introduced by John Pelan.

The Sign of the Scorpion — A 1935 Edmund Snell tale of oriental evil.

The Singular Problem of the Stygian House-Boat — Two classic tales by John Kendrick Bangs about the denizens of Hades.

The Smiling Corpse — Philip Wylie and Bernard Bergman's odd 1935 novel.

The Spider: Satan's Murder Machines — A thesis about Iron Man

The Stench of Death: An Odoriferous Omnibus by Jack Moskovitz — Two complete novels and two novellas from 60's sleaze author, Jack Moskovitz.

The Story Writer and Other Stories — Classic SF from Richard Wilson

The Strange Case of the Antlered Man — 1935 dementia from Edwy Searles Brooks

The Strange Thirteen — Richard B. Gamon's odd stories about Raj India.

The Technique of the Mystery Story — Carolyn Wells' tips about writing.

The Threat of Nostalgia — A collection of his most obscure stories by Jon Breen

The Time Armada — Fox B. Holden's 1953 SF gem.

The Tongueless Horror and Other Stories — Volume One of the series of short stories from the weird pulps by Wyatt Blassingame.

The Town from Planet Five — From Richard Wilson, two SF classics, *And Then the Town Took Off* and *The Girls from Planet 5*

The Tracer of Lost Persons — From 1906, an episodic novel that became a hit radio series in the 30s. Introduced by Richard A. Lupoff.

The Trail of the Cloven Hoof — Diabolical horror from 1935 by Arlton Eadie. Introduced by John Pelan.

The Triune Man — Mindscrambling science fiction from Richard A. Lupoff.

The Unholy Goddess and Other Stories — Wyatt Blassingame's first DTP compilation

The Universal Holmes — Richard A. Lupoff's 2007 collection of five Holmesian pastiches and a recipe for giant rat stew.

The Werewolf vs the Vampire Woman — Hard to believe ultraviolence by either Arthur M. Scarm or Arthur M. Scram.

The Whistling Ancestors — A 1936 classic of weirdness by Richard E. Goddard and introduced by John Pelan.

The White Owl — A vintage thriller from Edmund Snell

The White Peril in the Far East — Sidney Lewis Gulick's 1905 indictment of the West and assurance that Japan would never attack the U.S.

The Wizard of Berner's Abbey — A 1935 horror gem written by Mark Hansom and introduced by John Pelan.

The Wonderful Wizard of Oz — by L. Frank Baum and illustrated by Gavin L. O'Keefe

Through the Looking Glass — Lewis Carroll wrote it; Gavin L. O'Keefe illustrated it.

Time Line — Ramble House artist Gavin O'Keefe selects his most evocative art inspired by the twisted literature he reads and designs.

Tiresias — Psychotic modern horror novel by Jonathan M. Sweet.

Tortures and Towers — Two novellas of terror by Dexter Dayle.

Totah Six-Pack — Fender Tucker's six tales about Farmington in one sleek volume.

Tree of Life, Book of Death — Grania Davis' book of her life.

Triple Quest — An arty mystery from the 30s by E.R. Punshon.

Trail of the Spirit Warrior — Roger Haley's saga of life in the Indian Territories.

Two Kinds of Bad — Two 50s novels by William Ard about Danny Fontaine

Two Suns of Morcali and Other Stories — Evelyn E. Smith's SF tour-de-force

Ultra-Boiled — 23 gut-wrenching tales by our Man in Brooklyn, Gary Lovisi.

Up Front From Behind — A 2011 satire of Wall Street by James B. Kobak.

Victims & Villains — Intriguing Sherlockiana from Derham Groves.

Wade Wright Novels — *Echo of Fear, Death At Nostalgia Street, It Leads to Murder* and *Shadows' Edge*, a double book featuring *Shadows Don't Bleed* and *The Sharp Edge.*

Walter S. Masterman Novels — *The Green Toad, The Flying Beast, The Yellow Mistletoe, The Wrong Verdict, The Perjured Alibi, The Border Line, The Bloodhounds Bay, The Curse of Cantire* and *The Baddington Horror.* Masterman wrote horror and mystery, some introduced by John Pelan.

We Are the Dead and Other Stories — Volume Two in the Day Keene in the Detective Pulps series, introduced by Ed Gorman. When done, there may be 11 in the series.

Welsh Rarebit Tales — Charming stories from 1902 by Harle Oren Cummins

West Texas War and Other Western Stories — by Gary Lovisi.

What If? Volume 1, 2 and 3 — Richard A. Lupoff introduces three decades worth of SF short stories that should have won a Hugo, but didn't.

When the Batman Thirsts and Other Stories — Weird tales from Frederick C. Davis.

Whip Dodge: Man Hunter — Wesley Tallant's saga of a bounty hunter of the old West.

Win, Place and Die! — The first new mystery by Milt Ozaki in decades. The ultimate novel of 70s Reno.

Writer 1 and 2 — A magnus opus from Richard A. Lupoff summing up his life as writer.

You'll Die Laughing — Bruce Elliott's 1945 novel of murder at a practical joker's English countryside manor.

RAMBLE HOUSE

Fender Tucker, Prop.   Gavin L. O'Keefe, Graphics
www.ramblehouse.com   fender@ramblehouse.com
228-826-1783   10329 Sheephead Drive, Vancleave MS 39565